LUCKY In LOVE

A Novel of Romance and Disaster in World War Two

JOAN LA BLANC

Northampton House Press

Other Novels by Joan La Blanc:

INNOCENCE OF ANGELS
MINISTRY OF ANGELS
ODYSSEY OF ANGELS
ORDINARY ANGELS

Cover image is adapted from a Pennsylvania Railroad poster now in the public domain. Design by Naia Poyer.
LUCKY IN LOVE Copyright 2019 by J. H. La Blanc. All rights reserved.
Published by Northampton House Press. First trade paper edition, 2019, ISBN 978-1-937997-93-9.
Library of Congress control number: 2019934128
9 8 7 6 5 4 3 2

LUCKY In LOVE

CHAPTER ONE
11:30 AM, Monday, 6 September 1943

In the attic bedroom of a shabby Victorian cottage by the Chesapeake Bay, Gail Graham slathers her red thighs with white goo from a blue Noxzema jar. And stifles hopes of getting an early train from Washington. Last night, her father-in-law had promised they'd leave right after breakfast. Yet here it is almost noon, and he's nowhere in sight. Given the eight-hour trip home, her anxiety's at panic level. This weekend has been the worst since she married his son.

At 25, Gail is tall and angular, not quite flat-chested, but hardly as voluptuous as Jerry might have wished she was. Nor does her auburn hair fall in the sensuous waves of the calendar girls he'd lusted after. It's so short and curly he'd often called her "Orphan Annie", not fondly, but in a sneering tone. If he could see her now—skin so fair that even after two days, Saturday's sunburn is still flaming—maybe he'd take it back.

Well, too late. He's dead. Killed, not in action but a drunken accident. And even if he weren't, she'd no longer give a damn about how he regards her hair. Or her bosom. Or any other part of her body.

Finished slathering, she tucks the cream into her suitcase and gets into the same traveling clothes—white blouse, blue seersucker jacket and skirt—she wore for the trip down on Friday. As she pulls on bobby socks, Gail notes Jerry's sister studying her from the other bed. In contrast to her own boiled-lobster skin, Pixie's is the golden brown of a fresh-baked biscuit. Her hair's gold, thick, lustrous and wavy. She's seventeen, and from birth has been told she's adorable. Consequently, she regards all less attractive, less sleek young women with pity. Including the cousins who have packed the family cottage this weekend. And Gail, of course, even more so, since she's the widow of her illustrious older brother, Staff Sergeant Jeremiah Robert E. Lee Graham IV, United States Marine Corps.

After setting the suitcase by the door, Gail is studying her blistered nose in the mirror above a decrepit chest of drawers when Pixie says, "Are you really half-Italian, Gail? I mean, I'd think someone with Italian blood would get a marvelous suntan, not burn up the way you did."

She winces at the reference to last night's faux pas, when Jerry's mother introduced her to friends at the Fair Haven Yacht Club as "Jerry's widow, one of the Boston Bennetts." Startled, she'd blurted, "No...I'm one of the Portsmouth Benedettis." Which had led to Mrs. Graham's observation that, "But that sounds so...so Italian. And you don't look Italian."

Sighing, she explains again now. "That's because I take after my mother. I'm the only one of five kids that inherited her Norwegian coloring."

Pixie appears to ponder this biological tidbit. "But...why didn't you let Mummy go on thinking you're from that nice family Jerry told us about? Now all our friends know you're Italian."

Turning from her inflamed image in the pitted glass, she regards Pixie's smooth young face. "In your social circle, is it a sin to marry into an immigrant's family?"

The girl kicks off the covers and half-sits, hair tumbling around her face. "It's simply not done, that's all. Why, we don't even know any Italians. I saw some once, when we drove up for the World's Fair and Daddy got lost in the city. In the most awful slum." She shudders. "So crowded. So filthy. It was the middle of summer, but we kept the windows rolled up so we didn't smell them. Besides, they looked so...so sinister, we were scared they'd attack us."

Trying not to let anger color her tone, Gail says, "There's no one like that in my family. Or even in Portsmouth."

"Then maybe Jerry didn't know they were foreigners."

"Oh, he knew. He knew their names, too, because Franco and Pietro Benedetti run the best restaurant in town. He was probably just ashamed to tell his family.

"Well, at least I didn't get pregnant before he went overseas. Think of the scandal if I'd had an Italian-looking baby! You know…with a mop of greasy hair and a big nose, like a gangster! How'd you explain that to all your WASP friends in Virginia?" Smarting, she yanks the sheets from her bed and bundles them to take downstairs.

"Don't do that," Pixie warns. "That's Ruby's job." She yawns hugely and swings golden legs to the floor. "By the way, tell her to bring me some coffee. Good and hot. With plenty of sugar, you hear?"

Gail shrugs, aware there's a protocol to dealing with Negro household help. The nineteenth-century feel of it makes her bristle. Without answering, she tosses the sheets down the stairs, grabs suitcase and purse, and clatters down.

In the entry, the quiet of the house, the stale residue of the morning's bacon feel smothering. It's even worse in the kitchen, where no fans dissipate the late summer steaminess. Ruby, the colored housekeeper, is wiping inside the refrigerator with baking soda. Breakfast dishes fill the sink; the table's cluttered with the weekend's leftovers. Gail assumes they'll go home with the Grahams. Or with Ruby and her husband Billy; the couple does all the work at the cottage, which for the wife means eighteen hours a day in the kitchen, while Billy keeps grounds, vehicles, boats and beach pristine.

Nonetheless the black woman's smile is warm. "Morning, Miss Gail. Fix you some bacon and eggs? Or a nice ham sandwich?" She gestures at a platter where pinkish-gray shreds cling to an enormous white bone. "Still some cheese left, and plenty of tomatoes."

"Sandwich sounds good, thanks." Gail returns the smile

and kicks the bundled sheets toward the wringer washer on the service porch.

"No need of you to do that." Ruby lifts a homemade loaf from the pie safe and saws off thick slices. She spreads Miracle Whip and mustard, cuts a plump tomato, layers yellow cheese, then hacks chunks from the ham. The result is a sandwich so fat Gail despairs of getting it into her mouth.

Ruby bisects it, corner to corner. And lays out a fan of pickles on a Blue Willow plate. "Iced tea with that?"

"Yes, please." Watching the housekeeper's efficient moves, Gail's tempted to ask about her life. But social interaction is obviously not part of the protocol. All she knows is, Ruby and Billy have a small boy and a smaller girl; they play with the Graham kids in the yard but can't join them on the beach. Another fact of Southern life that increases her need to get home to New Hampshire.

Ruby sets the plate on a chipped Tole tray and follows with a glass of dark tea. "Thanks," Gail says. "Uh...is Mr. Graham around?"

"No, ma'am. The missus, she's down on the beach, but he's off to that club of his. Why don't I carry this out to the porch so's you can get the breeze off the water? Help cool that awful burn of yours."

"I'll take it, thanks. You've got enough to do here." She gestures at the clutter awaiting disposal. Once more, it seems, she's relieved the woman of a household duty. Fortunately Pixie isn't around to shake her pretty head at her Yankee sister-in-law's latest breach of etiquette.

Then she remembers the girl's order that Ruby bring her coffee. Tempted to ignore it, she decides that while it might save the servant a trip up two sets of stairs, it might also get her in trouble. Sighing, she adds, "Oh by the way. Pixie wants a cup of coffee. Nice and sweet, she said."

With no change of expression, Ruby nods and heads for the coffee pot on the range.

Walking carefully, Gail carries the tray through the entry hall and onto the enormous porch. Even in the shade, humid heat blasts her; Ruby's promised breeze is a myth. Ahead is a strip of weedy grass, and a sign PRIVATE BEACH—NO COLOREDS stands beside rough-hewn steps down to the narrow sand strip.

A clutch of Graham women and children lounge by the amber shallows of the Chesapeake. Farther out, the water's sullen gunmetal. A lone sailboat hovers, shimmering. The horizon's vague, with no sign of a far shore, only a pink edge to the glaring eastern sky.

Gail seats herself in one of the rockers along the rail, balances the tray in her lap, sips the too-sweet tea, and bites carefully into the sandwich. Sweet mingles with salty in her mouth, textures of meat and tomato and cheese combine. All Ruby's meals have been delicious. The local blue crabs are new to Gail's New England palate. One of the few pleasant surprises of the weekend, but compared to the others, of so little consequence, she's lost the ability to appreciate it. All her energy now is focused on getting to Washington, to the station, and onto the first New York-bound train. So she can be home by midnight, grab six hours sleep, and greet the opening of school tomorrow with the calm dignity the nuns expect of their lay teachers.

Most of all, she's anxious—no, *desperate*—to escape the saccharine Southern hospitality of this gregarious family she'd been in such a hurry to marry into the year before.

One to whom she now feels no further allegiance. Thanks be to God, she'll put these egregious obligations behind her the minute Mr. Graham shows up to drive her to Union Station.

He can't get here a minute too soon.

CHAPTER TWO
2 PM the same day

From the minute they leave the Navy Yard, Matt Ogleby, Lieutenant, Submarine Force, U.S. Navy, regrets he hasn't followed his instinct and flagged a cab to Union Station. Earlier, pink-cheeked Ensign Walter Wilson had promised he'd get him there in plenty of time.

But now Wilson says, "First, though, we gotta stop off at the Gradys. Not long. Just one little drink."

The side trip was not in Matt's Plan of the Day. He groans at the prospect of yet another hour with Ron Grady, of another damned party. Even with people he admires, such social events are torture. But Grady's the OinC of the BuShips unit where Matt had been stationed until midnight last night. For Wilson, who's still attached, this party or whatever the hell it is, is mandatory. For Matt, if he wasn't already trapped in Wilson's car, he'd skip the whole damned thing.

But he has to ask. "Why? Ron and I said everything we had to say when I checked out yesterday."

"All I know is, Dixie ordered—you know how she is—she ordered me to bring you by on the way to the train." Steering the 'forty-one Plymouth convertible, Wilson grins at a carful of girls at a red light. The top is down, of course, with Matt's stuffed seabag bouncing on the back seat.

Having recently turned thirty, which he figures is old enough to be wiser than he feels, Matt considers the younger man a jerk. In the four months he's known Walt, the ensign's only job seems to be accompanying Grady to parties, laughing at his lame jokes, and spending as little time as possible at a desk.

Meanwhile everyone else in the unit grows numb about the endless reports of trouble on subs in WestPac. Those that actually make it back to Pearl, that is. Trying to figure out why so many keep disappearing keeps Matt awake nights.

In the BuShips office, Wilson's annoying but harmless. On the other hand, Grady's prior service is too full of horror stories to dismiss. After four years at the Naval Academy and seven on active duty, though, Matt knows there's nothing he can do about inferior superiors. Except escape.

As he will after today's last unavoidable contact with this pair of useless assholes.

* * *

The Gradys' luau fills the flagstone yard behind the narrow brick house with a fashionable Georgetown address. As Matt steps out, layers of smell envelope him: the smoky tang of roasting pork, wisps of expensive perfume, cigarette smoke, and something fishy on a canapé tray held by a colored maid in a white uniform. Overhead the city sky seems filtered through thick glass. Steamy light washes the bricks and glints off row house windows behind them. Even in the shade, the late summer air feels too thick to breathe.

As Wilson hustles toward their host, Matt ambles toward the serve-yourself bar, nodding at two other guys from the unit. He's the only one in uniform; everyone else is wearing gaudy Hawaiian shirts, the woman, sarongs and sundresses. As usual, Grady's wife is picture-perfect in an off-the-shoulder number. Detaching herself from the suck-up ensign, she glides over. Cherry-red lips kiss his cheek. Reputedly an ex-movie star, she never runs low on glamor and charm. She and Grady are rumored to have met on the set of a Mickey Rooney film, where he was a stand-in. Now he's a plumper, sillier version of the chubby-cheeked star.

Matt wishes again he could ask the men lost in *Wolf Fish*

about Grady. Pointless, of course. He certainly wasn't the first skipper to go off his nut on patrol. To put his boat in a near-fatal situation, let the exec save his ass, then fill official reports with self-aggrandizing lies, as he suspects Grady's done. Ironic, Matt thinks, that his sub too went missing, after a really gung-ho skipper took command.

Grabbing an iced beer from a galvanized tub, he surveys the guests. Dixie always includes aspiring actresses to entertain the unit's bachelors. The wives or girlfriends look drab compared to Dixie's lacquered, busty starlets. Clustered away from the main group is a coterie of brass from other BuShips echelons, well-muscled older guys with clipped silver hair, smooth tans, Academy rings like the one Matt owns but seldom wears. The smell of rank is on them, even in those ridiculous flowered shirts. He glances at his watch, then at Wilson, who's belting down something pink from a tall glass.

Grady approaches, glad-hands him, leads him toward the brass for introductions. One by one they wish him well in his new assignment. One guy, younger and taller than the rest, says, "Ogleby…You the boy they call Lucky?"

Matt thinks *admiral,* and turns on a non-committal grin.

Grady says, "Two close calls aren't enough for this guy. Now he's going for number three. This time in a new boat."

The young admiral's well-trimmed eyebrows rise. "What's the difference between a new sub and an old one? They all stink of diesel. Besides, if I'm going down with my ship, I want a chance to get off. Even if it means ending up in the drink."

"Think that's the best way to go?" The man winces; before he can answer Matt adds, "For me it'd be dead in the water, disabled but surfaced. With a Jap plane so low you can see the pilot grinning while he strafes you. There'd be something satisfying in that."

This isn't party talk; the older man's scowl is gratifying. Muttering, "Nice to talk to you," he retreats to the bar again.

Behind him a Filipino mess steward is knifing into a charred suckling pig. Nearby two slim young women in skin-tight sundresses chat up a couple of bachelors. They're all laughing, swigging those pink drinks. Matt sips beer, which he dislikes too much to ever get drunk on. Pretense suffuses the air like smoke from the barbecue.

At quarter to three, the doorbell rings. The maid hurries inside to answer, and returns escorting the newest man in the unit. Framed in the doorway, Ensign Ben Finkelstein appears even taller and more handsome than usual. The khaki uniform complements his natural ruddiness, his clipped dark hair, blue eyes, smooth-shaven cheeks.

Behind Matt a girl asks, "My goodness, who's the dreamboat?"

In a stage whisper Wilson says, "The Hebe."

Matt's disgusted, but he's heard him call Finklestein worse.

As the new arrival walks down the brick steps, Matt steps forward to shake his hand. "Good to see you, Ben. Thought you had the duty."

"I do, but not till four. So I can't hang around."

"Lucky for you."

Though he's known the junior ensign only six weeks, Matt feels more rapport with him than with anyone else in the unit. Not just because Finkelstein's an engineer. Though he has no history in subs, he asks smart questions. Takes the job seriously. Doesn't goof off.

Matt asks, "Say, would you mind dropping me off at the station on your way back to the base?"

"Sure. What time's your train?"

"Four. Latest I can leave DC and not be UA at Portsmouth."

"Glad to. Give me half an hour to kiss ass first. Okay?"

Thirty minutes crawl by as Matt makes small talk with men from the unit while Finkelstein makes social rounds. Has a lemonade, samples shrimp canapés and roast pig. Matt fidgets, aware Wilson and Grady are joking about Jews, pork and shellfish.

"Looks like he doesn't keep Kosher," Wilson says out of the side of his mouth.

Grady laughs. "Wonder if he's been clipped?"

"Maybe one of Dixie's girls can find out."

The circumcision snickers are barely suppressed. Matt swallows the last of the beer, which is warm as spit now. Disgust with his fellow officers borders on nausea.

Finally, after nodding at more rounds of Bon Voyage wishes and relaying insincere thanks to the Gradys, he trails Finkelstein through the house. The younger man insists on lugging Matt's bag to his '35 Chevy before they climb in and head back through the city.

The air is thick with haze. The Washington Monument and Capitol dome are dulled by humidity and exhaust fumes. DC's supposedly choice duty, but Matt's never left any posting with so little nostalgia, even after four months of TAD waiting for a new boat. He'd hoped for Mare Island or New London, both areas he knows. Portsmouth, New Hampshire, might as well be the back of the moon.

"Spent summers there when I was a kid," Finkelstein says. "A lot cooler, but the beaches aren't much." His expression turns soft. "Didn't stop me from having a dip, though. See, we always stayed at this big old hotel where the river runs into the ocean." He frowns. "My father always registered as the Franklins, not the Finklesteins."

Matt frowns. "Why was that?" Then it hits him.

"More acceptable. Hell. What's more American than the Franklin family from Philadelphia?"

So it's not enough just to look Gentile. He's at a loss for a reply, but his chest tightens with regret for the insults at the party. Surely Finklestein hasn't missed them all. Finally he says, "Sorry. And they say we're the good guys." Which feels sententious and empty, especially when the younger man shrugs and keeps driving.

By now he can see the big station ahead; relief softens his regret at leaving the ensign to the bigots. It's 3:35 when they pull over near one of the arched entrances. Matt steps out while the other heaves the bag from the trunk.

A portly redcap hurries over. "Take that for you, cap'n?"

"Please."

He hefts the overstuffed canvas bag onto a dolly. "What train?"

"Four o'clock to New York."

"B & O? Or Pennsy?"

Matt pulls an envelope from his jacket, scans the ticket the Navy supplied with his orders. "Uh, the Pennsylvania."

"Follow me then, cap'n."

Matt grabs Finkelstein's hand and thanks him for the ride. Wishes him good luck. "And if you ever get to Portsmouth, give me a call."

The ensign murmurs something Matt loses in the blare of a passing car's horn, and waves goodbye. Before the porter can disappear in the mammoth station, Matt rushes to follow him to the train that will deliver him from this hot, miserable city.

Also known as the Capital of the Free World.

CHAPTER THREE
3:45 PM the same day

With fifteen minutes until train time, Gail bolts from her father-in-law's Lincoln Zephyr, grabs the suitcase he hands over, and braces for his hug. Too close, too long, capped off with a wet cheek kiss reeking of Bourbon.

She calls "Thanks for everything," to Mrs. Graham and Pixie in the back seat, then trots toward the entrance. Behind her the big car roars off into traffic. Her relief feels like ice water to a desert wanderer.

As she hurries across the crowded concourse toward the boarding gates, she spots a sign with the Pennsy's red keystone logo. The Congressional Limited, non-stop to New York. Beyond, a string of streamlined stainless steel cars stretches toward an electric engine at the front.

Not sure it's the right train, she shows her ticket to a roaming conductor.

He scans it, nods. "Still plenty of seats forward, miss. But hurry. We pull out at four sharp."

Incredulous at her luck, she races past ten coaches as conductors begin taking up steps, slamming doors, barking out "All Aboards" against a backdrop of the distant ding-ding of the locomotive bell. Finally, breathless, she follows a pack of sailors and troops up the steps into Car 6. After the miasma of grease, dust and hot metal smells, air conditioning is a fragrant balm on her scalded skin.

Inside, the line of blue plush seats offers so few empties she decides to try the next car forward. Midway up the aisle, however, she spots a naval officer wrestling a sea bag onto the overhead rack. He shrugs off a khaki jacket with gold on the epaulets, and on his chest, rows of service ribbons under a vaguely familiar emblem. As she approaches, she assesses him as colorless enough to be an innocuous seatmate. One who won't ask a lot of personal questions or fall asleep on her shoulder.

She hesitates beside the seat as he settles into the one by the window, loosens the black necktie and sets a book on his lap. He glances up with an expression that's half do-I-know-you? And half, do-I-want-to? No wonder he's dubious; her blotchy, blistered face must look like a case of leprosy, and she reeks of Noxzema.

She asks anyway. "Excuse me, sir. Are you saving this seat for someone?"

His smile is polite, neutral. "No, ma'am. All yours."

She murmurs "Thanks," sets the overnight case in front of the empty seat, and lowers herself onto it. Straightens her skirt, then improves her posture. Breathes deeply and relaxes for the first time since she'd left home Friday morning.

After a minute, the officer gestures toward the suitcase. "Ma'am, would you like me to set that in the rack so there's more room for your feet?"

She smiles as graciously as she can without cracking the tight sunburned skin of her cheeks. "Thanks, but it's fine where it is. Kind of you to offer."

His irises are more gray than blue, with close-cropped hair receding at the temples. A lean face is etched with faint lines. He appears travel-rumpled but comfortable. Not spit and polished and pressed, the way Jerry had always been in his greens. This fellow's older, maybe thirty, with a weary air. As if he's already seen enough war to last a lifetime.

Still, a grin lights his eyes. "Easy to be kind to pretty young ladies traveling alone." His gaze drops to her left hand. He adds hastily, "Even married ones."

Wondering if this is a line he's used before, she says, "Actually, I'm a widow. My husband died in the South Pacific last winter. A Marine."

His expression sobers. "I'm sorry. Killed in action?"

"No. The telegram just said he died in the line of duty. Then I got a letter that explained it was a Jeep wreck on Samoa. Marines train there before the next landing."

"I've heard that somewhere."

"Anyway, I don't tell anyone he was killed in action since he really wasn't." Except his family, she thinks. Gilding his image, just as Jerry had reframed the truth of her national origins to make the marriage more acceptable to his family. An electric current of betrayal jolts her again.

"I see. Still, it must've been a shock. Were you married long?"

"Since last Christmas. And I only knew him a month before that…a wartime romance. So, it wasn't as if we'd been childhood sweethearts. I mean, now it's almost as if…well, as if we'd never met."

Hearing the bitterness in her tone, she hopes the guy hasn't noticed. The train gives a jolt and slowly glides from the station. So quietly, so smoothly she barely feels the motion. Well, of course. This is how luxury travel's supposed to be. When he doesn't comment again, she says, "So tell me, sir. If I ask what branch of the Navy you're in, will you think I'm a spy?"

His chuckle's unexpected. "Didn't you see the insignia on my jacket?"

"You mean that pin with the whales?"

"Dolphins, actually. If you couldn't tell from that, you'd make a damn poor spy."

The giggle sounds louder than she'd intended. "Why? What is it?"

"Submarine Force."

"Oh. So you're a sub-MAR-iner."

"Right. Except we'd rather be called sub-mar-INERS. In case the other makes us sound inferior."

"Sorry. I've lived in Portsmouth, New Hampshire all my life. It's full of... submar*in*ers. But I've never known any personally."

His eyes widen. "That where you're going now?"

"Yes. Probably should've taken an earlier train. It'll be midnight before I get home."

"Huh. Had the same idea a while ago. I'm headed there too. Never stationed there before, though," he adds. "Except for sub school in New London, always been on the west coast. And Pearl."

"Pearl Harbor? My goodness. Were you there when it was attacked?"

"No. Friends of mine were, though, so I've heard what a hell it was."

She winces. "I can imagine."

He says no more, just gazes out the window through a blur of dust pocked with old raindrops. To continue the conversation, she says, "I have a friend who's married to a submarine officer. I think he's the engineer. Is that like the engineer on a train? I mean, would he be considered the driver?"

He turns a quizzical glance on her, as if trying to decide whether she's pathetically ignorant, or trying to be funny. The slow shake of his head tells her nothing. But he speaks patiently and clearly, as one might to a dullard. "No, ma'am. The engineer keeps things running. See, every piece of equipment's vital. One faulty valve can take you right to the bottom. By the way, which boat's he in?"

Heat rises on her cheeks as she realizes how dumb she must sound. "Mm, can't remember. But it's some sort of fish."

Emerging from the covered station into pale, fuzzy sunlight, the train clicks across a network of switches, gaining speed as it veers onto a northbound track.

He laughs. "Hey, they're all named for fish. Do you know his name?"

"Donovan. Dan Donovan."

"Oh... *Wolf Fish*. That it?"

"Sounds familiar. Do you know him?"

He nods. "But not well. Met him at a wetting down party at Pearl. Then saw his name in a list of...uh...."

She nods. "I know. His boat's missing in action."

A flash of green draws her attention to elephant-eared weeds tall as Jack's beanstalk beyond the window. They enclose the yards of decrepit tenements along the right of way. Laundry droops from sagging porch lines; an occasional potted geranium's the only spot of color. The contrast between that dismal world and this swift, elegant train sends a shiver through her. "Anna's hoping it's been captured, not sunk."

His grimace suggests neither alternative would be good.

Hoping it doesn't come across as intrusive, she says, "I bet you've seen some action."

"Ironic you mention it. Twice now, I've been transferred off boats just before they went missing. Guys I work with have started calling me Lucky. Worries me. Like it might be a jinx in the end."

She blinks; her blistered nose itches. "What's your real name? I mean so I don't have to call you Lucky all the way to Portsmouth."

His lip twitches in amusement. "Matt. Matt Ogleby."

She extends her hand. "Gail Graham."

His grip is firm, gentle, brief. "Like the cracker?"

She's heard that one so often she rolls her eyes. "Exactly."

He clears his throat, twiddles the pages of the book on his lap. "So what brought you to Washington? A weekend at the beach?"

"Gee. Why would you think that? Must be my beautiful tan."

"Sorry. Looks so painful, I had to ask."

"We don't have big beaches in New England, so I'm not used to sunbathing. I tried to catch up too fast at this place in Maryland. Fair Haven."

He nods. "Been there a time or two. When I was at the Academy."

She doesn't know what he's referencing, but feels she should. "Uh…the Academy?"

"Annapolis. The Naval Academy?"

"Oh, *that* academy."

"Besides, sun's a lot stronger this far south. And being a red head…no wonder you're fried. Well, you'll know better next time."

She wants to shout *there won't be a next time!* Not with the Grahams.

He riffles the pages of the book again. "So what do you do in Portsmouth? I mean besides avoiding the beach?"

The stab at humor touches her. "I teach English. In a private school for girls. They call it an academy too. Even have uniforms: St. Margaret's Academy for Young Ladies. Anything else you'd like to know?"

A faint blush suffuses his neck above the khaki shirt with two silver bars on the collar. "Didn't mean to pry. Anyway, what does a private school teacher do in her spare time? Or don't you have any?"

"Well, sometimes I work in my father's restaurant. It's one of those historic taverns where waitresses wear serving-wench costumes and the drinks are named for Revolutionary War battles." She closes her eyes so she can't see his reaction when she says, "But the specialties are Italian. Like my dad." Having just unfurled the family flag, she steels herself for a hint of recoil in Matt Ogleby—the usual narrowing of the eyes or a stifled sniff of disdain as he mentally retreats from interest in her family. Or her. "I suppose now you'll tell me I don't look Italian."

He gives her a frown. "Don't look Italian? Why'd you say that?"

"Well, some people feel deceived when they find out my maiden name's Benedetti. Like I've put something over on them. I hate that. But it happens now and then. I mean, since I married a man with a *real American* name."

Without comment, he glances out at a grade crossing where traffic's backed up behind lowered gates; the warning bell changes tones as they fly by. Gail wonders if mentioning the Doppler Effect would impress him. Before she can work it into a coherent sentence, he says, "If you have any spare time, how'd you like to show me around while I'm at the base? That is, if I ever get a day off."

Her glance drops automatically to his hand. He's not wearing a wedding band. But that doesn't mean anything: Jerry had refused to wear one because he'd known a man whose finger had been ripped off when the ring snagged on a recoiling cannon breech.

"Well, that depends." A deep breath. "On whether you're married. Or engaged."

Surprise widens his eyes. He shakes his head. "Neither. Used to be. Married, I mean. Only a couple of years though. So don't worry. I don't have a girl waiting for me somewhere."

"Sorry. Guess I'm just wary because Jerry jilted his high school sweetheart when he married me." Another deep breath to clear the air. A divorcé? Or a widower? Why hadn't he said? "Anyway...sure, I'll show you around. Not that there's much to see. Except Lake Winnipesaukee, and the Old Man of the Mountain, and Mount Washington, and...."

"Gosh, the Old Man of the Mountain! Always wanted to see that guy."

She studies his expression. A slight twitch of the lips, a glint in the eyes. "That *guy*? But...it's not a real man. I mean, it's a rock formation."

Now he grins. "I've seen pictures. I'm not expecting a hairy hermit in a cave."

His offbeat humor relaxes her further. Jerry would never have made such a joke. She laughs; their gazes lock briefly.

Still smiling, Matt turns to the window again as they overtake a train on a parallel track—five dusty gray passenger cars towed by a steam locomotive. A grin creases his face; he waves. From the open windows in each coach, smiling kids return the wave for the half-minute before the Limited pulls ahead.

His gesture impresses her. "Gee, that was nice of you."

"Thought it'd give them a thrill. See, when I was a kid, it was a big deal if somebody on a train waved back. Especially the engineer."

"Where was that?"

"In Iowa. Outside a little burg called New Liberty. Right smack in the center of the state. Both my brothers are in the service now, but my dad keeps the farm going."

These slivers of history add to her impression of him as comfortable. Curious about why he's no longer married, she rehearses ways to discreetly pry. Meanwhile he turns to the book on his lap. It's new and stiff; he forces it open, the way she always warns students not to lest they break the spine. "Well, Gail Graham, if you'll excuse me, got to catch up on some reading before I start the new job."

"Military secrets. So I shouldn't look over your shoulder, right?"

"Not unless you want to be shot as a spy." With another congenial grin, he turns back to the volume. A glance tells her nothing of the content, but the text is dense, full of italicized words she assumes are names of ships. Or subs. About which she's never been the least interested. Until now.

But he's scowling at the pages, as if he needs glasses. Or is troubled by what he's reading. Not my business, she tells herself. Besides, if we travel all the way to Portsmouth together, we'll share more stories.

Meanwhile she relaxes against the seat as a monotonous blur of utility poles, stanchions, signal towers and the industrial backsides of small towns flash by. Before long, the rumble of the wheels, the rhythmic click of the rails, the distant hoot of the horn lull her into a drowse so relaxing she begins to drift. Happy to float in the wake of the emotional waves that have battered her all weekend.

From time to time some new sound—a southbound train rocketing past on the next track, a curve, the conductor punching tickets—jolts her awake again. She nods off again in the shadows of Baltimore's brick and granite rectangles, on a long girdered bridge over a wide river, and at Perryville, where a crowd of boy-faced sailors stare up with lonely eyes.

Once or twice she senses Matt's glance and a faint grin, as if they share some unspoken secret. She can't imagine his. Hers is simply the relaxing effect of his undemanding presence. So restorative she's content not to project to the possibilities of the rest of the trip, or of the next day. These quiet hours, the enforced relaxation on this train are exactly what she needs to recover from the holiday outing. A *so-called* holiday with Jerry's fine Virginia family. And more harsh truths about him than she'd discovered on their three-day honeymoon.

Well, her father had warned her, hadn't he? Considering him overly suspicious, however, she'd disregarded his refusal to bless their marriage, or to attend the wedding. Eloping had seemed so romantic at the time. Now she's forced to conclude Pop had sized Jerry up better than she had.

Not that she'll ever let him know, of course.

CHAPTER FOUR
5:45 PM, the same day

Given the content of the Naval Institute Press book, Matt has to force himself through its accounts of twentieth-century submarine disasters. Not just American but British, German, Japanese, Russian. A catalog of risks he's all too familiar with. Especially on the basis of reports he's evaluated these last months at BuShips. The litany includes defective valves, painted-over air intakes, green signals that fail to turn red, and of course, human error. All sorts of sorry human error. And in cases in which evidence lies at the bottom of the sea, all that often remains are mere theories about why a boat went missing.

The party conversation at the Gradys', the mention of his luck, combine with these accounts to unnerve him further. Raised in an unsuperstitious family, such discomfiture is new to him. Not what he'd expected to feel on route to a brand new boat. He pictures her taking shape at Portsmouth, still too embryonic to be named, launched with only a hull number. Joining her now, he'll be there to supervise the installation of her fire control, engineering, and dive systems. When the crew reports aboard, it'll be his job to weld everyone into a cohesive unit. So body and soul, he'll know her from the keel up. As risks go, this duty offers a minimum. Until they join the Fleet to hunt down Japs.

As the train rolls through northern Maryland, he yawns and closes the manual, marking the place with his mother's latest letter. Beside him, his new seatmate's eyelids are closed, head lolling on the seat back, hands limp in her lap. Barely discernible under the burn, freckles sprinkle her cheeks. The dimples he'd noticed earlier are no longer visible. How old? Early twenties? Probably not yet wise in the ways of the world, despite the brief marriage. Her air of innocence…it makes him recoil to imagine her under some skin-head gyrene, all muscle and bluster and *espirit de corps.*

Later in the trip, if they're together all the way to Portsmouth, he can find out more. Open the door by sharing his divorce story. Well, not the whole thing. The real truth makes him feel like a pussy-whipped fool.

As he conjectures, a white-jacketed Negro enters the car and strolls forward, tapping a brass gong. "First call for dinner, ladies and gents. Two dining cars. No waiting."

Gail jerks upright, blinking. Looks at her watch, blinks more, yawns. Pulls a flower-printed hanky from her bag, and blots her nose. "Goodness. Are we there?"

He shakes his head. "Not even halfway. Good nap?"

"I guess. Must be more tired than I knew."

He tucks the book into the seat beside him. "Any idea what time the Boston train leaves Grand Central?"

"They say if you want to catch the one at eight, you have to get a cab from Penn Station right away. It's a rush."

"Maybe we'd better eat before we get to New York." Then, afraid he's assuming too much, he adds, "Or would you rather have dinner alone?"

For a moment, no response. Until a cautious smile lights her eyes. "I've never eaten in a dining car. On the trip down, I had sandwiches my mother packed. So, yes, thank you."

"Good. Well, then, it's a date. Maybe when we get to Philadelphia…"

"I can't wait."

She sounds so sincere, his imagination uncurls itself like a newly-awakened cat. In Iowa, heat lightning might or might not presage rain for the withering corn crop, but it always gave hope, even while too distant for thunder.

With a sigh, he opens the book again to distract himself from drifting into fantasies. She's not his type, anyway. At least, not if you consider Marcie his type—blonde, blue-eyed, petite, with big tits and an uncanny way of undermining his moral resolve. Only after the divorce had he been able to recognize her as the quintessential female predator With marriage on her mind, even if she had to get pregnant first. Thank God he'd been spared that trap.

Now, as is usual when he revisits that sorry episode, he shudders at his naiveté. A deep breath sidetracks more pointless introspection. He recalls Graham's mention of Dan Donovan's wife. Or widow.

He turns to her again. "Say, Gail. Just thought of something else. While I'm at Portsmouth, could I meet this friend of yours? You know. Dan Donovan's wife?"

Her brows rise slightly. "She'd probably like that. Since you knew her husband."

"Good. " Tempted to explain further, he swallows the next question. "Well, guess I'd better do some more reading." He taps the book with an index finger. Reluctantly turns to the marker, but keeps losing his place. The heat lightning's close enough now to be distracting.

It's ten to six when the strolling waiter returns to announce last call for dinner. By now they've glided through the first Philadelphia station, alongside a river where racing sculls stir the reflection of what could pass as a great Greek temple.

Gail points. "Any idea what that building is?"

"Art museum. Went there once when we were here for the Army-Navy game." Before she can ask who *we* consisted of, he adds, "Halfway through Philly now. So maybe we should find a dining car. I mean, if you're hungry yet."

She nods. "Starving, actually. A long while since lunch. What do you recommend?"

"Maybe some consommé. With a club sandwich."

"Right now, I'd settle for a Spamwich."

He grimaces. "Ugh. Don't even mention Spam on a train like this." When her eyes widen in what looks like alarm, he realizes she's taken him literally. He reaches over to pat her hand, the merest touch. "Sorry, kidding again. I'm always in trouble for joking around."

Her laugh sets his mind at ease, but her expression sobers as the train crosses parklands and the river, arrowing east through an industrial sprawl. Ranks of dismal brick houses enclose narrow streets where only an occasional skinny tree adds a touch of green. Within minutes they enter another station on the express track, slowing between platforms filled with drooping travelers. Beyond, they pick up speed on a straight stretch, through more neighborhoods dense with those cramped brick row houses.

Rising from the seat, Matt squeezes the book into the rack beside the sea bag, then takes his uniform jacket from the seatback. He's buttoning the front when Gail gets to her feet. "I know you're an officer, Matt, but what rank are you?"

"Lieutenant senior grade. About halfway up the ladder to captain."

"I think Anna's husband's a Jaygee."

"That'd make me an Essgee then."

Her smile widens. "Really?"

"Full lieutenant. Anyway, lead on."

She's about to step into the aisle when it's blocked by a large colored woman in a white uniform. A wizened little woman with a painted doll's face under an elaborate platinum wig clings to her arm. A red silk dress droops on the frail, stooped frame; a rope of pearls hangs like a noose around her neck. A cloud of honeysuckle trails them. Matt winces; it's the sickly-sweet fragrance Marcie always doused herself with. He follows as Gail steps out behind them. There's no way to pass, so they shuffle behind the pair toward the rear of the coach. And the dining cars, presumably somewhere farther back.

"Say, Gail. Care for a cocktail before we eat?' he asks.

Her nod is definite. "I'd love a rum and coke."

By the time they reach the vestibule door, three more passengers are in the aisle. Gail pauses. "Matt, mind waiting a minute while I freshen up?"

He assumes this is a ladylike way to say she needs to use the head. "Sure, but it'll save time if I go on and get us a table. Order our drinks too. Join me when you're done. Okay?"

She hesitates, one hand on the lavatory door. "Well...okay."

"See you in a few minutes then." A sudden impulse leads him to touch her arm as she steps into the head. Then, reaching around the nurse and her tottering charge, he wrests open the heavy door to the vestibule. "After you, ladies." His tone is gallant despite his plan to squeeze past as soon as he can and beat them to the dining car.

With infinite slowness, they step across the uneven gap between moving cars. As he opens the next door, the train leans into a long curve to the left. The squeal of wheels on rails rises to a prolonged, penetrating scream. Acrid fumes of hot grease and steel penetrate his lungs. Even after he's entered the next coach, the shriek assaults his ears, the stink persists. Alarm jolts him. Long before the Navy, he'd learned the telltale sounds and smells of distressed bearings in farm machinery. He glances behind him, intending to turn back.

No go. Too many passengers crowd the aisle to push past now.

Ahead of the two plodding women, the crowded coach begins to shake. The shaking grows worse. He grabs a seat back to steady himself. Instinct and training prime him to crouch for self-protection, to brace for impact. But even as he does, he understands it's too late: whatever's about to happen, there's no escape now.

He hits the deck, squeezes his eyes closed and tries to pray. But the only words that come to him are, "Our Father...Our Father."

CHAPTER FIVE
6:06 pm the same day

I n a signal tower overlooking the confluence of the
Pennsylvania Railroad's main lines in northeast
Philadelphia, Ed Dobson focuses binoculars on the
cantilevered bridge across the Delaware. Haze from industrial
stacks along the river obscures his view. Just as caution tempts
him to override the green signals on the New York tracks, he
makes out the smoke plume of the inbound Cape May train.

Three minutes late, it rounds a curve and crosses the mile
of rubbled wasteland faster than usual on its way into the city.
Six dull green cars rattle behind a workhorse steam locomotive
with *Pennsylvania-Reading Seashore Lines* on the tender.

As it rumbles past the tower, the fireman tosses a wave up
to Ed. Vacationers from Jersey shore resorts pack the coaches.
Someone hurls a brown paper bag from an open window in
the last car. It somersaults along, spilling waxed paper, banana
peels and drink bottles onto other detritus littering the ballast.
In a few heartbeats, the train is gone, leaving only trash and
sulfurous coal-smoke in its wake.

As it recedes in late-day murk to the west, Ed checks the
board to make sure the Limited's cleared to cross the Seashore
Line tracks as it swings northward.

Lights all green. He relaxes enough to light a Camel, but
maintains his focus on the inbound rails. Frankford Junction's
a pulse point on the Washington-to-New York line. At least
one north or southbound train crosses the shore line tracks
every half hour, so timing has to be spot-on to avoid close

calls. With eight packed trains currently underway between Union and Penn stations, the safety of at least four thousand passengers is in the hands of men like him, in towers all along those 237 miles. Despite the automated signal system, his worst nightmare is still two trains carrying six or seven hundred holiday passengers colliding at a combined speed in excess of a hundred miles an hour.

He spots a headlight approaching from the west and checks the clock. Limited's right on the minute.

When the rest of the train materializes, he feels the admiration the big electric locomotive always evokes. Painted a green so dark it's almost black, its slender curves are highlighted by narrow gold racing stripes. They meet below the headlight and the red Keystone emblem, then flare out on either side like the cat's whiskers they're said to resemble. Double-ended, with cabs facing both directions, its peak 8500 horsepower derives from the pantograph connecting it to the high-tension catenary overhead. Since it doesn't haul the deadweight of fuel, it's capable of up to a hundred and twenty miles an hour. On this non-stop run it cruises at eighty, even leading sixteen coaches. In the six years it's been in use, the GG-1s have exceeded all expectations. They're such a dependable workhorse, the Pennsy has built a whole new hydroelectric dam on the Susquehanna to power its fleet.

For most of his years with the line, Ed had been a steam engine fan. Until 1927 when, choking in the smoke of hundreds of locomotives, the borough of Manhattan passed an ordinance prohibiting any exhaust-emitting engine from entering the city. Initially the Pennsy had dealt with the restriction by switching incoming passenger trains to small electric engines at a North Jersey point known as Manhattan Transfer. From there it was a quick trip under the Hudson and into Penn Station. But since the advent of the GG-1 in 1937, it's even quicker.

Despite the tingle of pride as the long streamliner approaches, Ed focuses his binoculars on the cars' undercarriages. In the forward cab, the engineer gives him the high sign as they speed past. All seems well, until Ed's scrutiny snags on a smoke plume trailing from the forward trucks of Car 7.

He gasps, "Holy Christ!" and reaches for the phone even before he notes the orange tongues of flame that confirm his worst fears. Overheated bearings in the junction box have burned off the lubricating grease and ignited the packing. As these heat to red-hot, they can knife through the axle connecting the wheels. The result, at high speed, can be catastrophe. Known as a "hot box", it's an old problem on railroads, though kept under control by scrupulous oiling.

And today, by an immediate emergency stop.

Clutching the phone, he shouts, "Redboard the Limited," to the next tower up the line. "Redboard, redboard! Hot box forward on seven!"

"Jesus. Right away," says the signalman who answers.

By now all sixteen coaches have uneventfully crossed the shore line tracks and entered the long curve to the left. Up the rails beyond the next tower, a stalk of green lights blossom yellow, then red as the train approaches. Ed exhales, one hand still on the phone. But before he can take another breath, with a crack like thunder Car 7 jerks upward, exploding from the coupling with 6, and yanking Car 8 off the tracks behind it.

It all happens so fast he's not sure he's actually witnessed what he's afraid he has. For the space of a heartbeat, he mentally replays the rapid-fire images. Only then does it hit him: Dear God, this is no mirage: Car 7's front axle has sheared, catapulting it into the air.

Still hurtling forward, the coach rises at a steep angle, scrapes against the signal tower, and ricochets into an overhead stanchion. High-tension lines snap with a fierce flash of blue lightning.

As the metal-skinned car screeches underneath, the steel stanchion becomes a giant can opener, peeling back the roof above the windows. Behind it, Car 8 follows a similar destructive path. Finally, reduced to masses of crumpled steel and shattered glass, the two self-destructing coaches run out of forward momentum. As they finally grind to a stop, metal and glass shards, chunks, fragments and splinters rain down onto the right-of-way.

A cloud of dust and smoke rises above the debris.

Hands shaking and unable to catch his breath, Ed forces himself to assess the wreckage. The GG-1 and the first six coaches have coasted away from the ruined cars before the automatic air brake system stopped them. Four of those leading cars are upright, the last two canted, derailed, but still in line. At the train's other end, six more cars are zig-zagged across all four tracks. Only the last two remain upright and on the rails.

Still trembling, he focuses binoculars on the scene. Alongside the wrecked coaches are bodies, some moving, but most ominously still, strewn along the debris field. Train crewmen race toward them from the engine and cars at the rear. Even at this distance, he hears screams.

Farther away, a siren wails.

Horror floods him as he stares down from his elevated vantage point, like some impotent little god. Shock stifles his breathing, causes his stomach to lurch. Has God ever known this sense of helpless futility? Maybe back in the 1880s, when an excursion train with kids from city orphanages ran off the bridge over the Delaware after the engineer failed to notice it was open for a ship. Before Ed was born, but his mother's emotional recitation of the tragedy had made it as familiar as any Mother Goose bedtime tale.

The phone rings. He gulps a deep breath to clear his mind and enable experience and training to coalesce. As they take control, he'll combine them with the expertise of his co-workers to try to keep this wreck from being as bad as it looks.

No, his gut tells him: No matter what he or anyone else does, this is still going to be a hell of a lot worse than it looks. A cataclysm that will forever replay in his memory. Like the Delaware River bridge tragedy, a horror movie he can't stop watching.

Ed's not Catholic, but crosses himself anyway.

CHAPTER SIX
6:10 PM the same day

The cataclysm hits with such stunning suddenness that Gail doesn't realize the train's jolted to a stop until she finds herself on the floor of the tiny bathroom. By now the end-of-the-world thunderclap has subsided to a cascade of lesser sounds: falling splinters of glass, the groans of tortured metal, and the thumps of heavy machinery settling, with a final sigh like a dying gasp.

With her ears ringing, all she can hear is the faint trickle of water. The acrid stench of burning grease, however, pervades every breath she takes.

Too numb to assemble these unrelated sensations into an explanation, she grips the edge of the basin and cautiously pulls herself upright. Her first impression is that the coach is no longer level but canted to the right. The narrow window looks down on a weedy embankment strewn with chunks of coal, old railroad ties, and all manner of other trash. From a tangle of end-of-summer weeds, fronds of goldenrod reflect the low-slanting sunlight. She can see neither ahead of the train, nor behind, just this glimpse of a dismal wasteland beyond the tracks.

In the bathroom, the light above the basin has gone out. The round mirror is now divided by a neat crack, curving top to bottom. Water dribbles from the faucet and swirls slowly down the drain. She grabs her purse from its path, rinses her gritty hands under the thin stream, then dries them on a limp roller towel above the toilet. When she tries to turn off the faucet, it doesn't move.

As she assesses the situation, muffled voices outside the lavatory rise into a gabble of alarm, fear and shock. There's no smoke, flames or heat, but the burning smell suggests the car may be on fire. Panic cuts through her shock. She has to get the hell out of this closet.

But when she pulls on the door handle, nothing happens. She pounds on the door. "Help! I'm trapped in the lavatory!"

She waits; no one responds.

Breathing deeply to calm herself, she tries the door again. Still wedged tight, immovable. She pounds again, harder. Raises her voice, calls more loudly.

From outside, screams and cries for help make her wonder what the other passengers may know that she doesn't. Fear clutches more tightly, making her heart race, squeezing the breath from her. She pounds again, longer, harder, yells with all the force in her lungs.

Finally a male voice calls, "Don't worry, miss. Have you outta there in no time. Stand back, now, so's we can kick it in."

She backs as far away as she can in the cramped space. At the kick the door screeches and flies inward. A burly sailor grins down. "Y'okay, miss?"

It takes her a moment to say, "I think so, thanks."

"Can you walk?"

"I guess. But…what's happened?"

Behind him, a taller sailor points to a window in the door through which her seatmate had walked only a few moments earlier. "See that? Car behind us blew up and took the rest of the train with it."

When she peers out her gaze follows a debris trail along a section of twisted rails to the remains of a stainless steel rail car. Resting at a 45-degree angle against a standard carrying overhead signals and power lines, its roof is peeled back like the lid of a Spam can. Behind it, another coach is also a derailed mass of mangled steel and shattered glass. Severed wires dangle above the wreckage, flaring white-hot sparks.

Farther back, other coaches appear undamaged, upright but scattered across all four tracks like a game of Pickup Sticks. At the far end, two other coaches are still upright on the rails.

Before she can wonder whether Matt's in one of the wrecked cars, her gaze takes in a new scene from hell—lines of bodies apparently tossed from the wrecked coaches onto the other rails. Too distant to see clearly, but few seem to be moving.

Sick at heart, she turns away with the acid sense her new friend might have run of luck. She swallows and gulps another deep breath before she's able to whisper, "My seatmate was in one of those cars. On his way to the dining car."

The first sailor shakes his head grimly. "Lord help him in that mess. But don't worry, my mate and me—we're Navy corpsmen, medics—we'll look for him. Now, go back to your seat and wait for somebody to tell you what to do. Okay?"

Nodding, she turns away from the horrific scene behind them, and slowly picks her way forward. The aisle is full of passengers retrieving belongings jolted from the overhead racks. A child wails, a woman breaks into sobs; a man loudly curses "the stinkin' Pennsy", adding, "Bet it was a bomb. They better get us outta here before the next one blows us all to hell."

Behind her one of the sailors says, "Sir. Doubt it was a bomb. Now go back to your seat and wait for someone to tell us what to do."

But how does he know that? Wishful thinking? If so, it's enough to calm her.

Clutching seatbacks for balance on the sloping floor, she doesn't notice the young blonde down the aisle. Until she grasps Gail's hand and pleads, "Excuse me, miss. What's gonna happen to us now?" Her thin face is pale, mascara-rimmed eyes wide with terror.

Gail shrugs, and barely manages to murmur, "Don't worry. The railroad will take care of us," then proceeds forward on shaky legs. When she reaches her seat, they topple her into it. She lands on Matt's Navy hat and the manual he'd been reading, which have been knocked down from the overhead rack. On the floor, her suitcase has slid under the window. She kicks it aside and removes the hat and book she's sitting on. Inside the hat, his name's printed in block letters. The book is splayed open, and an envelope has dropped out. She scans the return address on the unopened letter: *Mr. & Mrs. J. Ogleby, RFD 3, New Liberty, Iowa.*

Oh, his parents…who will notify them? The tears that jump into her eyes are a shock. Why, she asks herself, is she so affected by the possible death of a man she's known for only two hours? After all, nothing had happened between them. For her, only the relief of his undemanding company. And while they'd talked of seeing each other in Portsmouth, no promises had been made, no intentions expressed. The connection had been only the gossamer strands of a spider web.

Still, with this evanescent story cut off as if by the blade of a guillotine, she feels a sense of loss too heavy to be logical. New tears sting her eyes.

Trying to distract herself, she gazes out the window at distant stacks belching yellow smoke, rusty gasometers, a cantilevered bridge. From afar the wail of sirens approaches. And on a bridge ahead, a three-car elevated train rolls eastward, just as if this is any ordinary Monday evening and passengers aren't gaping down at the dismembered streamliner on the tracks below.

Her sense of time is skewed. It seems hours before a conductor enters from a forward car. Even as he says, "Please stay in your seats," panicked voices pepper him with questions.

He holds up his hand. "Don't worry. We're in no danger. But don't try to get out. Live wires are down all over the place." Before he can say more, the corpsmen persuade him to pry open the door at the end of the car so they can help with casualties. He's reluctant, but brings a crowbar. A couple of soldiers jump up to join the rescue effort, then follow the sailors out through wrecked couplings. Shaking his head, the conductor stares after them with haunted eyes.

By this time, besides a score of ambulances, city fire engines and red police cars are converging on the scene along with curious residents of a nearby neighborhood. From her seat Gail can't see what's happening, but imagines rescue crews crawling up on the wrecked cars to force their way inside. The carnage they'll find tortures her imagination, confirms her worst fears for Matt. She reminds herself he's a Navy officer trained for emergencies. Possibly he's helping with the injured, or trying to get back to Car 6 to resume the journey with her.

But the hopeful images fall flat. Don't even hint that he's safe. Still clutching his hat, she tries to picture him unscathed and smiling. As she waits for this image to comfort her, the blonde from down the aisle teeters up on platform sandals. Her voice is rough, her accent almost a parody of comedic Brooklynese.

"Please, miss, can I sit with you a while? That rabbi next to me, he keeps whining them awful Jew prayers. Gives me the willies."

Gail glances up at the small, close-set eyes, hair the color and texture of straw. Pity fills her, but she makes her voice strong. "Okay. But if my friend comes back, you'll have to let him sit there."

"Thanks a lot." She plops into the aisle seat. "Where is he anyway?"

Her throat clutches. "Went to the dining car. If I hadn't had to use the rest room, I'd be with him now." She jerks her head toward the rear. "Back there in the wreck."

"Ooh, lucky for you. Not so lucky for your sweetheart, though. "

She nods. Out of nowhere, a whole-body shiver starts her trembling. "How about you? You alone?"

A serious, worried nod. "See, I went down to Virginia to see my hubby before he goes overseas." Her eyes fill. "I was so worried about him. But Jeez, here I am, in a train wreck myself. Holy Mother of God." She crosses herself. "What's gonna happen to us?"

"I can't imagine." With effort, Gail withdraws a hanky from her purse and blows her nose. "At least we're in a city where there's lots of help."

The girl introduces herself as Adele something-or-other, then adds, "Yeah, right. Suppose it'd happened on that bridge over that river a ways back? We'd be in the drink now. Goners."

Gail shudders at the gloom and doom image, but isn't reassured that the present reality isn't as bad as it could have been. Or that a man who'd twice escaped death on submarines wouldn't be undone by something as prosaic as a civilian accident. The irony accentuates the randomness of the catastrophe that's cut short this journey. Talk about a bolt from the blue.

Seemingly unfazed by Gail's failure to respond with more than the occasional murmur, the new seatmate natters on and on. Evening shadows darken into a light-splotched night. The air in the coach grows stale and hot; no one can open windows, and only a few cool drafts waft through the open door at the rear. Feeble emergency lights glow at either end of the car; searchlights play on the wreckage; acetylene torches spark as they hiss into twisted steel. On another track, a work train arrives with cranes and generators.

Around seven-thirty, a man in a blue Red Cross uniform with a flashlight and clipboard comes through the coach to ask if any servicemen need to notify their bases about being late.

Gail gives him Matt's hat so he can list the information inside, points to his sea bag in the rack, then crowds both his book and hat into her suitcase so they don't go missing later. When the journey resumes. When things return to normal.

But when the sailors climb back aboard, one leans over her seat. "Things are bad back there, ma'am. I wouldn't count on seeing your friend anytime soon."

"No." She can barely whisper. "He's a Navy officer. A submarine man. Maybe you saw him and didn't know who he was."

A slow shake of the head. "Sorry, ma'am. It's so bad you can hardly tell men from women. Least there's lots of help from a shipyard. And a couple of hospitals sent ambulances, so they're getting casualties out fast as possible. Still, there's bodies everywhere."

"No," she says again, before she remembers to thank the men.

When they proceed forward, Adele resumes her tales of life in Brooklyn. "The most exciting thing I ever seen was when the Hindenburg flew right over. Same day it blew up. Of course, we didn't know it was gonna do that. Couldn't believe how sad it made me feel."

As the screechy voice drones on, Gail wants to scream. By now her knees are aching, though she can't remember hitting them, and a dull ache grips her forehead. Worse yet, the possibility of Matt's loss has congealed into a *fait accompli,* an inescapable absence. It retreats only when a railroad official comes thru the car announcing that a relief train will take them to Penn Station.

"So everybody needs to collect your luggage and move forward to the first four cars. See, this one and the car ahead," he explains, "they're off the tracks. But lots of seats up front. Just follow the conductor."

A spate of new questions erupts from passengers, mainly about what time they'll get to New York. He checks a gold pocket watch on a chain. "Might be three hours. But better late than never, they say."

A wan, dispirited cheer trickles through the coach. All Gail feels is the horror that she'll be moving on without the man whose brief presence had lifted her from the doldrums of the past weekend. Leaving him behind. Knowing nothing of what's become of him since he followed the doddering women into Car 7. If she never sees him again, he'll still be the one shining segment in this dismal weekend. The only detail of it that she won't make every effort to convince herself it never happened. Or if it had, that it wasn't meant to be. A fluke caused by her father-in-law's failure to deliver her to Union Station for an earlier train. One that would have gotten her to New York by now, in plenty of time to catch the next New York, New Haven and Hartford to Boston, then the Portsmouth local so she'd be home long before midnight.

But mainly, on none of these trains would she have met the submarine officer who'd sparked new life in her, then disappeared as effectively as he might have on a doomed boat. Leaving her to perpetually miss something she'd never had anyway.

It makes no sense. None at all. But that didn't mean it still didn't hurt.

CHAPTER SEVEN
8:30 PM, 6 September

G uided by the conductor's flashlight, passengers from the derailed coaches drag their luggage toward the four forward cars. Two tracks over, a steam engine chuffs past northbound. In the aisle behind Gail, another official explains, "Power's out between Trenton and Wilmington, so we'll be towed to Trenton. And hook up again. After that, it'll be a quick trip to New York."

"I just bet," Adele whines as they navigate the off-kilter vestibule between cars 6 and 5. "I don't believe a damn thing they say."

Gail shrugs, keeps moving. By now the excited dread has receded, leaving her conscious of hunger, fatigue, and pinpricks of pain. It's a long walk, especially with the added weight of Matt's tome in her suitcase, and cars 4 and 3 are full. She's ready to collapse into a single seat in 2, but Adele urges her to keep going so they can sit together. Finally, in the coach behind the engine, there's an empty double in front of the two sailors who'd freed her from the lavatory. Their presence is strangely comforting.

From here, she can see nothing of the wreck behind them, but images she'd glimpsed earlier are etched in her memory like woodcut depictions of hell in some old volume of horror stories.

Finally, all the stragglers are seated. The relief engine is switched onto the same track. It backs up noisily and jolts into a connection with their original locomotive. The coaches behind rattle backward in sequence. Up front, the steam locomotive strains; the cars jerk a few feet forward. Until the telltale whine of drive wheels spinning on dead center mandates another attempt. Once again they lurch forward. This time their speed gradually increases.

In the seat behind Gail, the sailors comment on what a heavy load an electric engine must be for what looks like no great shakes as a locomotive. "More like the Little Engine that could," says one. A loudmouth farther back quips, "Maybe we should get out and push." Another male voice yells, "Get a horse!" Nervous laughter titters through the car. Adele shrieks at the humor of the remarks. Gail finds nothing to even smile at.

Finally accelerating, the relief train draws away from the other scattered coaches of the Congressional Limited. And the victims probably still trapped inside the wreck. Horrific images play like an endless newsreel in her head.

Fortunately, though her voice is annoying, Adele is a distraction. "Jeez. It's like we're refugees," she says as darkness deepens and their speed increases. Up ahead the whistle wails. Always a mournful sound, especially tonight. "Like we're on a train to nowhere. And we're the lucky ones. We got off easy."

Gail nods and twists her hanky. Mile by mile, time thins the connection between her and Matt. In its place is a dark horror she's never known before, even when she'd learned of Jerry's death. Regardless of how it had happened, he'd been a Marine prepared to die. If Matt had died, it was accidental, all the bad luck he'd previously eluded finally swallowing him. Like a predator too often cheated of its prey.

So wrong, so wrong. Her own good luck had kicked in only because she'd had to pee. Of course she'd euphemized the reason—to freshen up, not pee. Had he realized? Had he even had time for conscious thought as Car 7 was caught up in sudden violent destruction? Or had it all happened as lightning was said to hit—in a heartbeat, a split second, too fast for evasive action, self-protection or even prayer?

She slowly becomes conscious of Adele's speculative study. "This guy that was with you. You and him, you only just met, right?"

She manages a nod; her throat constricts.

"But you liked each other, right?"

She shrugs as if it's no big deal. "We were going to have supper in the dining car…"

"Huh. So…Want to say a prayer for him?"

Does she? "I guess it wouldn't hurt." How facile the collects in chapel at St. Margaret's, that smooth flow from the Episcopal Common Prayer book. Or with her pious Catholic older sister, the rosary in her fingers. Their Congregational mother had taught them "Now I lay me down to sleep" as toddlers. And her father had bragged about lighting a candle for Jerry after he'd died: "Even though he was a Protestant." But nothing in her life has prepared her to deal spiritually with this situation.

"If you want, I could say a rosary," says Adele.

From her reluctant exposure to Catholicism, she believes the rosary ritual is mainly penitential. But says, "That'd be kind of you. Thanks."

Fingering the beads, Adele prays all the way to Trenton. At least her lips move; Gail can't hear the words. Only when they pull into the station does the girl kiss the crucifix and slip the beads back into her purse. Just in time for the conductor's announcement that the Red Cross has refreshments inside; they'll be there for twenty minutes. "But when you hear the whistle, get back on so's we can get underway right away."

The brick station is dingy, dim, and bitter with old tobacco smoke and age. At oilcloth-covered tables, women with Red Cross armbands are handing out Cut-Rite-wrapped sandwiches—your choice of sardine and egg or pimiento cheese—along with doughnuts, and coffee, and Dixie ice cream cups.

Gail and Adele carry their picnic to a bench on the platform. Across the tracks, an electric engine and a string of red coaches are stopped at a mobbed platform. The air is sultry, heavy with creosote from the ties, the greasy metal smell of all railroads, and an overlay of what could be burning feathers. Adele suggests a nearby pillow factory might be on fire. In spite of herself, Gail giggles.

The lunch is so dry it sticks in her throat. Forcing herself to swallow, she observes that the I-think-I-can engine has been turned loose to chuff off into the darkness beyond the station. Atop their old locomotive, the rear pantograph unfolds, connecting to the overhead wires. Train crewmen walk the track, shining flashlights under the coaches. The engine begins a deep-throated hum. Yellow light blinks on inside the cars.

Still teary, Gail digs into the Dixie cup with the flat wooden spoon. The sweet vanilla cold momentarily distracts her from the growing weight of tragedy.

By the time passengers re-board, air conditioning has begun to banish the dank closeness in the coach. Taking her seat, Gail feels more hopeful. The engine horn honks twice, the bell dings; they begin to move as smoothly as they had leaving Union Station. Almost as if nothing cataclysmic has happened since. Almost as if on the final leg of a planned journey. Almost normal except for other trains stopped at other crowded stations—Princeton Junction and Rahway and Elizabeth and Newark—in the shimmer and smelly industrial fogs of North Jersey.

The New York skyline is glowing in the distance when the train slides into the tunnel under the Hudson. Chattering cheerfully about having survived the wreck, passengers collect luggage and prepare to spring out at Penn Station. Adele prints her name and address on an envelope so she and Gail can be pen pals. Gail writes hers on a page from her diary, but with no intention of staying in touch.

As they roll into the huge station, she's surprised at the crowds surrounding immobilized trains at every platform. One of the sailors explains that owing to the blocked tracks in Philly and the power outage, no scheduled runs have left since six. Now thousands of holiday travelers are desperate to get out of the city.

With a "follow me" gesture, the taller corpsman beckons Gail and Adele to stay with them as they step down from the coach. On the platform, the mob pummels them with questions: "Were you in the wreck?" "Are you the only survivors?" "How bad was it?" But mainly, "How soon till we get out of here?"

Adele basks in this quasi-celebrity status. She keeps tossing answers, and seems ready to give an interview to a man with a PRESS card in his hatband. But Gail and the sailors keep pushing ahead. Adele catches up at the front of the train, where a chalkboard indicates these four cars are "Section 2 of the Congressional Limited." Nothing mentions the fact that of the five hundred plus who boarded in DC, only about a hundred passengers have just arrived. Late but safe.

By now it's after ten. Numb, Gail follows the sailors to the upper level where crowds in the vaulted concourse swarm like refugees fighting to board the last train to freedom.

At the subway entrance, Adele gives them all tearful hugs and heads toward Brooklyn. Gail hasn't expected to miss the girl's constant chatter, but is relieved at the prospect of the sailors' company to Grand Central, then on to whatever Boston train they can get. For a moment she's nagged by the need to be at school by eight the next morning. Then decides if she has to, she'll show up late and risk the wrath of the headmistress.	One of Jerry's favorite obscenities--"Tough shit"—pops into her mind.

At Seventh Avenue, they push through more massed humanity to a ragged line of taxis. Finally they engage one that's just disgorged a gaggle of soldiers. The air inside is thick; old cigar smoke and whiskey fumes barely mask a residue of vomit. It takes the cabbie fifteen minutes just to get away from the station, and then he wants to hear about the wreck.

Gail closes her eyes as city lights whirl by, as men's voices drone on, as the cab wiggles in and out of traffic. The dull pain in her head escalates to a sick headache.

After the turmoil of Penn Station, Grand Central is an oasis of serenity. A relief, because the next Boston train doesn't leave till two AM, a local that will take almost five hours to reach Boston. Armed with this information, the sailors, Jake and Sam, escort her to a long bench in the waiting room, and take off to buy tickets. When they come back, they're waving a Special Extra edition of the *New York Times.*

Sam, the taller one, extends the front section to her. She winces at the bold italic header splashed across three top lines: *More than 50 are killed in wreck of speeding Congressional Limited in outskirts of Philadelphia.* Under it is an aerial photograph of the devastation, with columns of details.

She hands the newspaper back, shakes her head. "I'll look at it later. Too tired to make sense of it now."

"We can read it to you, if you like," says Jake.

"Not right now, thanks."

Shrugging, the sailors seat themselves on the bench, passing the paper back and forth and murmuring to each other. Gail closes her eyes, trying to ignore the suspicion they want her to read the account. Want her to know what they know. What the reading public will know. As if this is a step she has to take to put the day in perspective.

No, she thinks; not now. Complicated enough her memories of the hours since Friday morning when she passed through this station on route to Washington, to Fair Haven, to the Graham cottage, to the constant reminders of Jerry. And the ignominy of his lie about her Italian background. The only segment of this odyssey she cares to remember are the hours earlier today when the Congressional Limited was still beautiful. When she'd shared a seat with Matt Ogleby. And tasted the sweet hint of possibility.

Now those memories seem pointless. What she needs to do is clean them from her mental slate. Go home to her chaotic family and her structured job at St. Margaret's. Rewind the hours since Friday morning and move on as if they were only a movie she'd just watched.

Otherwise, she'll be forever haunted by an insistent whisper of *might have been.*

CHAPTER EIGHT
Tuesday, 7 September

It's eight-thirty by the time Gail unlocks the '39 Ford coupe she'd inherited from her husband. Closed up at the Portsmouth Boston & Maine station for four days, it reeks of leaking oil, threadbare upholstery and years of Jerry's cigarette smoke. As usual, it balks at starting. When she finally coaxes it into life, driving even these familiar streets demands all her attention.

Earlier, calling home from South Station had pushed her deeper into the nightmare sense of the previous evening. To begin with, her mother didn't realize Gail hadn't come home the night before, assuming she'd tiptoed in after midnight. As for the wreck, somehow she hasn't heard about it, though the kitchen radio is almost always on. And when Gail had asked her to call St. Margaret's to say she'd be late, she'd asked, "Why? Were you injured?"

A weary sigh. "I'll fill you in when I get home, Ma."

"Just as well. Can't talk now anyway. Got to get Frankie off to school."

Ma's main concern, it seems, is that "the baby" start first grade on time. Once she'd been the mother of Gail and her siblings, Charlotte, Pete and Rosalie. But the past six years, it's been all Frankie. She barely even worries about Pete in the Army Air Corps. Now she doesn't realize her second-born could have been killed. If she had been, Gail wonders, would that have transformed Ma into the all-inclusive maternal parent she'd once been? Or have her first four kids had all the mothering they're entitled to?

Despite her battered mood, the short drive somehow reaffirms her life. Sunlight sparkles through leaves of sugar maples lining the streets; kids in new outfits are walking toward the grammar school with new book bags, new lunch pails, new best friends. Yellow buses are picking up high school students from corners where they wait in gender-distinct clusters. All very normal for the day after Labor Day. Except that today Gail's turned into Alice-down-the-Rabbit-Hole, where nothing feels normal.

Halfway down the block is her family's home—a big Craftsman bungalow, painted yellow on a street where other houses are classic brick colonials on neatly-landscaped lots. This front yard's a jungle of overgrown orange marigolds and purple asters; a crumbling flagstone path leads through a colony of garden gnomes, trolls, replicas of the Seven Dwarves, scalloped bird baths, silver gazing globes and Italianate sundials. At least the goats are gone; her father gave them up after the neighbors took him to court. His only public lunacy now is driving the pale green Pierce-Arrow, a vintage limousine that emits exhaust heavy as a war zone smoke screen.

Parking in the street, Gail walks around to the back door. Sheets droop on a line strung between trees; the washing machine churns away in the cellar. With the *New York Times* clutched in hand, she calls, "Ma, I'm home."

Below, her mother's at the Maytag, guiding towels through the wringer. In the glare of a naked bulb, she looks about seventy. Her thinning gray hair wisps in limp strands and she's wearing a faded housedress. Times like this, no one would believe she's the attractive hostess who greets customers at the posh Coach House Tavern on the Boston Post Road.

Glancing up, she regards Gail with none of the relieved fondness a train wreck survivor might expect. "I'll look at the paper later. Took me half an hour just to get Frankie to stop whining and let go my hand at school. And I'm still working on the soup for lunch."

"Did you call St. Margaret's for me?"

Ma's face goes blank. "Oh Lord, it clean slipped my mind in all the commotion."

"Never mind, I'll do it now." Stifling a sigh, Gail ascends to the kitchen and dials the phone. She gives the secretary a quick sketch of the situation, and assures her she'll be there as soon as possible. A sliver of her consciousness wishes Miss Bullman will tell her not to come in till the next day. Still, when she hears, "Get here as soon as you can," she's not surprised.

Breakfast is a do-it-herself egg sandwich and half a cup of coffee so there'll be plenty for her father when he gets up around noon. He's rarely home from the restaurant till after midnight, which causes the rest of the family to tiptoe around so he's not disturbed. Today, with Charlotte working in Boston, Pete in the service, Rosalie in her last year at high school and Frankie in first grade, Gail's the only one home to tread softly.

Her mother's hanging out towels by the time she's changed into the white blouse and navy blue pleated skirt she wears to teach. Not exactly a uniform like the students wear, but close. Though she skips a shower, it's still after ten before she's ready to go. She closes the front door softly, hurries to the car and heads for Dover without letting her mother know she's off. If she hadn't noticed Gail's non-arrival the night before, Ma probably won't realize she's gone now.

It's an easy seven miles to the collection of Georgian brick buildings tucked into a hillside outside Dover. After four years of teaching, her routines are imbedded so deeply that even as fuzzy as she feels and as late as she is, they come naturally. She meets the new ninth graders in her home room, follows the day's schedule for her English classes, assigns the homework she'd planned the week before. Before she'd set off on the holiday weekend. Before she'd known Jerry's family more than superficially. Before her train had come to grief.

Like an automaton, she plods through the school day, following routines, interacting socially and professionally, but never mentioning the accident. Maybe if someone had inquired. But no one has, except indirectly, when Sister Julian, the headmistress, asks if she's all right. She doesn't mention the wreck, but Gail assumes that's her reference. She smiles. "Thanks for asking. I'm fine."

By the end of the day, however, she can no longer even pretend to be okay. It's not just the odd bumps and bruises or the itchy residue of sunburn, but a peculiar mental fog that short-circuits her connection to reality. She gropes her way through the first-day faculty meeting, then, driving home, stops at a news stand for the final edition of the *Boston Globe.*

The headline--*Death toll in Philadelphia train wreck rises to 79*—is augmented by the news that more than a hundred injured have been taken to three city hospitals. She's surprised that all the casualties were in the seventh and eighth cars: photos of their remains are the stuff of future nightmares.

Barely breathing, she turns to an inside page and scans a list of the dead. When she doesn't see Matt's name, she checks again. Then flips through the paper for an Injured list, but there is none. She's avid to know his condition and which hospital he's been taken to, but all she can think of is asking Anna Donovan to help: if anyone can, she'll find the missing naval officer. If he's alive, of course.

She intends to call as soon as she gets home. But by then it's almost six, and the house is in a state of chaos because it's Pop's night off from the restaurant. His mealtime presence is always dramatic; tonight it's worsened by Frankie's insistence that kindergarten was all the schooling he'll ever need.

The kid's final threat--"I ain't never going back and you can't make me!"—sends Pop into a tirade, which aggravates the tantrum. From infancy, fits of temper have been effective in getting the kid his own way. They still are. Pop shouts and threatens more of the discipline he never delivers. Ma cries and pleads. Rosalie's the only one who can quiet him, in this case by promising Gail will drive downtown for ice cream—*if* he stops crying. *If* he's a good boy. *If* he has a bath first.

In the calm after this storm, Ma finally remembers to tell Pop that Gail was in the big train wreck yesterday. Pop shoots her a worried look. "But you wasn't hurt, was you?"

She shakes her head and begins to explain. Until he snorts, "Train wreck! You talk about train wrecks, when we was kids, there was one in the Alps. On the main line to Switzerland. Two trains on the same track, they run head on in a tunnel. In a tunnel, mind you! Nobody walked away from that one. You was lucky, getting off so easy. You oughta thank your lucky stars."

All Gail can mutter is, "Oh, I do, I do."

As he rambles on about other disasters he's heard of, she realizes her adventure is only one small pebble Fate's tossed into the waters of his world. She may perceive it as a boulder, but only by having done something more spectacular than just surviving—say, by rescuing a famous movie star—would she have earned his attention. For now, at least in the bosom of the family, she's alone with her story. With no chance to call Anna until after she's driven down to the Friendly for the ice cream that will bribe her little brother into quasi-normal behavior. At least until bed time.

It's after eight before the kitchen's quiet enough for her to use the phone. And even then Pop warns that he has to make a business call, so she only asks Anna if they can have lunch Saturday. "See, I have to find a Navy officer I met on the train yesterday. The one that wrecked in Philadelphia?"

"What? You were on *that* train? Oh my goodness. Listen, I can't wait till Saturday to hear about it. How about coming to supper tomorrow night?"

Gail doesn't know Rev. and Mrs. Moss except by sight, but has always envied Anna her only-child status. That her father is an Episcopal priest is a bit off-putting, but her mother is a well-corseted little woman who doesn't wear lipstick but dots her eyelids with vivid blue shadow. "What time?"

"Early. Just come after school."

When she slogs up the stairs to the rear bedroom she shares with Rosalie, her sister's typing on the portable Clipper at her desk. Down the hall, Frankie's had his bath and his fill of ice cream, and is pestering Ma for a bedtime story. Shutting the door on the domestic chaos, Gail kicks off her shoes, stretches out atop the chenille spread and closes her eyes.

Normally, Frankie's evening tantrums roll over her. But now the nightmare sense of the past twenty-four hours is more acute than ever. That morning it had been new, her energy to deal with it fresh and her expectations comfortingly unrealistic, as it turns out. Despite her hope that Matt's alive, his condition and whereabouts are still a mystery. By now, she's read enough newspaper accounts to realize most of the injured are in critical condition, their survival in question. She hopes Anna will know how to find him; the only certainty is, she *has* to look. Has to know what's happened to him. And what will become of him now.

In some form or other, she needs to write a sequel to the horrifying ending of their evanescent friendship. Can't let the pieces of it just hang in the air. Almost like—no, much worse than—coming to the end of a suspense novel only to find the *denouement*'s been ripped from the binding.

However awful the details or unhappy the ending of this story, though, she can't let it go undiscovered. As if it hadn't really mattered. As if she doesn't care.

CHAPTER NINE
Saturday, 11 September

When she picks Anna up at the rectory, Gail's surprised at how much prettier her friend looks than she had only three days before. She'd understood the previous pallor, the circled eyes, the stringy hair: it's been only seven weeks since the C-section that had delivered her stillborn infant. And there's still the fact that her husband's Missing in Action. With such a double dose of loss, any woman might look like a refugee. Maybe today's improvement is only cosmetically-based, but still, making it happen has required some gumption from Anna.

She's curious, but as Anna gets into the car, her first words concern what she's learned about Matt. "I asked the base chaplain to see what he could find out. Not much; he's in a civilian hospital near the wreck site. But it's a start. Here's the address in case you want to write." She hands over an empty business envelope with scribbling on the back.

Gail glances at it before she shifts into Low. "Oh, it's an Episcopal hospital. Huh. Did he find out anything about his condition?"

Anna shakes her head. "Evidently all the injuries are serious." She shudders. "Easy to understand, looking at the newspaper pictures."

"The real thing was worse."

"I bet. Anyway, maybe someone on the boat he had orders to would know more."

"Maybe. Except I have no idea which one it was."

"That doesn't matter. It was new, wasn't it?"

Gail's supply of facts, however, is so miniscule, Anna finally stops asking and comes up with a plan on her own: after lunch, they'll look for the boat themselves. "I mean, if you're willing to drive."

Gail nods. "If you give me directions. Only thing I know about the base is where the Marine barracks are."

Anna's glance across the seat is quizzical. As if she's curious about Jerry Graham. Though they have Portsmouth High in common, since graduation their paths have diverged— Anna's to Mass General School of Nursing, Gail's to New Hampshire State College. What binds them now is a missing submarine officer, not personal history.

They catch up over lunch, after some low grade mutual complaints about being twenty-five, but still living in their parents' homes. In Anna's case, the worst of it is her mother's observation that she's still "pining away". Meaning, she thinks Anna's not putting her losses behind her quickly enough.

Gail laughs at the irony of their gripes. "Gosh. If I ever pined away—for any reason—Ma'd be too busy with Frankie to notice."

Anna's smile is wan. "Actually, first chance I get, I'm moving out. Not just from home, but this town. Too many memories. That way I can pine away in private." She breaks off a piece of a crusty roll, dips it into the Chianti, pops it into her mouth. "Sometimes pining's the only thing you can do."

The comment leaves Gail speechless. As an English teacher, she's usually quick with words. But now none come to mind that express her horror at this remark. All she does is nod, pretending to understand her friend's anguish, yet secretly relieved her own isn't as intense. She wants to find Matt, but God knows, she isn't *pining* for him. She hadn't pined for Jerry, even before she'd known all his warts.

After lunch, Gail drives them to the shipyard, flashes her ID at the Marine sentry, then follows Anna's directions to a fenced-off area along the river. She stops when another sentry

holds up his hand and strides toward them. Behind him a
chain-link barrier screens a black hull tied to a skinny finger
pier. Though it's draped with ladders, hoses, gangways and
machinery, even Gail recognizes the conning tower as part of a
submarine.

The Marine leans in her window, asks what they're doing
in a top-secret area. Across the seat, Anna waves her ID. "Sir,
my husband's the engineer on *Wolf Fish*. I'm looking for a
friend of his who was in that train wreck Monday night."

As she speaks, Gail gets out her ID again and reaches
Matt's hat from the back seat in case she needs to prove she's
not a spy. Though her father's an enemy alien, when you get
right down to it. God, suppose they question her?

"His name's Ogleby, Lieutenant Ogleby," Anna adds. "All
I know is, he had orders to a new boat. I assume it was this
one. Is there anyone here who might know?"

Having apparently been trained to deal with saboteurs, the
skinhead corporal seems flummoxed by a civilian's innocent
request. After some dithering, he returns to the sentry post and
talks on a phone. Anna and Gail wait, murmuring speculations
to each other. Now and then, sailors in dungarees amble
ashore, eyeing them as they pass.

After a suspiciously long while, as if he's checking with the
FBI, the corporal hangs up the phone. Three minutes later, an
officer in rumpled khakis emerges from the sub and jumps
down to the pier. His posture suggests fatigue and impatience.
The Marine points; he nods and plods over to the car.

Anna murmurs, "A lieutenant commander. Probably the
skipper. He'll know. Now let me do the talking, okay?"

When the officer stops at Gail's window, she's struck by
the pungent oil-smell radiating from him. He touches his cap.
"Good afternoon, ladies. Understand you're looking for
Lieutenant Ogleby?"

Anna nods. "Actually, my friend is. They were together
on that train that wrecked Monday night in Philadelphia. She
wasn't hurt, but he was in one of the ruined coaches. The only

thing we know is, he's in a hospital down there. We hoped you could tell us more."

He leans in closer to Gail. "You a family member?"

"No, we'd only just met. But I have his hat and a Navy manual that fell out of the overhead rack. I want to return them, if possible. But I'd really just like to tell him how sorry I am he was hurt."

The man sighs, glances over his shoulder at the sentry. His face is pleasant, though overgrown with stubble and smudged with black grease. He shakes his head, morose. "Sorry, ladies. All I know about Mr. Ogleby is, they've cancelled his orders and sent us someone else. From what I hear, he was banged up so bad, he's off the active-duty list. Meaning, I guess, he'll be hospitalized indefinitely. Not good news, I know."

Anna asks, "Will he go to the naval hospital down there?"

"I assume so."

"Anyway, thanks for seeing us."

He touches the bill of his hat, backs away. "Good luck, ladies." He turns, ambles back toward the sentry post, the gate in the fence, and the sub that Matt Ogleby had so briefly been assigned to.

On the way home, Gail asks Anna's advice about the letter she'll write Matt. "Now that I know more, I'm anxious to start. Maybe even this afternoon."

Anna's response is disappointing. "Today's too soon. Not a week since the wreck. People with serious injuries need at least ten days before they get over the shock and start to heal. Same with major surgery." Her laugh's ironic. "I learned that in nursing school, but it only sank in after the C-section last month."

Feeling inadequate, Gail murmurs, "I can't imagine what you went through."

"Neither could I, before it happened. Anyway, accident victims are usually in so much pain, they get morphine around the clock. So they sleep a lot. Even awake, they're in a daze. If you write him now, it might not mean anything. I'd wait till next week sometime. Maybe Thursday."

"Oh…any other suggestions?"

"No. Except I assume you like this man."

"He was nice," she says, aware she's using past tense. "I mean, not a wolf. And easy to talk to. Funny. I hate to think something awful happened to him."

"Put that in the letter too. And later, if he stays in Philly, maybe we can go down to see him."

"Go down? You mean…on the train?"

"Well, sure. The paper says they've cleared the tracks and trains are running normally. And it's an easy trip. See, I've been there. Back when I was engaged to Bob Hallowell. Fact is, we broke up that very weekend. So I know my way around the city."

Gail sighs again, and brakes in front of the staid brick rectory. "Well, that'd depend on whether he wanted us to come. I'd have to take time off from school too. I'll think about it, Anna."

The other girl opens the car door, laughs as she steps out. "Gail, he may not remember you, or anything about the wreck. That can happen. But I promise he'll be happy to have female visitors. Especially you."

For the next eight blocks, Gail mulls over the advice. But when she gets home, the house is empty, and so abnormally peaceful she takes it as a sign she's meant to write today. For inspiration, she reads the letter Matt had left in the Navy manual. From his mother in Iowa, it's a homely report on the corn crop, area relatives, and his two younger brothers in the service. Its contents deepen Gail's sense of the man she'd known so briefly. And adds new energy to her intention to connect with him.

Once she begins, the letter's easy to write. The hard part will be waiting five days to mail it.

CHAPTER TEN
Friday, 17 September

Clutched by the familiar dream again, Matt flinches awake as overhead lights flare and the night nurse begins the day's first torture. Not the major one, just enough to confirm he's survived the night. With only an hour till the shift change and a ward full of patients, she seldom lingers. Still her smile is cheery. "Good morning, Mr. Ogleby. How are we this morning?"

"Alive," he growls, and opens his mouth for the thermometer, bitter with the alcohol they keep it in. The blood pressure cuff pinches his good arm. Cold fingers clasp his wrist as she counts the pulse. Then she unwraps his lower belly, peers at the catheter and the bottle draining it. Charts his overnight output, then wraps him up again. He feels like a baby after a diaper change.

Finally she withdraws the thermometer, records more numbers. "And how's the pain today?"

He can't tell if it's better or worse than yesterday. The dull ache in his chest has receded by unnoticeable degrees. Except when he moves suddenly and disturbs the damaged ribs. The arm in a cast is numb; the same with the leg in traction. The other, the left, is always on fire. Except after a morphine shot. He loves these. Until they start to wear off and the dream takes over.

"I could use a shot," he says.

Her lipsticked smile frames horse teeth in a cheerful, pockmarked face. "Drink some water for me. Then I'll see you get it."

"Water's too lousy to drink."

"You need it, Mr. Ogleby. Urine's too dark. Come on. Just a few sips."

The promise of morphine is enough to start him sucking on the glass straw she holds to his lips. Until the chlorine cocktail turns his stomach. Gagging, he pushes her hand away.

But she's true to her word. She injects his butt, then moves to the next patient. Waiting for relief, he remembers chlorine fumes in a submarine indicate battery trouble. That he's a sub man is one of the few facts he knows with certainty. Along with the information on his dog tags. The recent stuff is a sink hole that's swallowed everything but his identity as a patient in some hospital in Philadelphia. Docs have told him he was in a train wreck, but his own recall only goes back to riding through downtown DC to Union Station. The why and when and who of it elude him. All he's sure of is, he's had a brush with death.

The effort to remember weakens as the opiate dulls his nervous system. He lapses into an oblivion sweeter than sleep.

Until the dream sneaks back in. Once again he's trapped in rubble, explosions all around, sirens wailing, lightning flashing. The usual people hurry by. A stream of refugees, or citizens in a bombed city racing to shelter. Some faces are familiar—men he's served with, high school chums, girls he dated. Or wanted to. Once in a while even Marcie, her expression colder than anyone else's.

As usual he calls for help. As usual no one even glances his way, just keep moving. As if he's not there. Or has died and is nothing but a corpse. He keeps calling but no one ever responds. Not even people he recognizes. No names, just faces from a splintered past flashing around him as he lies there. Unable to move, to be seen, to be heard. If not dead, he might as well be.

Two hours later, an orderly with a food tray wakes him. Still numb from the shot, he breakfasts on what he can pick up with his left hand—bacon and dry toast, a few slurps of coffee brewed with that awful water. Then the morning shift sweeps in. An elderly crew: nurses, orderlies, even a gray-haired doctor evidently pulled out of retirement by wartime manpower shortages. They add the indignities of an enema, a new catheter, fresh bandages and a sponge bath. The jolly practical nurse who bathes him follows up with a shave. "So you'll look real good for the folks down there at the Navy hospital."

By now he's aware his condition's stable enough for the move to the service hospital. A few days earlier, a jittery civilian chaplain had visited, prayed, given him communion. And named his many blessings. "Do you know how lucky you are, lieutenant? See, every passenger in those two coaches was either killed or injured. Most worse than you. Because you were in the front of the one that went airborne. And weren't trapped under the seats piled up in the back. So they got you out fast. And your blood's O-positive and donors are easy to find, so you didn't bleed to death. Otherwise, you might be one of the dead. See, the Lord really had his hand on you."

Despite this evidence of good fortune, Matt's left leg is gone. He can't pinpoint the moment when he became aware of the loss. Now, however, as he tries to ignore the poking and prodding, the staff's comments make him feel like a mad scientist's experiment. A collection of body parts held together with gauze, stitches, wires, adhesive tape. Torso, right arm, right leg from some anatomical warehouse. Unfortunately, they've run out of good legs, so he's stuck with a partial on the left. He hasn't been able to see what remains, but it's evidently not a lot. Still, they say he's lucky, because the Naval Hospital here is the center for amputee care east of the Rockies.

By the time the torture crew moves on, he's been sponge-bathed, wriggled into a clean gown and bathrobe, and pronounced ready to leave. Other patients in the ward grumble that they're still stuck in this old place, with lousy food, ugly nurses and windows too grimy to see through. One even calls him, "Lieutenant Lucky."

It's after ten when two sailors swing into the ward with a gurney. They waste no time sliding him onto it. By now the morphine's worn off and every twitch of damaged muscles sends needles of pain through his body. The broken ribs are the worst, though a doctor's told him not to worry. "See, the impact that ruptured your spleen only cracked them. So they didn't puncture your lungs. Or your heart. They hurt like hell. But they're not going to kill you."

There's that good luck again.

The gurney ride down to the ambulance is another form of torture, every bump an electric shock. Finally they roll him onto a loading platform, into high sunlight and a brief tinge of fresh air laced with exhaust and chemical smells. A trolley rattles by, a plane drones overhead; cars honk, and somewhere a radio is blasting out *Boogie-Woogie Bugle Boy*.

Inside the ambulance, he faces the small windows in the rear doors. One of the sailors drives, chain-smoking and taking every corner like a race driver. The other sits in the back with Matt. Without looking up, he opens a newspaper, says, "Tell me if you need anything." He's young, a third class Pharmacist's Mate who'd probably rather be on a battlewagon in the Pacific. Nothing like the First Class on Matt's first boat who'd doctored the whole crew for weeks at a time. He can't imagine this greenhorn ever rising to assume such responsibility.

It's a long ride, with more traffic lights than he can count. Each is an agony of sudden stops and jack-rabbit starts. His hunch they're on Broad Street is confirmed by glimpses of City Hall when they swing around it. The gingerbread tower reminds him of Army-Navy games. Staying in a hotel down the block with his parents and Marcie. Back when he really was lucky. Sudden, acute nostalgia combines with pain to bring him to the edge of tears.

The trip goes on and on, assuming the substance of a new nightmare. Finally they roll through a sentry post and back up to a loading platform. Inside a big, dim building, he's wheeled to an elevator and borne steadily upward. He's seen this hospital from the stadium; its twin towers rise above the South Philly slums and dumps like some glorious Art Nouveau cathedral. He hopes he'll be on one of the upper floors; they wheel him off at Nine. Those above, he suspects, are reserved for top brass. Probably penthouses with views of the city, beautiful private nurses. Gourmet meals, morphine on demand. Visiting hours all day long. Still he's lucky to make it to within three floors of the top.

There it is again: he's one lucky sonofabitch.

The room's on the south side of the building; the bed faces a double window. The head is raised enough that he can make out the trees of a park across the street. Beyond are the utilitarian gray cranes, masts and stacks of the Navy Yard, even a slice of the familiar stadium where he cheered for Navy. Back when football contests seemed life or death.

Once he's been settled in the high bed, a new corpsman and a Navy nurse who outranks him by two pay grades bustle in, rubber soles squeaking on polished tiles. Commander Steinhart's a no-nonsense gal with a lined face and enough gray in her hair to suggest she was in the first war, maybe even the Spanish-American. Her words are clipped, bitten-off. "Okay, lieutenant. Let's have a look at you."

He groans at the prospect of another exam. "Can I have a shot first?"

Her face hardens; she leafs through the chart that came with him. "A pain shot? Says here you had one at oh-six-hundred. Civilian hospital's turned you into a damn dope fiend. Listen, mister, in the Navy we do things by the book. In your case, every six hours. So not for another hour. Meanwhile enjoy the view. Lucky for you, this room was empty."

He tosses off a left-handed salute, murmurs, "Aye-aye, ma'am." And abandons hope.

Bending over him, she peers at the incision in his chest while the corpsman peels off other dressings. Her profile's stern and craggy, like that of The Old Man of the Mountain.

He finds this simile curious, since he's never been to New Hampshire. Yet now he wants nothing more than to drive into the White Mountains and stare up at it. For about a minute this unexpected notion distracts him from the latest round of poking, prodding, clinical questions. And the suspicion he's an anatomical experiment who no longer owns his body.

When the corpsman manipulates his right leg into traction, he grits his teeth to avoid screaming in pain. Not just in the damaged leg but from the one that's gone. How can that be? How can you lose a body part and still feel it? A doc at the other hospital had explained phantom pain, but the level of it now brings tears to his eyes. It takes all his will not to cry out as they work on him. He doesn't, of course. It will only get him a sarcastic rebuke from Commander Stoneheart.

Her parting shot is, "Well, none of your injuries shows signs of infection. Things could be worse, you know."

What could be worse? Maybe to lose both legs, both arms, both eyes? And the family jewels? Yeah, he's lucky, all right.

Meanwhile, there's the next shot to look forward to. Thank God for morphine. Thank God for occasional minor miracles.

CHAPTER ELEVEN
Wednesday, 22 September

Now that his shots have been reduced from four a day to three, Matt's perception of hospital routines has taken on a dismal new dimension. Mainly because he's realized how few minor annoyances it takes to transform a tolerable day into a shitty one. Today begins to deteriorate before reveille, when a nurse interested in his vital signs interrupts a delicious dream of a nameless but compliant young woman he's only begun to explore. After that, the downhill slope grows steeper: breakfast is cold oatmeal, cold coffee, no butter for the cold toast, and worst of all, no bacon. And shortly thereafter, an episode of what his mother calls "the dire rear."

The corpsman who cleans him up is overly friendly, excessively interested in the posterior regions of his body. Most ominous, however, is the reaction of the surgeon who makes rounds later. He studies the remains of Matt's left leg with a storm-cloud scowl. He confers quietly with Stoneheart, then asks the usual questions while he probes the flesh above the knee: "Can you feel that?" "Can you move this?" "How's the pain compared with the other leg?" Finally he murmurs to the nurse, "I don't like the look of this. Let's get some pictures and see what's going on." He scribbles some chits, adding, "We'll talk more after I see the X-rays."

Speaking the shorthand of medical professionals, the pair leaves the room. Matt's alone again with the congenial corpsman. And the suspicion some new medical problem's going to challenge his luck.

What the fuck? he thinks as the sailor wraps the stump in new dressings. Behind him the view from the window is of clotted gray clouds, slashing rain. The sash is raised just enough to admit a breeze redolent of a nearby oil refinery. Heavy, petroleum-rich, the smell's familiar, not acrid as diesel nor pungent as gasoline. And not unpleasant to a submariner.

The corpsman has another reaction. "God, that awful stink again." He slams the window closed. "Now, Mr. Ogleby, I'm gonna get a gurney and take you down to X-ray. The ride's real scenic."

The long upside-down trip jolts and sways, setting off twinges in his ribs. As an officer, he goes to the head of the line. But then there's a long wait to make sure they've got clean pictures and don't have to redo them. By the time he's rolled back into his room, the chow tray's waiting, the corpsman eager to help him eat.

Jesus. Creamed dried beef. Shit on a shingle. Today there's no shingle of toast, but mashed potatoes glistening with the crystals of saltpeter. Or so it's rumored in Navy establishments where lust is said to be chemically controlled. Matt's heard the legend so often he no longer gives a damn if it's true. The canned peas with it taste like coffee grounds, and the tapioca pudding has the slimy texture of frog eggs. He's never had slop like this on any sub, even in a war zone. The only good thing about it is, afterward he gets a shot.

Despite the blare of radios from other rooms, he drifts into a nap as soon as the attentive corpsman has helped brush his teeth. And reminded him he's off duty at three, "In case you want anything in the meantime." His smile is suggestive.

Faggot son of a bitch, Matt thinks.

The sleep is a deep, pain-free oblivion. Still, he's not too drugged to surface when the surgeon and Stoneheart return with his X-rays. In an apologetic tone, the doc says, "Sorry to

tell you this, Lieutenant, but you need more surgery."
According to the badge on his lab coat, he's LT M. Snyder,
MC, USNR. "See, the initial amputation just removed the
worst damage to the leg. To control the bleeding. Same with
the splenectomy. After the wreck, civilian surgeons only had
time to stabilize your injuries. Now the stump's healing. But it's
so mangled, it'll never be in shape to anchor a prosthesis. See,
it's easier if the knee's still intact. But this one's too bad to
save. Sorry."

Matt interprets his shrug as "Tough shit."

"Anyway, surgery's scheduled for Friday morning. Should
be a simple procedure." Another thin smile. "Any questions?"

"How much is coming off this time?"

"Just the mangled part." One finger touches the bandaged
stump just above the remains of the kneecap. "Don't worry.
We won't get anywhere near your genitals."

Matt's smile is wry. "And another thing. Afterward, can I
have pain shots whenever I need them?"

Stoneheart gives him a sharp look but doesn't contradict
the surgeon's affirmative answer.

Oh Shit, shit, shit, Matt thinks as they leave. He pictures
the pair enjoying martinis in some local officers' club. While he
lies here, waiting for more of his body to be chopped off. So
far he hasn't asked about his future, but this whole floor's
populated by amputees and paraplegics who specialize in
scuttlebutt. Now and then one rolls his wheelchair into the
room to shoot the breeze, mooch a smoke, play a little Acey-
Deucy. Matt doesn't smoke, but saves the Luckies the Red
Cross hands out for uninvited visitors.

One in particular, a Hellcat pilot who crash-landed on a
carrier, is so eager to share what he knows, he's told Matt all
about the Navy's Master Plan for patients with useless or
missing body parts. "See, first they get the rest of your body
in shape. Then they fit you with a peg leg. When you can
hobble, they ship you to a hospital near home so's you can
practice. Then you get a medical discharge and a fat pension

for life." To the flyboy with two empty pajama legs, this apparently sounds like hog heaven.

But when Matt tries to imagine life as a civilian, his gut constricts and the pain that never stops chewing bites even deeper.

Eventually he sleeps again, not peacefully now but trapped in The Dream, the usual nightmare as the shot wears off.

He wakes after four when a new nurse comes in to do his vitals. She's not pretty but smells of the lavender soap his mother favors. Leaving, she calls his attention to mail on his nightstand. The envelopes are already slit so he can get at the contents. Sometimes by shaking them out, sometimes with the help of his teeth and his good hand. Most are get-well cards from relatives in Iowa, and a slick Hallmark from Dixie and Ron Grady. Also a note from Ben Finkelstein promising to stop by next time he sees his parents in Philly. "Would have been there by now, but they haven't let you have visitors yet."

No visitors? The unexpected news sharpens the knife of apprehension further.

Last is a thick business envelope forwarded from the first hospital. It encloses a letter from his mother that came before he left DC. And a sheet of linen stationery, with a blue-monogramed *GBG* and small, precise writing, also blue. He skips to the signature: Gail Graham. Not a name he knows.

Dear LT Ogleby… You may not remember me, but I sat with you on the train before the accident. We were both going to Portsmouth and planned to have supper together. You went back to the dining car while I used the lavatory in our coach. What happened next was horrifying; I wasn't injured but had no idea what had happened to you. Until last weekend Anna Donovan helped me locate you. Now I'm thinking about coming to Philadelphia to return your hat and the book you were reading. They dropped out of the overhead rack when our car was derailed. The enclosed letter was in the book; I'm sure you want it. Please let me know when Anna and I can visit. In the meantime, I'm so very sorry you were injured. I hope you're recovering.

He reads it again, sniffs the note for a whiff of perfume, but gets only the clean smell of paper. No trace of the girl who wrote it. A girl he has absolutely no memory of on a train he can't recall either, except for what he's read in the papers and heard from hospital staff. For him it's still a fogbank after he left Finklestein's car at Union Station. On the last day that his body and mind were whole and undamaged. Before he became a ruin, useless, without a future.

What had he and this girl talked about those two hours? They'd planned to eat together, so maybe there'd been a spark between them. The promise of more? Or just the hint of future friendship? He hopes she was decent looking, at least. But nothing comes back.

Yet despite this latest frustration, he has a faint connection to someone who'd shared the experience. Obviously only a part of it, the pre-chaos hours. Not much to generate hope. If the Navy doesn't want him in this shape, what woman will? Even when he was whole, Marcie didn't.

Nonetheless, as evening blankets the city and fresh rain smears the lights beyond the window, the slight lift from the letter lingers. Maybe not every day will be as shitty as this one.

In the passageway, corpsmen are delivering chow trays. The aroma suggests spaghetti even before the sailor lifts the plate cover. And there it is, one puny meatball dead center on the tangled red strands. The medic cranks up the head of the bed and tucks a napkin under Matt's chin. "Look, Mr. Ogleby. Garlic bread too. Bet you thought you'd get no bread with one meatball." He guffaws at his own humor.

Matt manages a wry smile at the reference to the popular song. "Gee. They're gonna saw off the rest of my leg, but I get bread with the meatball. Must be my lucky day." He's tempted to add, "I guess cold comfort's better than no comfort at all," but by now the sailor's headed toward the door.

Just as well, Matt thinks. He'd have missed the point anyway.

CHAPTER TWELVE
Saturday, 2 October

As she and Anna walk from the taxi toward the lofty main entrance of the Philadelphia Naval Hospital, Gail's heart races, slowing her breathing. Her only prior experience with any hospital was when her mother had Frankie six years before. In contrast with dismal Portsmouth General, this one resembles a luxurious art- deco Miami Beach hotel. Even Anna seems awed. She pauses to stare up at the twin fifteen-story towers, the twelve-story section connecting them and a spate of low-rise satellites, all yellow brick with terra cotta and stainless steel accents.

"Gosh," she says as they walk on. "This is beautiful. If your friend has to be laid up a while, this is as good as it gets."

"I guess." Gail shudders in anticipation of seeing Matt again. Not as he'd been when they'd met, but as he is now, whatever that means. All she knows is, his right arm's in a cast. The Red Cross nurse who'd answered her letter said only that his injuries were "extensive." But also, "Compared to other victims of that wreck, he's lucky."

Guided by Anna's innate knowledge of medical facilities, they find Miss Howard in her second floor office, follow her to an elevator, then to the door of Matt's ninth floor room. In the corridor outside, men in wheelchairs are lined up like passengers sunning themselves on the deck of an ocean liner. Gail notes uneasily that all are missing limbs or parts of limbs, and are openly leering at her and Anna. She's reluctant to return their stares for fear of betraying pity or shock.

Miss Howard has warned them to control their reactions when they see Matt. "His morale's already low. Don't make it worse by talking about the war. Or the train wreck. Or anything else that might upset him."

"I'm a nurse myself," Anna interrupts. "I've seen so many injured men at the Portsmouth hospital I know the drill. Don't worry about us."

"Does he remember anything about the wreck yet?" Gail asks.

They turn a corner and almost collide with an amputee jolting along on crutches. Miss Howard shakes her head, setting frizzy brown curls trembling. "And he might never. Amnesia's common in trauma victims."

"Suppose he asks about the wreck?"

By now they're at the last door on the corridor. "Don't tell him any more than he wants to know. Now, if you'll wait here, I'll see if he's ready for visitors." She knocks, pushes the door open. Even after she enters, her crisp, authoritarian voice is audible above the cacophony of nearby radios. Gail catches whiffs of cigarette smoke, stale coffee, pine oil disinfectant. Anna looks nervous, paces. Gail takes this as a sign she knows more about Matt's condition than she's said.

"Is anything wrong?" she asks.

"Oh, just that this—you know, another Navy hospital—it takes me back to Dan when I met him. He'd been in a motorcycle crash. He was smashed up so bad he worried about being unfit for duty. This man may have similar concerns."

Before she can ask more, a corpsman emerges from Room 921 carrying a basin piled with stained gauze, gives them a flat glance, and takes off down the passageway.

A minute later Miss Howard reappears, smiles thinly and tells them they can go in. "Just remember what I said about hiding your feelings. We'll talk more at lunch. Noon in the staff dining room. Second deck." Looking relieved, she bustles off to other duties.

Anna signals Gail to go in first. In the dim room, she's so dazzled by sunlight at the double windows, she doesn't see the patient in the bed just inside the door. Until she turns and there he is, propped on pillows. His right leg's in traction. His right arm is in a cast, with only the fingertips exposed. And under the blue bedspread, there's a valley where the hill of his left leg should be.

She barely stifles a gasp, and changes her mind about the line she'd intended to open with. Suddenly, asking "Is this seat taken?" seems as corny as the dialogue between Phyllis Thaxter and poor, shot-up Van Johnson in *Thirty Seconds over Tokyo*.

Matt's left hand, the only obviously undamaged appendage, is extended. "Mrs. Graham?"

Clasping it, she widens the smile, nods. And feels like a character in a British war film, keeping a stiff upper lip as she regards her horribly-burned aviator fiancé. So far as she knows, Matt isn't burned, but he barely resembles her seatmate on the train. His face is sallow and deeply lined. His hair straggles over his ears. His lips are smiling, but his eyes are dull. Like someone on the cusp of hopelessness. It's all she can do not to break down and sob. But she doesn't. Her job's to restore this broken man's will to live, not send him into a suicidal depression.

Turning loose his hand, she holds up the Filene's bag she's brought. "Here's your Navy hat and the book you left on the train." She turns as Anna advances into the room. "And this is Anna Donovan. I wrote you about her. Remember? Her husband's engineer on a submarine. You know…the man who drives it?"

If there are degrees of blankness, his eyes register a rising level of it. Anna grins and shakes his good hand gently. "Glad to meet you, Matt. Just wish the circumstances were different."

"You and me both, Mrs. Donovan. So your husband's in *Wolf Fish*. Still missing?"

"Yes. But it's only been three months. The Japs are bad about notifying us about prisoners, so it might be a while yet before I hear anything. By the way, where did you meet Dan?"

"At Pearl a few months back. At a wetting-down party."

"That must have been right before they left on the last patrol."

As they get into details, Gail sets the shopping bag beside the night stand and pulls a steel armchair closer to the bed. Listening, she tries to translate the acronyms peppering their conversation. Until Matt turns back to her. "Sorry about all the Navy talk. But we know a lot of the same people. Including the biggest asshole in the whole service."

Anna smiles and eases into another chair between the bed and the sun-bright windows. "He means the old skipper on *Wolf Fish*," she tells Gail. "Almost got them sunk a couple times. Then he got orders to Washington and an old friend of Dan's took over. Ironically, the new guy was CO when they went missing."

Matt sighs. He shifts in the bed, apparently with difficulty. Anna asks, "Where do you hurt, Mr. Ogleby?"

"Huh! Where don't I? Worst of it's where they took off the left knee last week. Plus, talking about Ron Grady always sets off this intense pain in my butt."

Anna laughs aloud. "Sorry, Gail. Navy men don't always talk like preachers."

Gail smiles to dispel the possibility she comes across like a prissy old-maid schoolteacher. "Don't worry about it."

A sudden silence fills the room. Until Matt murmurs, "Anyway, uh, Gail, I thought seeing you'd bring back my memory. Maybe it has a little, but…well, I still don't remember being on that train. Except now I realize you're one of the people I keep dreaming about."

"Oh? Good dreams?"

His expression turns bleak. "Not really. More like nightmares. Not specifically about the wreck, just something awful in the background. Bombs exploding. People trying to get away. The way I picture the Blitz. Maybe because I was pinned in the wreckage an hour before they got me out. Or so they tell me. Anyway, in the dream, I can't move. Can't do anything."

"How awful," she sighs. "Do I try to help?"

"No, you just run by with the all the others. So tell me-- what happened to you in the wreck?"

In her second letter, she's written as much as she recalls of the two hours they'd shared, as well as a synopsis of the following night. "Nothing really. Only some bumps and bruises. Two sailors from our coach went back to help. Later they told me not to count on seeing you anytime soon." Despite her resolve to Be of Good Cheer, tears puddle in her eyes. She blinks them away. "Sorry. I'm being silly. I mean… here you are all banged up and I'm good as new. But the way it happened, well, sometimes I feel responsible." She finds her hanky, blots her eyelids. "As if I should've asked you to wait while I used the lavatory. Because if you had, you'd be fine now too."

He averts his gaze, shakes his head. "Didn't know that." He shrugs. "Just one of those things. Like being transferred off two boats just before their last patrols. My lucky streak finally ran out. You had nothing to do with it."

She blows her nose as daintily as possible. "Do the doctors think you'll recover your memory?"

"Possible. But not probable. A staff psychiatrist says it's too painful. Not just the accident, but losing my leg. At the first hospital they tried to save it so I'd be fit for duty again. But all they could do was stop the bleeding. Don't know how those surgeons dealt with so many casualties." He inhales a deep breath, gestures toward the emptiness where his left leg used to be. "Anyway, if ever want to go to sea again, I'll have to turn pirate."

It takes a moment for the remark to register. When it does, she's horrified at the laugh that erupts from her, sharp as the yip of a dog. Instinct prompts her to reach for his hand, lower her head to the bed and hide her face in the harsh chemical smell of whatever they wash the sheets with. Tears behind her eyes burn closer, despite her awareness she's indulging her own feelings with no regard for his.

"Well, Mr. Ogleby, at least you haven't lost your sense of humor." Anna's tone is light, likely the result of years of hiding shock, sorrow, sympathy. Probably a skill they teach in nursing school. Gail, however, has no idea what to say next.

Until she remembers another detail from the wreck. "By the way, Matt. Did you ever get that big bag you left on the train? In the overhead rack? When we had to leave our coach, I told the conductor about it. I just wondered."

"You mean my sea bag. Yeah, it caught up with me the other day. Not that I'm going to need it any time soon. Or the hat either. Thanks for my mom's letter too."

"The Red Cross lady told us your parents were here last weekend. From Iowa, right?" Anna asks.

His nod is grim. "Had to see for themselves I was alive. Spent more time on trains getting here than they did visiting. Which was probably merciful, being I must look like the living dead. Mom sniffled the whole time."

Gail wants to ask more about his family, but even with no medical training, recognizes that he's tiring. Or needs a bedpan. So when Anna mentions they're meeting Miss Howard for lunch, Gail gets to her feet with a curious mixture of relief and regret.

While they're still in the doorway, Matt asks, "You girls'll be back, won't you?"

Anna nods. "At two. After your nap."

Grinning—or is it grimacing?—he touches his brow with his free hand. Feeble, but still a salute.

CHAPTER THIRTEEN
Later the same day

G uided once more by Anna's innate sense of hospital layouts, they take the fire stairs down to the second floor. "Wish I could get my hands on Matt's chart," she says as they emerge in a broad corridor redolent of steam and hot food. "So I can see what he's dealing with. Besides the obvious damage. As it is, I'm sure the prognosis is guarded."

The term sounds ominous. "What's *guarded* mean?"

"That with so many injuries, he's at risk for complications. Mainly infection. And bedsores, from being immobilized. And what they call battle fatigue. See, that nightmare he talked about, it happens to men who've been in combat too long too."

"My goodness. It sounds so terrible, I wonder if he knows he's lucky to be alive."

"Especially since his future in the Navy's not exactly rosy."

At lunch, Miss Howard elaborates on the Navy's plans for Lt. Ogleby. Not specifically, but the general policy regarding amputees. Once their injuries are healed, they're fitted with artificial limbs, acclimated to using them at a hospital near their homes, then granted a medical discharge. No more war for gimpy heroes.

Anna looks horrified. "But in Matt's case, that'd be such a waste of talent! I mean, he's an Academy man. In line for command. Of course, an amputee couldn't handle active duty on a sub. But with all his knowledge, all his experience, there must be a desk job he'd be good at."

Miss Howard blots her mouth on a lipstick-smudged napkin. "I might agree, Mrs. Donovan. But we're seeing so many amputees, it wouldn't be feasible to send them all back to duty."

Anna shakes her head. "Even in the Revolutionary War, George Washington organized a Corps of Invalids, so injured men could continue to serve. They couldn't fight, but they could still stand guard."

"Well, in this war, we don't have the manpower to rehabilitate them, even for guard duty. Or desk jobs."

"Has anyone asked Lieutenant Ogleby what he wants?" Gail says.

Miss Howard's bushy brows shoot up. "No. If we did that, it would imply he has options other than those available for his situation. And give him false hopes."

Anna's glance over the rim of her coffee cup is skeptical. It's only when the other woman rises to return to work that she says, "You should still ask him. No Navy man wants to be stuck in a desk job. But it's still better than being kicked out of the service, especially in wartime."

After Miss Howard leaves, they dawdle at the table, let a steward keep refilling their cups while they explore the issue further. As if they can come up with a solution no personnel expert's thought of. Afterward, they pretty up in a ladies' room, then find their way back to Matt through corridors reverberating with a baseball game from radios in every room. Except his.

Despite the din outside, he's sleeping, twitching, breathing ragged. Anna finds a recent issue of *Life* on the nightstand; Gail picks up a *McCalls'*. One she's read before, but a good distraction. They tiptoe back to their chairs near the bed, leaf through the periodicals. From time to time Anna regards him with narrowed eyes, as if professionally assessing his condition.

Wondering about the nurse's observations, Gail tries to imagine the torture of being so restricted by injuries that you can't sit up or take care of your basic needs, let alone stand on your own two feet. Like an infant, needing others to do everything for you. Even in sleep his face is anxious. Until the slam of a nearby door startles him awake. Has he been caught in the entrapment dream again?

Matt slowly blinks back to consciousness. Watching, Gail decides he'd probably rather stay semi-conscious, no more than half-awake for perpetuity. She smiles to hide the pity she doesn't want him to detect. Finally she says brightly, "Well, Lieutenant. About time you woke up."

He reaches for a water glass on the night stand, barely manages to bring the straw to his lips. Anna rushes to help. "Sorry. Been waiting long?" he asks.

"No. Thought about waking you, but I figured you needed the rest," Gail says.

"Should have anyway. I can sleep anytime. But I never have visitors. Only my parents last weekend. Nobody else yet."

Anna asks, "If you were nearer home—Iowa, right? Would that help?"

He stares as if he suspects she's leading up to some momentous but unwelcome news. "You mean in a place full of Great War vets waiting to cash in their chips? Shot up in battle. Or gassed. Not survivors of train wrecks."

She ignores the remark. "Well, if that's not it, what do you want? I mean, once you've recovered. Once you're on your feet again."

"Feet?" His laugh's sardonic. "You mean my *foot?*"

"Well, okay. Or your peg leg." Anna covers her mouth as if hiding a smile.

Matt's grin is reluctant. "Okay, then. I want to go to New Hampshire, to the yard, like I had orders to last month. Sure, sea duty's out of the question. But even if I have to *hop*, I can still man a desk. Hell, that's all I was doing the last four months at BuShips. No reason I can't shuffle papers at the Navy yard there."

Anna's gaze meets Gail's across the bed. "Sounds reasonable. But you'll have to convince a medical board you can handle that duty. See, you have a right to express yourself, not just hold still for whatever they decide. Even if it's sending you home to Iowa."

If he takes hope from her words, his face doesn't show it. "Yeah, I know it's a pipe dream. Maybe if I'd been wounded in battle. But this way...forget I mentioned it."

Anna frowns. "Why? Because you were on a civilian train? But you were on orders, weren't you? I mean, it's not as if you were racing a motorcycle. Or driving drunk."

He nods. "I was supposed to report to the Portsmouth yard by 2400 that night."

"And the Navy arranged your travel, right?"

Another nod. His eyes narrow, as if to focus on the issue.

"As far as I can see, what happened to you was in the line of duty. So you should express your feelings. I mean, tell them you want to go to Portsmouth anyway. Even in a desk job."

"What makes you think the Navy gives a shit what I want?"

Anna sighs but maintains the smile. "Because even with only one leg, you can still be valuable to the sub force. The way we're losing boats, we need every man we can get."

Matt's sigh is heavy. "Excuse my French, Mrs. Donovan, but you talk like a damn Polyanna."

Gail gasps at his bluntness, but Anna's expression remains cheerful. Maybe for a nurse, handling insults is as routine as emptying bedpans. "Well, then, any other ideas?"

"Yeah," he grumbles. "Put me out of my misery."

Anna blinks quickly, her inhalation a gasp.

"Because if this is all there is," he goes on, "I mean, another year like this, then months on crutches with the peg leg...and for what? So I can hobble around the family farm pretending I don't notice the pity?" He shakes his head with new grimness. "If that's not a living death, what is?"

Anna shakes her head. "I agree, Matt. Pity's a killer. I've been getting it from my parents for months now. Ever since Dan's boat went missing...and..." she swallows hard, "...and I

...lost a baby. So next week, I'm leaving for a job in Maine. Mainly to get away from all that pity."

It takes him a moment to come back with, "Sorry. I mean, about your losses." He sighs. "But at least you can change something. The way I am now, I'm as trapped as I was in the damned derailment."

"Well, at the moment. But in a couple weeks you'll be able to sit in a wheel chair. Move around. And after that, stand up and learn to walk again. Okay, it'll be a long haul, but once you're vertical again, the world will look better."

Cynicism is cold in his gaze. "Mrs. Donovan, I'm sure you know what the hell you're talking about, *medically*. But I'm thinking about afterward. Being useless the rest of my life. That's the entrapment I'm talking about."

Anna sighs, shrugs, seems at a loss for words. Then, "Matt, I know how you feel. As if things will never be right again. Sure, I say I expect Dan's boat'll turn up. But every day that passes the odds get worse. Sometimes I wish I could lie down and die. Or walk into the ocean and never come out."

Without missing a beat, he shoots back, "At least you can *walk* into it."

Anna sighs again, says nothing for a moment. Then, "Don't know if Gail's told you, my father's an Episcopal priest. Sometimes I'm tempted to preach too. You know—'count your blessings' and all that. But even when I'm most hopeless, a little voice in my head says the Lord has a plan for me I can't possibly imagine. I don't want to count on a miracle. But who's to say there's not one in my future? Or yours."

"Huh. Like your husband's boat turning up at Pearl with all hands safe? Or for me, growing a new leg? What do you think?"

She blinks slowly, draws a deep breath. "I think the Lord has more up his sleeve than we can imagine. Maybe something even more far-fetched than growing a new leg."

He shifts in the bed, wincing with what Gail interprets as pain. Or is futility more agonizing than physical pain?

"Well," he rejoins, "the only miracle I'd go for's staying in the USN. Until we win this war, at least. Otherwise, put me to sleep."

Until now, Anna's expression's been steadfastly cheerful. But when she sighs again, her face is sad. "Tell you what, Matt. Next time we meet, if you still feel this way, I'll push your wheelchair into the ocean myself. Okay?"

He seems to be stifling a smile, which strikes Gail as a hopeful sign. Otherwise, they've come to an impasse. Anna's no-nonsense speech has shocked her again, though maybe it's the best way to handle despondent patients. Whereas Gail can only sniffle and gaze moon-eyed at the guy.

After that, uneasy in the silence, she sneaks glances at her watch. Until Anna returns to her nurse persona, asking how often he gets pain shots and what the staff's doing to provide him with exercise. Then she says, "Getting back to Ron Grady. I knew him when he was CO of Dan's boat. Nobody aboard respected him."

The new topic seems to spark Matt's interest. "Why was that?"

"Because he was a coward. Went out of his way to avoid going after enemy ships off the coast of Japan. Once he sank an empty old tub, turned the deck gun on survivors, then lied in his official report. On his last patrol, a Jap destroyer got on their tail, depth-charged them for eight hours, did such damage they barely made it back afterward. Then to Pearl, finally Hunter's Point. Took them four months to put the boat back together. By then Ed Zimmer was CO. Know him?"

"Met him a couple times. Heard good things, though."

She nods. "First patrol with him, they made a name for themselves. But then..." She shakes her head with patent sorrow. "At least I know if there's any way they can make it back, Ed'll find it."

"Yeah. A good guy. While the Asshole's living high on the hog in Georgetown." He falls silent a moment. "You know, if his wife hadn't insisted I come to their damn cocktail party that day, I'd have been on an earlier train. So right now I'd be working my butt off on the new boat instead of lying here in this worthless body. How's that for irony?"

Anna crosses her legs, rearranges her skirt. "Funny. When I first met Dan, he was so bitter about being injured, I preached it was all part of the Lord's plan for him." Her grin is rueful. "He didn't take it well. So I won't hand you the same line, Matt."

"You already have, Mrs. Donovan.'

Their gazes meet; both smile. More so than before, Gail's aware of her outsider status. She and Matt aren't nearly the pair that he and Anna are. Or could be, with a shared jargon, common friends, similar losses, even a mutual enemy. True, she's not officially a widow. And next week she's going to a Maine coastal island to work in a civilian medical clinic. But if the ties that bind are strong enough, maybe they could have a future together. Gail's not quite sure how she'd feel about that.

The mood, the connection's broken when a skinny, stiff-starched civilian nurse squeaks into the room on thick crepe soles. "Sorry, ladies. Sixteen hundred. Visiting hours are over."

Gail rises dutifully, but Anna doesn't move.

"Can you come back tomorrow?" Matt asks.

The nurse warns them again about visiting hours, and swishes out.

Gail says, "Wish we could. But we're getting an early train. I have school Monday morning." She raises the Filene's bag, sets it back on the floor. "Now. Don't forget your hat and that manual you were reading."

"Probably never need either one again. But thanks for bringing them."

Sighing, she gathers purse and jacket. Her throat constricts with the likelihood she may not see this man again. As if to confirm it, he says, "Wish you luck on that island, Mrs. Donovan. Lots of U-boats off Maine. See, Atlantic convoys make up just off Portland, so the wolf packs are waiting. If you see any, let me know. I'd be glad to hear from you anyway."

"I'll keep you posted."

"You too, Gail," he adds as if suddenly reminded of her presence. "And keep writing, okay?"

"Sure." She intends to give him a fond smile. But an impulse beyond good sense moves her to lean down, take his face between her hands. And kiss his mouth. So quickly, she wonders if he'll even notice. Or if he does, he can ignore it, if he chooses.

Instead, as she starts to straighten, his good hand on the back of her neck pulls her down for an even longer kiss. So deep she can taste the hunger, the sudden intensity. In only a heartbeat, it overrides the practicalities of the situation, stirs up an irrational craving for more. Deep in her core, desire pulses like the first sparks of an awakening volcano.

Even as she wonders whether it's mutual, the nurse sweeps back in. Her, "Okay, Mr. Ogleby. Playtime's over. Tell your girlfriends goodbye," is caustic.

Barely breathing, Gail backs away from the bed. Matt whispers, "Will you come again sometime?"

She nods. "If I can." Their gazes hold; Anna shakes his hand, wishes him well.

The nurse intervenes, pops a thermometer into his mouth. "Really, ladies, I can't do my job with visitors hanging around in total disregard of the rules."

Gail retreats, but Anna says, "Listen, miss. I'm a nurse too and just as overworked as you are. But that's no excuse for rudeness. Especially to an officer's visitors."

Anxious to put this contretemps behind them, Gail edges toward the door. Above the thermometer, Matt's gaze follows her. He waves with his good hand and murmurs something unintelligible in response to her "Take care of yourself," and Anna's, "So long, Matt." The nurse shoves the door closed the moment they step outside.

"Bitch!" Anna sniffs. But as they head toward the elevators, she smiles wickedly. "Well, that kiss should've raised his heart rate. If nothing else."

It takes Gail a moment to catch on. "Oh don't be silly. He's a helpless invalid. Surely he couldn't ...you know."

At the elevator doors they merge with a crowd of departing visitors. "Listen," Anna murmurs. "I've known of men on their death beds who still lusted. It's the last part of the male body to die."

Despite her resolve not to, Gail blushes, wondering where the kisses might have led without the nurse's intervention. Or Anna's presence. Once, the answer would have horrified her. But after her marriage, however brief, naiveté no longer shields her from the inevitability of sexual attraction.

In the descending car, she's aware of the conflict in her emotions. On one hand she regrets having to leave; balancing it is relief at returning to normal. This blend is made even more curious by the new element introduced by the kiss: Romance? Or plain old desire?

She's still pondering as they wait for a taxi outside. When Anna asks where she wants to eat that evening it takes a moment for her to say, "Let's try an Automat. Saw one near the hotel."

Once they settle into the cab, Anna says, "Too bad Matt's going to be laid up so long. A romance with him won't be easy."

Gail blinks and inhales the old leather, motor oil and burnt tobacco ambiance. "My goodness, Anna. It was only a couple of kisses!"

"Really?" Her friend's tone is dubious.

"I was just being friendly. Saying goodbye. You know. By the way, does he remind you of Dan?"

She smiles, her gaze wandering toward the window. "No. Not really. He may be a submariner, but he's a lot...uh, well, I guess you could say *tamer*. Fewer rough edges. Dan was the sort of man mothers warn their daughters against. "

"Apparently you tamed him."

Anna's gaze remains distant, her expression thoughtful. Then she turns with a bright smile. "Temporarily, at least. Some men are never tamed. I doubt you'd have anything to worry about with Matt, though. Except the distance between you. That could be a problem."

Gail shrugs in mute understanding of that and other challenges to a romance in these days, these circumstances. As she tries to think of a comment, the cabbie screeches to a stop at a red light. Squinting back at them, he speaks through the stub of a cigar clenched in his teeth. "Hey, ladies. Mind if I turn up the ball game? Don't wanna miss the last inning, what with the Phillies so close to winning the pennant."

In unison, Anna and Gail say, "Sure, go ahead," and settle back to think their separate thoughts. From there to the hotel, the frenetic commentary of the announcer overrides further attempts at conversation. Gail's relieved; she wants to cosset the warmth of those kisses, not discuss what they portend. Or listen to a lecture about potential problems. Needless anyway: the reality of Matt's situation had hit her only a few minutes into the visit. Now, however, their parting has given it a lively new dimension. The sheltered girls in her English classes would call it Romance. On the other hand, Anna, more earthy, more pragmatic, would likely identify it as Lust.

For Gail, it's a promising hybrid of both.

CHAPTER FOURTEEN
Later the same day

I t takes Matt a good ten minutes to come down from the electric high of Gail's kisses. Until the crotchety nurse's rough handling hastens his return to the world of pain and discomfort. But, for the first time, he declines the shot she offers. Once she leaves the stirring returns, to banish his sense of himself as nothing more than a hopeless cripple. After four weeks, finally a glimmer of hope. Only a candle glow, but enough to light a path out of the bog of self-pity.

And why? he wonders. Because the tall, freckled girl had ignited a flame? Or because her friend preached at him to believe all things are possible? The kiss had been a surprise, but Anna's pep talk had been what he's come to expect of nurses. From his observations the past month, she's typical—crisp and strong and positive. Perfect for the job, perfect as a submariner's wife, even his widow. She's the Rock of Ages, anchored in faith. Even as he'd accused her of being a Polyanna, admiration had tempered his annoyance.

On the other hand, Gail seems a different breed of woman, more kitten than cat. All soft edges, vulnerable in her innocence, she appeals to his protective instincts. Then there's this other thing, a promise only in concept—that glimmer. That possibility. That interest in *more*.

For a few minutes before Joe Beck wheels himself into the room, Matt savors the fresh energy in his shattered body. He wants to wallow in it, chase its tentative promise that his productive manhood can be restored. That he'll again work in a worthwhile cause. That he'll love and be loved, partaking of life's ordinary blessings. The ones most men take for granted. Like getting laid now and then.

Before he can dig deeper, the double amputee's wheelchair bumps open the door. As he rolls inside, he barks, "Hey Ogleby, got any smokes?"

Matt gestures toward the bedside cabinet with his good arm. "But not your brand."

Beck roots into it, comes up with two packs of Camels. "Listen, today I'd even settle for Kools." He rips into one, fishes matches from his bathrobe pocket, soon has a cigarette going. As he inhales, his facial muscles relax. Not quite a smile, but an improvement over the previous scowl. Unusual for the guy. Normally he's annoyingly cheerful.

Observing the other's nicotine-based relief, Matt wonders if he should take up the habit to replace the morphine he's already sorry he declined. "Bad day?"

Beck nods, exhales. "Never thought I'd say it, but my girlfriend's a first-class bitch." His expression turns bitter again; he takes a fresh draw. "Shoulda known something was up when she brought her old lady today. Jeez. What a pair!"

Matt's disinclined to hear Beck's complaints, but there's no escape. "What'd they do, steal your smokes?"

Disgust supplants simple annoyance on Beck's features. "Worse. She called it a filthy habit. Said she—Cheryl, that is—she won't put up with it. Never bothered her before! It's the old lady's influence. See, she owns the building where Cheryl's got an apartment. We're supposed to live there. After we're married, of course." He smokes again, faster. "Jesus. What've I got myself in for?"

Matt's missed the backstory to this drama, but isn't interested enough to ask questions. Or offer advice. All he can think of is, "Is it too late to ditch her?"

Beck shakes his head, continues the rapid-fire smoking. "If I believe her, it is. See, claims she's knocked up. Guess she could be. 'Cause last time she was here, said she wanted to cheer me up. Huh! Thought she just wanted to see if a guy with no legs could still do it." His laugh's harsh, ironic. "And there I was, just dying to prove it. Oldest game in the book. And I fell for it."

Matt considers more intrusive questions, but says only, "She's from Pittsburgh, right?" He doesn't care, just needs to move this discussion to less personal territory.

Beck nods morosely.

"So…when was that?"

"Six weeks or so." By now the air is thick with smoke and tension. "Jesus. Shot down again! Just when I thought I had life by the short hairs. You know?"

At this point, all Matt knows for sure is the other man's faith in life after the Navy. In the absolute freedom of a disability pension. To be able to drink as much as he wants, never have to work again, and get laid anytime he feels like it, which he believes will be incessantly. And to be forever revered as a war hero. Now this ironic shoot-down, starting with his being forbidden to smoke.

"Tough," Matt mutters. "But it could be worse." As he says it, he's aware it's one of those meaningless things people say when they know the other person wants a quick fix, not a philosophical discussion.

Beck nods vaguely, lights up a fresh butt, rolls himself over to the window and stares out at a watery pink and purple sunset. Matt yawns, fidgets. From radios in other rooms, cheering reverberates along the passageway. Somewhere in the city, a baseball team has won an important game. He has no idea who's playing, and less interest in the outcome. Much easier to picture Gail and Anna back in their hotel room, just down Broad Street from City Hall. Only a few miles away, but suddenly remote, distant. Already ancient history. Their visit, her kiss too fleeting to matter to the course of his life. For a few minutes it had pushed his useless body and its various aches into the background. Now gloom settles into him again as Joe Beck continues to smoke and berate himself for the twist of fate that's shot his glorious future out of the sky.

Maybe he's right, Matt thinks. Nothing works out the way you hope it will. So what's the point in making plans?

By the time chow trays come up and Beck leaves, he's back to the hopelessness that's become a habit the last few weeks. He can hardly wait for the relief of the day's last shot.

CHAPTER FIFTEEN
Sunday, 3 October

The dream features the same old plot. Except this morning it has a new denouement. It begins with the usual parade of characters hurrying past, ignoring him. Then, near the end of the procession, Gail Graham suddenly recognizes his predicament and walks toward him. Her expression is determined. Until she smiles and stoops to embrace him. Like Prince Charming's kiss on the comatose Snow White, the gesture sets him free of his entrapment.

Reviewing it on waking, memory seeps in, slowly at first and imperfectly—their shared seat on the train, fragments of conversations, that distant heat lightning, his intention to treat her to dinner. Even the waiter with the gong.

Another significant bit is his offer to go ahead and get a table while Gail uses the rest room. Finally, dawdling into Car 7 behind the old woman and her nurse.

Even without images, he knows what comes next. He dreads details, but the screen goes blank after he steps into the doomed coach. The docs have said detailed recall is unlikely anyway. This much—those two retrieved hours, with Gail—are enough. Not the total picture but sufficient to hint at the rest.

Just like that, laying claim to his recent past frees him to believe in his future. A transformation so amazing that, wallowing in it, he stares at the dark windows until the first glow of dawn shreds the clouds. Around him, the institution's awakening for another day of its healing mission. Now, for the first time, he can visualize it putting him back together.

Like Humpty Dumpty, he thinks with a smile. Reassembled not by all the kings' horses or men, but by a young woman—nothing like Marcie—who could have sat anywhere in those sixteen cars that day. But had chosen the seat beside him. For no reason except pure chance?

Unless this is what Anna Donovan refers to as a trick God had up His sleeve. The smile widens as he pictures the deity watching Gail and himself the morning of the wreck. And determining that they're decent souls, battered by events and in need of human love. That they're both en route to Portsmouth, NH, is the puzzle piece that convinces Him to intervene. Reaching into a voluminous sleeve of His shining robe, He grabs a slip of paper—no, more likely a parchment scroll— inscribed in gold calligraphy with "See to it that Gail Graham and Matthew Ogleby meet on a train today."

He flags a passing angel. "Here," He says in His awesome voice. "Make this happen."

The angel, Matt imagines now, would be a Navy man killed in the line of duty. Perhaps a submariner trapped in *Squalus* the pretty May morning in 1939 when she was test-diving off Portsmouth. And a faulty valve flooded one engine room so suddenly and massively that no emergency maneuver could bring her to the surface. Down and down she went, watertight doors sealing off the engine room, trapping the men inside in order to limit flooding. And save the others aboard.

Matt sighs, the familiar story always poignant. Especially when he imagines one of those sacrificed men—maybe a motor mac he'd met at sub school—now the Lord's right-hand man in charge of other submariners. As he plucks the scroll from the divine hand, he gives a brisk salute, a crisp, "Aye- aye, sir," and bustles off with the orders.

God is pleased. But only until that evening, when He realizes His neglect to specify *which* train is going to complicate the star-crossed romance He has in mind for the couple.

As Matt hears the approach of medical personnel in the hall, a wry notion crosses his mind. Maybe even the Lord and all His guardian angels can't think of everything. The apostasy would horrify his mother. Likely Anna Donovan too, who might judge it sacrilegious. He's still grinning when the last night shift nurse barges in to take his vitals. She seems annoyed at his good humor. Her cold hands and scowl are almost enough to plummet him back into the blues.

But not quite. Not now that he has this image of the Almighty taking such personal interest in his life. It makes sense; it wasn't good luck that kept him from sailing in those doomed boats. Or bad luck that put him on a train that would come to grief. Rather, some overarching plan he might never fully grasp until his last day, when he can fly over his life and appreciate terrain he's been too close to in the actual living of it.

After four weeks with only morphine to ameliorate hopelessness, the wild notion comforts him, almost as much as Gail's kiss. And his restored memories of her. Not nearly as miraculous as sprouting a new leg. But close enough for government work.

CHAPTER SIXTEEN
Thursday, 14 October

Back in his room again after a nerve-racking session with a clumsy technician determined to saw off a limb along with the cast, Matt stares down at the white, withered stick that used to be his good arm. He squeezes the tennis ball that's supposed to exercise his hand back to normal. Skeletal after weeks under wraps, the limb bears two scars from surgery he has no memory of, probably at the civilian hospital. One puckered red track itches above the wrist; the other's just above the elbow. Since the x-rays have been explained, he knows about messy compound fractures.

So far his remaining leg hasn't healed enough for that cast to come off, but even this much progress seems monumental. By now too the lateral incision in his chest has healed enough to no longer need dressings. And mercifully, his ribs no longer twinge when he coughs or sneezes. Or laughs, though he's done damned little of that recently.

He's wondering if the corpsman who brings noon chow will urge him to eat with the right hand. No one asks if he needs help these days; he's gotten so good with his left, he's no longer a high-priority patient. At least not when it comes to eating.

Bathroom functions are another matter. Weeks before, wrapping up his tour in BuShips, he'd had no idea how quickly and completely the human body can be smashed into uselessness. Or how long it takes to restore one that's been reduced to a quivering bundle of raw flesh, exposed bones and jangling nerves.

Someone knocks on the door, then pushes it open before he can answer. Not the kid with chow, but a crew-cut, Joe College ensign he's never seen before. Soon after Anna and Gail's visit, he'd asked Stoneheart to arrange an audience with someone from the Medical Service Corps so he can talk about staying in the Navy. Since this man wears the Corps' oak leaf insignia on his sleeves, Matt reckons he's about to have his hearing.

But before Matt can begin to make his case, Ensign Shuttlesworth jumps into the issue. He carries a clipboard, but doesn't glance at it. "Lieutenant, I understand you're unhappy with the Navy's plans for your rehabilitation."

Matt hesitates, aware of the other officer's faint sneer. The guy's so young he probably doesn't even shave every day. His uniform's so obviously new Matt figures him for a ninety-day wonder. Fresh from some Ivy League V-12 program and ready to tackle the Jap, or the U-boat menace to North Atlantic convoys. Certainly not a broken-down O-3's hope of deviating from the official policy on amputees.

Matt nods. "I believe I have the right to disagree with any decision about my future."

The other guy shifts his weight from one leg to another. Impatience radiates from him like heat from a fever. "Technically, sir. But not yet. Not while you're still recovering. After all, it's only what? Six, seven weeks since you were injured? Even your good leg's an unknown quantity." He taps the clipboard with a fountain pen. "We have strict standards for amputees. To qualify for limited duty, you have to be able to walk with only a cane for support. You're months away from even thinking about that. And the stump of your left knee…hell, according to your chart, it's not healed enough to support a sock, let alone a prosthesis. So…" His shrug is articulate and dismissive. "You've got a long way to go before you can think about staying in the Navy." He turns toward the door.

"Wait a minute, ensign."

The guy looks back with a *what-now?* sigh. As if he's late for lunch with some hot-shot admiral who's about to promote him to aide-de-camp.

"That mean you'll come back when I'm in better shape?"

A curt nod. "Just don't look for me anytime soon."

"How long? A month? Two?"

"More like six." He pauses, one hand on the door. Then, with an impatient sigh, he pulls up a chair and squats as if poised for a quick get-away. For a moment, he actually scans the papers on the clipboard.

"You know, lieutenant, most of our patients are only dealing with amputation. You, though, are recovering from four major fractures, a splenectomy, some minor fractures and two surgeries to remove the mangled parts of one leg. So when you do get a prosthesis, it'll be for an above-the-knee amputation. Which means you'll never walk normally.

"Plus, before you ever start physical therapy, your right arm has to be in shape to support your upper body, and the right leg has to be able to bear the weight of walking. Meanwhile you've lost tone in all your muscles. Besides which, your age is against you. At thirty, the body doesn't recover as quickly. Or regain strength as completely." He shakes his head morosely. "Because the sort of prosthesis you'll have uses twice as much energy just for walking. So, even if you get good enough to run a race, stamina's still going to be an issue. Hate to tell you, but you're facing an uphill battle all the way."

The facts have come so fast Matt can't sort them out. All he's been able to hear is Bad News. For a moment he teeters between frustration and anger. Then he draws a deep breath and clenches his good hand into a fist; the other can only limply clasp the tennis ball. "Okay, Ensign. Thanks for giving me the straight skinny. But I'm still going to try. No matter how long it takes, I want to stay in the Navy. And be stationed at the Portsmouth Navy Yard. See, I had orders to a new boat there. As exec." He arms himself with a fresh breath. "Okay. There's no chance I'll ever go to sea again. But I still want to work there. At a desk. Trouble-shooting, solving problems, coming up with solutions based on my at-sea experience. No reason I can't do that."

"I doubt the Navy'll see it that way."

Matt shrugs. "Maybe not. But it's worth a try. And another thing—I want to convalesce at the hospital in Boston. I have friends up there, so I'll be close to the action."

The younger man stares with a mixture of pity and contempt. "Really, sir, the retirement policy's so generous, I don't see why anyone would want to go back to duty. Especially a submariner."

When the man pronounces it *sub-MAR-iner*, Matt decides the next time he talks to someone from MSC it won't be this bird. "Maybe that's why. Because most sub-mar-INERS in this war don't have any choice about their future. See, when you're dead in the water and the depth charges are going up your ass, you'd give anything to get out. Including an arm or a leg. Maybe both."

As he delivers the impromptu speech, he realizes it must sound cornball, even irrelevant to this young whippersnapper. No surprise that the polished face registers no emotion. "Well, if that's what you want, you need to make it official."

For the next few minutes, he writes furiously on a form on the clipboard. Then hands it over, along with the pen. "Read this, then sign and date."

Matt glances through both the text and the ensign's additions, then with his left hand scrawls a distorted version of his signature and *14 Oct 43*. The younger man retrieves his pen but doesn't check the document before he gets to his feet. "Okay, Mr. Ogleby, lots of luck. You need all you can get when you ask for the moon."

His exit is quick, and his parting shot hangs in the air like a cheap aftershave.

Stewing in the wake of this encounter, Matt reminds himself he hadn't really expected good news, just not to be talked down to by a JO. Since his casts are beginning to come off, he's taken heart that he'll soon be moved from bed to wheelchair. Meaning the worst is over, and the rest of the healing process will be rapid.

Instead, he's just heard "six months." *Six fucking months.* Not till April.

It's after chow before he stops seething. And then only because the mail includes three pages of Gail's neat script. He's surprised at her strong reaction to passing the wreck site on the way home, given that she hadn't been injured. Wonders what he might feel, since he can remember nothing more than the run-up to the cataclysm. But, he resolves, if he ever gets a chance, damned if he won't ride that same train again to confront any demons still lurking in the shadows.

For now, though, her mention of another visit lifts him to a sunnier place. "Maybe the day after Thanksgiving, if that doesn't interfere with your plans."

Plans for what? he wonders. Doesn't she know he can't go anywhere?

He reads it twice more, then settles himself for the usual post-prandial nap.

He's drifting closer to sleep when another knock on the door rouses him. His "Come in," is reluctant in case it's someone else with crappy news.

Instead, it's one of the blue-uniformed Red Cross volunteers. They show up daily with books, newspapers, games, comics, cigarettes and activities designed to sustain the morale of long-term patients. This gal's pushing a cart piled haphazardly with supplies.

"Lt. Ogleby," she begins hesitantly, then introduces herself. "I'm Mrs. Schwartz. How would like me to make a portrait of you?" She nods toward the cart. "Nothing fancy, just a sketch. It'll look like charcoal and pastel, but it'll only be grease pencil and crayon."

"Oh, is that what you have there? Art supplies? Hoped you were moving in with me."

Her eyes—deep brown in a well-seamed tanned face— widen. Her hair is pure white, long enough to be cinched back in a turquoise-studded barrette. She could be as young as thirty, as old as fifty. Instantly he regrets having reacted the way half the horny guys on the floor would.

"Sorry." He draws a deep breath. "A portrait, you say?"

She nods. "Wouldn't take long. Half an hour, more or less."

He's tempted enough to glance at samples of her work. He can't tell if the likenesses are accurate, but they look professional, not the efforts of some do-gooding amateur. "That's something my mother might like. Maybe for Christmas." He clears his throat as a preamble to turning down the offer. "Only problem today is, I need someone to write a letter for me." He elevates the newly-uncast arm, now in a supportive sling. "See, my right hand still doesn't work. So…"

Her expression registers only graciousness. "Well, if that's what you need, I can do the portrait another time." She returns the samples to the case and withdraws a folder of stationery from the jumbled contents of the cart. She pulls a chair closer, and settles into it. "Now. What do you want to say?"

After dictating, "Dear Gail," he describes the meeting with the MSC officer. Then assures her that Thanksgiving weekend's fine; he'll reserve a room at the Bellevue. "Normally the Army-Navy game's here and downtown hotels are full. But this year they're playing at West Point, so there shouldn't be any problem."

As he dictates the words, he's aware they're more impersonal than if he were writing this himself. He hopes Gail gets the deeper sense of his final comment: "Really looking forward to seeing you again."

After he finishes, he gives Mrs. Schwartz the address, then wishes he'd asked her to leave it with him to put in the outgoing mail. Because, even with his right arm as feeble as it is, he'd be able to underline the last line. Once, twice, maybe even three times. Too late now, though; the volunteer has it ready to go. She asks, with a grin, "Shall I write S.W.A.K. on the envelope?"

Abruptly embarrassed, he blurts out, "I don't know her well enough for that."

"Sorry. Just wondered." She rises quickly, smooths out creases in the uniform skirt, neatens the hodgepodge on the cart. "Okay, Mr. Ogleby. I'll see you next week. So whenever you feel like sitting for a portrait, just say the word."

He nods, smiles, thanks her for helping. And tries to imagine how it feels to walk out of here, catch a bus or the subway, and head for home. A place where the challenges of life are ordinary, its discomforts related to such minor maladies as headaches, sort throats, colds, constipation. Not the fact that in order to achieve his present goal, at the very least he's going to need one well-functioning leg and two good arms. Right now all he can count on is his left arm. Which is not nearly enough to achieve what the Navy will require to let him stay in.

He sighs and squeezes the tennis ball harder.

CHAPTER SEVENTEEN
Saturday, 26 November

By the time the taxi reaches the hospital that morning, apprehension is nibbling at Gail's newly-polished fingertips, rumbling in her stomach and quivering through her body. Back at the hotel, Aunt June had suggested all this was related to meeting Matt's parents. Whereas Rosalie thought it was more likely caused by being in love and not knowing if it was requited or not. Gail had said that was silly, because there's no such word as *requited,* only Unrequited. She doesn't know if this is true, but her sister trusts her because she's an English teacher.

Without anyone to lead the way, Gail's not sure she can find Matt's room. But once she gets off the elevator, it comes back to her. This time the clustered wheelchair patients in the hall leer so openly she wonders if her slip's showing, or if she has a run in one nylon. Trying not to appear flustered or grim—grim being even worse than flustered—she walks resolutely to the end of the long hall

The door's closed, but she can hear voices inside. She knocks timidly, gulps a breath and waits. Almost immediately it's flung open by a large older man she guesses is Matt's father. He's bald, but his grin is just like Matt's.

"Mrs. Graham?" he asks.

She nods, extends her hand. "Mr. Ogleby?"

"Come on in. We're dying to meet you." He takes her hand limply, as if he's not sure what to do with it.

Inside, the bed's now next to the window, and Matt's in a wheelchair at the foot. His mother rises from a side chair, greeting her with a nervous smile. She's not the countrified little farm wife Gail expects, but tall enough to look her in the eye. Her powder blue suit has a homemade look, but her handshake is warm and welcoming. "Glad to meet you, Gail. Take off your coat and I'll hang it away."

As she sheds the heavy winter garment, Gail relaxes enough to notice the difference in Matt since the first visit. Not only is he sitting up, but his remaining leg, though propped up, is no longer in a cast. He's in a dark blue robe; his hair's close-trimmed, his color good, his smile wide.

Barely breathing, she shakes his hand too. In the taxi, she'd planned to rush over and kiss him. But, scrutinized as she is by his parents, decides a handshake is more appropriate. Until he pulls her down and presses his lips to hers for so long the Oglebys exchange knowing looks.

"My goodness, Matt," she exclaims when he finally turns her loose. "Six weeks has made a big difference. You must be feeling a lot better."

His grin is mischievous. "Still waiting for the new leg to grow, though."

Mrs. Ogleby gasps. "Why, Matthew. What a strange thing to say." Her tone is gentle but with an admonitory undertone.

Gail tells them, "When we were here last month, my friend Anna promised him a miracle. Her father's an Episcopal priest and she believes in them."

"Well, we're Methodists and we do too. But nothing like...I declare! Growing a new leg!"

"Just a joke, Dottie," Mr. Ogleby puts in. "Now, let's all sit down and get to know each other." He waves Gail into a steel chair close to Matt. "So, how was your trip, Gail? Or shall I call you Mrs. Graham?"

"No, Gail's fine." She sits carefully, smooths the pleated skirt over her knees. "It wasn't what we planned. My aunt and my sister and I, I mean. Aunt June—she's my uncle's wife—she's the Women's Page editor for the newspaper up home, and she has a good car with a C gas ration card. So we decided to drive. It didn't look far—only six inches on the map. But south of Boston we got into snow, the heavy wet kind. So we left the car in Providence, and came the rest of the way by train. I wanted them to come with me this morning, but they couldn't wait to go shopping at Wanamakers."

Even as she relates the story, she realizes she's talking too much, too fast. Telling more than they want to know. A simple "The trip was fine, thanks," would have been enough. But with the Oglebys and Matt seated across from her, the oblique sunlight at the window feels more like a spotlight, their questions an interrogation. Yet none are confrontational, just curious and friendly, as farm folks are reputed to be. Matt doesn't join in but watches like a spectator at a ping-pong match.

Before long, however, Mr. Ogleby takes over the conversation, volunteering information not just about the farm but "the nice folks we're staying with here. See, the Red Cross has a list of rooms near the hospital. Only a few blocks north on 17th Street, so we can stroll down anytime."

When he pauses to fish a cigar from the pocket of his plaid flannel shirt, his wife warns, "Howard, don't you dare light that smelly thing in a sickroom. Tell him, son."

Matt sighs, but his eyes go on smiling. "That's right, Dad. Cigarettes are okay, but you have to smoke cigars in the sunroom."

Ignoring them in a way that recalls Gail's own father, he stuffs the cigar back in the pocket, then goes on about how they'd always come to Philly for the Army-Navy game back when Matt was at Annapolis. "Don't know why they're playing at West Point this year, but we can catch it on the radio. Red Cross is throwing a party, so it'll be almost as good as being there. Won't it, son?"

Matt's smile broadens as his gaze connects with Gail's. "Yep. And almost as good as growing a new leg."

Mrs. Ogleby's comment is just a mutter, but Gail can hear more disapproval. Undeterred, her husband says, "Came every year he was there. The last two, Marcie was with us. His high school sweetheart. They married the weekend after he graduated."

Gail fakes a so-what? tone. "He told me about her on the train that day."

"He did?" Brows raised, he glances at his son. Matt's nod confirms the half-truth. "Well, anyway, she's a nice girl. Married again now, but we still get a Christmas card every year."

Matt's tone borders on bitter. "Listen, Dad. Just because she still sends Christmas cards doesn't mean she's nice. And there's no need to mention her now."

Mr. Ogleby clears his throat, scratches at the fringe of hair along the back of his head. "Well, I just thought maybe Gail'd be interested, seeing she's been married too."

The logic of this statement escapes her. "Yes, I was. But only for three days. Then he went overseas and died before he ever got into combat."

"Sad," says the older man. "Divorce is sad, but death's even sadder. How long since it happened?"

"Last January. Funny you mention him, because I'd been visiting his family when I met Matt on the train. One of those coincidences that later seem like the hand of Fate." She adds the last line to solidify her presence here today. Unable to read the older man's expression, she goes on: "By the way, Mr. Ogleby, I understand you were a submariner in the first war. Did you ever consider making the Navy a career?"

"Oh Lord, no. Folks needed me on the farm. Not that I wasn't tempted. Best year of my life on that boat. Nowhere near as big as the ones today, but they got the job done. L-boats, with gas engines. After the war, the Navy laid them up in the yard here—" he jerks his head toward the south, which she interprets to mean the Navy Yard—"and now they use them for training at New London. At the sub school. Right, son?"

Matt's nod is minimal.

"Kinda sorry he won't be able to stay in either. Think he really wanted to serve in a big new boat fresh off the ways." Another quick glance, another brief confirming nod.

Gail arms herself with a deep breath. "But a man with all his experience… couldn't the Navy still use him?"

"In the shape he's in? Listen, if you'd ever been on a sub, you'd know they're no place for a cripple. Besides, we need him on the farm. Even with one leg, he'll work harder than any hired hand."

By now Matt's expression has gone from flat to bleak. She realizes he might be more comfortable if she changes the subject, but can't resist chasing the issue. "But if he could… say in a desk job…don't you think he should?"

Mr. Ogleby fidgets, gaze on his son. "Well now. If that's what he wanted. Of course, be hard to keep the place going without him. But it'd be his call." With a loud sigh, he shifts focus to his wife. "Wife and me, we only want what's best for him. Isn't that right, Dottie?"

Dottie's vigorous nod leaves no doubt. "Just for him to be happy and safe. That's the main thing."

Sensing his parents expect Matt to agree, Gail lowers her gaze to the imitation leather purse in her lap, something for her nervous fingers to pick at.

All he says, though, is, "I know exactly what you want, Mom."

The ensuing silence becomes stifling. Until Gail puts in, "At least he'd be safe on the farm, compared to a sub. But in a desk job, wouldn't the risks be minimal too?"

"Minimal to none," Matt agrees. His parents don't even glance at each other.

With the silence thickening, Gail's relieved when Mr. Ogleby reaches for a newspaper on the bed. Makes a big show of unfolding it, then reading aloud a list of both teams' starting players for the big game. He can recite their strengths, weaknesses and records. And is quick to predict another Navy victory. "As usual, we've got the better team."

When this pep talk falls flat, he fiddles with the brown Philco on the night stand until he finds the station that will air the Great Contest. Matt's reaction to his father's zeal is to shift in the wheelchair, scratch the arm that had been in a cast, and glance at Gail with the pleading look of a trapped animal. He's saved only when a corpsman enters. "Sorry, folks. Time to get the patient ready for chow. If you'll excuse us."

She assumes this means getting Matt into the head for some private function. Just as she'd excused herself to "Freshen up" while Matt went on to the dining car on September 6.

The meteor of memory leaves a trail of regret as it flashes through her. It fades only as she follows his parents down to a second floor cafeteria that Mr. Ogleby calls a gedunk. It's steamy, noisy and fragrant. Besides doctors, nurses, corpsmen and ambulatory patients, it's full of visitors in blue and gold outfits that proclaim their allegiance to Navy's team. Some are waving "GO NAVY" or "BEAT ARMY" pennants.

When he sees the line at the counter, Mr. Ogleby sends Gail and his wife to find a table while he buys lunch. As they clear leftovers from the only one available, Mrs. Ogleby chatters about their last visit, right after Matt was transferred from the civilian hospital.

"It was such a shock, seeing him like that. Now all we can think about's keeping him safe, of course. Especially with one of his brothers overseas in the Army, and the other with orders to a carrier."

Unable to imagine having three sons in harm's way, Gail says, "My brother's in the Army too. The Air Corps."

"A pilot?"

"A mechanic. He expects to go overseas any day now. Probably to England. Uh...do you know where your Army son is?"

"Anzio. You know...Italy?"

Gail nods, aware the horrifying campaign is stalemated, Yanks bogged down in winter mud, unable to retreat or advance.

"His letters don't say much, but you can read between the lines. It's a...well, only word for it's a hell-hole, if you'll excuse my French. Nothing we can do. Except pray, of course."

"Of course." Scanning the crowded room, she spots Mr. Ogleby at the register. "The friend who came with me last time, her husband's missing on a sub in the Pacific. She keeps saying he's all right. But I think she's just trying to keep her hopes up."

Mrs. Ogleby's nod is wistful. Who better to understand whistling in the dark than someone with three sons in the service? To Gail, motherly love is a country she can't imagine visiting, let alone inhabiting.

Before the conversation becomes complicated, Mr. Ogleby returns with a tray piled with burgers, fries, shakes. His complaints about the wait persist even as they work through their food. Then it's the cigarette smokers at a nearby table who irritate him. Still, as soon as he bolts his burger and fries, he retrieves the cigar from his shirt pocket and lights up. This time Mrs. Ogleby doesn't protest; she seems caught up in some issue below the surface of their conversation.

Sure enough. As Gail slurps up the dregs of her milkshake, Dottie says, "Now, Gail. Maybe it's none of my business. But I get the idea you're... well ...sweet on Matt."

Taken aback, Gail blots her lips with a paper napkin and tries to shake off what feels like an accusation "Actually, I wouldn't say I'm sweet on him. I'd just like to know him better. So I'm hoping he'll go the Navy hospital in Boston when he gets the prosthesis. It's only an hour from Portsmouth. But if he goes back to Iowa, I'll probably never see him again." She shrugs. "But it's up to Matt. What I want's beside the point."

Mr. Ogleby exhales a cloud of smoke, briefly fragrant before it begins to smell like smoldering garbage. "Well now. Have you told him this?"

"I mentioned it when I was here before, after he told me he wants to stay in uniform. But he may have changed his mind."

She's on the verge of saying more when Mr. Ogleby's dubious expression stops her. Suddenly his parents are on one end of a tug-of-war rope, she on the other. Or maybe they're standing in front of Solomon, all claiming the same baby. She hates being adversarial with these salt-of-the-earth folks; they only want what she presumes most parents want—for their son to be safe. And back in the bosom of the family where they can keep him that way.

"Anyway," she says again, "it's really up to Matt." Which sounds fair and rational, as she herself hopes to be perceived no matter how this contest eventuates.

When they get back to Room 921, the sunroom football extravaganza is about to begin. From every doorway radios blast out a cacophony of cheering young voices and the brass blare of marching bands. Matt protests he can wheel himself, but his father insists on pushing him down the long hall. When they invite her and Gail to follow, his mother says, "If you don't mind, son, I'd just as soon listen right here in your room."

Gail adds, "So would I, thanks."

After the men leave, they settle into chairs near the windows; neither moves to raise the volume on the bedside radio. Outside, low sunlight bathes the park across the street, the Navy yard beyond and the rivers that flow through the sprawling cityscape of bridges, shipyards and industrial stacks streaming horizontal smoke ahead of a brisk wind.

"Well, this is nice," Mrs. Ogleby says as she squints out. "Now we can chat."

Chat is a word Gail's mother uses derisively to describe empty social conversation. In this case, Gail's uneasy that it might turn personal and lead to the other woman's observation: "…but you don't *look* Italian." Followed by ill-concealed shock.

Instead, the older woman edges into mention of her bonds with Matt, not just those any mother feels for her firstborn, but in her case, those enhanced by three miscarriages before she'd conceived. New to this territory, Gail can only murmur sympathetically now and then. What she'd really like to know are details of Matt's marriage, but doesn't ask. Curiosity like that might make her seem scheming. God forbid.

Eventually, relaxed by the sunlight at the windows, she begins to yawn.

Her eyelids are drooping when Matt's wheelchair bursts into the room. Cradled between his knees, a paper cup of popcorn tilts on the turn.

"Halftime, ladies" His voice is ebullient. "Now, Mom. Dad's still at the party, but I'm ready for a nap. So… he wants you to come down and keep him company." The yawn is exaggerated.

Mrs. Ogleby looks startled, but smiles and rises from her chair. "Good idea, son. So you rest, have some private time with Gail." Her tone is too enthused, her smile too toothy to be sincere, but they mark her as a good mother who knows her place. Which is to comply with what her son wants, at least in this case.

After she leaves, Gail helps Matt into bed, cranks it up until he's half sitting, then pulls up the covers, drapes his robe over a chair and raises the volume on the radio. As the clamor of half-time at West Point fills the room, however, he asks, "Hey, why'd you do that?"

"So we can hear the game."

"That what you want?

She laughs. "Not really. I don't understand football. And I care less. But I thought you did."

His grin warms her heart. "Just wanted to get rid of my parents. Been here three days now and we've run out of small talk. Bet they've been bending your ear too."

She reduces the volume until the game is the buzz of a distant fly. "Only about how much they want you to come home to the farm."

He grimaces. "Fat chance. Come hell or high water, I'm going to Portsmouth." He extends his hand; when she clasps it, warmth surges in her, old but familiar. And more compelling than she'd expected.

She takes a steadying breath and pulls a chair closer to the bed. "Okay. But is that a possibility?"

His shrug looks as if he's trying to shed an unwanted cloak. Pessimism abruptly overrides passion. "Sure, it's possible. Just going to take a damn long while. And a hell of a lot of work. I mean once I get the leg, I have to be able to walk with just a cane. Right now, I can't even hop." Another shrug. "Maybe in another six months."

Seating herself, she reaches for his hand again and makes her expression cheerful. "That's not long. Just till June. It's only starting to warm up in New Hampshire by then. Just in time for the three-legged races."

It takes a moment for the joke to register. He gapes, then grins.

"You have to admit, we'd be a natural."

The smile fades. "But six months is a while for a girl to wait for a cripple. Especially one who may or may not show up."

"Isn't that what women do when men go to war?"

He blinks, shrugs.

"Without any guarantees they'll come home safely. Right?"

"Yeah. Especially in the Sub Force. Why? Think that's what might've happened to us if I'd ended up in Portsmouth instead of the wreck?"

"Could be. At least this way, if you don't stay in the Navy, I'll know where to look for you."

"Would you do that? Come to Iowa to find me?"

She gives him a broad smile so he can regard this conversation as nothing more than banter. "If you invited me."

His gaze shifts to the windows behind her. "Sure. If that's the only way we could get to know each other. See, I don't remember every detail of that day on the train. Except the feeling I had about you." He clears his throat, squirms in the bed. "I mean, that you're a girl I want to know better."

Aware of a rising blush, she regards her newly-polished pink nails biting into her palms. "Well, then. That settles it. Because I feel the same way."

The relief on his face morphs into another smile. He extends his hand again. Clasping it, she lets him pull her toward him, across the divide between chair and bed, between the amorphous possibilities inherent in any developing relationship, and their mutual need.

The kiss doesn't surprise her. Until the initial hesitance turns serious. Heat builds between them. But recedes only when he backs off. "Except it can only happen if they send me up there to convalesce. You can't keep making the long trip down here. Especially in winter. And I'm sure you're kidding about coming to Iowa."

She gives him what she hopes is an enigmatic smile. "You'll find out."

For another moment he holds her gaze; in his eyes she reads questions he won't ask, in search of answers she can't yet provide. The future is now a catenary of these linked unknowns, the only certainty that both are driven to discover more of each other's reality.

The kissing resumes; she moves closer, eventually onto the bed beside him. Heat returns, subverting all other concerns. Until once again, he breaks away. His voice is rough. "Say, Gail. How'd you like to crawl under the covers with me?"

She backs off, interpreting the invitation in the context of her Jerry memories. "Let me take off my skirt first, so the pleats don't get mussed. Okay?'

"Take off anything you want. It won't bother me."

Self-conscious, she turns her back to unbutton the waistband, unzip and step out. Draping the garment over a chair back, she smooths the slip over her hips and raises the covers enough to slide into the narrow space beside him.

Before she can cover herself again, he pulls her against him. The lines of his body and the masculine scent mingle with the aroma of the popcorn on the bedside table. He's unexplored territory, especially the shortened leg she hasn't seen but fears somehow hurting. Only on the far horizon of these sensory perceptions is she aware of the unlocked door and the chance of an ignominious discovery. At the moment however, that she and Matt are alone in a bed with loving on their minds outshines all dark realities.

Yet even as they're swept to a point of no return, she's brought up short when he pauses to regain his breath. Even more so when he asks her to turn on her side facing away from him. "So we can spoon. Won't look as bad if someone comes in."

She's heard about spooning but never experienced it with Jerry. Of course not—the main event at maximum speed was always his goal. Shoving that memory aside, she turns to face the window. Even as she does so, Matt's arms encircle her, pulling her to fit against him. At first she expects he'll slide one hand inside her panties, the other into her bra. But he only presses her more tightly to him, moving against her so she feels the unmistakable solidity of his desire. It stirs a longing for more—to be touched, explored, penetrated. But he makes no move toward anything further.

The reason occurs to her only after he gasps, clutches her more tightly, then eases off. And asks her to grab some tissues from the nightstand.

She thrusts the box at him and bolts into the bathroom. Her mirrored image regards her with an astonished stare while she wets a wash cloth in hot water. Embarrassed at her own naïveté, she waits to recover her composure before she returns to the bed. He welcomes her with an abashed grin.

"Sorry, that wasn't what I had in mind. Really. Just wanted to hold you."

She forces a casual smile. "It's okay. According to Anna, this happens a lot in service hospitals."

"You mean conduct unbecoming an officer?"

"No. Wounded men trying to feel alive again."

"Well, whatever you call it," he sighs. "I'm embarrassed as hell." Averting his gaze, he two-points the used tissues neatly into a wastebasket in the corner. "Hope you can forgive me."

For a moment she's too uncomfortable to comment. For another moment, she considers assuring him that she regards the incident as an act of love. But even imagining the words, the naiveté, the romanticism and the self-delusion in them makes her recoil. She says only, "Nothing to forgive, Matt."

She returns to the bathroom, washes her hands again, and fluffs up her hair where it was mashed against the pillow. Emerging, she smiles. "Now, if you don't mind, I'll put my skirt on and come back to the bed. Only this time on top of the covers. So we look respectable."

"Yeah, I'd hate like hell if my folks thought I took advantage of you."

Aware he's watching, she pulls the skirt up over her stockinged legs. "Be worse if they thought I was the one who took advantage. A schemer trying to ensnare their son." She smooths the covers and places herself carefully beside him, all pleats neatly in line. "As for what happened, actually I wouldn't have minded if you'd...well, if you'd gone further."

"Further? Like the whole nine yards?"

"Does that mean...you know...all the way?"

He nods. "It's a sailing term for using all the canvas—the sails—on a ship. Picked it up at the Academy. Never found it useful on a sub." He inhales deeply. "In these circumstances, it wasn't what I had in mind. One of those things people do when they're desperate. When they think there's no hope. Kind of shoddy. Irresponsible. Not the way I think of you."

Though it's hardly a declaration of undying love, the impromptu speech reveals more of the man than she might have learned on a hundred movie dates, in a thousand letters. Touched, she leans to kiss his cheek. "Well..." she breathes, suddenly content in the moment, even with their future prospects obscured by distance and his crippled state, and the imminence of winter. "Then I can wait for the rest."

His kiss is undemanding, tasting of new promise. She's deep in it, when she becomes aware of a moving tide of sound—cheering, whistling, whooping and male voices belting out "Anchors Aweigh"—advancing along the hall. Matt reaches across her to raise the volume on the radio and grab the cup of popcorn. "Here. Pretend we've been eating this."

Just in time, she catches the final score: Navy 13, Army 0. So when his parents push open the door, she can appear innocent, sharing popcorn and the triumph of his alma mater, with no hint of demon lust. Still, her pumps are under the bed and the tissues box is empty.

For the few seconds they scrutinize her and Matt, she realizes his mother doesn't recognize these signs of their sexual encounter, but his father's passing glance is wiser. Almost a nod of approval.

"Damn fine game, son," he says. "Sorry you missed it."

"There'll be another next year," Matt yawns. "I can wait."

As the day dims and sunlight at the windows thins into red-gold stripes, Gail realizes the visit has begun to feel final. Passing Matt the popcorn cup, she yawns and glances at her watch. "Oh my goodness. After four. Last time I was here, a nurse chased us out right on the dot. Remember, Matt?"

"Oh yeah. Old Stoneheart."

Gail laughs. She rises from the bed, brushes popcorn crumbs from her skirt, and slips into her shoes. "Anyway, I'd best get ready to leave." She snatches up her purse and retreats into the bathroom to comb her hair and swipe on fresh lipstick.

Satisfied she looks too ordinary to be perceived as a temptress, she emerges to find the Oglebys settled into chairs by the bed. They seem hunkered down, as if they're staying for supper, maybe even until Lights Out. Today, especially for family, there may be no definite visiting hours. She envies them. As she tucks her scarf around her neck and slips into her coat, she wishes they'd invite her to join them. But neither makes a move. She's not surprised; the stand she's taken on Matt's staying in the Navy conflicts with their wishes; she's no longer an ally.

But Mr. Ogleby's tone is friendly enough. "See you again in the morning, Gail?"

"Wish I could come back. But we're taking an early train so we get home as soon as possible."

His nod seems relieved. "Well then. Think you'll be back before Christmas?"

Her gaze turns to Matt's. "Well, maybe. If we don't get a lot of snow. Besides, my brother in the Air Corps's coming home. I'll have to see how things go."

Matt shoots her a sad smile, holds out his arms. "Then come over here and give me a proper goodbye."

Returning to the bed, she eases down beside him for an embrace, so warm, so comfortable she's immobilized by reluctance to leave. Despite the promise she'd felt earlier, the bumper crop of unknowns produces a renewed sense of improbability. Tears she hasn't felt rising spring to her eyes when Matt kisses her.

"Hey," he whispers. "A train wreck couldn't keep us apart. Neither will a couple of snowstorms. Remember that, okay?"

"I will. It's just that…well, I hate to leave." A deep breath, a couple of quick blinks clear her focus. The smile she manages isn't much, but it's better than sniffling.

"Maybe next time, I'll be able to leave with you. Might still be in a wheelchair, but not permanently." Another kiss, fond and deep. "Meanwhile, write every chance you get. Okay?"

By now his parents have caught on. Peripherally, she can tell they're nudging each other and whispering. Finally, feeling the inevitability of the moment, she kisses Matt's hand and rises from the bed. As she smiles down, his expression sags, giving him a weary, troubled look. Too late, she wonders if their carnal encounter has strained some injured part of his body. Doesn't ask, of course, but knots her scarf and walks over to shake hands with his parents. Both rise but make no move to hug her.

Pulling on gloves, she murmurs, "It's been good to meet you. Hope you have a good trip home." Too late, she notices her double use of "good", wonders if they'll judge her for it. No; she's already done something more egregious. Opposing their wishes is what they'll remember her for.

Still aiming a fixed smile at Matt, she murmurs more goodbyes and walks resolutely from the room. In the hall outside, she's caught up in a raucous celebration of a Navy victory she neither understands nor gives a damn about. As she reaches the elevators, she wonders if any of these cheering souls cares a fraction as much as they seem to. Or are they merely grateful to have something to occupy their thoughts besides war, and wounded bodies, and the enormous black maw of the future?

Boarding the Down car, she's aware that the weariness of her body has begun to override all such unknowns. Thank God for fatigue, she thinks. Now all she has to do is find her way back to the hotel, and the ordinary decisions awaiting her there. Like where to eat supper. What to wear for the trip home. And how to sanitize her visit for June and Rosalie.

But mainly, how to find her way through a hurricane of new memories.

CHAPTER EIGHTEEN
Thursday, 1 December

As usual, the morning's Physical Therapy has sucked so much strength out of Matt all he can do after noon chow is flop on the bed like a zombie. At first, with the goal of building strength in his arms and upper body, it had been merely exhausting. But for the past four days, his arms have supported the rest of his body on the parallel bars, while he learns to trust what staff calls his "good" leg to bear weight for the first time in three months. The leg isn't good at all, though, except in comparison with the one that's gone; as soon as the foot touches the floor, an electric current of pain shoots through muscles, tendons, ligaments and bones that are still trying to heal.

After fifteen minutes it's enough to make him scream. Or at least grunt and curse under his breath. The arm that was broken isn't in great shape either, though everybody promises the more you use it, the easier it gets. Supposedly to cheer him up, doctors, nurses, corpsmen and now the physical therapists keep reminding him he's not alone in this torment. As if the collective pain of others can somehow diminish his.

He only has to look around the enormous gym to see hordes of other men working through similar or worse challenges. Some are paralyzed, but most are amputees, quite a few double, even triple. One has no intact appendages, just four stumps of varying length. Blown off *Arizona* at Pearl, he's said to be one of the lucky survivors. Others are Marines from Pacific invasions, fly boys who crashed during training flights, sailors smashed up in car wrecks, a CPO who lost a leg to a

Brooklyn streetcar, and a chief warrant officer strafed by one of our own planes.

So far he hasn't met anyone else who's been in a train wreck. Whenever anyone asks, he makes sure they know he was on orders when it happened. No one seems to care, or notice the irony of a submariner coming to grief in this way. In fact, most of the guys he talks to have their own tales of irony: "I'd only been on the beach five minutes when the shell got me," or "We were just mopping up after we secured the island." *If Only* is the rampant sentiment for victims of war and civilian life alike.

Sprawled on the bed, he leafs thru mail that's accumulated since Monday: a note from Finklestein: he's got orders to Sub School and will stop by en route to New London. A tinted scenic postcard of Chicago's Navy pier his mother sent on the way home, and yesterday's four-pager from Gail, the best of the bunch. Her writing is crisp and colorful, especially the segment dealing with the train trip home:

"We took the Baltimore & Ohio this time, the Royal Blue streamliner, not to New York but Jersey City. It takes a different route, and doesn't go past where we wrecked. In Jersey City, you ride a ferry across the Hudson with a spectacular view of Manhattan. And on the other side, special buses take you anywhere in the city."

She's similarly descriptive of the Christmas pageant taking shape at her school. About their personal involvement, however, she's more reticent.

"It was wonderful to be with you again and see the progress you've made. Those few hours have given me hope you'll be able to stay in the service, with the rest of your convalescence in Boston where I can get my hands on you —so to speak—every weekend. For the time being, though, I'll just have to dream about it."

The letter activates his discomfiture about what he's come to consider the nasty little incident in his bed. Anxious to make amends, he's been trying to find a way to let her know he wants something better for them. Like a hotel room for a night, or even better, a weekend. With champagne, candlelight and room service. Privacy, comfort, and a deepening intimacy.

This romantic fantasy has the feel of a wedding night. Not like his first, nor Gail's either from what she's mentioned. But marriage isn't a viable option yet. Not while his future's still clouded. And they haven't had time to unwrap their private selves beyond the needs of their bodies.

Restless despite the fatigue, he stares out at the slice of the city visible from the bed. Sunlight fleets in and out of thinning clouds; a tanker noses under a high bridge on the river that converges with a wider stream near the Navy Yard. And beyond, a four-engine R5D transport rises from an airport; he pictures it carrying others to some exciting harm's-way duty. While he's stuck in the same dead center that's held him captive for almost three months.

He wants to answer Gail's letter, but even if he manages to find a comfortable position for writing, what progress can he report? What cheerful words can mask the foreboding that today nothing seems possible?

His eyelids droop, but real sleep hovers just beyond his grasp. Jesus, now he can't even relax when he wants to. He almost wishes Joe Beck would burst in and gripe about his girlfriend again. But Beck's gone to a veterans' hospital in Pennsylvania, from which he'll soon be discharged into the glorious civilian community. And the pregnant new wife who won't let him smoke.

He's considering wheeling down to the sun room for the new *Popular Mechanics* or *Astounding* when someone knocks on the door. He barks, "It's open!" in a tone he wishes he could soften when Mrs. Schwartz, the Red Cross volunteer, pushes her cart in.

"How are we today, Lieutenant Ogleby?"

"Okay," he grumbles. "Wiped out from PT. But I've felt worse. Why? Want to sketch me?"

"If you're up to it."

"I guess. If I don't have to sit up. Or get out of bed."

She studies him, turning her head this way and that as if assessing angles. "Would you mind if I rolled it up little so you're not so flat?"

"Go ahead. Don't want to look like a corpse."

She cranks up the bed's head until he's half-sitting. "Comfortable?"

He nods, watching as she assembles art supplies from her cart—a pad of rough gray art paper, a handful of fat black pencils from which she peels curlicues of paper to expose the lead, and a yellow box of Crayolas. She arranges these on a chair, then seats herself facing him in another, pad on her lap.

"Okay to talk while you work?" he asks.

She nods. "I'll let you know when I need to do your mouth."

Observing her focused expression, he thinks of casual questions: is she a commercial artist? How long has she been a volunteer? Then, noticing a wedding ring, he asks if her husband's in the Navy, where she lives and where she's from. Her answers are minimal but informative; she's married to an Army doctor stationed in England, and lives with his parents in North Philly. Even more interesting, as a child she was brought to America by the Friends' Service Committee when Germany was suffering under the punitive measures imposed after World War One. He'd assumed from her white hair she's older than he calculates she is now.

Her expression is unreadable, her answers terse. Before he can ask more, she says, "Tell me about yourself, Lieutenant. Did your friend from New England come down last weekend?"

He nods. "My parents were here too. So we didn't have much time to...uh, visit." His face heats as the sexual memory intrudes.

"You met her on the train the day of the wreck, right?"

"It was crowded and she was late, so she asked if she could sit next to me." A deep breath clears mental clutter. "Funny. Right then, I knew there was something different about her. I mean, see, she's a redhead and she had this terrible sunburn, so I felt...I don't know, not exactly sorry for her, but....anyway, then she told me her husband had died in the South Pacific. A marine." He pauses to clear his throat. "The way she spoke of him was…I don't know…not with affection or grief or really anything. So I wondered if it'd been a happy marriage." His face warms again as he verges into a theory he hasn't put into words before.

Mrs. Schwartz's expression remains neutral as the grease pencil moves, as her focus flicks between his face and the evolving image.

"Anyway, then we found out we were both going to Portsmouth. She lives there and I had orders to the yard, so I asked if she could show me around." He laughs. "*She* thought *I* thought the old Man of the Mountain was a real person. Like a hermit."

Mrs. Schwartz smiles, as if she's heard the joke before.

"She was easy to talk to. I mean, not like a stranger. She even told me her father's Italian, but she resembles her maternal family.   Evidently since she married Mr. Graham, some people are shocked that her maiden name was Benedetti. Even tell her, 'But you don't *look* Italian.' At least her in-laws did. I think she was offended."

The woman pauses in her sketching. "It sounds rather like not looking Jewish."

He hopes his eyes don't reveal his surprise. For a second he searches her features for clues to her ethnicity. Obviously, as people must do with Gail. Chagrined, he says only, "Huh. Never thought of it that way."

Her deep brown gaze rises to meet his. "You never had to. Not only is your name American, you look American too. No one ever pigeonholes you as anything else, do they?"

He's unable to answer except to nod. He wants to speak but is stymied by the ignorance of his assumptions. The silence is loud as certain realizations weave a curtain between them.

Until she says, "But getting back to your friend. Gail, right?" He nods. "Were you shocked when you found out she's half Italian?"

Was he? Not nearly so much as he'd been a moment before when confronted with this woman's probable Jewishness. "Only that she was worried about it. I guess because of the way her husband's family reacted. As if she wasn't acceptable. Of course, they're Southerners. Maybe they have more prejudices."

A faint smile turns up the corners of her mouth.

"Anyway, I won't see her at Christmas, so I want to send her a nice gift. I have something in mind, but I don't know if it's…well…appropriate. Can I ask your opinion?"

She shrugs, sketching. "Sure."

"Well, I was thinking about something like a…well, a nightgown. I don't mean anything…you know…cheap. Or sheer. Maybe white, with long sleeves and a high neck. And a little lace here and there. How's that sound?"

Her nod is positive. "Like something you could give your mother. Or your sister." The half-smile touches her eyes. "Or a girl you esteem, maybe even enough to marry."

He wonders if he's protesting too much. "Well, I wouldn't go that far. We'd have to know each other better first."

"Yes, of course."

Embarrassed by issues he hasn't foreseen, he can't find the next words.

"Well, however you intend it, it'd be a lovely gift." She's sketching faster now, squinting at the image. "Meantime, why don't I look around and see what's available?"

"Something good, though. Something she wouldn't buy for herself. I'll reimburse you, of course. Not much to spend my pay on, here."

"Of course. Now, can I get you to stop talking and give me a little smile? So you don't look like the Old Man of the Mountain?"

The request amuses him; compliance is easy. She works quickly, but he has no way of judging her skill. No matter; his mother will love it even if it looks nothing like him.

"Almost ready for the next step," she tells him. "Coloring it in. And if you like, I'll put you in uniform, not pajamas and robe. Khakis, whites, or dress blues?"

"Khakis. There's a jacket in the closet so you can get the ribbons right. And the sub force insignia. Mom wouldn't know the difference. But my dad would."

By now the earlier weariness is seeping back into his body. As she works with the crayons, he finds his most recent pay envelope in the nightstand and extracts a crisp new twenty. "Think this'll be enough?" She looks startled, so he adds, "For the nightgown, I mean."

"Oh, I'm sure."

"On second thought, I'll give you fifty. If there's any left over, keep it. Not just for the portrait, but for shopping for me. Okay?"

The laugh is unexpected. "Suppose I run off with it? Suppose you never see me again?"

"Wouldn't be the end of the world. See, I've already lived through that."

She looks up from her work, expression sobering. "Yes, I guess you have, Mr. Ogleby. Now; want to see what I've done with your face?"

She explains she still has a few touches to add at home, but even so he's surprised at the likeness. Pleased, even flattered. "You're very talented. If you did this for a living, you'd be famous."

As she packs up her supplies, she mentions matting the portrait, backing it with cardboard and presenting it in a mailing envelope. "Next week, or the one after, depending on how long it takes to find a nightgown. But don't worry; I'll be back. Of are you planning to leave?"

The laugh sounds sardonic. "If I do, it'll be feet first."

Her expression shifts to reproving, but she says nothing. As she wheels the cart out, he concludes she's heard that one before too. In a hospital full of wounded, death is never far from anyone's thoughts. Possibly not even as the worst thing that can happen. After all, they've already lived through the end of the world. Now all they have to worry about is the rest of their lives.

CHAPTER NINETEEN
Thursday, 15 December

After catching up with Ben Finklestein for an hour, Matt's too weary to move from wheelchair to bed without collapsing. Which would give the lie to his earlier claim that he's making progress with the crutches. And any day now will be fitted with the prosthesis that'll put him back on both feet again. And soon after, return him to active duty.

"Well, not a hundred percent active," he amends. "Nobody wants a crip on a sub. The most I can hope for is limited duty. Like BuShips, but without Ron Grady."

Finklestein snorts with laughter, the sort you enjoy after an asshole like Grady's become ancient history. "Just hope he doesn't follow me to New London. See, when I got orders to the school, he said he wouldn't mind teaching there."

"Jeez. Teach what? The art of incompetence?"

More laughter, hollowed out by reality. By now they've covered everything Matt remembers about sub school plus every question Finklestein has come up with, from "What was the worst of it?" to "Were you a believer before you went in?"

He stifles a yawn. "Must've been. Based on my dad's experience in the first war, of course. For you, though, I'd think working with Grady would've made you want to get as far from subs as you could."

"Actually, all those damage reports just whetted my appetite. Mainly from an engineering standpoint." He shakes his head; Matt interprets the gesture as incredulous admiration. "You know, how they keep going against all odds. Like *Squalus*." More head shaking. "That she could sit on the bottom for three months, then be raised and rebuilt, and sent out to join the fleet as if nothing ever happened. And serve with distinction."

"Of course, she wasn't heavily damaged, just flooded. She was just lucky the McCann chamber could make it from New London in time to get the survivors out. But it's tough shit for boats that go to the bottom in the Sea of Japan."

"Speaking of luck, any thoughts about what happened after you left DC?" By now Finklestein's heard every variation of Matt's Good Luck story, including the truth that he'd done nothing to deserve being spared, three times now.

"You mean the remarkable irony of cheating death in high risk situations, only to end up like this in a civilian accident?" Of course that's what he means. Matt recalls a previous discussion of Grand Design before there was any irony to it. Back when it all felt like fortune so good you knew better than to trust it.

The ensign nods. "Still wonder if Fate's spared you for some higher purpose?"

"Damned if I know. "

Before they can dig deeper into the existential mystery, someone knocks. Mrs. Schwartz comes partway in, then sees Finklestein. "Oh, sorry. Didn't know you had company."

Finklestein rises instantly from the chair. His smile is warm, dimpled. "Don't leave on my account, ma'am. I'm not really company. And I've got to be going anyway."

She looks at Matt for permission, then enters with her portable studio. Before he can introduce them, she extends her hand to the visitor. "Liesl Schwartz."

They shake. "Ben Finklestein. I was stationed with Matt in Washington. Fact is, I drove him to the train that day. Always wondered what would've happened if he'd missed it."

"Well, don't rush off. I want to show him something. Won't take long."

Matt nods and he takes to the chair again, but more alertly now, upright and at attention. Mrs. Schwartz plucks a legal-size manila envelope from a precarious pile on the cart, hands it to Matt, and follows it with a John Wanamaker bag. He goes for the contents of the envelope first: his portrait, of course, neatly matted, signed and perfect. He holds it up so Ben can see; the other man comes over to study it at close range.

"Gee. You did this?" he asks the volunteer.

She shrugs. "Grease pencil and crayons. Should be pastel and charcoal. But they get messy unless you spray them."

"It's beautiful. How much do you charge?'

Her laugh is girlish. "No charge. Just something we do for patients."

"Oh, you have to be a patient?"

"Theoretically. But once in a while someone on staff wants one too. In that case, I suggest a donation to the Red Cross."

He stares at the portrait a moment longer, then focuses on her. "If I donated, would you make one of me?"

"Uh…maybe next week. See, I'm done for the day. This isn't a good time."

His smile wilts. "I'm leaving for Sub School Sunday morning. Could you do it tomorrow?"

She shakes her head. "Sorry. I work in my father-in-law's dental office Fridays."

"And you're in a hurry to get home, right?"

Her gaze goes to the rain-speckled windows, city lights blossoming through the murk outside. "It's a long trip. And I've been here since nine this morning."

"Where's home?"

"West Oak Lane. Up at the end of the subway, with a bus ride after that. Then three blocks walk."

His face brightens. "West Oak Lane! Say, I'm going to Elkins Park. So I could give you a ride. Right to the door. Save you the subway at rush hour. What do you think?"

Her smile is hesitant. "Well, I guess so. But this time of day, it won't be my best work."

"I'm sure my parents'll think it's wonderful. And I'll give the Red Cross a huge donation."

As she unpacks her supplies and Finklestein settles into a pose in the chair, Matt lurches to the bed on one crutch. Stretching out, he has an impression of weariness in the woman that he hadn't noticed before. Profound, as if it stems from more than the day she's winding up.

But as she begins sketching and she and the junior officer chat, another impression increases. At first he thinks he's imagining it. But before long it solidifies into a three's-a-crowd sense that he's become irrelevant. He can't see the volunteer's full face, but her voice has taken on new animation, while color floods Finklestein's cheeks.

Something has begun to bloom here. Not exactly a bud opening, but something lavish and bright that contrasts with the intruding murk of the winter afternoon. He can almost taste it, like chocolate on his tongue.

He tries to reason with this strange perception for the twenty minutes it takes Liesl to produce Finklestein's image, as conversation flows between them. Not an extraordinary stream—his life, hers, the mundane, the banal—but each word is colored with an animation the subject matter hardly merits. The connection is so innocent, yet so powerful, Matt feels like a voyeur, wanting to interrupt but unwilling to break the spell.

It falters only when Liesl detaches the paper from the pad and hands it to Ben. To distract himself from the drama, Matt burrows into the Wanamaker bag and withdraws the nightgown she's brought. But the ensign's praise of his own portrait is so lavish, Matt's observes only that the gown seems adequate. It's silk, with lace. Or maybe rayon? He tucks the tissue paper around it and slides it back into the bag.

Finkelstein bounds over, portrait in hand. "Ogleby, look at this, will you?"

Matt glances at the flattering likeness, smiles, nods. "She's good all right. Mrs. Schwartz, do you have an envelope he can take it home in?"

"I'll pick one up before we leave." She moves swiftly, replacing supplies on the crowded cart. She seems more breathless than one would expect from the chore. "What about the gown, Mr. Ogleby? Is it what you had in mind?"

"It's perfect, thanks."

'All right, then; if you give me the address, I'll send it to your friend. In a nice box."

Before he hands it over, he scribbles Gail's address on the outside. Then a new impulse moves him to slip his portrait in with it. His mother already has a dozen pictures of him; this should be Gail's. "Do I owe you anything?"

Her hands tremble as she takes it from him. "No, no. You gave me more than enough. I put the sales slip and the change in with the gown. Wait. I'll get it for you."

"Didn't I tell you to keep whatever was left?"

"Yes, but it was too much." She hands him a fistful of bills and coins. "If you want, give it to the Red Cross. Or Navy Relief. They do good work too."

"Well, thanks. I appreciate everything you've done." As he takes the money, he feels her attention straying back to Ben, still standing nearby, smiling down at his portrait. Like someone admiring a treasure: a kid with a new bike, a Navy man at the first glimpse of his first ship. Or someone giving the lust in his brain permission to take over the rest of his body.

With a flurry of parting phrases to Matt and a quick exchange with Ben about their rendezvous later, Liesl pushes the cart from the room. As the door thumps closed behind her, Ben sighs and sinks back into the chair, picture still in hand. "Wow. Can't get over how talented that lady is. Must've had professional training."

"You can ask her on the way home," Matt suggests. "Sounds like a long ride."

"Better part of an hour this time of day. But not out of my way. Least I can do after she made this for me."

"Lots of time to find out all about her, then. Or has she already told you she's married to an Army doctor in England?"

Finklestein's expression changes subtly, morphing into something akin to a glower. "She mentioned it. What's that got to do with anything? I'm only taking her home, for God's sake. Not to a hot pillow joint."

Matt smiles at the colloquialism. "Sure."

"Jesus, Ogleby. Get your mind out of the gutter."

"Not the gutter. It's that other place where everything's rosy. And feels good. Where it's eat, drink and be merry, for tomorrow we die. Or go off to sub school."

The scowl darkens Ben's face as he rolls up the portrait and thrusts it into his uniform jacket. He gets to his feet abruptly, shakes out his raincoat and shrugs into it.

Matt holds up the cash. "See this? I told her not to bother bringing change. It's from a gift she bought for a…well, a friend of mine, But here's the change anyway. Every penny of it. That's the kind of woman she is. Mrs. Schwartz, I mean."

Finklestein snorts. "Think I don't know that? Think I pegged her as a whore?"

Matt hesitates, incubating a reply that won't add to the wall suddenly rising between him and the only man he'd regarded as a friend at BuShips. God, that's the last thing he needs. "Sorry, Ben. Guess I'm just envious. Because you've got two good legs, and a car, and you're going to be a submariner, and you can drive a woman home. And do basically whatever the hell you want. Christ. What I wouldn't give to be that free again."

Ben nods, tension draining from his features. "Look, Matt. I know what you're saying. But don't worry. I'm not going to do anything crazy. Or rather, I don't *intend* to. Of course I'm tempted." A grin lights his eyes. "And I don't have a lot of experience with that kind of thing." A casual shrug. "So who knows what's going to happen?"

Matt's about to remind him of a Yiddish saying Finklestein himself had once quoted: *When the schlong speaks, the brain goes out the window.* But he settles for a more innocuous platitude of the sort issued by older, presumably wiser friends: Or parents, especially parents. "Well, just be careful."

"Don't worry. I'm not nineteen."

Feeling awkward about having interfered, Matt grabs the crutches and volunteers to walk the other man to the elevators. "I'm not as good with these damned things as I have to be, so I need all the practice I can get."

"How soon till you get the prosthesis?"

Matt shrugs and struggles to rise to a standing position; as usual pain jolts him. By now he's learned to react with nothing more noticeable than a sharp intake of breath. "Sometime after the first of the year, they tell me. The stump has to finish shrinking before they measure you for the wooden leg."

Finklestein winces and holds the door open so Matt can precede him into the noisy corridor. "After it shrinks, then what?"

"I want to go to the hospital in Boston. Then limited duty at the Portsmouth yard. But if I can't pass the physical, well, back to Iowa. To hop around the farm the rest of my life."

They proceed at Matt's clumsy pace past the parade of wheelchair patients watching for chow trays, nurses taking vitals, visitors leaving; through clouds of cigarette smoke and patches of boogie-woogie from radios. Until they reach the crosswise corridor with the passenger elevators; Finklestein edges into the crowd. "Keep me posted?"

"Wilco. And vice-versa. I'd ask you to come see me after sub school. But if I'm not out of here in three months, I'll be in a nut ward somewhere."

A Down car pings to a stop. With a mini-salute and a grin, the ensign pushes aboard. Matt watches till the door closes, then hobbles back to his room.

The walk leaves him shaky. Still, sagging on the crutches, he stands at the windows staring down at cars streaming out the gate, at the red squiggles of tail lights on the wet paving. It's dark now; he wonders which car is Ben's; from nine floors up, they all look alike. For a moment he wonders too whether the other will actually have an adventure. But his curiosity has drained along with the day's energy. Besides, he can hear carts coming and smell something like roast beef. His mouth begins to water.

Suddenly, chow blossoms into the most important event in his life. As he tosses the crutches aside and arranges himself in the wheel chair, he imagines this is a preview of his future: sitting with his father at the kitchen table while his mother dishes up supper. The high point of everyone's day. Night after night into infinity, this is what he has to look forward to.

"Jesus, no." Clenching his fists, he summons the same shreds of resolve he requires six mornings a week to lift weights, pull himself up on overhead rings, clutch parallel bars and hobble to the end and back. Over and over, the monotony as bad as the pain. Everybody seems to be making more progress than he is, maybe because they're younger. Or were well-muscled to begin with. While he's the ninety-eight pound weakling people kick sand on at the beach in the ads for body-building the Charles Atlas way.

Whistling no tune Matt can name, the duty corpsman pushes into the room with his covered tray. "Good news, Mr. Ogleby. Everybody's favorite tonight. Yankee pot roast."

"I can hardly wait." The sailor doesn't react to the sarcastic tone, probably hears it so much he doesn't notice. "Best thing that's happened all day."

"I'll bring the ice cream later. So it don't melt."

"Swell."

He uncovers the plate and digs into the mashed potatoes, sloshing them thru the gravy moat around a crumbling castle of beef. For a moment it's rich with the flavors he expects. Almost immediately, however, they fade into a tasteless mush, alternately salty, or sweet, or sour. This happens a lot lately, not at every meal but often enough he's asked a couple doctors if it's normal. One told him, "Sure, for someone who's been hospitalized as long as you have." Another: "You're just bored with eating off a tray. Once you can go to a mess hall, it'll be better."

Maybe, he thinks. But Stoneheart's explanation is the most logical, chillingly so. "The morphine's dulled your taste buds.

See, even if it doesn't turn you into a dope fiend, it takes half the fun out of life." A look of self-righteous *schadenfreude* had lit her face. "I won't even mention what else it'll do."

He eats every crumb of the meal including tasteless canned green beans and a salad of pallid lettuce drenched in orange slime, then both ice cream slabs—chocolate, vanilla and strawberry. But all this heavy sustenance does nothing more than fill his belly for the night.

Well, that's something, he thinks. You've got to keep your strength up. So at every meal he will dutifully eat everything set before him in an effort to get back some of what he's lost since his own Day of Infamy. He doesn't expect to recover it all, just enough to convince the Navy he's still worth his salt.

If indeed he still is.

CHAPTER TWENTY
Saturday, 24 December

By the time Matt phones that morning, Gail's been sucked into a sense she's the family Cinderella, but one with no prospect of rescue from a fairy godmother or a handsome prince. It's not enough she's washed all the dishes from last night's supper. Or fried up the bacon for Pete and Frankie's breakfast. That is, when they finally decide to come downstairs. Worst of all is, Ma wants her to pull shreds of meat from the stewed chicken carcass cooling in a puddle of congealed fat. Later, when Charlotte calls from the station, Ma also expects Gail to pick her up, then go to Woolworth's for wrapping paper, and Laidlaw's Market for vegetables for the Christmas Eve soups. And anywhere else her mother's need dictates.

When the wall phone rings, her mother grabs it. Her eyes widen, her voice turns reverential. "For you, Gail. Person-to-person. All the way from Philadelphia."

Her heart flutters; she wipes wet hands on her apron. "I'll take it in the hall. Hang up when I start talking, Okay?"

"Now don't be too long. In case Charlotte's trying to call."

As she hurries to the front hall, "Screw Charlotte!" crosses her mind. Another obscenity she'd learned from Jerry, though his was usually directed at his sergeant-major, the Corps Commandant, or President Roosevelt.

When she lifts the receiver, an operator confirms Gail's identity, tells the caller his party's on the line. The next voice is thin, laced with static: "Hi. That you?"

Already racing, her heart bangs faster. She nods, as if he can see her. "Yes. And is that you, Matt?"

"In person." He sounds breathless too. "So...how are you?"

Clamping her hand over the mouthpiece, she yells at her mother to hang up, then eases down on the next to last step on the stairs. "I'm well, thanks. How about you?"

"Better. Physical therapy's hard work, but seems to be paying off. In fact, I'm getting around so well, I've signed up to go home with a retired chaplain. For Christmas with his family. In some town north of the city. Just overnight, though. To get out into the world again."

She laughs. "Are you going stir crazy?"

"You could say that." A pause; he clears his throat. "Say, did you get my present yet?"

"Present? Oh, you shouldn't have. I mean, I haven't sent you anything."

"This isn't for Christmas, just for...well, you'll figure it out when you see it. Couldn't get to a store myself, so a Red Cross volunteer chose it. She was going to mail it too, but I guess parcel post is slow right now. Anyway, hope you like it."

"Oh thank you, Matt. Whatever it is, I can hardly wait." A silence, backgrounded by muted male voices, laughter, holiday carols, and the sizzle of long distance. "Are you calling from the hospital?"

"The sunroom. There's a phone in here and every patient on the floor's waiting to use it, in case you hear them cutting up. I probably shouldn't hang on anyway, 'cause I've got to finish dressing before the padre picks me up. Blues, white shirt, service ribbons, shoes and socks. Well, *one* shoe anyway. So far I've only managed shirt and trousers. Nurse pinned up the empty leg. Must've lost a lot of weight, the way things are hanging on me." He takes a breath. "What are your plans for the day?"

Ignoring a twinge of sympathy, she forces a laugh. "Plans? Nothing much...mainly helping Ma make supper. My brother in the Air Corps got home last night, and my older sister's coming up from Boston. Later, after the restaurant closes, my father will take everybody out to look for a tree. He always waits till today so he can get one cheap." Matt's chuckle tells her he's amused, not shocked. "After supper we'll decorate it, then go to Midnight Mass. Except I'm going to Anna's father's church instead. Because I've never really felt Catholic. Even on Christmas Eve."

Another laugh. "How will your dad handle that?"

In spite of mild anxiety about that very issue, she says, "I don't give a damn. This year, his other kids will do what he wants. Anyway, after last year, nothing I do will bother him."

"Gosh. What'd you do last year?"

Hesitant about crossing into personal history, she says, "Eloped with Jerry. Well, not exactly eloped. But we drove down to his parents in Virginia and got married. Because Pop had forbidden me to even go out with him." A deep breath transports her to 1942, then back again. "Anyway, what about you; where were you last Christmas?"

His voice turns flat. "Somewhere in the Pacific. Between Perth, Australia and Pearl Harbor. Must've been an ordinary day. Because the only thing I remember's Christmas dinner. We ate real well on that boat."

She pauses on the edge of another possibly sensitive area. "Uh…was that one of the subs you got off before it was lost?"

"*Bluefin*. The first. Left her at Pearl when I got orders TAD to another boat. Filling in while the exec was in the hospital."

"TAD?"

"Temporary Additional Duty. In this case, three months. Just long enough to jinx her."

"Oh, Matt," she sighs.

"What?"

"Oh, just that there's so much we don't know about each other. If you ever get to Chelsea, we'll have a lot of catching up to do."

"Right, Gail. Except it's not *if* I get to Chelsea, but *when*. Besides, for me those two hours on the train before….you know…I learned everything important about you. The rest is only the fine print, At least for me."

"The fine print. I like that." She skips to another matter. "That reminds me—do you have a photo I could have?"

In Philadelphia, the noise level rises. Holiday spirits, she imagines, from the spiked eggnog. "Funny you ask. Didn't know if you'd want it, but there's one in with the gift. Now you have to send me one of you."

She groans. "All I have is a studio shot from college graduation."

"Well, I'd rather drool over one in a bathing suit, but I guess it'll do."

She laughs. "I'm not a pin-up girl, Matt."

"Close enough for me, sweetie." He quickly adds, "By the way, how'd your school play turn out?"

"Well, the dress rehearsal was okay. But it snowed yesterday and the roads were bad, so we postponed it till next year. Other than that, it was perfect."

"Sounds like my life. Other than having only one leg, everything's perfect." A muffled conversation, then, "Gee Gail, I hate to ring off, but a smartass gyrene claims I've been hogging the phone for an hour."

When she pictures a Marine like Jerry hovering nearby, it's easy to imagine a smartass.

"Anyway, I'll call again soon's I get word about the pegleg. For now, though, hope you and your family have a fine Christmas. I'll be thinking about you." A tone of wistfulness tints the last line blue.

"Same here, Matt. Have fun with the chaplain. Thanks for calling. Oh, and for the present. I know I'll love it."

"Just remember, though—it's not just a gift. It's…well, sort of a promise." His reluctant goodbye is followed by the click of disconnection.

As she hangs up, she observes her reflection in the rococo mirror opposite the stairs. The letdown she feels shows on her face, as if she's stifling tears. Yet she has no reason for disappointment; it was a good call, with news of an unexpected gift, a surprise package in the mail.

While she's still crouching on the step, Pete comes charging down the stairs, Frankie riding piggyback. Noise explodes around them, filling the house like the smell of stewed chicken in the kitchen. Ma comes in to remind her Charlotte might be trying to call, then, "Who was it? That crippled Navy guy you went down to see?"

Gail rises slowly, nods and trails Ma back to the kitchen with a resurgence of the Cinderella feeling. Familiar, a hangover from childhood, but more noticeable today because it's Christmas Eve. And she's heard from Matt, whose presence, even at a distance, makes her feel esteemed. Last year, Jerry had made her feel desired, which she'd mistaken for love. What Matt gives her, however, is something new.

Most surprising, it's something she's done nothing to earn, except perhaps to notice him when she had only intuition to guide her.

Or as her romantic younger sister might imply, it's actually the mysterious hand of fate leading her to true love. Whatever the source, she's eager to follow it away from life here in the only home she's ever known.

Twenty-five years is long enough, she thinks. Even if Matt doesn't turn out to be the handsome prince with the glass slipper, she needs to leave.

CHAPTER TWENTY-ONE
3 PM, Christmas afternoon

When he reaches the brick steps from the front porch, Matt pauses and inhales the nippy air. Breezy, spiced with wood smoke and exhaust from Pastor Muller's Oldsmobile warming up in the drive between the parsonage and the tall-steepled church next door. Pink and lavender clouds line the sky; golden sunlight winks off snow piled along the cleared sidewalks of Penn Hill, Pennsylvania. Situated in rolling countryside north of Philadelphia, it's one of several picturesque villages that straddle Route 29 between the city and Allentown.

Yesterday, on the drive from the city, these towns and the surrounding farmlands had welcomed him like a holiday greeting—snow-covered hills, well-tended farmhouses, neat red barns and herds of sleek Holsteins, all a vibrant change from the view from his hospital windows. Later, he'd basked in a low-grade euphoria generated in the warm embrace of the pastor's family and a supper of local dishes—spaetzele, sauerbraten, red cabbage with apples, homemade rye bread, shoo-fly pie. All so mouth-watering he'd tasted everything and happily stuffed himself.

Afterward, sated and sleepy, he was ready to retire to the Spartan first-floor guest room. Except by then it was time for the Christmas Eve service next door. Grateful for the hospitality, he had to go. Not a long walk, not a lot of steps, but tricky in the snow. Still, those sentimental moments with apple-cheeked, red-robed kids singing "Heilege Nacht" by candlelight, were well worth the effort.

In contrast, however, was the long night afterward. Even huddled under layers of patchwork quilts, he'd shivered in a room where the radiator never got more than lukewarm. By morning he'd been chilled to the bone, and aching in all the parts of his body damaged in the train wreck: ribs, right arm, right leg, stump of the left. Pain he'd thought healed was burning there again. And all he had to deal with it now was aspirin.

Nonetheless he'd persisted in being a good guest. Had eaten heartily of the scrapple, apple pancakes and eggs for breakfast. Hobbled back to the church for a morning service, watched Muller's grandkids tear into their presents, even expressed pleasure at the hand-knit cardigan—Navy blue with brass buttons—Mrs. Muller had made for him. Afterward, he'd stuffed himself again at another "seven sweets and seven sours" family feast.

Now, two hours later, he's finally recovered enough to handle the trip back to Philly. Surveying the distance to the car, he swings the crutches down the steps to the brick walk across the front yard. The pastor's gone ahead to open the passenger door, while his wife and fourteen-year-old grandson wave from the porch. After talking to Matt to the exclusion of everyone else at dinner, the boy's decided to become a submariner. And never ride another train.

Matt's almost reached the Olds when one crutch tip hits an icy patch. The fall's actually a soft tumble that lands him on a pile of crusted snow, with most of the downward force absorbed by his gloved right hand.

In a twinkling, the others reach his side, grab his arms to help him stand. He says, "Wait a minute, let me make sure I'm okay." With so many aching parts, it's hard to tell. A quick assessment convinces him he's not damaged anywhere except his hand. Unless it's so bad he can feel nothing else.

He nods anyway. Pastor and Rudy take his arms, hoist him upright, then install him into the front seat like equipment through an access hatch. Blessedly hot air pours from a dashboard vent.

Pastor Muller stows Matt's bag and crutches in the back seat, then climbs behind the wheel. "Sure you're all right, Matt?"

"Yeah. Just embarrassed." He waves to Mrs. Muller and young Rudy hovering anxiously outside, smiles and gives them a thumbs-up so they won't worry. Nice people, the whole family—a pair of married twin daughters, a lot of grandkids, all so short and plump that Matt, even at barely six feet, has felt like a skinny giant in their midst.

Squinting into the low sun, the pastor backs out the drive, then heads south through that snow-sparkled Christmas village. On the way north, he'd told Matt all about the German immigrant farmers who'd settled so much of the state. Two hundred years later, their native tongue is still spoken in most homes, along with heavily-accented English. "Bet you noticed," he'd said. "Twenty years in the Navy, and I still talk Dutchy."

To help him remember the local cuisine, the pastor's wife has sent him back with half a shoofly pie and a Mason jar of corn relish. To enhance what she regards as "all that dismal institutional food."

He'd groaned. "As full as I am now, I won't eat again for a week."

The sun blazes out, sinking below the hills, and the sky purples into darkness as the pastor drives toward the city's sprawling outskirts. The Olds' heater keeps pouring out hot air, but Matt's shivering again, and more conscious of pain than he's been since right after the wreck. Bombarded by the clergyman's boundless cheer, he finds it difficult to reply, but eventually concludes he doesn't have to. The older man would rather talk than listen, even after preaching two Christmas sermons.

The last part of the trip is the entire length of Broad Street with interminable traffic lights at almost every block. When the pastor says, "I read somewhere this is the longest street in America," the only response Matt can produce is, "Huh!"

Halfway down Broad to the Navy yard, he's surprised that the yellow moon of City Hall's tower clock shows only four-thirty. It feels later, as if he's been gone for a week. When Pastor Muller asks if he's tired, he says, "A little. Not used to being with real people anymore." He concludes with a half-truth: "But it was wonderful, every minute of it."

Muller chuckles, shifts to neutral and coasts to the next red light. "Well, we've had enough of you fellas to the house, we know what you need. A change of scene. And chow that's not hospital dreck. That's German, by the way. Dreck. For you, though, might've been too much so soon. Just three months since you were injured, that right?"

"Closer to four. Maybe at my age, you heal more slowly."

"Your age?" Muller grins. "What are you, twenty-five?"

"Thirty last August."

"Looks young from where I sit. But what you went through, it must take a lot out of a person. I mean, not just losing the leg, but all the other injuries."

Listening, Matt tries to appreciate the retired chaplain's observations. But his hand's on fire now; the surging agony overrides other small bites elsewhere. All he can do is nod when appropriate and try to breathe through it, deeply, not shallowly as instinct urges. To reassure himself he's not seriously damaged, he manages to wiggle the fingers. Though possible, it's a new torture.

God. If he's broken some of the myriad small bones that comprise the hand, there'll be a major problem. Without it to lean on, he won't be able to manage a crutch or continue physical therapy for weeks, maybe months. Then there's all that other pain; what does it mean in terms of his overall recovery?

It after five when the pastor pulls up close to the hospital entrance. "Think you can walk the rest of the way?"

"I'll give it a try." Matt wills strength into his voice, but it's still shaky.

Murmuring, "Atta boy!" the minister grabs the crutches from the back seat, opens the passenger door and holds them at the ready, as he's done before. Matt reaches, but pain shoots through his wounded hand until he has to let go.

"Ow. Ow! Sorry. Can't manage it."

Pastor frowns, nods. "I'll go in and get a chair. Wait right here."

With the door closed again, heat returns. He watches the older man hustle toward the entrance with the confidence of someone who knows routines, where to find a wheelchair, and personnel who can help. Matt hates it that he's lapsed into this dependency again. But even if his hand were working, he suspects he wouldn't be able to hobble in now.

Muller's gone a long while before he returns pushing a wheel chair. Matt manages to get into it, awkwardly balancing crutches and bag on his lap as they set off toward the entrance. Each bump jolts new agony through him, while the clergyman's tone becomes ever more upbeat, ever more chirpy. Inside, the lobby's almost empty; an elevator waits with open doors. They rise to nine without any stops, then hiss swiftly along the corridor to Matt's room. On the way they pass a corpsman taking vitals.

"Evening, doc," the chaplain says. "Any chance you can help me get this man into the sack?"

"Yes sir. Soon's as I'm done here." The kid studies Matt. "You jake, Lieutenant?"

Matt nods. "Will be once I hit the sack, thanks."

As they enter Matt's room, the light-spangled view from the windows surrounds him with a sense of homecoming. And relief. Still in the wheelchair, he shrugs off topcoat and jacket while the chaplain goes to find a nurse. The corpsman enters while he's trying to unbutton the shirt with his left hand. He soon gets Matt into pajamas, into the head, into the bed. Finally he takes his vitals and probes his swollen, throbbing hand.

"Can't tell without x-rays," the sailor says, "but don't seem to be anything broken."

He's one of the chattier corpsman, but he leaves when the chaplain returns with Miss Steinhart. Her manner, as usual, is brusque. She takes his vitals too, and concludes with, "Mr. Ogleby, you've had far too much fun while you were away. BP's up, pulse is elevated and you're spiking a fever. Too much Christmas cheer, I reckon."

He grits his teeth as she examines his hand and listens to his recital of symptoms with her customary unapologetic absence of sympathy. He's relieved; if she seemed worried, he'd know he was a goner. Nonetheless, she retreats to summon an MOD for a closer look.

"Thanks for all the help," Matt tells the pastor, "but don't feel you have to stay. Long drive ahead of you."

"No hurry. Want to make sure we haven't set you back."

He manages to smile up at the round pink face above the dog collar. "I'll be fine once I get a shot for this." He holds up the damaged hand.

"Sure sorry about that. Wife and I should've been watching you closer. Especially on the ice."

"The whole visit was wonderful. I'll always remember your hospitality."

"Well, we'll be praying for you. Sometimes the Lord's timetable's hard to understand. Easy to get impatient. Just have to keep praying. And trusting all things work together for good."

Matt's sick of upbeat bromides, but says, "If my mother were here, she'd say the same thing."

The older man sneaks a glance at his watch, but makes no move to leave. When the nurse returns with the duty doctor, he backs toward the door, but still doesn't exit.

The MOD's a young lieutenant in a blood-spattered lab coat with a stethoscope around his neck and a frazzled air, as if he's seen too many banged-up sailors today. Still, he's patient, his examination gentle and thorough.

"Can't feel any broken bones, but I'll order x-rays to make sure. Pretty sure things are only sprained, so we'll immobilize the hand in a soft cast and let it heal gradually." He glances over at the nurse. "As for your other pain, anyone ever tell you it takes damaged tissue and bones a year to return to normal? Your injuries are superficially healed, but you've asked too much of your body. Your orthopod'll probably put you on bed rest until you're back to normal. Tonight, though, I'll order shots as often as you need."

Stoneheart's fleeting grimace is a tacit critique of pain shots. Even on Christmas.

The doc scribbles on the chart, passes it to the nurse; she nods; both leave. As soon as they've gone, the pastor takes Matt's left hand, and recites another string of upbeat scriptural clichés, concluding with "The Lord watch between me and thee while we're absent one from the other."

Matt nods. "Thanks, Padre. Thanks for everything."

Then finally, *finally* he's alone. In the ensuing silence, he replays the doctor's observations and tries to derive optimism from them. But all he can feel is hurt and fatigue, and a sense he's no longer in the race, the one he's been running full tilt to get back to the quasi-normalcy the Navy requires for limited duty. The notion exacerbates the physical torment. Until Stoneheart returns with a hypodermic, a roll of gauze and a padded board.

First, the shot, in his thigh. Then she begins to wrap gauze to hold the hand against the board. Wrist to fingertips and back again, firmly but not tightly. Her touch is sure and deft. "Now. Where else do you hurt?"

He groans. "Everywhere. How can you hurt this bad and not be dying?"

"Huh. You can be dying without any pain at all. This is just your body warning you to take it easy, give it a chance to heal. If you don't, even morphine won't help."

The first ripples of the drug trickle into him, like a warm current in an icy sea. "Listen, I just want to get back to duty. Even a desk job."

"What's your hurry? Way I hear it, war won't be over anytime soon."

"Still want to get out of here."

She smiles, collecting leftovers from her errand of mercy.
And Matt feels himself sliding away into the gentle arms of his
old friend Morphia. The room fades, the nurse's next words
blur, memories of the pastor's family grow dim. Pain, nibbling
at his body, is the last to recede. But soon it's gone too, along
with the shreds of consciousness.

The ultimate gift of Christmas, 1943 is a state of blessed
oblivion.

CHAPTER TWENTY-TWO
Monday, 26 December

Matt's gift arrives at the Benedetti house with the afternoon mail. By now the flurry of holiday excitement has faded. Charlotte's gone back to Boston, Pete's out with his high school chums in Gail's car, and Pop and Ma are at the restaurant, setting up for New Year's Eve parties. Which leaves Gail and Rosalie to babysit Frankie.

It's snowing again and he's bored with his mountain of Christmas toys, all except the Flexible Flyer sled. He's had the sniffles, so Ma doesn't want him to go out, but he's determined to escape. And whatever he's determined to do, or get, is what he invariably does, or gets. Known as "Having his own way", the euphemism for "tantrum" is a family joke.

After lunch, the girls bundle him up and send him outside with orders to sled only on the small slope behind the house, so they can watch from the kitchen window. At first all is well. But with him, "well" is always temporary. Within minutes a pack of neighbor kids have joined him, not to sled but to pummel each other with snowballs.

For a few minutes they're only children having cold fun. Soon, however, the action turns into an Arctic version of the Battle for Guadalcanal. When she realizes Frankie's on the losing side, Rosie goes out and drags him in. His nose is bleeding. Tears stream his frostbitten cheeks, and he's cursing "them lousy sonsabitches what ganged up on me."

It takes both sisters to get him upstairs and into a hot tub. His protests are so loud, Gail barely hears the doorbell. Downstairs, the mailman hands her a brown-paper wrapped package. Tied with string, it could be just another parcel post package mailed too late for Christmas delivery. Except for the Philadelphia postmark.

By the time she goes back upstairs, Frankie's playing quietly with a fleet of tiny boats. Assuming it's safe to leave him, Rosalie follows Gail to the bedroom, and watches as she picks at the knotted string. "That from Matt?"

She nods and sits on the edge of the bed.

Rosalie hands her the manicure scissors. "What do you think it is?"

"No idea. Maybe hankies. Really good ones, though, maybe monogrammed."

"Oh I hope not! Hope it's something more personal. Like a slip. You know. *Intimate.*"

As the string falls away, Gail peels off the wrappings around a satiny white box with *John Wanamaker, Philadelphia & New York* on the lid.

Inside, shrouded by neatly-folded tissue, is something white, with a French label. She lifts it carefully, letting it unfold into a long-sleeved nightgown. The square neck and cuffs are edged in fine lace, the pin-tucked bodice closed with tiny pearl buttons. Delicate, elegant, it smells of dried rose petals.

Having had a year of domestic science, Rosalie identifies the fabric as, "Handkerchief linen. Very expensive." She edges close enough to finger it. "Gosh, this beautiful. Must've cost him and arm and a leg."

Gail shrugs, mentally contrasting it with the slinky black number Jerry had given her for their wedding night. Even though it concealed nothing, he'd torn it off within seconds of the door closing. She'd left it in the trash can at a gas station in Salisbury, Maryland, on the way home after the honeymoon.

"Wanamakers has a lot of little salons with high-class stuff like this," Rosie explains from her recent experience with the department store. "June and I went top to bottom, all eight floors. Furs, Evening gowns. Accessories. This must've come from Ladies' Fine Lingerie. We didn't go in because a salesgirl was looking down her nose at us. As if we were hicks from the sticks."

Gail shakes out the folds, gets to her feet and opens the closet door. She holds the gown against herself and studies her reflection in the long mirror.

Rosalie's eyes widen. "Golly. That's swell enough to be a wedding dress. Think that's what he has in mind?"

Returning to the bed, Gail sniffs, "Don't be silly. He said it was sort of a promise. I guess he means in case he gets duty up here. You know. That we'll get to know each other better." For a moment, she indulges in a brief fantasy of herself as a bride. Then quickly comes back to the reality of the snowy afternoon, the ominous sounds from Frankie in the tub down the hall, and the big unknown of Matt's condition.

She refolds the gown, and is placing it back in the box when she discovers the big envelope under the tissue. And inside, Matt's hand-done portrait. She withdraws it, admiring the likeness conveyed in grease pencil on gray paper, with crayoned skin and eye coloration.

Rosalie peers over her shoulder. "Golly. Does that look like him?"

Gail nods, her smile involuntary.

"He looks nice. Not as handsome as Jerry, but nice. Kindly."

Gail rolls her eyes, resorts to a bromide of her maternal grandmother's: "Kindly and nice beat handsome any day of the week."

"Uh-huh. Well, I can see why you like him. But suppose he doesn't get duty up here? Then what?"

"He'll go home to Iowa. As a civilian."

Rosie plops down beside her on the bed. "If that happened, know what I'd do?"

Suspecting an unrealistically romantic suggestion, Gail asks anyway, "No. What?"

"Well, I'd go down to Philadelphia and get a room at that swell hotel, then make him come back with me in a taxi. So we can have a night of love before Fate parts us forever."

Gail's smile is bemused. "Hmm. Like the Japanese girl and the Navy officer in *Madame Butterfly*. That opera Pop's got on records? One night of love, before he goes back to his ship and his American fiancée, while the Japanese girl has a baby. Years later, when he comes back, he's married, and she's disgraced. So she commits hari-kari and he and his wife take the little boy back to America. That's what happens when you settle for one night of love."

"Well, maybe in an opera. But I bet if you got pregnant, this guy would marry you in an instant. And the child would unite you forever." She sighs in a quasi-tragic way, shakes her head sorrowfully. "Remember that Longfellow poem. 'Of all sad words of tongue or pen, the saddest are, *it might have been.*'"

Gail sets the portrait on the nightstand, then replaces the lid on the box and tucks it into the bureau drawer with her previous, now rather cheap-seeming lingerie. From down the hall, the noise has diminished, which strikes her as ominous, a sign Frankie's up to some quiet mischief. "Yeah, sure. Like Frankie's united Ma and Pop? No thanks. It reminds me of a sequel to that poem: 'If, of all sad words the saddest are *it might have been*, still sadder are these we daily see: *it is but hadn't ought to be.*'"

Before Rosie can answer, the water begins to run again in a tub already full to the brim. Looking alarmed, she races down the hall. Gail stands a moment staring at the gift box and replaying her sister's notion, extrapolating it into a Madame Butterfly plot twist. In her imagination, a child she and Matt might conceive on their night of love looks nothing like her little brother, with his olive skin, black hair and nose that will probably outgrow his face. No, their child's a sweet-faced, golden-haired little girl who always smells like Johnson's Baby

Powder and never spits up on her handmade dress. What Navy officer could resist such a baby?

She sighs. Resigned to helping Rosie deal with Frankie, she realizes that while fantasies slide easily into the imagination, she knows better than to trust them. Savoring this one offers only fleeting pleasure, like candy which, after a moment of delight, will lead to tooth decay, diabetes and fat hips.

Still, as she wrestles the squealing, wriggling Frankie out of the tub and into a towel, the image of her own child lights a dark corner of her mind. And sets her wondering if that absence could comprise one of the sad might-have-beens of her life.

No, she decides; more likely the presence of a love child would eventuate into another hadn't-ought-to-be. Like being married to Jerry. Surely Fate hasn't rescued her from that God-awful mistake only to lure her into something worse.

Surely not.

CHAPTER TWENTY-THREE
Thursday 29 December

Gail's thank-you note—actually a full-length letter—is still open on the nightstand, her photo atop it, when Liesl Schwartz enters Matt's room on her usual weekly rounds. She takes one look at him and approaches the bed. The head is elevated so he can sit up. But so far "strict bed rest" has meant just that, except for staff-assisted trips to the head.

Her eyes widen, her expression is dismayed. "My goodness, Mr. Ogleby. What happened? Last time I was here, you were ambulatory. Had a relapse?"

"Guess that's what it was. From falling on the ice." He holds up his right hand, still wrapped like a mummy's. "Nothing broken, just sprained."

She pulls a chair closer. "Is that why there's a bed rest sign on your door?"

He explains everything he's been told about the flare up that's only now abating. "Another week or so, they say I'll be ready for PT again. But meantime, I'm wondering, even if I pass the physical for LimDu, will I be able to handle it? Even just a desk job. Or am I too old to recover, ever?"

"What do the doctors tell you?"

He shakes his head. "Some say it's all up to me. Meaning I have to work even harder at PT."

"But why did it happen?"

He shrugs. "That's another thing. I was cold the night before, which could've caused muscle spasms. Or it was too soon for an outing. Or a combination of factors." He sighs. "The overall effect was, I went dead in the water."

"But you're recovering now, aren't you?"

"Slowly. Don't know what to expect when they resume physical therapy. That's the thing. Maybe it's a pipe dream to even think about staying in the service."

"Has anyone said that? Or is it just the way you're feeling?"

"No one's confirmed it. But it seems logical, all things considered." A deep breath arms him for an admission he finds painful to make even to himself. "The thing is," he begins, "Gail and I have this…I guess you'd call it an understanding. If I get duty at Portsmouth we'll…well, we can get to know each other better. That's what the nightgown was about. By the way, she said you have good taste."

"Happy to help."

He clears his throat, sips chlorine-laced water from the glass on the nightstand, then props Gail's picture against it. "But it all depends on whether I get to Portsmouth. And the way I've been feeling this week, I have serious doubts I can qualify, no matter how hard I work on it. "

Her gaze wanders to the watery sunlight at the window, her face registering a sorrow he can't wholly attribute to his tale of woe. Maybe she's just more sensitive than he realizes, or has heard worse. Then the dark eyes focus on him again. "But you'll keep trying, won't you?"

"Sure. But in the meantime, I think Gail should know I'm having doubts. So, I want you to write her for me. Don't know how long this'll be out of action…" He holds up the bandaged appendage…"but she needs to know now."

"Hmm. I don't agree, Mr. Ogleby. If I were you, I'd wait a while to see if things improve."

"I've thought of that. But that'd give her six or eight more weeks of false hope. I say it's easier to tell her before she…I mean, before things get serious between us." He waits but she only sighs and compresses her lips, as if to stifle another comment. "So…will you write it for me?"

"Can't you wait till next week? It might make a difference."

"Why? No time today?"

"No, no, there's no hurry." Her eyes brighten, her cheeks flush. "See, your friend's letting me use his car while he's in New London. Says he has no need of it there. He's such a kind person, and it makes the trip home so much easier. So I have plenty of time, if you want to dictate it now."

"Yeah. Want to get it over with." Watching her assemble writing equipment from her cart, he mentally regurgitates her assessment of Finklestein's generosity. The suspicion he'd had the day they'd met takes on new dimension, converting his black-and-white memory to sunny Technicolor. Conflicting judgments flitter through his brain. Until finally Liesl's as ready to write as he is to dictate thoughts he's strung together the past four days and nights of Strict Bed Rest.

Though occasionally she suggests alternate wording, the gist remains the same—the level of pain he's experiencing has convinced him he may never qualify for limited duty. Or if he does, he won't be able to handle even a desk job. Because—he has to face it—he's been damaged beyond his body's ability to heal. He'll keep trying, of course, won't abandon the effort without giving it every chance. But his prospects aren't promising; she shouldn't count on a future with him.

That's the crux of everything: *Don't count on a future with me.*

"I hate to admit that," he adds for her to copy; "but I want to be honest about my chances."

"Maybe you should ask her to come down for another visit," Liesl interposes.

The deep breath he exhales emerges as a sigh of regret. He shakes his head, but doesn't comment.

She reads back the note aloud. The inevitability of the words touches off sorrow that exceeds his expectations. Even thanking her is an effort. After she leaves, he stares at the darkening windows, lights blossoming in the familiar city beyond. An end-of-the-road sense swells in him, so strong he tries to imagine the consequences of refusing further PT. And the prosthesis that it's preparing him for. Of resigning himself to perpetual invalidism, a process that will culminate in his transfer to a hospital closer to Iowa, then back to the farm… in the best wheelchair a grateful Government can supply.

His parents will be pleased.

As for him, better if he'd stayed on *Bluefin* to her end, he thinks now. Or died with those seventy-nine others on the Congressional Limited. He's read the list so often the names have become familiar, a roll of innocents who'd chosen seats in cars seven and eight. Or like him, were heading to and from the dining cars.

Confronting the end of his career, he wishes Fate had spared him this ignominious whimper of defeat.

But like most of his wishes, its futility leaves him still aching, still uncomforted. And with too much time to imagine where all this is leading. Which is nowhere he wants to go.

CHAPTER TWENTY-FOUR
Tuesday, 9 January 1944

After the flurry of packing that follows Dr. Grimm's six-weeks-of-quarantine edict, Aunt June's dinner that night is a peaceful hiatus. Or as peaceful as it can be with Pa ranting that Frankie really needs to go down to Boston, to Children's Hospital. "Your mother can't take care of him for six weeks," he tells his two younger daughters. "It'll kill her!"

"Calm down, Pop," Rosalie murmurs. "She only has to do what she always does around the house. The nurse'll take care of Frankie. Night and day, whatever he needs."

"Besides," Gail says, "the doctor says it's a light case. If he were in Boston, you couldn't see him every day."

"What, see him every day? You mean behind the front door? Don't call that seeing him."

Pietro brings a fresh beer, massages his brother's stooped shoulders. "He'll be fine, Franco."

"Like them kids was fine back home when we had that epidemic?"

"That was whooping cough, not scarlet fever."

"Same thing, you ask me."

Smiling the conciliatory smile she's affected during twenty-some years of Benedetti family gatherings, June goes around collecting dirty plates from the lace-spread, candlelit table. Gail and Rosalie join in to help. Even after a three-course dinner, the adjoining kitchen is neat and attractive. So unlike the one at home, even when things are put away.

Maybe the absence of children has something to do with Aunt June's ordered symmetry, though Gail's heard rumors of multiple miscarriages. Years before, when no one discussed reproduction with their kids. Yet they'd heard the whispers, and deduced what they could.

Of course, June and Pietro's apartment—the second floor of a genteel Victorian in the Riverview section of town—is compact, easy to keep spotless, with a maid who comes in every day. This serene ambiance is enhanced by upscale French Provincial furnishings, Aubusson carpets, floral still-lifes, elegant draperies. There's only one spare bedroom, however. So while Rosalie and Gail share the guest room's twin beds, Pop will sleep on a cot in the office at the restaurant. So far he's so up-in-the-air about Frankie he hasn't even griped about being discommoded.

As temporary accommodations go, it's as good as it gets. Or will be, Gail thinks, once they're used to suitcase living, to using tables for desks, and to an unsettled, distorted normality. Tonight she's so busy grading sophomore compositions about New Year's resolutions, she doesn't remember Matt's letter until she finishes. It had been in the day's mail she'd picked up when she and Rosie were hastily moving from the diseased homestead.

At first she only scans enough to realize a Red Cross volunteer wrote it after Matt injured his right hand. *"Nothing serious, but I'll be immobilized till after New Year's, so I can't write or have physical therapy for a while. Meantime, I hate to say it, but I'm having doubts about getting limited duty at Portsmouth, or anywhere else. The present setback is so painful and unexpected, I wonder if I'll ever qualify even for a desk job. Of course I'll continue to pursue that goal, but without the previous optimism. After I get the prosthesis, leaving the service might seem the best option after all. Gail, I'm sorry, but in the interest of honesty, you need to know that my present status leaves little room for optimism."*

After the signature is a PS—*"By the way, thanks for the picture."*

Gail drops the letter, and shakes her head as if to deny its contents.

Rosie peeks from under the comforter. "What's wrong?"

She hands the letter over. "See for yourself." Suddenly the world has become even more hostile than it had been an hour before, when her main concern had been adjusting to the long quarantine.

Rosalie reads twice, hands back the sheet. "Oh that is so sad. That poor man. But after all he's been through, maybe it's normal to give up hope. I know you're disappointed. But gee, you got over Jerry's death, and that was worse. At least you don't have a lot of memories with Matt."

Gail comes close to saying, "You'd be surprised," settles for, "A few. Enough." Wishes she could tell everything, but her virginal sister would be shocked. She wishes too she could talk to Anna, at least pour out her heart in a letter. Maybe tomorrow. Tonight all she can do is let regret sour her outlook while her future melts like crayons on a hot radiator. The result is a twisted mass of lesson plans, term papers, and the expectations of her superiors at school. For ever and ever. Or at least the next thirty-some years until she can retire.

Rosie turns over in the bed. "I still say you should go back to see him before he leaves Philadelphia."

Should she? "It'd just make me feel worse."

"But if you did, maybe it'd give him back the will to live."

"I don't think he's lost that. Just the will to stay in the Navy."

Rosie sighs dramatically. "You know, maybe if you promised to let him have his way with you, he'd change his mind about coming to Portsmouth."

Gail's surprised to hear herself laugh. "Now that's just silly. I mean, promising to sleep with someone for a...a *reward*. Besides, I think he already knows that."

Another of her sister's sighs. "I guess the rules are different when you've both been married before. Things aren't so....well, special. The way it is with your first love."

Gail's tempted to tell Rosie that for her, lovemaking with Jerry was only special before it ever happened. Whereas what had taken place with Matt, though not technically intercourse, had been incredibly special. But her sister is still too starry-eyed, too steeped in *How do I love thee?* clichés to believe romance could perish overnight.

But who knows? Maybe her life will play out differently; maybe she'll sail through marriage with all illusions intact, never to know the dark side of any man's nature. She might even marry one of the rare guys for whom sweetness and light isn't just skin deep.

Gail hopes so anyway. Tonight, however, she can't tell Rosie that marrying Jerry had been a mistake on so many levels. And that the tragedy of his death has probably saved her from the ignominy of divorce. None of which matters now that she's learned that the bright blossom of a happy ending with Matt is withering on the vine.

Someday, when this news has cooled and receded into her past, she'll write a poem about it. She can't decide whether it will be ironic and sharp, as Edna St. Vincent Millay might make it. Or pensive and wistful in the style of Emily Dickinson.

More likely the reclusive Emily, she thinks. Edna always had so much fun.

CHAPTER TWENTY-FIVE
Wednesday, 25 January

G iven how long it's been since he'd dictated the letter with Liesl, Matt's almost given up hearing from Gail. He's not surprised, surmises her non-response is indeed an answer, her way of tacitly agreeing. Maybe its message is even, *so why stay in touch at all?*

Then, out of the blue when he returns to the room after the morning's PT, there's the envelope with a Portsmouth return address. Even before he digs into the chow tray, he rips into the letter.

The first paragraph is an explanation of her tardiness in answering—her brother's scarlet fever has made her a displaced person. Then she turns philosophical: *"Setbacks such as yours may be a natural part of recovery from numerous injuries. I can't imagine how weary of pain and fatigue and isolation you must be."*

Further on, she seems to accept the new status quo: *"I wish I could promise to visit you in Iowa. But given the difficulty of getting even to Phila., it seems unlikely. The best I can do is promise to stay in touch. While I regret the loss of a possible future with you, we might not have had one anyway even if we'd both arrived safely in Portsmouth last September. By now your boat might have left, and we'd be parted by the war, with no guarantee of a reunion".*

The last paragraph underscores her regrets, while the closing—*"Fondly, Gail."*–doesn't even promise to remember him always.

Reading it through once more, he addresses the tray with the sense it contains nothing new, nothing special, nothing to remove his focus from the fact that he'll be going back for an afternoon torture session, all to guarantee that his abbreviated leg will be in shape for the prosthesis he'll soon be measured for. That the rest of his body will be strong enough to handle using two legs again. And that his muscles won't contract and shrink into uselessness before he does. Yet nothing promises the happy ending he's been hoping for.

By now the widespread pain he'd felt at Christmas has backed off, though echoes of it remind him he'll never be a whole man again. He may work his ass off, but he'll never be useful. Never be normal. Never live as most men do.

He's a damned *cripple,* for God's sake. And always will be.

And now Gail knows it too.

CHAPTER TWENTY-SIX
Wednesday, 6 February

I t's snowing again when Gail parks in the drive alongside her parents' house and carries in the sacks from Loblaw's. As usual now when she delivers, she crosses the porch to the front door, rings the bell and sets the bags inside the storm door so her mother or the nurse can pick them up without breathing contagion on her.

While she waits for someone to appear, she withdraws mail from the wrought iron box on the doorframe. On top is a letter from Matt; the scrawled address looks like his penmanship. Her heart jumps: if his hand has healed enough that he can write, perhaps he's more optimistic about the rest of his body.

Before she can open it, her mother appears behind the door. Since Frankie's illness, she's become a gray wraith; hair and wrapper, even her facial skin are like ashes. Behind her, the live-in Irish nurse is pink and sturdy, a study in perpetual cheer. In her arms, Frankie struggles to get down, get outside, get into the snow. He whines so loudly Gail hears hear his pleas for hot dogs and ice cream even through the door.

"Not today," she calls, digging through the mail for the latest batch of get-well cards. Four more, most from Ma's family in New Haven. She sets them atop the groceries, then backs off so Ma can take them inside. Later, Pop will stop by with ice cream and whatever new toy the boy has decided he needs. In Gail's estimation, Frankie's previous spoiled-rotten state will be beyond correcting by the time he's well. Her parents believe, however, that it won't matter. Because he'll be an invalid the rest of his life; he'll deserve all the spoiling he can get.

Her chore accomplished, Gail waves, backs away from the door and slogs to her car. Snow's coated the windshield in just the few minutes she's been here. It's piling up on the roads. At the Riverview house, hers is the only car in the drive, so she'll be alone with Matt's letter. Stuffing it in her purse, she pushes through a small drift to the entrance and lets herself into the lavender-tinged antiquity of the foyer. Deep in the big old house, someone is playing the piano, so haltingly she can't identify the music. No lights dissipate the late-afternoon dusk; a haunted feeling follows her up the steps to June's apartment.

At the top of the long stairs, she turns on every lamp from landing to living room, then settles herself on the rose brocade sofa with Matt's letter.

"*Dear Gail....I have read and re-read yours of 15 January with the deepest regret for my inability to honor my promise to come to Portsmouth. I find this ironic after my brave words at Christmas, especially since my visit with the pastor's family made me realize how much I long for a home and family of my own. Until then I'd been proud of my will to recover. Now I've learned what 'pride goeth before a fall' means. What shot me down was the assumption I could control the rate at which I healed. Not that I hadn't been warned—several medical people had advised that a full recovery might not be possible no matter how much I worked. Pain and weakness, however, have finally made the truth clear.*

"*Gail, I thank you for understanding. I remind myself it's easier to accept such a contretemps now than later. As things stand, my hand has recovered, so I'm still trying to get in shape for the pegleg. Once I'm fitted for it, they'll send me to a convalescent unit either here or at Great Lakes Naval Training Center north of Chicago. Then it'll be back to the farm. Naturally, my parents are thrilled. As for me, I'm sad but resigned. After 12 years of letting the Navy decide what to do with me, I should be used to it by now.*

"*Gail, I hope we can stay in touch. I'd like to think you'll visit me in Iowa, but it may be that we've missed our chance. Then again I remember what Anna Donovan said—the Lord has more tricks up his sleeve than we can ever imagine. That remains to be seen. But for now I have to accept the truth that my future is not as a naval officer but a crippled farmworker."*

When she finishes reading, tears puddle in Gail's eyes. She feels as if the world has stopped turning, and she's stuck in a winter of incessant snowfalls and the tedium of school. With an empty place in her heart where the hesitant promise of loving Matt had been pulsing the past five months. And all she can do about it is read and re-read his letter on the off-chance she's missed some hopeful message between the lines.

It's fully dark before June comes home, still in the elegant tweed suit she's worn to work that day. Pietro, Rosalie and Pop are busy at the restaurant, so it will be just the two of them for supper, with a tuna casserole the maid started earlier. June lights the oven and sets the table while Gail throws a salad together. Then, carrying a crystal decanter of sherry and two glasses, they head to the sofa in the front room.

Downstairs, the novice pianist tip-toes through a Beethoven sonata, while June recounts details of the Officers' Wives' Club luncheon she'd covered that afternoon. "With a fashion show and a card party afterward." The smile enhances her resemblance to Dinah Shore. "Just think, Gail, if you marry Matt, you can come to all these affairs yourself."

A deep breath arms her to speak the contradictory truth without tears. "Sounds lovely. But it's not going to happen. Matt's given up hope of staying in the Navy. So he won't be here for duty. And we won't be getting married."

June's smile inverts to a look of distress. "But I thought he was doing so well." As Gail fills in the blanks, her aunt's delicate features register deep sympathy. "Oh my dear. I'm so sorry," she says. "You must be terribly disappointed."

Gail sips more wine, nods, compresses her lips to deflect a stronger urge to weep. Downstairs the music becomes agitated, as if the pianist is venting frustration.

"But it may be that after such a long hospitalization," June goes on, "Matt's afraid he'd be a burden. And he's trying to spare you."

Gail's laugh is sardonic. "Maybe he would be. But the way things are at home now—even before Frankie got sick—they're already a burden." A shrug. "After we go back, it'll even be worse. Frankie'll be impossible."

June studies her; the lamplight flickers as if the power may go off. Snow gusts at the bay window. "Is he the problem?"

"One of them." She sighs. "See, I turn over half my salary to Pop. So does Rosie. He claims it's our obligation. Still, we do more housework than Ma does. And whenever there's an errand to run, well, there I am with my little car." Another sigh, another dollop of that crisp sherry, before she speaks more repressed truth. "I should have moved out after Jerry died."

June nods, as if deducing that Matt's withdrawal from Gail's life has given her more reason for disappointment than just the loss of romance. "You can still move out. I'm sure they don't need half your salary to maintain the household. Then you could get a room, maybe closer to the school. Say in Dover. And establish yourself as an independent woman."

Independent woman. Gail absorbs the phrase.

"Or, you could teach somewhere else. You know, with four years' experience, you can go anywhere. Portland or Boston, or....well, anywhere you want. To a school that lets you wear lipstick and jewelry. And sweaters."

Gail smiles, nods, sips.

June helps them both to more wine. "Then there's military service. At the base, my main contact's the Public Information Officer, a WAVE ensign. With your degree and your writing talent, you could qualify for a job like that. Really, Gail, there are lots of things you could do. Lots of places you could live besides with your parents. And lots of interesting men you could fall in love with. Or at least date."

Gail winces at her aunt's advice; is June implying—or is she herself inferring?—that she's been expecting Matt to rescue her? The question's troubling. As wine blurs conversational boundaries, she considers changing the subject, asking June about the lost pregnancies rumor.

Before she can, however, June says, "You know, I worried about this when you married Jerry. As far as I know, you didn't date much in high school. Certainly not the way Rosie's doing now."

"Of course not. Pop wouldn't let us, neither Charlotte nor me."

June's smile is minimal. "Easy with Charlotte. She never liked boys. Or vice-versa."

"Well, that's not Rosie's problem. She's so beautiful, she can have any guy she wants." Another mirthless laugh. "As for me, though...well, do you know how Pop once described me?"

"Tell me."

"He said I'm not as smart as Charlotte or as pretty as Rosie, but I have dimples. And I'm sensible. He never even mentioned my greatest asset—that I don't look Italian."

June studies her with a wistful gaze. "Is that how you see yourself? The way your father described you? Or the way you feel about living at home?"

Gail inhales a deep breath before she wades into these rising waters. "Not completely. I mean, I know I'm intelligent. But marrying Jerry, that was stupid. So now, am I doing the same thing with Matt? Wanting a man to rescue me from my life?"

June's look remains pensive. "My dear, I couldn't possibly answer that. But he seems to be out of the picture. So this might be a good time to explore your options. Starting with a place of your own. Maybe a new job. Finding a new pattern. In other words, not leaving it to chance, or letting someone else make important decisions. Unless you don't mind becoming another Emily Dickinson."

Gail groans. "Even if I could write poetry like hers...no, thank you."

As snowflakes spatter the window panes, she and June drain their wine. Downstairs the amateur pianist has turned on the radio. The bass of a news broadcast rumbles through the floor. More war news; Gail's glad she can't hear the bloody details.

"Know what I'd like to see you do?" June says after a long silence.

"Turn into Edna St. Vincent Millay?"

June's laugh is musical. "Don't go that far. But besides teaching in a school that isn't run by nuns, let your hair grow. Wear red lipstick and paint your nails the same shade. Take up smoking. Go out dancing. Wear dangly earrings. Date a man with a convertible, and stay out all night. Use a few cuss words now and then. Frankie can teach you." She drains the wine in her glass. "Even if you end up an old maid schoolteacher, you don't have to look like one. Or act like it."

She's absorbing these notions when June jumps up and runs to the kitchen. Caught up in introspection, Gail hasn't noticed the warning smell of a casserole about to burn. Still, mesmerized by the snowflakes whirling in a patch of light from the ginger jar lamp, she doesn't move. Until a few minutes later, her aunt calls her to the salvaged meal.

As she carries her empty glass to the table, she senses she's turned a metaphorical corner. Yes, she's disappointed about Matt. But not immobilized, not trapped in the ruins of her hopes. Sure, she'll feel that way now and then, and miss the future she's begun to imagine.

But thanks to June, she's glimpsed alternatives. One day she'll ask what lessons tragedy—if indeed she's lost all those pregnancies—has taught her. Tonight, however, she's been blessed by the wisdom from another woman's hardships.

Ironic, she thinks. June has no children. But tonight she's been more of a mother to me than Ma's ever been, even with four other kids to practice on.

CHAPTER TWENTY-SEVEN
Thursday, 8 March

Maneuvering with crutches on the clumsy substitute for his left leg, Matt stows toilet items in the carry-on, tightens the drawstring on his sea bag, and settles into the wheelchair for a last glimpse of the city. For the last half year, this view has reminded him there's a world beyond his pain-filled prison. He'll miss these VIP quarters; after today, he'll be just another cripple who no longer needs constant medical attention as he hobbles along the road to elsewhere. Meaning, life after the Navy.

Once he'd hoped Elsewhere would be limited duty at Portsmouth. But since Christmas, those expectations have dissolved like a message scrawled in beach sand. Elsewhere now will be a convalescent unit either here or at Great Lakes. At least until he's adjusted to the thing he's staggered around on the past week. It's rumored that for an above-the-knee amputation like his, you need at least eight weeks.

Not that it matters how long it takes or where he is; the farm will be waiting. Meanwhile, his parents have improvised a downstairs bedroom and bath so he won't have to tackle stairs. And are planning a huge "Welcome Home" party. All he has to do is say When. To leave a Navy career for the life of a farm hand.

He sighs, checks his watch, wonders what's become of the sailor who promised to help him move. After 1100, edging toward lunchtime. Will they bring his tray here, or to the new unit? A strain of restlessness worms into him; *hurry up and wait* is a maxim of wartime life. But today the new mandate is *Get on with it; get it over with.*

Within minutes, Chief O'Toole, the Medical Service Corps rep on his case, opens the door. Behind him, a baby-faced Seaman Apprentice gawks at his piled luggage. The chief asks, "Ready to go, Mr. Ogleby?"

Grabbing crutches, Matt clambers from the chair and shrugs into the heavy bridge coat. "Ready as I'll ever be."

"All right, sir." He withdraws documents from an interoffice envelope. "Your travel orders. And something else you might want to see…Commander."

The single sheet he hands over is one of those terse BuPers documents he's read before, but not often enough: on 1 May, he'll be promoted to Lieutenant Commander. Happy surprise warms him, though all it really means in his present situation is an increase in retirement pay. Until he gloms onto another phrase the chief just used:

"Travel orders?" Mental alarms ping. "Thought I was going to the convalescent unit here. Or are they sending me to Great Lakes today?"

The chief wags his head. "Nope. Not Great Lakes. *Boston.* The Chelsea hospital. FFT."

Suspecting he's stumbled onto a huge official mistake, he says, "Boston? That can't be right. Yeah, I wanted to convalesce there. But that was before Christmas, the setback…and why 'For Further Transfer'?"

While they talk, the seaman loads his luggage onto the chair and pushes it into the passageway. Matt takes a last gander around the room that's sheltered him for six pain-filled months. Relief, or a weird nostalgia? He'll never forget it, whatever you call this feeling. As they head toward the elevators the wheelchair gang regards him with overt envy, calling out pleasantries like "Goodbye," "Good Luck" and "Get laid every chance you get."

Passing them, the chief says, "Because you're still on track for Portsmouth. Just have to qualify when you're done convalescing."

"Jesus! I never heard anything more, so I gave up on it."

At the service elevators, the chief rings for the VIP car, the one reserved for top brass so they don't have to mingle with the common folk. "Ever tell 'em you changed your mind?"

"Didn't *change* it. Just assumed I could measure up."

The steel doors swoosh open; they push inside. "Well, Commander, you never cancelled the request you signed last year. Not too late, if you want to change your mind now."

"No, no, not at all. God, this is unbelievable. Chelsea! And I'm going today?"

"Flight out at 1300. With some brass on an inspection tour. So, New England clam chowder for you tonight. I mean, if you're *sure* you want to go."

"You bet your ass I do!" The door opens on the ground floor. Hobbling across the lobby, Matt inhales the civilized smells of floor polish, fresh coffee, cigarette smoke and well-groomed civilians. Outside, haze from smoldering dumps blankets the city, trapping oily fumes from a nearby refinery. In the park across the street, the winter sun is a pale gold coin behind naked trees. Damp cold knifes through even the layers of blue wool.

They stop at a battleship-gray Navy sedan. While the sailor stows Matt's gear in the trunk, the chief helps him into the front seat, then takes the wheel. As he starts the engine, the sailor clambers into the rear. Still fighting disbelief, Matt stifles the urge to yell "Yippee!" when they pull away.

At the municipal airport, the plane he's to fly out on is parked behind a chain link fence where other military transports are coming and going. The drone of engines rises and falls. Exhaust belches into the wind as they swing around to leave, or nose up to the loading area. His is the smallest, a twin-engine the chief identifies as a Lockheed Electra. "Same model Amelia Earhart disappeared on, sir." He chuckles. "But don't worry. You won't be flying over the ocean. So even if you go down, they'll find you right away."

Matt grimaces. "That's a great comfort."

After a guard inspects Matt's orders, he instructs him to board and proceed to the rear. By the time he's navigated the steps and the narrow aisle to the cramped seat, he's winded by the exertion. Even more so by the adrenaline rush of the surprise flight. The chief stows the crutches, reminds him his orders are in the topcoat, then extends his hand. His grip is firm, his smile broad.

"Pleasure knowing you, sir. I'd wish you good luck. But even with only one leg, seems like you've already got enough of it for three men." His final gesture is a smart salute, even though they're inside the aircraft.

Matt returns it with a heartfelt, "Thanks, Chief." But by then it's almost 1300, and four commanders and a captain have straggled aboard. Their chatter suggests they've just enjoyed a two-martini lunch. Matt's impatience takes on a sharper edge as the others start to light up cigars, but are hastily warned not to by the crew chief.

Finally, an enlisted man makes sure he's seat-belted in and promises, "Coffee once we're in the air." The door thumps closed, engines sputter and catch, exhaust billows past the windows. Without further ado, they begin rolling toward the runway. The taxiing is long and rough as a jalopy on a dirt road. Finally they pause; the pilot revs the engines separately, then together; the plane vibrates as if about to disintegrate. This feels risky. Until Matt remembers it's standard operating procedure.

After a civilian DC-3 lands, it the Electra's turn to head into the wind, pour on the power and race down the runway. It unrolls beneath them alarmingly fast. Ironic, he thinks, if the plane that's lifting him to freedom were to crash. As if the bad luck of the train wreck was actually his last brush with *good* luck. At least the chief has assured him they'll be found quickly if they do go down. Or their bodies will.

The ground falls away. They rise above a line of trees along the murky Delaware, wheel over the Navy Yard and the airfield where they're building PBY seaplanes, over the twin towers of the hospital, and the stadium where he sat through all those Army-Navy games; over bridges, ships at piers, at anchor, or in drydock, then sprawling neighborhoods on both sides of the river.

Banking northeast, engines straining for altitude, they pass over railyards, lines of tracks, and a wide northward curve he thinks is where the Limited wrecked. Before he can see more the plane slips into cloud shreds, then surfaces above a puffy layer of gray cotton. The ground has disappeared; sudden sunlight is briefly blinding.

As promised, when they reach cruising altitude the steward comes around with paper cups of steaming black Navy joe. A high muckity-muck asks for bourbon. All Matt wants is information about the route they'll be taking: "Will we fly over New York City?"

"No, sir. We'll cross Jersey, then go up the coast, offshore all the way. Not much to see, but the most direct. Now, need anything else? Maybe a Hershey bar?"

Offshore…nodding, Matt tries to shove doomed Amelia Earhart and Chief O'Toole's predictions from his mind, sips the bitter coffee, and shifts his thoughts to this sweet new current in his life. This miraculous aftermath of months of gloom and doom and false assumptions.

Too bad he couldn't let Gail know. But as soon as he can after they land, he'll phone her. And greet her with, "Guess what? God had something up His sleeve after all!"

If anything can, this should counteract the Jobean lamentations in his recent letters. And restore her faith in the promise that all things work together for good.

It's certainly made a believer of him today.

CHAPTER TWENTY-EIGHT
Friday, 9 March

As she opens the front door, Gail winces at the fishy smell in the house. Of course: Friday night. Even before Uncle Sam decided meatless civilian Fridays would mean more for our brave boys, Ma had always served fish. Because Pop's Catholic and she's a good wife, a converted Protestant who observes his rules even when he's at the restaurant. And, Gail's certain, eating whatever he wants from the kitchen. Like rare prime rib any night of the week.

Shoving the door closed, she hears her mother upstairs giving Frankie his evening bath, and from the noise level, encountering the usual resistance. Since he's had scarlet fever, Ma's taken over all the care she'd previously left up to Gail and Rosalie. As if the disease has left him a porcelain statue too fragile to entrust to underlings. For her part, Gail sees no indication he's any less hardy, any less tough, any less willful than he ever was. If anything, he's more spoiled.

She drops purse and coat on a chair, calls up the stairs, "Ma, I'm home." Not because her mother cares, more to keep up appearances as the Dutiful Daughter. Tonight, after dinner with three other teachers from St. Margaret's, she feels less filial than ever. Probably the aftereffects of all the chat about future plans. Because it's the time of year to renew contracts. First, though, to decide if they *want* to. Or are there juicier opportunities over the horizon?

The one that interests most of them is joining the service. Except for Ralph Lescaullette, the music teacher who'd treated them to a fried oyster dinner at the Dover church where he's organist. At four-feet, eleven, he's too short for the army, though he often proclaims, "I'm not a dwarf, just the world's shortest giant." To which someone invariably retorts, "Or the world's tallest midget."

Until this evening, Gail hadn't pursued the empty, unsettled feeling that's haunted her since her talk with June. But now, as she heads toward the kitchen, it swells like hunger verging on starvation. When she sees the clutter of leftovers and dirty dishes on the table, it explodes into a full-fledged mandate to get the hell out of this house. No matter where. At the very least, leave southern New Hampshire. As Charlotte did when she took the library job in Boston. Gail doesn't think her sister has much of a social life, but at least tonight she's probably doing something more exciting than cleaning up the family kitchen, for God's sake.

After she commits the cold codfish cakes and creamed potatoes to the fridge, she loads Ma and Frankie's plates into the dishpan, sprinkles Ivory Flakes and turns on the hot water so forcibly she barely hears the wall phone ring. She wipes soapy hands on her skirt and reaches for it, expecting it'll be some young man yearning for Rosalie.

Instead it's a long distance operator, with a person-to-person call for her. From Boston. It takes her a moment to say, "Uh, this Mrs. Graham. Did you say *Boston*?"

"Yes, ma'am. Go ahead, sir. Your party's on the line."

"Gail?" When she doesn't answer, the familiar voice asks, "Gail, that you?"

She swallows hard. "Matt? My goodness. Yes. And is that you? In *Boston*?"

"Yep. Really me. And really here, at the Chelsea hospital. I was shocked too, it happened so suddenly, I thought I was going to Chicago. "

"Oh my goodness." Questions dart into her mind like hungry starlings into a spring meadow. "When did that happen?"

"Yesterday. Just put me on a plane and flew me up here. With no warning. Best thing that's happened since I met you."

"Oh, that's such good news. Does it mean you're coming here for duty after all?"

"Well, that depends. See, right now I have to get used to the leg. Then they'll decide if I'm good enough to hold down a desk at the yard. But even if I'm not, hell, I'll get a civil service job. So, one way or another, I'll be there."

The determination in his voice is even stronger than when they'd talked at Christmas. "How long will that take?"

"Six to eight weeks. It's a big program, not just so you can walk, but so you get used to a prosthesis for normal activities. And don't turn into a recluse. Or a beggar."

She smiles at the image of him holding a tin cup and a sign, War Veteran, outside Filene's, like so many after the Great War. "Oh Matt. I can't picture you as either. Anyway, when will I see you? I have a car, you know. I can drive down any time. Only takes an hour."

He chuckles. "Can you hold off another week? See, tomorrow they've scheduled meetings, then lots of PT. Sunday we're going to some famous church, then out to lunch. After that we have a couple hours to rest. But I won't have a whole day off till next Sunday."

"Oh, that long?"

"Sorry. Wish it were sooner."

She smiles. "Listen, a week's sooner than *never*. That's when I expected to see you again. Probably never. Yet here you are."

"Yep, here I am, despite everything." Another chuckle. "The Lord really did have something up his sleeve." A deep breath, with male voices in the background and a distant radio blasting out *Tommy Dorsey's Boogie-Woogie* in some echoing institutional space she visualizes as a dimly-lit barracks packed with stacked bunks and hairy men in various stages of undress.

"Anyway," he continues, "if I don't screw up, I'll take the train to Portsmouth next Sunday. There's only one each way, so I might need you to drive me back. That okay?"

"Sure. But why don't I pick you up *and* take you back? That Toonerville Trolley stops at every grade crossing along the line. Takes forever."

"I appreciate the offer. But see, they want us to use public transportation anytime we can. Besides, it'll do me good to get back on the horse."

She giggles. "Oh Matt. That local's nothing like the horse that threw you. A kid on a bike can outrace it."

His laugh's filled with optimism. "Anyway, that's the plan right now. So, could you meet me at the station and show me around?"

"Sure. What do you want to see? The Old Man of the Mountain?"

"Well, maybe next time. Right now, though, I want to see *you*. That's number one. Then the base, and the town, and your dad's restaurant, and oh, all the high spots."

"I'm yours to command. Just tell me where."

"And another thing." He clears his throat, as if he's nervous. "I'd like to look for a place to live. Nothing much. Just a small house somewhere near the base…?"

"What? A *house*? But…but you're not sure you'll even be able to stay in the service, are you? And if you do, won't the Navy provide quarters?"

"Sure, the BOQ. Since I got here last night, though, I realized I don't want to waste another minute in a Q. Okay, I can't go to sea again, but I can work on subs. And have a home of my own, and…and everything that goes with it. Hell, Gail, I'm almost thirty-one. High time I settled down, don't you think?"

She's not sure what he means by *settled down*, but says, "I guess so."

"I'll explain when I see you. I mean, if you're still willing to drive me around."

She inhales deeply to calm the fluttering of her heart. "I can hardly wait."

"Only nine more days. Piece of pie compared to the last six months."

The goodbyes take a while, but from the sound of things, he's on a pay phone with a dozen other guys clamoring to use it. Eventually, he hangs up; the line goes dead, and she's left holding the receiver.

As she dawdles back to the dishes, she realizes this wallop of good news has softened her brittle earlier mood. A surprise made sweeter because it's come out of the blue. Until now, she's assumed sudden news is always bad—of train wrecks, scarlet fever quarantines and Kamikaze attacks. Rarely the stuff of poetry, as this seems to be. Still, her fingers are crossed.

By the time she's wiped the red and white checked oilcloth on the table and draped the dishrag over the faucet, she's humming *I'll See You Again*. Just in time to smile at Ma as she plods into the room in an old house dress and the ragged felt slippers that accommodate her bunions. With a martyred sigh, she heads for the decanter of port on the sideboard and fills one of the juice glasses that came free with Quaker Oats and are painted with cartoon images. This one bears a likeness of Little Orphan Annie, whom Gail was said to resemble when she was young and her hair as orange.

Ma flops into her chair at the far end of the table and takes a long swig of the fortified wine. "Who was that on the phone?"

"Uh...my friend Matt. The Navy man I met on the train last year? He's at the Chelsea Hospital. He wants to come up next weekend."

"Huh. To see you?"

Gail nods. She pours herself a dollop of the ruby wine into a glass decorated with Red Riding Hood and the Big Bad Wolf. Briefly reminded of Jerry Graham, she adds, "And have a look at the base. In case he gets duty here after he learns to use the...the artificial limb." She expects her mother to comment that Matt's a hopeless cripple. But no; she's lost in her own thoughts. As usual when she gets into the vino.

At her end of the table, Gail realizes this scene is a foretaste of their later years, after Pop's gone to what he calls his "heavenly reward", the other kids have moved to their own lives, and she's her mother's only company, her only support. She shudders. Daunting, but not as much as it had been before this evening's discussion of alternatives to teaching at St. Margaret's. And even less since Matt's call, with its mysterious mention of a home of his own.

Still, she warns herself not to translate these coincidences into a promise of happily-ever-after. Not all surprises are shocks, but she's had enough of the latter to conclude that more are than aren't. It'll be nine days before she learns which category applies to tonight's news. For now, however, while she'd like to believe Matt's back in her life, she's aware that with or without him, she has to chart her future course on her own.

She likes the sound of *chart her own course*. It has a certain naval ring.

As she pours more of the sweet wine, *Screw Ma, screw Pa, screw Frankie* crosses her mind. She smiles with the secret satisfaction of planning a life they know nothing about. In a new job and a place of her own, where she can experiment with various forms of wild living that might shock the shit out of them.

Until now she's been good old reliable Emily Dickinson. From here on, however, she'll transform herself into Edna St. Vincent Millay, burning every candle at both ends. Maybe in the middle too.

Starting with Matt's visit next week.

CHAPTER TWENTY-NINE
Sunday, 18 March

As the Boston and Maine local chugs north through coastal Massachusetts, Matt observes that the crystalline sky has taken on a shimmer. From prior experience along the California coast, he knows this effect is due to the proximity of the ocean. Like a giant mirror, it reflects the sunlight back into the atmosphere, intensifying it. Today, however, he suspects his interest in seeing Gail again has sharpened his awareness. Actually, the passing landscape is mainly end-of-winter drab; only his expectations are electrically charged.

By the time they clatter into Portsmouth, he's fairly sizzling, despite apprehension that she won't understand this new urgency to put his plans into action. At least as much as he can while he's still at Chelsea. According to the schedule, he has another six or seven weeks of a program unofficially known as Life with a Peg Leg.

After the conductor announces "Portsmouth, New Hampshire, folks. End of the line," Matt pops a peppermint Life Saver into his dry mouth; not a day to risk halitosis. At the tiny station, he lets the other passengers precede him down the steps in case gravity hastens his descent beyond control. But he lands safely, if shakily, on the platform. The conductor hands down the crutch and wishes him Good Luck.

Even before he looks for her, Gail appears. In a tailored cadet blue coat, with her hair waving about her shoulders, she's prettier than he remembers. Best of all is her dimpled smile. Grinning, he sets off toward her, trying to walk steadily, as if he had two perfect legs. Instead, nervous, he wobbles on the crutch as if he'd never used one before.

They meet just beyond the squatty coal car, the least romantic setting he could imagine. Never mind; here she is, close enough to get his arms around. To plant a kiss on. And hold so close that he's enveloped by a sweet sense of homecoming, as if he's just finished a long journey, through storms and hostile territory. And has arrived safely in the arms of his own true love.

Tempted to blurt out some such sentimental phrase, he backs off a little. Allows himself to say only, "Gee, Gail, you're even prettier than your picture." She's also taller than he recalls, unless six months of medical torture has caused him to shrink in height as well as girth.

She murmurs, "Thanks, Matt. You are too." A quick blush. "I mean, you look a lot better than last time I saw you."

"Feel a lot better too." Then he notices her eyes are hazel, not the green he'd remembered. He's taken aback. As if it's immoral to forget details about someone you've had sex with. Even the ersatz kind they'd sneaked in his hospital bed last Thanksgiving.

For a moment longer, they breathlessly exchange questions. Like his, "Gee, it's nice of you to meet me like this. Hope didn't have anything important to do today."

And her, "Golly, no. Nothing I'd rather do." Until she clasps his free arm. "What do want to do first? See the base? Look for a house? Or meet my family?"

He stifles a quip about taking her to bed. "How much time do you have?"

She shrugs. "All day. Why? Changed your mind about seeing the Old Man of the Mountain? "

"Maybe next time. Today let's start with the base. If you'll drive me around."

Just beyond the hissing, snorting locomotive, she leads him to a black snub-nosed '39 Ford coupe with a base sticker on the bumper, red for enlisted. "Told you I would. If you can fit into my car. Your leg, I mean." She sounds as nervous as he is.

Among the legends he's accrued at Chelsea is that most civilians are uneasy with the logistics of prostheses, yet curious about how they affect ordinary life. Especially the sex act. A chief boatswain in his group had pressed one of the docs for details, only to be told, "You'll figure it out. Even quadruple amputees can when they really want to."

He mentally dismisses that advice and says, "Sure," with a bravado that belies the truth: he's not sure. The past week he's fallen on his ass twice in his zeal to prove the leg doesn't cramp his style. Others in the group have too, but he's one of the oldest, which makes him self-conscious about pratfalls. Now he manages to get his butt squarely on the seat, then manually lifts the artificial limb in and arranges it under the dash. Folding his good leg alongside is the easy part. The only thing that goes wrong, he loses the crutch and it clatters to the ground.

Gail lunges to retrieve it and stows it in the back seat before she gets in. She starts the engine and smiles over at him. "Well, okay, I'll take you to the base. Don't know where everything is, but Anna showed me the way to the fitting-out piers."

"Ah, the fitting-out piers." The familiar term connects him to other yards, other bases. And his lost career. As he anticipates the sight, he inhales deeply, to forestall nostalgia. "Hope I don't get all choked up."

Gail's expression registers no surprise. "It'd be natural, though. Especially if you never expected to be here."

Her empathy touches him. "That's right. I gave up hope. Until they put me on that plane the other week."

"Yeah. I did too. Gave up hope, I mean. Yet here we are."

He can't answer for the fullness in his throat. Finally he coughs. "Anyway, I saw you have a base sticker. Was that your first husband's?" Too late, he realizes he's called the jarhead her *first* husband.

If Gail notices, she says nothing. Just "Yes." She coasts up to a blinking red signal. There's no cross traffic, so she drives through, veering left onto a four-lane highway.

"How'd you meet him?"

"Another teacher at school was dating his buddy and recruited me for a blind date." She shrugs so casually he gets no clue to her feelings. Up ahead a sign indicates they're on US Route 1 North. "This is the Boston Post Road. My father's restaurant's a mile south. If you don't mind, we'll have lunch there. Have to warn you though, everybody wants to meet you. Pop and my sister and my uncle and his wife. They're all working today. Hope you can stand it."

His laugh is involuntary. "Hey. Do you have any idea what I've gone through just to be here?"

As they chat, he senses the same easy-going rapport that had connected them on the train last year, then during her hospital visits. Still, he's nervous about this one. Which, when you come down to it, is generated in the issue of whether this girl's as interested in him as he is in her. For someone who's survived two years with Marcie, the loss of countless sub force friends and a major train wreck, working out the next part of his life's equation shouldn't be daunting. Yet it feels like some new calculus that might have stumped Einstein.

As he'd expected, the most memorable part of the base tour is the fitting-out pier. Even on a Sunday morning, work is proceeding on the boats there. The sub he had orders to last year is long gone by now, but the Arsenal of Democracy has kept churning them out. One of these looks ready for commissioning. Or so it appears through the chain link. Sailors and officers in stained work uniforms scramble up and down the gangway, in and out of the conning tower and torpedo hatches. When he rolls down the window, the familiar perfume of dank tidal water, diesel oil and machinery suffuses him with emotion. He's embarrassed when the overflow fills his eyes.

He blinks as the sentry approaches his window and snaps a quick salute. "Sorry, sir. Y'all can't park here. Off limits except to crew."

"We'll move directly. But first, do you know who's skipper of this boat?"

By now the Marine has evidently recognized the Sub Force insignia on Matt's jacket; he relaxes. 'Sorry, sir. No idea. But I could call and find out."

"That's okay. Just thought it might be someone I know. Thanks anyway,"

They exchange salutes as Gail reverses away from the secured area. "Okay. Want to see the rest of the base?"

He shrugs, grins, pats her shoulder. "I guess. Except right now it feels like an anticlimax."

Without commentary, she identifies the few other places she recognizes—administration building, hospital, chapel, officers' club, and at the eastern end of the island, the looming naval prison. Otherwise, she drives in silence. At first he wonders if this is a retreat from the glimpse of his fragile emotions. Then it seems more likely it's her way of respecting them.

Finally, emerging from the base, she stops at the first intersection. On the right, a shabby business section faces the river. Its bars, pool halls, tattoo parlors and dance halls advertising Girls! Girls! Girls! are mirror images of those outside other bases he's known. All strategically located to snare lonely sailors as they head out on liberty.

Gail gestures towards it. "Downtown Kittery. My aunt— the one who works for the paper—she tells me the best place to find a decent rental near the base is Kittery Point. So let's drive around and see if anything strikes your fancy. Okay?"

He nods, abruptly conscious that he's edging into the rest of his life, the part that had so suddenly slipped away from him last year. Its parameters have changed. Diminished. But it's still wider and broader and higher than his expectations of life as an Iowa farmer. It ain't heaven, he thinks, but it's a damned sight better than that bucolic purgatory.

He grins across the seat at Gail. "And if nothing does, you can always take us down the garden path."

The look she returns is half shock, half delight. After a line of traffic passes, she turns toward town. "You know, Matt. I can hardly wait to get to know you better."

He reaches over to pat her hand on the gearshift knob. "That's going to take a lot longer than one afternoon." And wonders if she's gotten the message he'd hoped the white nightgown had introduced. He can't tell. He likes her uncertainty, her hesitance to rush to a conclusion. Just another of the ways she's unlike Marcie. Or any other girl he's known. Which convinces him further that they're destined for each other.

Or, as he's becoming fond of saying, "paired in the Lord's sleeve". He makes a mental note to thank Anna Donovan for the phrase.

If, of course, they ever meet again.

CHAPTER THIRTY
Later the same day

Scribbled details about the house in Kittery Point Estates fill a page in Gail's pocket notebook. To make sure they're accurate, she repeats them back to the real estate person on the phone in the restaurant office.

Then Mrs. Abercrombie asks, "When would you like to see it?"

Pushy salespeople make her nervous. "I'll talk to my friend and let you know. "

"Fine. Just remember, Cape Cods are very desirable. This one'll go fast."

Returning to the dining room, she spots her father in a booth across from Matt. Between them are a basket-wrapped bottle of Chianti, two goblets and a bowl of bread sticks. Pop's smoking a cigarette and his glass is almost full. But Matt's is empty except for a red sheen. She's surprised he hasn't waited the few minutes she's been on the phone.

As she approaches, her father's gravelly voice announces, "Now *that* was a train wreck, lemme me tell you! Nobody walked away from that one like my Gail done. Too bad you wasn't so lucky."

Before Pop realizes she's behind him, Matt catches her eye and winks. "But when you consider how many people died in just those two cars," he says, "I could be a lot worse off. A peg leg's no picnic, but at least I'm alive." He pours another glass. "By the way, want to see it?"

Her father says, "Sure. Being it's different from them regular wood ones the pirates wear." His laugh has the hearty ring he affects for special customers. Horrified, Gail gasps. As usual this afternoon her dad's wearing his good black suit, white shirt and black tie embroidered with the red, white and green flag of Italy. Time and again, Pietro's warned him such a display of an enemy standard could cause trouble. But he always retorts, "If it ain't a swastika, nobody'll give a damn."

So far he's been right. Besides, nobody who knows Franco Benedetti is ever surprised at anything he does, even when it's in the worst possible taste.

Before Matt can make the first move to reveal the artificial limb, Gail steps closer. "Pop, that's a terrible idea," she whispers, gesturing around the busy dining room. "Customers don't want to see something like that when they're eating."

Pop shrugs, stubs out his half-smoked cigarette in a Souvenir of Sicily ashtray and rises from the booth. "Seen it yet yourself, Gail?"

"Good heavens, no. And I don't intend to now."

Taking the ashtray with him, her father wanders off; she slides in across from Matt. "Please say you were joking."

He shakes his head and grins. "I was only going to pull up the trouser leg to show him the false foot. You can see the whole thing anytime you want."

Rolling her eyes, she points at the glass. "I take it that's not your first." Even as she speaks she winces at the temperance-crusader tone.

"Second. See, soon as he brought the bottle, he started toasting things. Like the U.S. Navy, and America the Beautiful, and his mother, God rest her soul. Didn't want to get off on the wrong foot with him. So I kept drinking."

"The wrong foot? " She giggles. "What else did you talk about? Besides train wrecks."

He has a short swig. "Well, I told him my brother's defending his homeland, so we talked about Anzio. Said he'd been there lots of times."

"First I've heard of it. Thought he never left his village till he and Pietro came to America as teenagers. My dad…sometimes stretches the truth."

"Don't know about that. But we got on real well. By the way, he's already ordered. Specialty of the house, he said."

Ravioli, she thinks, with a couple of meatballs, more bread crumbs than meat. She opens the notebook. "So…Here's what I found out about the house on Admiral Dewey Lane. First the rent—a hundred, fifty a month, plus utilities. I was right; it's expensive."

He chuckles. "Not bad for a brick house with a garage, in a nice section like that. Besides, with the back pay I've got on the books, it'd be cheap at twice the price. What else?"

To someone who barely clears one-fifty a month, the next item feels like a stumbling block. "You have to sign a year's lease and pay the first and last month's rent in advance."

"No problem. How many rooms?"

"Five. Two bedrooms, tile bath, kitchen with refrigerator and stove. Knotty pine book shelves and fireplace in the living room. Dining room has a chair rail and crystal chandelier. She said it's a perfect place for all the entertaining naval officers do."

"Huh. Not this one! Last thing on my mind. Anything else?"

"She can show us this afternoon, if you want."

His eyes narrow as he sips again. "Well, I'd like to. Except by the time we eat, I'll be dead in the water." A casual shrug. "Happens every day, even without wine. They say you have to expect it with a heavy prosthesis like this." He sighs. "Sorry. Maybe you could look at it for me next week?"

"I'll set it up for tomorrow after school."

He reaches across the rustic pine tabletop to clasp her hand. "And if you like it, just sign the lease and pay the rent." He glances around, lowers his voice. "Remind me to give you the cash when we're back in the car. Wouldn't look right if I handed it over here."

She's momentarily baffled, until his reason dawns. She shakes her head at the absurdity, but doesn't argue. "Don't you want to see it yourself? Or look anywhere else?"

"Nope. Even from outside, it felt like home. Can't wait to move in. Except it'll be two weeks before I have another day off. And I'll have to buy furniture."

"Nothing in storage?"

"No. The only time I ever lived off base was in San Diego. A furnished apartment that was way too rich for my blood." His gaze turns distant.

"Was that when you were married?"

The nod's so minimal, she takes it as a signal the subject is off-limits for further discussion. He pours the last wine from the bottle and quickly belts it.

As she regards the man across the table, she's aware she understands him no better than she understands how submarines work. Which is not at all. Oh, she's got the basic sense of him, that he's smart and honorable and good natured. But there's this other quality, this steel core of resolve to get what he wants. It both attracts and repels her. And ignites memories of Jerry Graham.

Before she can pursue them further, Rosalie arrives with the antipasto and the water glasses. When Matt asks for more Chianti, Gail shakes her head and orders coffee instead. She expects him to protest. But no; his reaction to her younger sister's lush beauty has evidently cleared his mind of such concerns. The waitresses' low-cut peasant blouses are designed to produce this effect in male customers, though her sister stirs it up even wearing school clothes. Unlike Gail, she looks Italian, but in her case it's an exotic asset.

Though he has three cups of black coffee, Matt yawns all through the main course. Gail tells herself he's probably had nothing to drink for months now, so the wine's hit him hard. She makes a mental note to warn her father never to do that again. It's probably one of his ploys to test Matt's mettle, see if he can hold his liquor, the way "real men" do. He'd prized that in Jerry, at least until he'd eloped with Gail.

Once they finish eating and are in the car again, she turns on the radio in case there's any war news. Instead she finds only shows like Uncle Bill's Children's Hour, a sermon by a New York evangelist, and a gospel chorus concert. After Matt falls asleep, she switches to the New York Philharmonic broadcast of a Brahms symphony. He doesn't comment even when she stops at red lights and jolts him awake.

But as she pulls up at the Navy Yard gate, she rouses him to show his ID. Besides, she needs directions to the hospital. He blinks, straightens his tie, sits upright.

"Sorry. Rude of me to nod off like that. Sorry, Gail. Hell of a way to repay your kindness."

She gives him a reassuring smile. By the time she finds the convalescent officers' quarters, he's alert enough to call her attention to a gray jitney ahead of them. "Went out to Provincetown last Sunday in one of those buggies. All the guys in the unit, I mean. For a shore dinner."

"Was it fun?"

"Compared to a train wreck, what isn't?" He grins across the seat. "All part of the program to make us comfortable as civilians."

"Oh. Is that why you want the house…so you can live like a civilian when you're off duty?"

"Something like that. Anyway, I'll call tomorrow and see if you like it enough to sign the lease."

"I thought you'd already decided."

He nods, expression turning serious. "But I want *you* to like it too. See, I don't intend to live there by myself."

She inhales the car's old oil-and-cigarette ambiance as the statement sinks in. Not a complete surprise, but still…

Finally she says, "Oh Matt. It's too soon to talk about…well, something that serious. We're only just getting to know each other."

"Yeah. But that's how I feel. Whether you do or not." He breaks off and points to a parking spot close to the entrance. After she's turned off the engine, he adds, "You told me once—actually that day on the train—you said you only knew your husband a month before you got married."

Tight-lipped, she nods, gazing at a cluster of sailors waiting for the base bus. "And I don't intend to make that mistake again."

"No, of course not. And I guess he died before you really got to know him."

Her face warms. "Well actually, no. That happened on…uh…what he called our honeymoon. You see, we were married Christmas afternoon, had a reception, then left for Norfolk. In this car."

She waits for questions, but gets only a puzzled gaze. "Anyway, it took three nights in tourist cabins all along Route 17." A deep breath arms her to add the rest, or as much of the rest as she can bear to speak. "Until then, I'd been in a romantic haze. T*hen* I got to know him."

When Matt doesn't comment, she sorts through memories for one innocuous enough to add to her explanation. "The worst of it was how much he drank. And the way he changed when he did."

That hadn't really been the worst of it, just the only part she can admit now.

His expression downshifts toward *troubled*. "Changed? How?"

She forces her voice into casual range. "Well, I guess you could say he got…uh, *mean*. Didn't act drunk, just mean."

"Did he hit you?" Matt asks quickly.

"Goodness, no!" She averts her gaze so he can't read her eyes. "It was more the way he talked." She swallows the part she's reluctant to remember, let alone speak aloud. "I'd never seen that side of him before, when we were dating. Even when he drank a lot."

"Were you afraid?"

The question's so fraught, she feels as trapped by Matt's inquisition as she had by Jerry's incessant, often brutal lust. "Look, Matt. He wasn't a bad person. Because before his unit left Norfolk, he did all the paperwork so I'd be his official next of kin. So I could get an ID card and his GI insurance after he died. And this car."

For the next few minutes, Matt stares out the window at the gray clutter of the Yard. "He died on Samoa, didn't he? While they were training for combat? In a car accident?"

She swallows hard before she can answer. "Yes. Later I had a letter from the sergeant who was with him that night. They'd just gotten orders, so they were celebrating. In a borrowed Jeep. With enough Bourbon to choke a horse. And a couple of native girls." A fresh breath helps her continue. "Jerry was driving. Lost control and turned them over. Nobody else got a scratch. But his neck was broken." She shudders, presses her eyes closed to block a sight she can only imagine, yet finds haunting.

It feels like a half hour before Matt says, "Okay, honey. I get it. Except for one more question."

She tenses. "What's that?"

"Was he ever rough with you, in bed?"

Gripped by sudden panic, she swallows hard; her face heats. She nods without speaking.

Matt inhales sharply and clenches his fists. "Was it rape?"

"No, no. Of course not. By then we were married. Anyway, it only happened when he'd had too much to drink."

He shakes his head slowly, jaw tightening.

"Look, Matt. I don't want to give you the wrong impression. He wasn't like that all the time. We had three nights on the way to Norfolk, and it was only when he drank. I mean, that he got rough."

After a long silence, Matt says, "I hate speaking ill of a man you once loved. But seems to me you're well out of that marriage. No wonder you're in no hurry to get into another. Anyway, take as much time as you need to get to know me. So if you decide I'm not the one, it won't be because you don't know all my secrets. Okay?"

Suddenly, sharing the odious personal details of marriage to Jerry gives her uneasy sense of having opened a closet full of decaying garbage that's now spilling out to pollute this new romance.

She inhales deeply to clear her consciousness, forces a tiny smile. "Okay, Matt. Next time you come to Portsmouth, I want to hear *your* secrets. Starting with your marriage."

But he says, "Why wait, sweetie? I'll tell you right now. Unless you're in a hurry to get home."

By this time. avoiding further discussion has begun to feel life or death. "But don't you have to go in? For roll call or muster, or something?"

"They won't miss me till midnight. So let's talk now. So we don't have any secrets. Nothing off limits. All right?"

Sighing, she gazes out the windshield at passing cars, a jitney, a city bus with a sign for North Station. Beside her, Matt sits more upright, folding arms over his chest, as if he's as averse to sharing personal failures as she is. But is determined to do it anyway.

"Her name was Marcie Maxwell." His voice is so low she has to strain to hear it. "She was year behind me in high school. Prettiest girl in the whole school. Blonde, and built like a brick outhouse." He shoots her a quick grin. "If you know what I mean."

"Heard it from my brother in the Air Corps. *Stacked,* right?" As she speaks, her hands outline a curving female form.

His grin is reluctant. "Anyway, we dated my senior year. And when I was at the Academy, she came with my parents every year for the big game."

"I remember what they said when I met them. They seemed to like her."

"*Now* they do. Back then they thought she was a gold-digger, because she came from the wrong side of the tracks, the wrong kind of family. They thought she was seducing me." His laugh is testy. "I wished she was. But I knew her rules—not till after the wedding. So naturally after four years of raging lust, I was ready to do anything to get her into the sack. Including the big church wedding."

"I think that's why Jerry married me too. Except he'd only had a month of lust. Anyway, then what happened?"

Matt scratches his head. "Well, I had orders to a tin can, so we moved to San Diego. I went to sea and she started working in a bank, and if there was anything wrong, those weekend reunions kept me from noticing. Until we left for a six-month cruise to WestPac. And Marcie started spending money we didn't have for stuff we didn't need. Like a red roadster and new furniture and fancy clothes and jewelry and—well, anything else she wanted." His sigh is exasperated, "After the divorce, took me three years to get out of debt."

Gail's about to comment when he adds, "That wasn't the worst of it though. She started seeing other men. Finally got pregnant by some damned Four-F who claimed he wanted to marry her. That did it for me. The end."

"Yes, I'd think it would be."

"But you know the funny part?"

"Can't imagine."

"Okay. You didn't know Jerry when you married him. But I knew Marcie as well as you can ever know somebody. Least I thought I did. Now I realize all I really knew was how she made me feel. How pretty she was. How sexy."

As Gail absorbs his words, she's overcome by the weight of their respective admissions. Of failed marriages, foolish choices, dashed hopes, crushed love. She glances at her watch—quarter to five—wanting nothing so much as to hurry home and bury herself in book reports from her students. Focusing on the work at hand. Preparations for tomorrow's classes. On simple tasks requiring that she feel nothing.

"Well, thanks for telling me, Matt. But now I really do need to get home and start grading papers."

"Sorry. Didn't mean to keep you so long. Didn't realize how late it is." He glances at his watch, then at the darkening sky behind the hospital. "And now it looks like rain." In one quick motion, he leans the door open, grabs the crutch, and hauls himself to a standing position.

Exiting from her side, Gail clutches his free arm and walks with him to the three steps into the building. At the top, she pulls open one of the double doors while he hobbles up.

"I'd invite you in," he says with a grin, "but there's always guys running around in towels."

"Wouldn't want to see anything I've never seen before."

He touches her face, his gaze soft and fond as he leans closer for a light kiss. "Anyway, I'll call tomorrow night and see what you've decided about the house. Which reminds me." Extracting the billfold from his jacket, he hands over four one-hundred dollar notes. "This ought to be enough to seal the deal. I mean, if you think it's worth sealing."

She stuffs the money into her coat pocket as he gives her arm a final pat. Then he steps into a long hall where fluorescent lights reflect in green linoleum swirled with the circles of a floor polisher. Inside, he tosses her a wave, calls, "So Long, honey," and sets out along the shining passageway.

She lets the door close, watching through the glass as he limps away. She hadn't noticed earlier, but he winces in pain.

With a sigh, she hurries through a rising, sea-fresh wind to her car. As she navigates back to Route 1, she reviews the day's unexpectedly complex choices. Especially in light of her naïve expectations that she'd handle Matt's visit with all the sophisticated aplomb of an Edna St. Vincent Millay.

Somewhere in the nondescript towns north of the city, sudden rain slashes the windshield, is soon followed by wind-driven sleet pellets, and just as quickly, large wet snowflakes. Even before the New Hampshire line, the snow turns brittle and frantic, then abruptly stops. For a moment, she considers joining the family for Sunday night supper at the restaurant. But they'll want to share their impressions of Matt, so she heads home instead. Sidestepping a question Pop's likely to ask.

"So... is he serious about you? Or just another of them playboys, like that Jerry what's-his-name? Yeah, he done the right thing by you. But I still say he was a damn playboy."

Nonetheless he'd probably add, "God rest his soul," and cross himself.

Not tonight, she decides. Tonight she needs to ponder something more solid than romance. Like where she's going to teach next year. Not exactly the way Edna St. Vincent Millay might deal with the day's revelations, but it's all Gail Benedetti Graham can manage tonight.

CHAPTER THIRTY-ONE
Saturday, 21 April

Heavy rain collects in diagonal slashes across the windows, washes out the passing landscape and dampens Matt's spirits as the little train rattles north. Given this is the last time he'll have to ride it for a while, he's disappointed at the downturn of his mood. The day before, after he'd learned the review board's good news, he'd felt so festive he'd planned a celebration. At the conclusion, he intends to present Gail with a ring. The diamond's only modest, but the platinum setting makes it seem...well, not exactly the largest in Boston, but close enough.

Finally, if all goes well—meaning if she agrees to be engaged—maybe she'll also agree to spend the night. Or maybe just an hour or two; the rollaway in the house on Dewey Lane's too narrow for serious sleeping. For carnal activity, though, it'd be perfect.

Now, however, recalling his visit with Ben Finklestein, these plans seem an exercise in self-delusion. Finished sub school, promoted to jaygee, with orders to new construction at Electric Boat in Groton, Ben's on his way to the sort of career Matt might have had. But when he'd asked, "Ever hear from Liesl these days?" the younger man's expression had turned wistful. He'd nodded vaguely, as if the question warranted more than an easy yes-or-no answer.

"Well, we stay in touch. A lot of good that does, though, since there's nowhere to go from here." He'd sighed.

"Sometimes in life you get everything you want. Except for one thing." He'd extended his hand—open, palm up and empty. "Then it's all you can think about."

Embarrassed at having asked, Matt stifled a comment that his friend should have known a romance with a married woman had no future. Until now, about to embark on his own version of happily-ever-after, his awareness shifts to the one thing *he's* destined never to have—two good legs. And the sense of himself as a whole man.

But why now? After he's qualified for a shipyard desk job, found a place to live and a girl to love, why is he downcast? With pieces of his life coming together, why does the absence of a body part outweigh these other blessings? As the one thing he can never have, will it become for him what Liesl Schwartz is for Ben Finkelstein—the only thing he can think about?

Hell, no, he resolves as the rain slacks off and the train slows for Portsmouth. It's only a leg, for God's sake, not his dick.

At the station, the helpful conductor hands down Matt's suitcase. Maneuvering with a cane, he drags it to the taxi stand, and lets the equally helpful cab driver stow it in the trunk. And, at the house in Kittery Point, carry it inside, then hold out his hand for the extra-large tip Matt has ready.

Alone in the house for the first time, he wanders among the cast-off, makeshift furnishings. He'd seen them two weeks before, but not with the sense of belonging he has now, as he mentally hangs photos of submarines, and on the shelves flanking the fireplace, arranges his collection of books and the sailing ship models he intends to build when he actually lives here.

Finally, finding the phone connected, he calls Gail to report his arrival. And his plans for the evening: "Since it's our first official date, I've made dinner reservations at the Wentworth. At six." He doesn't mention his other excuses for celebrating, including that it's his first overnight at the house. And the ring.

"Oh, wonderful!" Her tone is so enthusiastic, his hopes surge. "I can't wait. What time shall I pick you up?"

He's not sure where the old hotel is. "Will five-thirty give us enough time to get there?"

After he hangs up, he unpacks the suitcase, then yields to the rising ache in his left hip. It's a regular visitor at this time of day, a signal he needs to get off his feet, give muscles strained by the weight of the man-made leg a chance to rest. At Chelsea they warned that for this kind of prosthesis, this need never abates. Sure, you build up stamina; you get used to that toothache in the hip. But it never retreats completely.

Always a reminder of that one thing you don't have. You may forget it when you dream of running, or kicking a football, or screwing in the missionary position. But only until you wake up, and truth hits you again.

He rests until five. Then, refreshed and relatively pain-free, shaves and gets into a clean shirt. By now the rain has let up and patches of blue dot the sky above the pines. From the kitchen window, he marks a full tide in the narrow inlet beyond the back yard. And later, when he opens the door for Gail, the air smells like bed sheets fresh from the farm clothesline.

Nostalgia tugs at him, but only until he gets a good look at her in a simple black silk dress, with classic pearls at the neck and on her ear lobes. Her hair is in a smooth page boy, her lips pink. The smile touches off her dimples. He's mesmerized.

"Gosh, you look wonderful," he says, adding a kiss. It ignites a fire that leads nowhere, at least not where he wants it go. Putting it on hold for the ride to the hotel, he assumes the persona of a genteel officer escorting a comely redhead into the stuffy elegance of the Wentworth's vast dining room-- a wonderland of crystal chandeliers, potted palms and linen-draped tables, presided over by seasoned waiters in well-worn tuxes. Most of the diners are equally old, celebrating having cheated death for another week. Music is provided by elderly gentlemen in white ties and tails; his parents would probably recognize the schmaltzy tunes they pump out, but he doesn't,

Their table is under a tall window with a downdraft that makes the candles sputter and drip. Through the dusk, he sees waves pounding the rocks of the promontory where the Piscatagua River flows into the Atlantic. When Gail says, "Anna watched Dan's boat leave from the porch here," he's tempted to speculate about how many other submariners had sailed out of here and not come back. Not tonight, he thinks with a pang. Tonight's for pretending life's always good.

When they've been seated, their laps draped with napkins and drink orders taken, he asks, "Ever been here before?"

Her grin's wry. "A couple times. When Pop and Pietro worked here. Started in the scullery, washing dishes, eventually became waiters. A big deal for a couple of immigrant kids. Eventually they saved enough to buy the Coach House. The rest is history."

"Rags to riches," he says admiringly. "You must be proud."

"Oh, I am, I am. Most of the time, at least."

Hoping to avoid another family story, he scans the menu's elaborate script. "Gee, everything looks so good, what do you recommend?"

"My favorite's the sea bass with Hollandaise. Rice pilaf. Shrimp cocktail appetizer, and the green salad with hearts of palm."

He nods. "I'll go with that too."

The menu, the setting, the occasion recall other social outings he'd endured since Annapolis had transformed him from an awkward Iowa lad to a polished naval officer. Now as he sips the Tom Collins and works his way through small perfect portions of perfect food, he watches other couples teetering across the dance floor like caricatures of urbane sophisticates in a Noel Coward drama. And wonders if Gail misses the diversions he can't offer. Which leads, of course, to the question of whether she'll accept the ring.

Finally after petits-fours and demitasse coffees, he orders champagne. He doesn't specify, "the best you have," because it might imply they serve anything *but* the best.

After the flutes are set before them, he raises his glass. But instead of a toast he says, "Now, Gail. Guess what?"

And she says, "What, Matt?"

"Take a wild guess."

She sighs, but with a smile. "Please. Just tell me."

"Okay. Yesterday I found out I've been approved for limited duty. Here, at the shipyard. Starting May first."

Her eyes go wide. "Oh my goodness. That's the best news ever! We should drink to that."

He nods and sips. "So, when I come up next week, I'll be here to stay. With all my worldly goods. I've already paid a corpsman to drive me up and carry my gear in."

"Gosh, you've thought of everything."

"Well, almost." He sips more of the bubbly, then, with a flourish, brings forth the velvet box from his jacket. He lifts the lid, extends it across the small table. "Sorry it's not the largest diamond in Boston. But it is the finest cut." The last line is pure fiction. "Hope you're not disappointed."

When her gaze shifts to his face and she says, "It's beautiful, Matt," tears shimmer. "I love it."

"So…does that mean you'll be my fiancée… until you get to know me better?"

Her nod is firm. "You could say that."

"Then may I put it on your finger?" The sincerity oozing from his tone reminds him of a used car dealer, but seems appropriate for the question.

She nods; grasping the ring, he slides it into place on her left hand. "I am truly honored," he says. "Now; do I need to ask your father's permission?"

"Don't worry about his. Just *mine*."

For a while, he's so elated, he barely feels the ache in his hip as they walk from the dining room, through the lobby, across the front porch and down the steps to the car. The wind is chilly, and a few fresh raindrops spatter the windshield. As she drives along the shimmering river, he begins to feel a strange sense he can only identify as *anointed*. So uplifting he says, "You know, dear, I'm so happy about—well, all this—I'd like to go to church tomorrow. To thank the Lord for everything he's had up his sleeve." He coughs to subdue more sentiment. "What do you think?"

She shrugs. "I'm not a regular Christian. But Christmas Eve, I went to Anna's father's church, and it felt...well, comfortable. It's Episcopal, in case that bothers you."

"Heck, no. I can't tell one denomination from another. Anyway, we should get to know him. So he can marry us when the time comes. "

Gail's laugh is so light he infers her shock is feigned. "Oh, Matt. Now you've gone too far. Let's just wait and see. Okay?"

"Well, okay. But tonight, why don't you spend the night? So we can keep celebrating."

More shock. "No, no. I couldn't. It'd violate the morals clause in my contract."

"Thought you'd given notice."

"Well, yes. But I'll still need a good reference. Besides, your bed's too narrow for both of us."

"Only for sleeping."

Her laugh is so happy he's convinced she'll change her mind. Until she says, "No, I really can't. I mean...well, you've been married. You know about...uh...that monthly thing that happens to women?"

He's tempted to tell her Marcie had used that excuse so often he'd eventually realized it was a ploy to avoid intimacy. With him at least. "Oh that," he says now. "Maybe another time."

"Promise? Remember, it's not fornication when you're engaged."

She laughs but says nothing, which leads him to conclude he may be trying too hard. There's that used car dealer persona again. God forbid. He reaches for her hand on the seat and resolves to stifle exuberance till they get back to Dewey Lane.

At the house, she walks with him to the door but doesn't volunteer to come in, even when he offers to make coffee and ignite the stacked logs in the living room fireplace.

He unlocks the door, says, "Well, guess I'll see you in the morning then. What time?"

"The service is ten-thirty, so…oh, probably ten. Afterward I'll make you a nice lunch, then drive you back to Chelsea."

"For the last time, thank God." Reluctant to let her go, but suddenly racked with the worst hip pain he's experienced in weeks, he pulls her to him for a kiss that momentarily takes his mind off the suffering. But as she turns to leave, he remembers some crucial information. "Wait a minute, honey. Forgot to tell you something."

She regards him with a glint of alarm. "Oh? What's that?"

"Oh. Just that…well…I love you, Gail. Can't believe I never mentioned it before."

Her inhalation is so deep it's almost a gasp, but her lips are warm on his.

"Funny. I was going to tell you that day in Philly. Except I figured you'd think I only said it because of what'd just happened."

She nods. "I did too. Besides, it was too soon." She shakes her head. "It isn't now, though. I love you too, Matt. I still need to know you better, though. Before I commit to forever and ever."

"Yeah, sure." He laughs with nervousness and mounting fatigue. "Well, see you tomorrow. Maybe we can hold hands in church."

As he watches the red rear lights of her car recede, he's left with the same gloom he'd had recalling Finklestein's comment earlier. Drifting in it, he turns off the living room lamp and prepares to rid himself of the cumbersome apparatus that tethers him to the fake leg. That done, he stretches out on the lumpy rollaway and waits for the easing of a pain that never recedes as swiftly or as completely as his occasional outbursts of hopefulness.

Of course not; if hope is the thing with wings, that One Thing He Can't Have is a vulture that never stops circling.

CHAPTER THIRTY-TWO
Monday, 30 April

Full of her own news, Gail barely notices the sweet scent of newly-mowed grass when she parks behind Matt's 1940 Chrysler. Grabbing the Filene's shopping bags from her car, she lugs them toward the house and opens the door with more anxiety than anticipation.

Because today marks the end of Matt's status as a patient and his official return to duty. Obviously, a time to celebrate his achievements, not rejoice in *her* wonderful job offer. Lest it switch the spotlight from him, she won't even bring it up. Besides, she still has to navigate tomorrow's interview. If the news is good, that's time enough to tell him. And find out whether he's as thrilled as she is. She very much doubts, however, that any job requiring her to spend the week sixty miles away will thrill him much.

Her heart rate steps up as she calls, "Matt? Are you here?"

"Be right there." An instant later he appears at the kitchen end of the hall, silhouetted in sunlight from the back windows, hopping toward her on two crutches. She drops the bags, holds out her arms and meets him halfway. The pungency of raw onions distracts her from his toothpaste-tasting kiss. "Do I smell something cooking?"

He laughs, kisses her again. "Yep. Tonight's chow-- Submariner's Surprise."

"You mean, you're making *supper*?"

His shrug is casual. "Not a big deal, sweetie. Basically corned beef hash. Anyway, wait till you see the new furniture." Taking her hand, he leads her into the bedroom and gestures toward the curly maple suite they'd bought Saturday. "Not sure where you wanted things, but we can move them around. So…what d'you think?"

She inhales the new wood scent and surveys the mirrored dresser, night stand, spindle bed, mattress covered in blue ticking. "Gosh, it's perfect. Or will be in a minute." She retrieves the bedding from the Filene's bags and sets it atop the dresser. All still precisely folded and fresh from her aunt's linen closet. "I was going to buy new sheets, but Aunt June insisted I take these."

"Aunt June—the one who looks like Dinah Shore?"

"And she's my godmother. Never had kids of her own, so… lucky for us, I guess."

His gaze lingers on her face like sunlight, unexpectedly warming. "Need help with the bed?"

"I can manage, thanks. Anyway, aren't you busy in the kitchen?"

"Nope. Everything's under control at the moment."

As she turns, her vision snags on something large and white in the tattered boudoir chair by the front window. Stepping closer, she discovers a bone-shaped plastic apparatus terminating in a black sock and shoe. So macabre, she retreats to his side. "Oh my goodness, Matt. Is that it? I mean, your…you know…your *other leg?*"

"Wore it all day. But the hip started to act up, so I took it off. Sorry if it startled you."

Gingerly, she advances again, Matt hopping behind her. "But what keeps it on?"

As serious as an anatomy lecturer, he picks up two large sheaths like shapeless socks. One's rubber, the other of knit fabric. "First you put these on the stump, to keep it from swelling." He elevates the latex one. "Guys at Chelsea called this the elephant condom."

She manages a feeble smile.

Next, he displays a wide elastic belt with dangling straps. "Then you slide the stump into the socket on the peg leg, and hook it onto these to keep it from flying off. And kicking a passing stranger."

She forces a wider smile. "Gosh, I had no idea it was so complicated. It's not really wooden, is it?"

"Not these days." He replaces the equipment on the chair. "Okay. Unless you want a demonstration, I'll get back to the galley now."

Before he leaves, she brushes a kiss on his cheek. Smooth, freshly shaved and faintly tinged with Mennen Skin Bracer, it tempts her to further affection. Except by then he's hopping back to the kitchen. So she unfolds the quilted mattress pad and flings it over the bed, then begins layering the smooth percale sheets, a blue lambswool blanket, and finally the white chenille spread, all faintly fragrant of lavender sachet.

As she follows the familiar routine, her gaze keeps shifting to the spectral appendage. That he needs it has been an abstract fact, like statistics about the population of Boston. Now, however, it's an inescapable reality that stirs pity deeper than any since the morning in the Philadelphia hospital when she'd noticed a valley where a hill should have been. That day the Red Cross nurse had warned her not to let sympathy get the better of her. Nor had she. Today, however, unexpected tears wet her cheeks as she tugs pillows into their cases and tucks the spread up over them.

Sniffling, she wipes her eyes and is about to head to the kitchen, when Matt blocks the doorway. He glances around, nodding appreciatively. "Looks swell, sweetie. Now the place really feels like home."

Setting the crutches against the wall, he hops over to the dresser, leaning against it and regarding her with a look so warm it makes her blush. Her heart rate quickens. And when he holds out his arms, she steps into his embrace with the sense of crossing into new territory. Well, not totally new. Just not yet explored.

That he can manage a long head-to-toe kiss is another surprise. "Wanted to do that ever since we met," he breathes into her hair. "For a while, thought I'd missed my chance." His lips find hers again, with rising intensity. "Now we need to try it lying down."

Swept on by her own rush of ardor, she follows him to the bed. There, details fall into place so seamlessly she concludes this moment has been pre-ordained by the Fate that led them to meet. Divinely directed, even the fumbling with clothing and maneuvering for a position that she'd never been able to imagine. Never mind the daylight at the windows, the cars passing on Dewey, the baking smells from the kitchen, or the disarray of the bedding she's just so carefully arranged.

This moment is where all their previous moments have been leading. Even haphazard as it is, it feels perfect. Even the words he gasps against her neck are perfect.

Of course, it ends too soon, but leaves a residue of promise. "Oh my," she sighs when she catches her breath. "What a nice surprise."

"About time, don't you think?" he says.

"But what about supper? Won't it burn?"

He chuckles. "If it does, I'll make more. We can eat anytime."

She's so relaxed she has to say, "Well, that's good. I mean...maybe if I spent the night, we could have it again for breakfast."

He gives her an incredulous glance. "Spend the night? What about that morals clause you always worry about?"

"Screw the clause. Besides, tomorrow's May Day at school. With all sorts of silly dances and poetry contests. Even a May pole, for God's sake. I don't even have to be there." She's briefly tempted to share her plans to get an early train from Dover so she can interview for the job in Portland. Not today, she thinks. This is Matt's day to celebrate having reached the goal of staying in the Navy, his last as a gimpy patient. His last as a Lieutenant Senior Grade. Tomorrow he'll put on his service dress blues restitched with the two-and-a-half gold stripes of a Lieutenant Commander, and drive his new car with hand controls down to the base. And become a functioning member of the Sub Force again.

But tonight he's made supper for them, and they've christened the new bed and later, will occupy it together for the first time. The day is too special to pollute with news he may not find as thrilling as she does.

She cuddles closer "Gosh, Matt. If I'd known this was going to happen...." She edges away, slides from the bed. "Be right back. Need some Kleenex."

"Bring the box. We may not be done yet."

As she heads into the bathroom, her sense of their romance takes on a new dimension—a feeling of being not only appreciated but respected and fulfilled. Essentially, *loved*. With a ring on her finger, a home that will become her own, and a man whose regard for her is unquestionable. Who even cooks. Corned beef hash may not be the food of the gods, but tonight it's the nectar of romance.

Most of all, she and Matt know each other's secrets, at least the awful things based on other partners. And their regrets. As for the Portland job, it sounds so good she'll probably be competing with a dozen other applicants. So why even mention it? Perfection has been so long coming, they deserve to savor it.

After smoothing her mussed hair in the mirror over the washstand, she grabs a new box of Kleenex from atop the toilet tank and, still wearing only her slip, hurries back to the bedroom. Matt's smile is inviting and his arms are ready to pull her down beside him again. Except this time, he's holding a rolled-up condom between thumb and index finger. "Sorry. Didn't think of this earlier. Too worried about how we were going to manage with...you know...my handicap. Now, though, seems like something we should think about. At least until we're married."

Recoiling in flashes of Jerry, she almost says, "I hate those things." Then remembers Portland, and the biological facts that life with her parents has etched in her mind. She forces a smile and a shrug, without moving closer. "That makes sense. But... don't you want to eat before your supper dries out? It smells so good. And I'm really hungry."

"Sweetie," he says patiently. "I've had chow every night since the wreck. I mean, every night since the docs decided I wasn't going to kick off. But this is the first night I've had *you*. So...what do you think?"

In an instant, the simple speech scours away traces of Jerry as well as her nascent curiosity about this man's culinary skills. Her heart races, then melts in a surge of heat more intense than any she's ever experienced. Sighing, "Oh yes...yes!" she hastens to join him under the rumpled sheets she'd recently arranged with such proud precision.

Just as if she no longer gives a damn about his special supper either.

CHAPTER THIRTY-THREE
Friday, 26 May

This balmy pastel morning, Matt expects his part in the day's schedule will be observing from shore as the new Balao-class boat begins the sea trials that will qualify her to join the fleet. And, as a member of the team responsible for installing her massive GM diesels, he'll sit in on critiques after she returns.

So far, the no-load tests at the pier have been flawless. But they're only part of the equation: no static trials, however stellar, can guarantee underway performance. It's a critical point for any new boat. And as yardbirds and crew shuffle onto the fitting-out pier and up the gangway, he's filled with envy so acute he hopes it doesn't show on his face.

Last to board is the skipper, LCDR Chuck Kellogg. Matt had known him at sub school, adding credence to the maxim that if you're at New London long enough you'll meet every man in the sub force. And after that you'll keep running into them somewhere in the world. Until you read their obits in *Navy Times.*

By now the engines are rumbling under the deck; pungent exhaust tinges the sea-fragrant breeze off the water. The familiar smell flashes Matt back to other boats at other piers— Mare Island, Pearl, San Diego, Midway, Perth—and kicks off a new pang of longing so sharp he clenches his fists to loosen its grip. It fades only when he realizes Kellogg's addressing him: "Coming along today, Commander?"

His first instinct is to remind the skipper that limited duty status precludes his going to sea on any vessel, except as a passenger. Or, unless ordered to by the CO. Is that what Kellogg intends? He stammers, "Uh…is there room?"

A quick nod. "On the bridge. If you don't mind a pull-down seat."

He tightens his grip on the cane, murmurs, "I'll manage," and follows the other up the gangway, then across the slatted wood deck to the conning tower. The ladder to the bridge is no problem: since he's joined the engineering team, he's had abundant practice—and boosts when needed—in short climbs. While his co-workers are aware of his limitations, no one's mentioned his disability. Some have even begun calling him "Lucky." The irony of the old sobriquet makes him wince. Has Kellogg asked him aboard as a troubleshooter? Or a mascot— a lucky penny, rabbit's foot, crossed fingers?

Nonsense; he's there because he's part of the team. And when Kellogg hands him a stop-watch and a clipboard, he recognizes his specific duty will be timing the engines' responses as they're put through their paces.

On the bridge with the CO, the Exec and a helmsman, he huddles onto the small metal seat hinged to the after bulkhead, and manually lifts the artificial leg out of the others' way. By this time, line handlers are casting them off while a yard tug stands by to escort them to the testing grounds five miles offshore. And by implication, to tow them back if something breaks down. A possibility the Navy recognizes from its long history with the combination of sea trials and random chance. The ignominy of being towed back to the pier is nothing compared to that of wallowing dead in the water, while the engineers try to revive some lifeless piece of machinery below.

It's been over a year since he's been underway. Still, the process is familiar as breathing—the terse commands to the engine room, the warning hoots of the horn, the increased pulsations underfoot, the rising exhaust cloud as they part from the pier and head out. The overarching thrill is being aboard a sub set loose for the first time. Ordinarily a helmsman's at the wheel. But today it's the skipper's privilege to take the first measure of his ship himself.

Abruptly aware the train wreck has cost him not only a leg but a chance to experience command, Matt feels that corrosive envy again. He quickly overrides it with the resignation he's been practicing in the new job.

As they move across the slack water toward the Piscatagua, he absorbs the scene with appreciation born of his previous supposition that he'd never experience it again—black hull cleaving the ripples, clatter of cars on the old iron bridge upstream, traffic flowing on the causeway across the river. All of it perfumed with eye-smarting diesel exhaust, the submariner's aphrodisiac. For others aboard, it's all ordinary; for him, another of the miracles that have brightened the dark months since he was injured. And offered him a chance to feel whole again. Well, *almost* whole.

At the merge with the river, the twin screws bite into incoming tidal currents with increased purpose. The tug follows at a respectful distance, like a faithful dog hoping for a pat. The hills of Kittery, the cranes of the shipyard recede; on the east end of the island, the naval prison looms dark and forbidding even in bright sunlight. And on the southern promontory, at the river's mouth, rocking chairs on the Wentworth hotel's porches nod in the breeze. He wishes he could tell Gail without confessing he's seen them from the water.

For a while after the boat enters open sea, Kellogg tests the engines separately on a slow, steady run toward the Isle of Shoals testing grounds. Offshore, the spring wind takes on a brisk bite; rising waves hiss along the hull. Satisfied with the results so far, he calls for both engines in an official speed trial. Underfoot, vibrations increase; the boat rises slightly. At each change, he signals Matt to mark the time required to raise the RPMs.

After the next speed increase, Matt's sunglasses fog with spray and his lips taste of salt. Behind them, a foam trail and a pall of exhaust merge with a haze that swallows the coastline, while the mechanical whale flexes her muscles and runs for the open sea.

Finally Kellogg rings for Full Flank, the maximum speed the diesels are designed to produce. In other subs Matt's known, this is about 24 knots. The hull steps up still higher and the wind freshens as the boat dashes eastward. The heady moment reverberates through his being like a shot of pure adrenalin.

Until just before they reach maximum RPMs, he senses a momentary hesitation in the engines' pulse beats. Barely discernible, it disappears so quickly he thinks he's imagined it. Especially when no one else seems to notice.

"Skipper?" He raises his voice above the diesels' thrum. "Thought I felt a hiccup before we hit max RPMs just now. Can you repeat the maneuver?"

Kellogg shoots him a startled look, but nods.

"Maybe just imagination. Won't hurt to double-check."

"Roger." Kellogg rings to reduce speed. The boat slows and settles lower. When it's barely making way, he calls for Full Flank, Emergency. A maneuver designed to get them out of harm's way with all possible speed. Vital in war zones when a boat's surfaced and an unknown blip appears on RADAR. When they race toward a crash dive before the enemy gets their range.

Matt closes his eyes to focus on the accelerating rhythm of the pistons. For a fraction of a second, there's that hesitation again, almost too miniscule to discern, certainly not to register on the gauges. He signals Kellogg to try again, then grabs a phone .

No one in either engine room has noticed the irregularity. Neither has the control room crew.

On the third try, however, the hiccup's more pronounced. This time it shows up on the board as a fleeting red flicker among the green Christmas lights. Long enough too for the engineer to pinpoint the problem in the forward engines.

For the next hour, they test them separately again. The hiccup only appears momentarily, near maximum RPMs, which might qualify it as too insignificant to pursue. Except everyone knows there's no such thing as Too Insignificant on a sub. If they let this or any other minor imperfection slide, it will come back to bite them in the ass. And at the worst possible time.

The rest of the trials go well. For further proof, they return to the yard powered only by the After engines, which also tests the steering mechanism. It's a slow trip, but the generalized tension has retreated, as confirmed by the engineer's presence on the bridge. He's a know-it-all jaygee who thinks they'll lick the problem in no time.

"But actually," he asks innocently, "how often do you have to run on only one engine?"

The other officers exchange glances. Even the helmsman rolls his eyes. Matt says, "Couple years ago, a boat on patrol took such a pounding from the Japs, one shaft was bent out of shape. She made it to the repair ship at Midway, but they couldn't replace it. So she limped back to Pearl. Yard there was too busy to do anything but patch her up and send her to Hunters' Point, still on one wing. It took them four months to put her back together."

Kellogg lights a cigarette, flicks the match overboard. The smell of fresh tobacco smoke is briefly refreshing. "What boat was that?"

"*Wolf Fish.* Ironically, they only had one more patrol before they went missing."

"Skipper was Ed Zimmer, right?" the XO asks. "Who was engineer?"

"Dan Donovan," Matt says. "Widow's a friend of my fiancée." There's that connection again; nostalgia softens him with a full-circle sense of his role here.

When the smart-ass jaygee adds, "Just goes to prove, one good screw's better than none," the ensuing snickers signal general relief that the trial's discovered nothing worse than a malfunction almost too minor to mention.

By now it's close to noon; fatigue has invaded Matt's body; his left hip aches and hunger gnaws his innards. Still, he no longer feels like an outsider or a good-luck charm. He even wishes he weren't going to be on leave the next month. A critical time for the new boat, when plenty of overtime guarantees she'll be commissioned on schedule, then sent down to New London to complete fleet training.

Without him, of course.

This part of limited duty leaves him feeling cheated: watching others sail away in a boat he's become attached to will probably feel like loving a woman who belongs to someone else. But as soon as the thought crosses his mind, his own experience insists that a man can get over a woman. This loss is much worse.

After they've returned to the fitting-out pier and are chowing down in the Building 15's conference room, Kellogg commends Matt for noticing the gremlin: "Good you were with us today."

He shrugs and peels soggy wax paper from the baloney sandwich he'd made that morning. "Someone would've caught it if I hadn't." He dismisses the notion of canceling leave so he can help find this bug, and directs his imagination toward how he's going to report the day's events to Gail. For supper, he'd planned to take her to the O Club. Now he vetoes the idea of a venue where, after Happy Hour, some half-looped shipmate might blurt out, "Sure good old Matt was with us on the sea trials today."

Maybe in her preoccupation with final exams, term papers, graduation ceremonies, the remark might fly over her head. Then again, she's such a stickler for societal rules, her trust in his Absolute Honesty could take a serious nosedive. Of course, in the future that could erode in the give-and-take of married life. But not before they even tie the knot, for God's sake.

Hopefully, by the time they get back from leave, it'll no longer be news. Maybe if today's incident had ended badly, that'd be another matter. Say, if his peg leg had tripped a sailor who'd gone overboard and been chewed up by a shark, it might have become a Fleet legend.

But as it is, he commits the memory to the All's Well that Ends Well chapters of his life. And turns his thoughts to other matters. Such as, whether Gail will want to spend the night after almost a week apart. He hopes this notion works out as well as the rest of the day has. Even without an ulterior motive, it interests him even more than all the Navy talk he's heard since he'd hauled his ass up to the bridge that morning. And for the next few hours, felt like a real submariner again.

CHAPTER THIRTY-FOUR
Sunday, 18 June

T he sleep that cocoons her is so deep that Gail's still in a stupor when someone raps on the bedroom door. Until Matt's mother calls, "Wake up now. Time for breakfast. Don't want to be late for church."

She doesn't give a damn about either, but makes her voice cheerful. "Be right down," she says, just as she has every morning since they've arrived at the farm Monday. The early start's been mandatory for the Scenic Wonders of Iowa tour his parents planned, so that Gail, as a teacher, can learn everything there is to know about the state. Whether she cares or not.

Since New Liberty's near the geographical center, by Friday afternoon they've covered all four corners in the family La Salle. A big, comfortable car, except that Gail has had to sit in the front with Mr. Ogleby so she can appreciate every remarkable detail of every remarkable site. Like Herbert Hoover's birthplace, the boarding house where Mark Twain lived during his riverboat days, the world's largest cereal factory, a couple of dams, acres of mysterious hills, and enough corn rows to reach to the moon and back. The worst part about it is, Matt's been stuck in the back seat with his mother.

Even at the house they haven't been alone. Or alone *enough*. It's a big four-square clapboard, four boxy rooms downstairs, four up. When they'd expected Matt home again, the Oglebys had converted a first-floor office to a bedroom, and a utility room to a bathroom so he wouldn't have to navigate steps to the second floor. They'd thought of everything. Except that he'd want to stay in the Navy. Gail suspects they blame her for that. The tour might even be their revenge.

So are the sleeping arrangements, a floor apart. Gail's been assigned his old room, now a shrine to his boyhood—walls covered with pennants from New Liberty High and the Naval Academy, along with photos of various teams he'd either played for or cheered on. On his desk are other pictures, including one of his wedding to the Hot Mama. At least Gail figures that's who the dimpled blonde is beside him under an arch of swords raised by other ensigns in dress whites.

Even before she unpacks, Gail turns that one face down.

Now, despite being with the family all week, she hadn't realized church today is mandatory. Still drowsy, she wears her plisse bathrobe down to breakfast. Since the others are already in their Sunday finery, she bolts syrup-drenched flapjacks, then races back upstairs to finish dressing. The coffee had smelled so bitter, her stomach roils. And until she brushes her teeth, her mouth tastes like garbage.

Nonetheless, they arrive at the First Methodist Church of New Liberty in time for her to scan a bulletin board thumb-tacked with photos of service members from the congregation. "Our Honored Dead" are displayed separately in a glass case surmounted by American flags. Matt explains who each is, or was once.

Despite the fluttering of hand fans with the picture of Christ in Gesthemane, the heat in the crowded sanctuary soon rises to stifling. Light-headed, Gail nods off during the slow-paced sermon by a spindly parson brought out of retirement when the regular minister joined up. Some folks in the congregation actually snore.

After the benediction, the crowd presses in to greet her. Well, of course. As the fiancée of one of their own, she's a celebrity. The young widow he'd met on the train that wrecked. And a New Englander, of all things. Some folks have never known anyone from the East Coast, so they pummel her with questions—does she like Iowa? Have they set a date? Where will she and Matt live after they're married? She answers with a frozen smile, dwindling energy, and the beginnings of a sick headache.

By the time she's shaken every sweaty hand, her temples are throbbing. Back at the house, her hopes of a nap evaporate when dusty cars swarm into the yard. She watches from the bedroom window as Matt's relatives stream toward the house bearing covered dishes. She's about to flop onto the bed, when Matt's father calls up the stairs: "Lunch, Gail. Come on down so we can say the blessing and eat."

Once again, she's on stage. To be inspected, interrogated, interviewed. The curiosity is friendly, just overly abundant, and from more relatives than she can keep track of. At church she'd met two aunts on Matt's mother side, their kids and grandkids, plus Aunt Bernice. The clan's matriarch lives with her widowed daughter Mildred, and sixteen-year old Donna, one relative Gail won't forget. If not for her nickname—Bella Donna—then for her thick makeup, skin-tight halter top and overly short shorts. Even more memorable is the way she clings to Cousin Matt. And bats mascaraed lashes at him.

Among Mr. Ogleby's brothers and their families, her instant favorite is Uncle Jim, because he's curious about why Matt was injured and she wasn't. "Never knew anybody been in a train wreck before," he comments. "Myself, I was in a plane came down once, but I walked away. Thought I'd be another Lindbergh, but never got the hang of landing. She threw me out when she nosed over with her tail in the air. Took it as a sign the Lord had other plans for me. Now my youngest boy, he's a Navy pilot." His smile never fades, but he swallows hard before he adds, "Flies a Hellcat, off a carrier in the South Pacific."

When it's time to eat, she follows Bernice and Milly to the line for the enormous spread on the front porch. She's hoping Matt will rescue her, but he's been herded by Bella Donna and some lesser cousins to a table across the lawn. There's a good breeze, but even in the shade of the huge maples surrounding the house, it's about two hundred degrees. A man ahead in the food line gestures toward the emerald-green stalks stretching to the horizon. "Here in corn country," he drawls, "they call this one of them days you can hear the corn grow."

She smiles. "Where I come from, they say it's hot enough to fry an egg on the sidewalk."

He gives her a pitying look, as if picturing her in some city slum.

Focused on loading her plate with potato salad, fried chicken, watermelon pickles, baked beans and deviled eggs, she just smiles and moves on. By the time she reaches the table, the food is melting into a brown sludge. The headache throbs more viciously.

Forcing herself, she takes small bites of everything, washing it down with iced tea and trying to look interested in the ladies' stories. Mostly about Matt and his brothers as they came of age on the farm. No brushes with the law, just surreptitious driving, smoking, and beer-drinking. That he was the one who got into the least trouble doesn't surprise her.

"Only thing he ever did that worried them was marrying for the wrong reasons," Aunt Bernice says with a shake of her Queen Victoria hairdo. "But he was fresh out of Annapolis, ready to take on the world. Guess he told you about it."

She nods, conscious of Milly's covert scrutiny from across the table. "I gave my father fits when I married. That was for the wrong reasons too."

"Everybody gets to make a mistake now and then," Aunt Bernice's tone is don't-argue-with-me self-righteous.

"Speaking of marriage," Milly says in her flat mid-western accent, "have you and Matt set a date yet?"

"We will when we get back. He wanted to make this our honeymoon, but I thought it'd be better if it was just the two of us."

The other women titter politely. "But it'll be soon, won't it?" Milly says. "Or doesn't he know about your condition yet?"

Condition? The word glares like neon italics in a black and white text. Tension tightens her muscles. She's barely able to say, "Uh......what condition's that?"

Milly laughs. "Generally referred to as delicate, if you catch my meaning."

Gail stifles a gasp. "You mean...Are you implying that I'm *expecting?*"

Milly shifts in the folding wooden chair. This smile seems forced. "Just an observation, dear. See, I work for the GP in town, and over the years I've noticed when young women come in with...well, various symptoms, they have a certain look. Around the eyes, mostly. I've seen it so often, I know what it means even before they have the test."

Seven years before, Gail had overheard a fragmented conversation between her mother and Aunt June when Ma still hoped her pregnancy with Frankie was only menopause. Evidently from long experience, both women had recognized The Look as an early sign. "And you're saying... I have it?"

Milly shrugs. "I could be wrong. But I believe you do."

For a moment Gail's tempted to explain her period's just a bit late. Averse to sharing even this intimate fact, however, she says, "But you only met me today; you don't know how I look. These others—you've seen them before, so you can tell when they change." She draws a deep breath and affects a lofty expression. "Excuse me, but in my family we consider it rude to ask visitors personal questions. And to accuse them of... improper behavior."

Aunt Bernice sniffs. "May be improper, dearie, but it's the way young people conduct themselves since that man Roosevelt got us into this horrible war. Like there's no tomorrow."

"Sorry, Gail," says Milly. "Didn't mean to offend you. Just thought...well, you've both been married before. So I assumed—well, it just seemed natural."

"It's all right," Gail says, softening her tone. But as soon as she can, she carries her plate to a big trash can by the house. Matt's still across the lawn with his cousins, and everyone else is occupied with other family members. While she may have fended off Milly's curiosity for now, the suggestion has left her shaken. And desperate to escape this mob of well-meaning but inquisitive farm folks.

Willing herself to appear calm, she holds her head high and marches up the steps to the back porch without looking to see if anyone's watching. Inside she strides past the kitchen and tiptoes up the stairs. This sudden retreat feels childish, but given the possibility that everyone at the picnic, at least the women, are snickering and speculating that good old Cousin Matt has had his way with her, hiding feels like her only option. Especially after she studies her face in the mirror and observes that her eyes seem more darkly circled than usual.

Telling herself this could be just a sign of fatigue, she kicks off her shoes and stretches out on the patchwork quilt atop the bed. And tries to ignore the likelihood that his aunts' consensus will be that if he's bedded her, it's because she invited him. Led him astray. Seduced him. Because everyone knows eastern women are fast. Especially the widows of Marines. Even those who teach at private girls' schools. And who may not look Italian, but are. In her case, only fifty percent, but that may be the half with the hot blood.

Washed by the distant buzz of conversation through the open windows, the shouts of the kids, the calls of the adults, and the occasional blast of jazz from someone's portable radio, she closes her eyes and wishes for sleep. But before long, the food she'd forced down begins rumbling in her stomach. When it rises in her throat, she flings herself up and races to the bathroom. She barely makes it to the toilet.

After the nausea passes, she brushes her teeth and creeps back to the bed. There, the possibility Aunt Milly knows what she's talking about stirs her to tears. No, no, her mind insists. She *can't*—absolutely *can't* be pregnant. Not when she's just signed a contract for the best teaching job in New England. Even if she and Matt marry immediately, she won't be able to work more than a month or two. Not that he'll mind. His approval of the Portland job has been grudging at best. He'll welcome this more than she does. Which is not at all.

For a while, regret sours all her emotions. Along with disgust with herself for not giving a moment's thought to contraception that first time. Even Jerry had been careful—and optimistic enough—to bring a gross of condoms on their so-called honeymoon. So maybe the ultimate arbiter of the morals clause is God, and now he's punishing her for immorality. Carelessness. Or all the collective small sins of her life. Whatever the cause, she's trapped.

But as the tears run their course, a hopeful thought emerges: maybe the nausea's not morning sickness, but old-fashioned food poisoning. She should have known better than to eat potato salad on a day as hot as this one. She grabs at the explanation like a drowning man going after a life ring. And reminds herself her periods have never been regular. So maybe all this gloom and doom is needless. Certainly there's no need to mention it to Matt.

Relaxing, she's drifting toward a nap when distant thunder stirs her awake. And galvanizes the picnickers below to gather dishes, chairs, card tables and kids, pack up and head home. In the west the sky darkens to bruise blue; sunlight fades, wind whips the maple leaves inside out and a steady procession of cars rolls out the lane. Suddenly aware this is Iowa and the approaching storm may be a tornado, Gail springs from the bed, swipes on lipstick and heads downstairs.

No one seems surprised to see her or asks where she's been, so she helps Mrs. Ogleby collect cloths and leftovers from the porch. Then, as thunder crescendos and rain cascades from the roiling sky, she joins the others in the kitchen. No one seems alarmed, or suggests seeking shelter in the storm cellar, even when the power goes off.

Later, as the rain fades to a drizzle, they take to the damp rockers on the front porch, drink iced tea, and talk, mainly about those who'd been at the picnic. If Cousin Milly's shared her suspicions about a delicate condition, no one mentions it. Nonetheless, Gail's relieved that she and Matt are leaving tomorrow. Beside her, he reaches for her hand and fondles it in what, for him, is a suggestive manner. All begins to feel right with the world again.

Low in the sky now, the sun breaks through. The air is sweet and fresh and cool; leftover rain drips from eaves and trees; a chorus of robins chirps evening songs. Suddenly touched by the moment, Gail's moved to say, "Gee, it's been nice to be with all of you," to no one in particular. And is surprised to realize she's spoken from her heart.

Matt squeezes her hand. Mr. Ogleby clears his throat and his wife says, "And it's really been grand having you."

Tears fill Gail's eyes at the warm-heartedness of these country folks. Still, she's not tempted to prolong the visit a moment beyond two o'clock tomorrow, when she and Matt have a train to Chicago, then the B & O overnight to Washington for the rest of the trip he's planned, to show her the nation's capital. So she can continue to get to know him. And decide when they'll be married.

Now that there's no urgency, she's looking forward to being with him in a nice hotel, in a glamorous city full of sights she really does want to see. Not an official honeymoon, just a reward for having endured Iowa. And not being pregnant.

Well, *probably* not.

CHAPTER THIRTY-FIVE
Thursday, 22 June

Rising from the bench in the vast, echoing sprawl of Union Station, Gail leans down. "Going to the Ladies' room, then get a magazine for the train. Need anything?"

Matt rattles the rumpled *Washington Post* a previous traveler left on the seat. "About done with this. So maybe a *Time*. Or *Argosy*. Thanks, sweetie."

She nods, and heads toward the far reaches of the waiting room. As he observes her listless gait, the contretemps between them takes on new life. Trying to ignore it, he turns to the back pages of the newspaper in case a sub loss is hidden there. Despite the astronomical number of missing boats, such news rarely makes the front page. When there are no bodies to bury, few civilians give a damn how many submariners are dying every week.

Or so it seems, given the cynicism that's soured him the last few days. And convinced him Gail's about to break the engagement. Not that he blames her, after the Iowa trip. To atone, he'd tried to book a roomette on the overnight from Chicago. None was available, only curtained-off bunks in an old sleeping car. His hopes for the hotel here had been dashed too when he couldn't produce a marriage certificate, so had to settle for single rooms a floor apart.

"Sorry, sweetheart," he'd said. "Didn't realize that in the District, fornication's not just a sin but a crime. Even with your fiancée."

He hadn't expected a guffaw, but she didn't even grin.

The next day, things turned worse. First, they didn't leave the Potomac River Scenic Cruise at Mount Vernon because Gail was too tired to climb from landing to mansion. Instead they'd stayed aboard the old sidewheeler all the way to a rickety amusement park on the Bay. And back again, with a cargo of hogs from every backwater village along the river.

Wednesday's city tour might have been an improvement… if the Gray Line bus had moved fast enough to get ahead of its own exhaust. If the blast-furnace city heat had abated; if humidity hadn't blanketed marble monuments and halls of democracy alike. No surprise Gail developed a sick headache by the time they reached the National Cathedral. Even before she suggested it, he hailed a taxi back to the hotel. Then cancelled the next day's museum plans and changed tickets for the trip home from Friday to today.

"Why don't you switch to the B & O too?" she'd said. "It doesn't go anywhere near where we wrecked last year. Besides, you get a wonderful view of Manhattan on the ferry from Jersey City."

"Sorry, dear," he'd said. "When I was in the hospital, I promised myself I'd take the Congressional Limited again someday. Like getting back on the horse that threw you? If you'd rather, though, you can take the B & O and we'll meet in New York."

Her sigh was long-suffering. But when she'd said, "No, I can handle it," he'd concluded her aversion to this train was evidence of what she *really* wants—to separate before he puts another ring on her finger. While they can part with only regrets, not a legal connection.

He sighs. Remembering Marcie, he tells himself that if an ending is inevitable, better now than later. Before Gail turns desperate and vindictive, and they end up wounding each other. The comfort he finds in this logic, however, is Antarctic.

When she hasn't returned after fifteen minutes, he translates her long absence into another sign of fading love. An ache sharper than mere disappointment stabs his chest, as if her rejection isn't just about his family. Or Iowa. Or this dismal glimpse of Washington. Maybe what's really eating her is that he's a cripple, not a whole man.

Maybe this, maybe that, he thinks as the minutes tick away. Almost like waiting for this train nine months before, Except then he hadn't known time was running out on the life he'd lived for thirty years. This new doomsday may be unavoidable, but it won't be a surprise.

He's in the midst of another sigh when it occurs to him that sighing never saved a sinking sub. Nor will it change Gail's mind. But as a naval officer, he's oriented to push beyond his own emotions and address every problem before it turns catastrophic. At the very least, *try* to find it, *try* to fix it. Not just stand by and let it happen, for God's sake.

When he finally spots her across the cavernous space, her expression is grim. As if she's steeling herself to administer the *coup de grace*. Still, he gives her a "welcome back" smile. Not that it thaws her: taking her seat, she neither responds nor explains her long absence, just hands him the magazine she's bought for him.

"Thanks, sweetie," he says. "Feeling okay?"

A brusque nod. "Just tired."

Just tired is her stock answer these days. Along with "I'll be fine once I can catch up on my rest." He pats her hand. "Well, tonight you can sleep in your own bed again. Unless you'd rather stay in New York and get an early train to Boston."

"Oh Matt, no. Let's keep going."

And get it over with? He should have known better, he thinks as he opens the shiny new *Time*. Gail sighs and begins leafing through her *McCalls*. Like two strangers, they read separately—or she does; his thoughts are stuck in this fogbank between them. This ominous *something* he can't even name.

When the Congressional Limited's announced, he flags down a redcap to lug their bags out to Car 6. Again, in seats halfway up the coach, they settle themselves with none of the banter he'd expected. More strangers today than before, when they hadn't yet met. When the future still shimmered with possibilities. Yet two hours later, he'd learned everything about her that mattered. Mainly, that she was nothing like Marcie, therefore safe to fall for.

Now, before the train begins to move, they return to their magazines. Matt's brims with D-day stories and optimistic reports on the invasion. From time to time, he finds himself absorbed, but only for a paragraph. Until he glances at the short story Gail's reading. A wartime romance, judging from the illustration of a comely blonde gazing into the eyes of a soldier too slickly handsome to be flesh-and-blood real.

Still, passion pulses in the picture, its promise frozen in color. Maybe this is what she'd expected with him. Instead, she got an earthbound cripple whose sprawling family has daunted her. Months before, when she'd resigned from St. Margaret's, he'd worried she might join the military. When she'd settled instead on teaching in Portland, he'd been relieved it was only sixty miles away. Not close enough to live together, but better than the alternative.

Reining in his runaway suppositions, he notices the train's making stops it hadn't in last year's high-speed dash to the unscheduled end of the line—Baltimore, Bel Air, Havre de Grace, Perryville. They're in a curve leaving Wilmington when a gong-toting waiter strolls through the car announcing the first call to dinner. One of his last memories of their first trip on this train, today it stirs regret. And the sharp truth he can't wait a moment longer to face this. Whatever comes.

He closes the magazine, manages a minimal smile. "Well, dear, dining car's open; want to eat now? Or shall we wait till we're closer to…where it happened last year?"

She shrugs, voice flat. "Whatever suits you."

"Might as well get it over with, then."

Her scrutiny morphs into a half-frown. "That sounds like a chore. Or going to the firing squad."

"Maybe because last time it turned out that way."

She winces just enough to notice. "Well, anyway, to keep things authentic, I'll stop off in the Ladies' Room while you go ahead and get a table."

He shakes his head. "Sorry. Don't want to tempt fate; this time I'll wait for you."

Leaving their seats, they're the only passengers heading rearward. While she's in the lavatory, he stands in the swaying vestibule, leaning on the cane to keep weight off the stump. On the five trains they've ridden the past ten days, he's tried to rely on the prosthesis instead of using crutches. Trying to prove—to Gail, his parents and himself—that he's as good as he ever was. Maybe Gail's the only one he hasn't fooled.

When she rejoins him, he notices the dead-white pallor of her face contrasting with the dark circles under her eyes. "Feeling okay?" he has to ask.

She nods, pulls open the heavy door and precedes him into a miasma of cigarette smoke in the next car. So she won't notice his halting gait, he says, "Go on, I'll catch up." Still, she takes the swaying aisle so slowly he's right behind when she pauses, clutches the nearest seat. And sinks gracefully to the floor.

Alarmed, he says her name, then calls, "Can someone help me?" to the half-empty coach. A few passengers are craning, but a Navy medical officer rises and hurries toward them. He's young, the two stripes on his blues still bright gold. He stoops to Gail's inert form, presses his fingers to her neck, looks up at Matt. "Is this lady your wife, sir?"

"Fiancée. Her name's Gail."

"Gail?" The doctor repeats the name loudly, then asks, "Has she been sick?"

"We've been traveling the last ten days. And she's been off her feed. Always tired. But not sick."

The younger man inspects Gail's lowered eyelids. "Might be anemia. Or low blood sugar. When did she eat last?"

Matt moves closer, bending until pain shoots through his hip. "Breakfast. Now, sweetie, can you hear me?"

To his relief, her lids flicker. She blinks a few times before she tries to sit upright. "Matt…What happened?"

"You fainted, ma'am," the doctor explains. "Remember?" With a deep breath, she struggles to rise.

"Sit still a while longer, ma'am. I'll help when you get up."

By now others in the car are staring, getting up, speculating among themselves. The doctor asks them to step back, then gives his hand to Gail and asks if she can walk to the dining car. She wobbles, but says, "I'm okay, thanks."

There's one more coach to navigate, Gail and the doctor ahead, Matt hobbling behind. In the dining car, a waiter leads them to the nearest table, holds the chair while the doctor guides Gail into it, then orders orange juice and chicken noodle soup. "With plenty of Saltines. How's that sound?"

She nods. The waiter bustles off. The medical officer adds, "I think she'll be fine, Commander. But be sure she sees a doctor soon as possible. Just in case."

Matt snaps an unofficial salute. "Will do, doc. Thanks for helping."

Alone at the table, he reaches across to clasp her hands. Surprisingly cold. "Sure you're all right now?"

Another nod. "Actually, I feel kind of silly. All that fuss."

"Good a doctor was right there. I didn't know what to do. Couldn't even kneel beside you. Don't try it again, okay?"

"I didn't try this time."

"I know. Just kidding. Seriously though, what do you think caused it?"

She averts her gaze, as if embarrassed. Because the fainting spell's related to some woman's issue, like what she calls her monthly?

Finally, inhaling deeply, she says, "Oh Matt. In the movies, when a woman faints for no reason, everybody knows she's…uh, expecting." Her face reddens and her eyes squeeze closed.

Surprise makes him stutter: "Expecting? Uh…what do you mean?" Recalling his buddy at the hospital, he almost says "knocked up". The term's okay between sailors. But not here. "You mean....*pregnant?*"

Another nod, eyes still closed.

Spoken quietly, the word is only one of thousands they've exchanged. Now the others recede and fade, while this one ascends in his consciousness, a star lighting the landscape of his future. His heart begins to race. "I wouldn't know about that, dear. I only ever went to the cowboy movies."

She shrugs and twiddles the ring on her folded left hand.

"So...Is that what you're trying to say? That you're...uh, *pregnant?*"

Her nod is almost imperceptible, but she unfolds the napkin at her place and begins to torture it. "I don't really know. I only said that because your aunt asked if I was. The one who works for the doctor? She said I have The Look. And well, the symptoms. So maybe I do. I mean, maybe I am." Her eyes fill and her lips quiver.

His mind chews on this new development. On some level he's speechless. But how can he be surprised? After all, like half-witted kids, they've enjoyed each other more often than he can count. Since early May they've gone the whole nine yards whenever they've felt like it. Usually with a condom, but not always. The memory makes him grin and reach for her hand again.

"What's funny, Matt? Think I'm joking? "

"Of course not. It's just the last thing I expected you to tell me."

"It's really not funny. If I am, then the child will be a bastard. And I'm a fallen woman. A back-street hussy." She shakes her head. "Just what people expect of Italian girls. They're cheap. Even ones who don't look like wops."

Still smiling, he says, "Well, it's your own fault. If you'd married me right after we got engaged, it'd all be on the up-and-up now. But no. You had to know me better. So now you do."

She stares across the table with the conflicted gaze of a child left with a piece of forbidden candy. "What…what do you mean by that?"

"Let me tell you a story." He forces his face into serious mode. "When I was a horny adolescent, my father gave me a talk. About how girls trick you into marriage."

Before he can explain, her expression hardens. "Are you implying—?"

"No, no, not at all," he says in a soothing tone. "If anything, I tricked *you*. Because now you *have* to marry me."

"No, I don't, Matt. I can stay with Ma's relatives in New Haven and give it out for adoption."

Shock slaps him in the face. "What? You wouldn't! I mean, why would you do something like that, when there's no reason we can't be married?" Then a new possibility floods his mind, so dire he can't speak it: *Maybe it's not his.*

New guilt rises as the innocence in her eyes reaffirms a truth he'd realized only an hour after they'd met: *Gail's not Marcie.* She's not trying to trick him into anything. He's baffled by her reaction, but his surety there's no guile in her is as strong as his conviction Jesus is the Son of God.

So he says, "Tell me, sweetheart: how can you even think of giving it away?"

Before she can answer, the waiter arrives with her soup and juice. When he asks, "Anything for you, sir?" Matt orders coffee and a hamburger. Then tries to find words to transform the situation into one he can manage. Or at least make sense of.

Gail opens the crackers and breaks them into the steaming soup. "Okay, sweetie," he says unsteadily. "Tell me what you really want to do."

She sips from the heavy spoon with the keystone logo on the handle. "Well, if I could find a doctor who'd do it, I'd have one of those…illegal operations. So I could take the job in Portland. Oh Matt, it's the best job I ever heard of!"

As she explains, all he can hear is "if I could find a doctor who'd do it…" New shock sucks the breath from his lungs, the words from his mouth. The only ones left are about as irrelevant as you can get: "Can't pregnant ladies teach?"

"Only until you start showing." She sighs, turns her gaze to a sun-dazzled river beyond the window. "I wouldn't make it through September."

Guilt rushes in like a rogue wave. "Oh sweetie. I'm so sorry."

Her look is heavy with cynicism. "Sorry? Why, Matt? Isn't this what you want? Someone to live in your house and take care of you? A wife who makes supper every night and washes and irons your shirts? And gives cocktail parties for your Navy friends? Isn't that why you wanted that house in the first place?"

Although he's tempted to protest, her vehemence convinces him this is not an argument he can win. On one hand he's pleased that now marriage seems inevitable. But his complicity in her distress is inarguable. New guilt heats him…because it's true, he wants a happy ending. Wants everything she's just described, plus a child. All he can say is, "Sorry, dear," again, as if tacitly admitting her assumptions are correct. "Wish to hell I knew how to make things better."

She shrugs again, sips soup without saying more.

He's relieved when the waiter sidles up with his lunch, hovers briefly to make sure he has condiments, refills their water glasses, then moves on. Matt watches his retreat, then asks, "Besides not being able to take the new job, what's the worst of this for you? What people might say?"

"No. Worse than that." She takes a long swig of juice. "Too bad even to tell you."

"Worse than having a baby out of wedlock? And giving it away?"

Another shrug, another tormented look.

"Tell me, Gail. Whatever the hell it is, just tell me."

The misery in her eyes is distorted by fresh tears. After a long, deep breath, she murmurs, "Having a baby I don't love. What's worse than that?"

"A baby you don't....? You mean...you're worried it might be deformed?"

"No. Just that it might look like Frankie. He was the ugliest kid I ever saw. Like he didn't have a drop of Ma's Norwegian blood, nothing but Italian. I couldn't understand how she could love him. If I ever had a kid like that, I couldn't."

Studying her mournful expression, he swallows coffee to soften the painful lump in his throat while his thoughts race to the logic of Mendel's Law. But all he remembers is that brown eyes are a dominant characteristic, which doesn't support his own take, that since their child will be three-quarters Anglo-Saxon and only one-quarter Italian, it won't resemble her brother at all.

As if it matters, he asks, "You mean, he looked like your father?"

"A hundred percent. Ma didn't want another kid. But right from the start she loved him more than the rest of us. Gave him everything he wanted, spoiled him rotten. Yet with me...and I look more like her than any of the others—she never even noticed I didn't come home the night after the wreck."

Mentally blending these fragments of her history, he shakes his head, bites into the burger, then anoints it with the pickle slices and all the catsup and mustard in the tiny cups on the plate.

"You're shocked, aren't you?" she asks between bites. "I mean, the way I feel?"

His "No, of course not," is rote, while his heart aches for her anguish. The only clue to its source is a memory from the day they'd met—when she'd told him she was half-Italian. It hadn't seemed a warning until now. Finally, he says, "Yeah, guess I am shocked, sweetie. I had no idea how much this— this whole Italian thing—how much it matters to you. God. Only wish I knew how to make it better."

"Just tell me you don't hate me."

His eyes sting with sudden tears "Jesus, Gail. Don't you know me better than that?" But as he speaks words of reassurance, he realizes the fear that grips her is so virulent, so old, so dark it distorts her perception. And, though he hasn't recognized it before, it's been there all along. Even if this out-of-the-blue pregnancy hadn't brought it to a head, even if they'd married and waited to start a family, one day she'd have to face it. Time alone won't take the sting from an issue he can't begin to make sense of.   At least with his white Anglo-Saxon Protestant mind.

When she doesn't answer, he finishes the tasteless food, drains the cold coffee, and asks, "Need anything else?" She shakes her head. Of course not. What she needs is nothing she can order in a dining car, nothing he can give, or even name. He summons the waiter, pays, then lets Gail precede him back to car six. Only as they wobble through the coaches does he realize the train has left the second Philadelphia station and is racing toward the curve where nine months and twelve days before it had been dismembered.

As had he. *As had he.* He shudders and keeps walking on what's left of his legs.

By the time they reach their seats, the train's leaning into what the newspapers had called "the dreaded Frankford Junction curve," wheels squealing on rails. The sound recalls his last memory before he blacked out. But now there are no acrid hot grease fumes, only a gentle swerve before a long straightaway through an area of factories and smokestacks, a distant river, an arched bridge, acres of brick row houses. No pain slashes him, except that of today's new reality.

For privacy, he lets her take the window seat. She huddles with purse on her lap. He offers his pocket handkerchief, waits while she blows her nose. Then, unsure how to proceed, closes his eyes and prays for guidance. Not "Tell me how to fix this, Lord," but "Help me do the loving thing."

Slipping his arm around her, he turns on what he intends as a reassuring smile, though her gaze is fixed on the industrial landscape outside. "Look, sweetheart, I have no idea what to do . Except tell you I love you, no matter what." He pauses, but she only blinks and wipes her eyes. "But before we decide anything, we need to find out if you really are. I mean, *expecting*. In case it's a false alarm. What do you think?"

Her "I guess so," is laced with doubt..

"So tomorrow, let's go to your doctor. And If you're not, then, well, you can take the job in Portland. And live happily ever after."

Her next glance is a half-frown. "I can't tell this to my family doctor, Matt. But maybe Aunt June's doctor can see me. He's a women's specialist in Rochester. As for happily ever, it sounds as if you're not going to be part of it."

"I'll be whatever you want, Gail." As he says the words, he hears the resignation in his tone. "Even if you decide not to...you know...keep it. " He shakes his head. "Or live with me. It'll be up to you."

"Oh Matt. Surely you want more than that."

"Of course I do. Hell, I want to marry you and raise our child and...well, that's *my* happily ever after. But I'll settle for being married. Even if it's in name only, I'll be on record. So no one will ever think of you as an unwed mother."

Her eyes fill, tears glisten on her cheeks. "Oh, I don't know. I just don't know."

"Then let's take it one step at a time, okay? That make sense?"

She nods, sniffles, blows her nose again. "If anything does."

As the train races northward he stares blankly at the shabby outskirts of the city he'd been so happy to leave. When his hopes had been focused on New England, the resumption of his career, and this woman he'd fallen for before he'd ever gotten to know her. And to whom he'd committed himself in total ignorance of this torture in her soul. Now all he can do is hold her close and hope his love is enough to see them through this labyrinth.

By the time the train rattles across the Delaware on an old bridge with the sign "Trenton Makes—The World Takes,"

Gail's returned to her magazine and he's thumbed through his twice. By now he's weary beyond the usual late-day weariness, as if some battle has usurped the energy he needs for this long trip. And further discussions of an issue he can only feel his way through. Like being on a sub in a power failure, groping in total darkness toward a solution that will restore the order of that small part of the universe.

He sighs again. And reminds himself he's no stranger to challenge. The problem is, this one's not only his to deal with. Moreover, though it derives from a situation he's basically happy with, he can't ignore Gail's existential torment. He may not understand it, but he has to respect it.

For love of her. He slips his arm around her again, with a silent prayer for compassion, tolerance, and whatever else this commitment is going to require.

Even if it involves living without her.

CHAPTER THIRTY-SIX
Tuesday, 27 June

As she regards the others around the table in a private room of Pop's restaurant, Gail pats Matt's arm, whispers, "Not bad for a shotgun wedding, is it?"

His eyes widen and he drops the crust of bread he's about to bite into. "Don't call it that! There's no coercion involved."

"Hope everyone sees it that way." Even as she speaks, however, concern for her family's opinion recedes like a spent wave. Like so many other worries. All thanks to the tiny white pills Dr. Humbert had dispensed Friday, after he'd confirmed her pregnancy.

"To prevent morning sickness and help you relax," he'd promised. They've done this so effectively that she's been able to regard the drama generated by their hasty wedding as if it's a scene in a movie.

Across the table, her older sister glowers at no one in particular. Generally described as "dumpy," today Charlotte's in a snit. Not just because Ma hadn't made her a dress like Gail's and Rosie's, but because no one asked her to be a bridesmaid. Nor had they invited her roommate to the wedding, so she'd have company on the train from Boston. In protest, she's in the shapeless blue seersucker number she wears to her library job. She already resembles Pop's mother, even to the moustache, but this outfit gives her the sinister look of a prison matron.

In a burst of drug-generated sympathy, Gail directs a smile at her. Charlotte's response isn't exactly warm, but the glower fades briefly.

Everyone else is gussied up for the occasion, including Frankie in a pint-sized tuxedo. Seated between Pop and Ma, he's fidgeted all through the wedding and the luncheon, so they've turned him loose, Now he's running around the table with a toy tommy gun, cranking out rat-tat-tat-tats at everyone in sight.

Gail's about to ask Matt if he could stand a son like that, when Charlotte grabs the kid for a hug. The smile she beams on him lights her eyes, beautifies her, transforms her into a woman Gail hardly recognizes. Amazed, she laughs. Even Pop seems funny today. She'd expected him to rebel against a Protestant ceremony, but the worst he's done is to wear the Italian flag tie with his tuxedo. Maybe having a wounded hero for a son-in-law impresses him. Or maybe she no longer gives a damn what he thinks. At least while she's still feeling the effects of the wondrous pills.

On the other hand, Ma's bedraggled, hennaed hair is streaked by a wide gray part, and the bosom of her plain black dress is food-spotted. When she hostesses here, she sports an ornate rhinestone necklace. Today she's insisted Gail wear it in honor of the something-old-new- borrowed-and-blue tradition. Gail agreed only to keep her happy, because the fake jewelry cheapens her green brocade sheath with the gardenia corsage at the shoulder. Normally green's her best color, but lately her skin's so sallow nothing gives her a glow.

On her left, her younger sister is more gorgeous than usual in a similar dress of rose brocade, with a rose corsage. At eighteen, she's newly graduated from Portsmouth High with a scholarship to Middlebury and a summer job on the paper Aunt June works for. Beside her, Matt's best man seems unable to stop smiling at her. Judging from the stars in her eyes, Rosalie's equally smitten. At supper the night before, she'd told Gail "That Ben Finklestein's the handsomest man I ever met."

And that was even before she'd seen him in the crisp tropical whites he and Matt wear for the wedding festivities.

If you can even call them festivities. With only four days to plan the ceremony in the parlor of St. Stephen's rectory, Gail had left everything to Aunt June, Ma and Rosalie. She hadn't realized Reverend and Mrs. Moss would be invited to the lunch, but they fit in, telling and and retelling Anna's part in Gail and Matt's romance, and assuring everyone Episcopalians don't object to drinking wine. And apparently not to shotgun weddings either.

Seated nearby, Aunt June and Uncle Pietro sparkle, she in a pale violet suit, he in his tuxedo, dark hair and moustache trimmed so he's more handsome than she's ever seen him. "He got the looks," Pop likes to say about his younger brother; "but me, I'm the one with the brains."

Surrounded by familiar faces, Gail feels increasingly mellow. Until she realizes someone's missing. Her next younger sibling's a mechanic at an Army Air Corps bomber base somewhere in England. Pete's in less danger than the pilots, but his absence brings sudden tears to her eyes. Despite the pills, she cries at everything these days. Another symptom of her condition?

Now, faintly nauseated by the combined fragrance of her gardenias and Rosie's roses, she pushes her plate away and stifles yawn after yawn. The doctor had warned the pills might make her drowsy. A small price to pay for relief from the emotional tail-spin of the past week. She can still identify those worries, but they've receded into a hazy distance where they're only as real as war stories about places she'd never heard of. Like Tinian and Saipan and other foreign-sounding specks of land in seas Matt once navigated.

Does he still miss being part of a sub's crew? she wonders. The possibility shoots her with guilt pangs about turning down his ideas for a honeymoon. "Don't bother," she'd said. "I'd just as soon go home and sleep for a month."

"But sweetheart. This is a celebration. We're not eloping, we're doing everything right." His expression had turned sheepish. "I mean, as right as you can once the horse is out of the barn. So it should be festive. At least for your family."

She'd taken another pill and told him to do what he wanted. Now, after the tiramisu is cut, toasts made and hugs exchanged, he hustles her to his car in a shower of rice, then accelerates out of the lot as if the well-wishers are a band of head-hunters. "Thought they'd never let us go. At least they didn't decorate the car." He swerves onto Route One faster than usual. "Let's get home and change for the trip. Can't wait to get out of these glad rags."

"Trip?" The word knifes through the pink haze. "What trip?"

"Just to Wolfeboro. Down on the south end of Lake Winnepesaukee? They say it's only thirty or forty miles. About an hour's drive."

"I know where it is, Matt. But these pills make me so sleepy, I need a nap."

"Don't worry; we can have one. And still get there before six. Maybe you've heard of it...the White Water Inn? Will recommended it. Bridal suite wasn't available, so they gave us the presidential instead. Teddy Roosevelt stayed there after he left office."

Unmoved by his pitch, she shakes her head. "Oh, Matt. Haven't we traveled enough? Can't we just stay home a while?"

"And we will, sweetie. I promise—starting tomorrow, we won't go anywhere till you feel better. But tonight's special. We'll have champagne. And a room service supper. With the pretty nightie I sent you."

Another sigh. "I can wear it just as well at home."

"Please, sweetheart. Just this one night? To make up for Iowa and Washington? And that mess last year." He winks at her across the seat. "You know...during the Army-Navy game?"

Benign resignation augments the drug, especially after she recognizes the boyish grin, the eagerness in his eyes. And intentions so good they'd never pave the road to hell.

Before she can answer, he adds, "Today…well, the wedding was fine. It just wasn't special."

"Maybe because we had the honeymoon first."

"Oh, that doesn't count. That was just—well, getting to know each other. This is a…well, the real commitment. It's why I sent you that nightgown."

Listening, she realizes that what he's trying to do is transform today's ordinary black and white moments to stained-glass memories. To sanctify them. To erase "shot gun" from their thoughts. Sudden tears warm her eyes. She swallows a lump in her throat. "Well, okay. Since you've gone to so much trouble. But promise we'll come home tomorrow."

"Sure…right after we see the Old Man of the Mountain. It's only a few miles up Route Three. As long as we're that close, be a shame not to. Then we'll turn around and head for home port. I promise."

She laughs in spite of herself. "Really? Sure you don't want to go a few more miles so you can get a sticker that says 'This car climbed Mt. Washington?'"

He shoots her a wide-eyed glance. "You mean, you can *drive* to the summit? Thought you had to take the cog railway. Huh…"

"Matt," she says, "Don't even think about it. At least right now. Maybe later this summer. Still seven months before…you know…before the baby comes."

As she speaks the words, the normalcy in them contrasts with her attitude before the pills. This is what a woman's supposed to feel—aware of the time yet to be accomplished before her body completes the child it's growing. And impatient to have it *fait accompli*. She's not ready to assess her view of impending motherhood as entirely normal, but she's relieved she's made this much progress. That some chemicals have lifted the cloud of fear that gripped her before. And brought her to the edge of hell.

Matt's smile lights his face and shines in his eyes. Once she'd expected that by the time they married, she'd know him as well as she knows herself. Now however, none of it matters.

Except the truth that he loves her with all of his being. In spite of her peculiarities, her emotional problems, even her Italian family, he loves her steadfastly, maybe even unreasonably. Certainly beyond her ability to speak of it.

Fresh tears arise from the depths of the new sweetness within her. It probably won't last, but even fleeting joy's an improvement over her previous state of mind.

CHAPTER THIRTY-SEVEN
Wednesday, 15 August

Matt's still at work when Anna Donovan arrives for her first visit since she'd come home the past weekend. Since then Gail's only spoken to her on the phone, just enough to intuit that her friend's on the verge of some momentous change. From Anna's letters during her months on the Maine Island, Gail knows Dan Donovan has now been officially declared Killed in Action. And that early in her time there, she'd witnessed a Nazi U-boat hit an offshore mine.

From a distance and on paper, Anna's life has sounded fraught with danger and intrigue. But when Gail had asked, "Are you back in Portsmouth to stay?" she'd said only, "It's a long story."

And now that she's coming for supper, Gail's anxious to hear it.

But when she opens the front door, her friend's first words are, "Gosh, you look wonderful! Positively blooming! How far along are you now?"

"Fifteen weeks, more or less." She beckons Anna into the hall, the first stop on what she intends as a tour of the house.

But Anna doesn't move from the doorstep, studying Gail's face with serious eyes. "That mean you're happier about the baby now?"

Gail flinches; she'd hoped Anna wouldn't bring up what she'd said two months before, in a letter she'd mailed before thinking. As soon as she'd dropped it in the box, however, she'd realized pouring one's heart out to a friend was better done in person, especially when the friend might be sensitive to the issue she's fretting about.

She fortifies herself with a deep breath and nods. "Aunt June's doctor gave me some pills for nausea. They actually make me feel better about everything. Besides, Matt's agreed that if I don't have maternal feelings when the baby comes, he'll consent to having it adopted."

Anna's gasp is barely audible, but the shock on her face is raw. She says nothing for a moment, then asks, "Does that mean he feels the same way you do? I mean, is he afraid he won't love it either?"

"No, not all. I mean, he's tickled pink by the prospect of fatherhood. But he's leaving the decision up to me."

Anna shakes her head and steps into the hall. "Oh, Gail. Only a really fine man would honor your feelings like that. I hope you appreciate what he's doing."

"Oh, I do. I do." She smiles to lighten the mood. "Now, let me show you the rest of the homestead."

When they glance into the bedrooms, Anna regards the furnishings with a nod but no change of expression, as if nothing's a surprise. Well, of course, Gail tells herself: after you've seen a sub blow up, friends' modest houses are hardly the stuff of poetry. Or maybe she's still horrified by the notion Gail might not keep the baby.

As they dawdle toward the kitchen, Anna asks, "Have you felt...you know...*life* yet?"

"I guess that's what it is. Or gas."

This smile seems forced. "And no more morning sickness either, right?"

"No. And if it comes back, I still have those pills. Now, let's sit and talk till Matt gets home. I want to hear all the details you didn't put in your letters."

But as they pass through the kitchen, Anna stops to inspect a book on the breakfast table. "My goodness. The *Better*

Homes and Gardens Cook Book! My mother's kitchen Bible. Was it a wedding gift from her?"

Gail nods. "How'd you know?"

"She gives it to every bride my father marries. Even women who've been married before. Even grandmothers. So...."--she sniffs the air—"are you making something from it tonight?"

"The salmon loaf with hardboiled egg sauce. Does she ever make it?"

Anna giggles and leafs through the book. "Only every Friday night since the war started. Don't worry, though. She never sticks to recipes anymore. Besides, it's one of my favorites."

Feeling slightly shot down, Gail heads through the dining room, where the table's covered with her best cutwork cloth, and three place settings of the good silver and china, along with candles in crystal holders that match the salt and pepper shakers. Too late she realizes she's forgotten to pick some roadside wildflowers—blue chicory and white Queen Anne's lace—for the vase that came with the set.

In the living room, they perch on the sofa so Gail can inspect Anna's photos of Hope Island and the folks she's written about during her stay. She can't see much of the terrain except a rocky shoreline, a harbor filled with lobster boats, and on a hillside overlooking the village, the mansard-roofed hotel where Anna had boarded. The pictures of friends are taken at such a distance all she can see are sunlit faces squinting at the camera. The only shot that stands out is of the doctor she works for and mentions more than anyone else. Combined with the fact that Anna's prettier than she'd been in October—gray eyes sparkling, cheeks flushed, lips bright with some vivid lipstick—Gail suspects she's found a new love.

After glancing through the photos once more, she hands them back. "Now tell me everything. Especially about this doctor."

Anna's eyes widen. "Well, as I said, it's a long story. But basically, after I got the final word about Dan....well, I let myself get silly over him. Jim, I mean. Jim Millett." She sighs, gaze going distant. "He's divorced, older. And he had polio, so he's kind of, uh, crippled. But he's just the kindest person. So... well, one night I ...uh, I threw myself at him." She shrugs, expression briefly bleak. "But he rejected me. I think he's still in love with his wife. Anyway, it was a bad night. The girl who ran the hotel—Jean; I wrote you about her: she was pregnant by a sailor from the U-boat? Some people in the area regarded her as a traitor, so when she developed puerperal sepsis after she had the baby—"

"Puerperal sepsis?" Gail asks.

"In the old days, they called it Childbed Fever. It used to be spread by doctors who didn't wash their hands between patients. In Jean's case, Jim suspects some of the staff were negligent. Someone even called her baby 'a little Nazi bastard.' Anyway, sulfa might have saved her, but Jim couldn't get enough. And she died." She breaks off, "She was an odd woman, but we were friends. So this is hard to talk about. A glass of water might help. Or a Coca Cola, if you have one."

Gail nods and retreats to the kitchen for a bottle from the fridge. She removes the cap and brings it to her friend, later realizing she should have offered a glass and ice. Or maybe rum, as in the popular song. Evidently a real conversational lubricant.

Anna sips, then sits holding the bottle, as if she doesn't want it to make a ring on the coffee table. Gail proffers a coaster with a picture of Mt. Washington from a souvenir set. "So go on," she coaches.

Anna sets the bottle on the coaster. "Anyway, the night she died, Jim and I were both grieving, which is when I—well, I tried to get him into my bed. The next morning, though, I realized I'd compromised our working relationship. Then her uncle decided to close the hotel. So it felt like time to come home."

"So...is this just a visit? Or a permanent move?"

Anna shrugs. "Not sure. See, after nursing school I was going to join the Navy. The Nurse Corps. But I married Dan instead. Now, though, now he's gone…yesterday I went to the base and filled out an application. Then I came home and dug up all the documents they need. Except I can't find my nursing school transcript. So tomorrow I'm going to Boston and get one from Mass General, then spend the weekend with Margie Halvorsen—remember her from high school?"

"That perky little blonde who dated football players and got invited to all the parties? People said she was fast, right?" She waits, but Anna only nods, so she says, "My goodness, you've had an eventful year. And golly, now the Navy…!'"

Anna brightens. "Actually, I'm hoping to get duty on a hospital ship in the Pacific. Mother thinks I'm looking for Dan. As if he's still alive and floating around just waiting to be picked up." Her laugh is mirthless. "Anyway, that's enough about me. Now tell me about you and Matt. Hope he doesn't think I'm here to keep that promise I made in Philadelphia. You know—about pushing his wheelchair into the ocean if he still wants to die?"

Gail's surprised she's brought it up. But she's long since realized nurses—especially this one—are no-nonsense people who don't sugar-coat words. "He hasn't mentioned it. In fact, since they transferred him to Chelsea, he's been optimistic about life. Passed the exams to stay in. Even figured a way to make the prosthesis work better. And he comes home every night smelling of diesel. Can't figure out why someone in a desk job would smell like that. Unless he sneaks onto the boat they're working on. I don't ask. Last thing I want to be is a wife who keeps track of every move her husband makes."

Anna laughs and sips more Coke. "Hate to tell you, Gail, but if he's anything like Dan, of course he's going aboard."

Alarmed, Gail says, "What do you mean, *of course?*"

"I'm just imagining how Dan'd be if he were limited to a desk job. Sorry. Didn't mean to imply Matt's as reckless as Dan was. He couldn't be, with his handicap. Even if he wanted to, he couldn't get himself in and out of a sub."

Gail's pondering Anna's improvised explanation when Matt's car swings into the drive. Walking toward the house, he leans on the cane more than usual and without the eager expression she'd expected. But it's the tenth day in a row he's worked late; he'd even missed church Sunday. Like everyone else in the ship supe office, he's caught up in the push to complete the new boats on schedule.

Narrowing her focus to see him as Anna might, she observes he's more tanned than she'd realized. As if he's spending a lot of time at the fitting-out pier. Is it reasonable to suppose he's never tempted to go aboard?

When he comes in, he and Anna exchange abashed hugs before he excuses himself to wash up. "And change into a shirt that doesn't stink."

"Don't do it on my account, Matt. I love that smell. Reminds me of Dan."

He shrugs, then settles beside her on the sofa. Gail brings him a bottle of beer. He tips it to his mouth as he studies her snapshots.

After a few swigs, he zeroes in on her recollections of the U-boat that hit a mine off Hope Island, and of the crewmen the Navy buried in the cemetery behind the hotel. "Did they mention anything about the damage that caused her to sink?"

"It was supposed to be top secret," Anna says, "but I figured out the first mine hit the forward engine room; the boat was surfaced at the time, getting ready to drop off a shore party in rafts. They were on deck near the stern, so they got off before she hit the second mine. That one was farther aft, and she went down fast."

As he stares at Anna, Gail reads the intense interest in his eyes and voice. This is meat and drink to him, the essence of his being. And a part of him she isn't privy to. "Do you know if they managed to recover any secret equipment, like a crypto machine?" he asks next.

She nods. "Something, maybe. But by the time they'd removed the first bodies, the wreck was unstable, and they couldn't get the rest. Then a nor'easter blew in, so the salvage ship and the minesweeper left, as if there was nothing more they could do."

Matt glances at the pictures again; his half-frown tells Gail he's still curious. Aware of kitchen duties, Gail remains standing while he asks, "What about the shore party? Did they ever find them?"

"Two made it as far as the lighthouse across the Sound, and a few days later, they found a dead man washed up on another beach. The fourth...well, turns out he'd lived in Portland, even spent summers at the Hope Island hotel. Since he knew the area, he was in charge of the saboteurs. But he killed his partner, then made it to an adjoining island and hid out till the Navy'd left. By then he was in bad shape—it was November, and cold—so he strung up a white flag, and Jean and her uncle went over and brought him back to the hotel." She pauses, then says, "Would you believe he and Jean were sweethearts before the war?"

"No!" Matt says.

"Yep, they sure were. The romance only ended because his family went back to Germany so he could go to seminary. After they found him, though, she wanted to hide him at the hotel till after the war. Main problem was he was so sick I had to get the doctor—Jim—from the mainland. Later, when the sailor recovered, Jim had to turn him in, or be accused of harboring a fugitive."

"Oh my goodness," Gail says as her imagination absorbs details Anna's letters hadn't included. "Obviously the romance heated up again...since she became pregnant."

Anna sighs. "Unfortunately, the Navy didn't believe his story—that he planned to betray the other saboteurs. So once he was healthy again, they sent a PBY from Brunswick and took him away. Later she heard he was shot trying to escape from a prison camp in West Virginia."

Gail sighs, imagining the story as a movie. "What a tragedy, the way they both died. But the baby's all right, isn't he?"

"He's the only good thing to come out of it. Jean's uncle and his wife are raising him."

Absorbed in the narrative, Gail suddenly realizes the smells from the kitchen now suggest something's burning. Hopefully only the baked potatoes, not the salmon loaf. "Excuse me," she says on her way out, "but I need to put the finishing touches on supper."

As she removes the overbaked casserole and the petrified potatoes, she's aware that the conversation has resumed in the living room. She can't hear more than the occasional word, just murmurs. So low that she suspects they're discussing her attitude toward the baby. Speculating on her mental state. Or comparing notes on other interests they have in common.

Now, as she did when they visited Matt in the hospital last year, she realizes he has far more in common with Anna than with her. And though the gulf in her knowledge has narrowed since they've been married, there's still so much she doesn't know or understand about the cramped, perilous life of a submariner.

While she breaks iceberg lettuce for a salad from the cookbook, she tells herself that what she does know is Matt's reality, far beyond the vital statistics on his driver's license or service records. She's privy to his innermost feelings, his entrenched attitudes. Like his commitment to her and her feelings about their child, and his job, though not necessarily in that order. She's aware he values his home life, and is faithful about informing her of changes in routines and including her in conversations about his work. Finally, he's shared his views of God, Jesus and the Heavenly Kingdom, and President Roosevelt and the conduct of the war, as well as other matters they don't have to discuss, but do anyway.

But at the table, the excluded feeling returns even after a spate of compliments about the meal, when Anna says, "Say, Matt. What did you think of the prosthesis training program at Chelsea?"

"Can't say enough good about it," he rejoins between bites of salmon loaf and sips of Chianti. "They covered everything. Really got us ready to rejoin the two-legged world. Leg's still a pain in the ass, but it beats hopping."

As Anna laughs and he goes into details, Gail tenses, hoping he's not going to mention the sexual enigma. He doesn't, but she's still aware that his amputation's another connection between them. And wonders, if the train hadn't wrecked, if they'd arrived intact in Portsmouth and gone their separate ways, perhaps dating or just being friends, would he and Anna have been drawn together by their mutual interests? Or just by Anna's more outgoing personality, her exciting life as a submariner's wife and a priest's daughter? Most of all by her one-hundred percent American background, untainted by the possibility she could have a foreign-looking baby.

After the meal, after coffee and cannolis from Pop's restaurant, after the clock on the living room mantel dings eight, Matt yawns widely and gives Anna a loose hug. "Hate to be a party pooper, but I've got to be on the job by zero-seven tomorrow. So if you don't mind, I'll head for the sack. Come back and see us again before you go overseas."

And she says, "Sure thing, Matt. Better be leaving myself, so Mother doesn't start worrying that I'm running wild with another sailor."

When Matt's gone to the bedroom, Gail walks Anna to the shabby '36 Plymouth. "What'll your mother do when you're out there in the Pacific, with all *those* sailors to run wild with?"

"God knows." She laughs, one hand on the door handle. "This was Dan's; would you believe his cigarettes are still in the glove compartment? Every now and then I sniff them to remember how he smelled. Besides the diesel, of course."

"Matt probably helped with that, didn't he?"

Anna's nod is sober. "He's such a good man, Gail. Glad you two ended up together. Really enjoyed seeing you in happier circumstances than last year."

"Same here," Gail says, feeling awkward.

"Listen, I'll be back from Boston Tuesday, so maybe we can get together for lunch before I leave for OCS. Meanwhile, I envy you. A baby on the way, and all the excitement of marriage to a submariner without the risk he'll sail away and never be seen again."

"We went through that the day we met," Gail says. "At least the part about possibly never seeing each other again."

Anna's smile is wistful. "But the Lord had something else up His sleeve, didn't He?"

"Matt has a theory about that. He thinks our meeting was divinely ordained from the start. Except after the wreck, the Lord realized He should've had us take an earlier train."

Anna stares into the pink-streaked twilight sky. "On the other hand, maybe He wanted you to experience it together. The whole thing." She shrugs, grins. "Maybe one day we'll figure it out. In retrospect, of course."

Gail nods, laughs. "I might even make a sampler—one of those old fashioned things with 'Remember the Lord's sleeve' cross-stitched on it? To remind me when I start to forget. Or begin to doubt."

Anna pulls her over for an embrace. "Make one for me too, will you?" The smile fades as she slides in, slams the door, cranks down the window. "Because I need to remember every bit as much as you do. Maybe even more."

Gail waves as the car pulls away, gears grinding as Anna shifts into second before it rounds the curve and disappears among the pines up the street. Suddenly tearful for no reason, she heads back in, tiptoes past the bedroom and returns to the remains of the modest supper, still languishing on the table like forgotten dreams. As she clears them, the tears become an irresistible flood. Stacking dirty dishes in the pan, she turns on the water to muffle the sound of weeping. So if Matt's still awake, he won't hear. And wonder whether she's as happy as he is.

And if not, why? What more can he do to make her happy? And why should he even try? Doesn't she have everything a woman needs to be contented?

Sighing, she sniffles and plunges her hands into the suds for the comfort of dealing with a matter she can actually feel and touch. And do something about.

CHAPTER THIRTY-EIGHT
6:30 AM, Friday, 17 August

Matt's intent on leaving the house before Gail wakes. Getting into leg and uniform in the bathroom, he skips the usual shave, doesn't even make coffee in his attempts to sneak away unnoticed. Last night he'd warned her he might be late getting home today because he has to sit in on the meetings after the *Spearfish* sea trials. This morning he prefers not to discuss that half-truth further.

When he'd first mentioned this—a hell of a lot more casually than he was inclined to—her expression had turned disappointed. "Matt, no! Tonight we're having a surprise party for Ma's fiftieth birthday. I'll pick you up after work so we can get to the restaurant before she does."

He'd sighed, but pretended to greet the news with cheer. "Well, then, I'll just have to get the skinny later. What time are you thinking about?"

"Four-thirty."

"No problem. By then we should have most of the results."

Her expression had softened at this news. Still, this morning, uncomfortable about the deception, he's unnerved when she pads into the kitchen just as he's leaving to rendezvous with the Gladwells.

Her hair's sleep-tousled, eyes bleary, robe still untied. "Oh sweetheart. Weren't you going to kiss me goodbye? Or even say So Long?" Her tone is disappointed, but not aggrieved, not disturbed.

He turns back, lunch pail still in hand. "Sorry, dear. You looked so peaceful, I hated to wake you."

"Please, Matt. Don't ever go anywhere without telling me. Even if you think you're bothering me. I almost lost you once, remember?"

"Worry wart." He smiles. As she walks into his arms, his conscience starts sending out SONAR returns. Because he's trying to convince her he's just leaving for a routine day on the base. Well, not quite routine; Gail knows the new boat's performance will be on trial today. If she passes, the Navy will accept her. It's the culmination of the construction phase, the official start to *Spearfish*'s naval service. Everyone's caught up in the importance of these tests, even wives.

Another of Gail's beliefs is that he won't be observing the boat's performance first hand. That's the part that requires a sin. Not exactly a lie; he'll just withhold the whole truth. For her own good, of course—so as not to inject a strain of worry, considering her delicate condition.

This is not his first experiment with well-intentioned deceit: he hasn't yet confided the thrill of riding along on the engine tests back in May. He hadn't known about the pregnancy then; it just made sense not to alarm her without a valid reason. Particularly because, of all the underway tests a new sub undergoes, that had been one of the least risky.

Today's risk is higher, so concealing it is even more vital. Because this time he won't just be on the bridge for surface runs, but below, in the control room during the timed crash dives.

Maybe if she hadn't heard about the *Squalus* disaster during such testing, she could absorb this truth without flinching. But she has. Besides, she knows as well as he does that he's not supposed to be aboard any boat underway. Bad enough he's on and off this one at the pier. That might give her the notion he can't control himself anytime he's close to a sub. Like an alcoholic at a dime-a-drink Happy Hour.

God forbid she ever figures it out.

Smiling, he gives her a proper kiss, juicy enough to suggest he's interested in more than submarines. Or will be tonight, Then, backing away from the embrace, he steps out the door to meet his ride to the base, to the office, and eventually to the fitting-out pier. There a tug will be standing by with steam up to follow *Spearfish* out to the Isle of Shoals testing ground, then stand by during her dives. In the unlikely case a gremlin turns up.

"Stay out of trouble today, Matt," Gail calls. As if on some level, she's already figured it out. And is letting him go anyway.

He loves her for more reasons than he has fingers to count. But right now, mainly for this one.

CHAPTER THIRTY-NINE
3:30 PM the same day

F resh from the shower that afternoon, Gail lifts the new maternity dress from the hanger and regards it with a pleased smile. It's blue dotted Swiss, with a smocked top, empire waistline, white collar and a red silk rose at the neck. She's not actually showing yet, just plump in places that used to be flat; everything in her wardrobe is tight. Beyond comfort, though, she wants to affirm the pregnancy publicly, starting with her mother's birthday dinner. Not that anyone will be surprised; the truth had come out at the wedding reception.

She's combing her hair, admiring the page-boy the new length makes possible, when the jangle of the nightstand phone makes her jump. As she picks up, she expects it to be Matt, saying he's ready to go. Instead, it's Bonnie Gladwell's honeyed Southern voice. The engineering office secretary, at the yard. Except that now, even when she says only, "Mrs. Ogleby?" it sounds strained.

"Oh, hello, Bonnie. Thought you might be Matt, saying he can leave early. We have something planned."

The pause before she says, "Mmm, sorry," doesn't seem significant, just noticeable. "No, that's not it. There's been a...well, a problem with the boat. And everybody in the building's on tenterhooks. I mean, trying to figure it out."

Gail's senses immediately take on a new intensity. "A problem? Serious?"

"Don't know details. Except they lost contact. And no one's said anything since." Gladwell inhales so deeply Gail can hear it over the line. "Anyway, when you come to the base, come to the O Club instead of the office. Some of the wives will be there, and a chaplain. So we'll get word as soon as it comes in."

"A chaplain? Sounds ominous."

"No, not really. After all, they were conducting all sorts of tests. So probably something went wrong and now they're fixing it. That's why they do so much testing, you know—to catch problems while the boat's still close to home."

"If that's all it is, why didn't Matt call me himself?"

This pause is longer. "Well, he probably didn't want to tie up the line. Or maybe the office was too noisy. Anyway, I'll see you at the club, okay?"

As she agrees, anxiety begins to assert itself: in trembling fingers as she applies lipstick, a haunted look in her mirrored eyes as she studies her hair again. And the stepped-up pounding of her heart, like a drumbeat accentuating tension in a movie.

Silly, she tells herself. Nothing could possibly happen to the fine new boat that Matt regards with such paternal pride. Nor to the men aboard, yardbirds and Navy personnel she's come to regard as friends. Besides, even if *Spearfish* is in peril, he isn't even aboard; it's one of the cosmic compensations for his having been crippled in the train wreck.

So why, she wonders, do Bonnie Gladwell's words keep reverberating in her memory like the voice of doom?

She's been ready for half an hour, but doesn't leave the house till quarter to four. Driving to the base, she's slowed by reluctance to learn more, to darken the afternoon brightness with some ominous new knowledge. She's heard enough *Squalus* tales to imagine the day five years before when dependents clustered on the shoreline, waiting as word filtered in about the new boat sent to the bottom by a faulty valve.

But that was back in 1939. Matt's always assured her they'd learned so much from that tragedy nothing similar can ever happen again. Besides, they've made so many improvements to the McCann rescue chamber that virtually no submariners need ever be lost. At least if the boat's not below crush depth.

Crush depth. Another of the many terms she's picked up but can scarcely bear to ponder. Especially in light of the loss of another sub too, a small training boat from New London that went down without explanation last year. The next day divers spotted her, lifeless on the bottom, a victim of crush depth.

She's wondering how Matt can stand living with so much potential for disaster, when a Marine sentry stops her at the gate. Usually they note the blue sticker on the bumper, salute and wave her on. Surprised, she holds up her dependent's ID. "I'm picking up my husband," is all she says, but it's apparently enough.

His salute is brisk, his expression blank as he motions her on.

Driving the familiar streets to the club, she senses that this Friday afternoon doesn't feel like others, when personnel are hurrying to leave, to start liberty or get home. Today everything seems to be moving in slow motion. Or not at all, as it is at the fitting-out pier where the boat's been berthed. But even there, there's no clue to what's happening, only visual affirmation of the craft's absence.

Increasingly uneasy, she parks at the Officers' Club. Inside, the bar is strangely empty, considering it's Happy Hour. A steward directs her to a private dining room where other women—wives of crewmen and yard workers, she assumes— huddle at tables. Bonnie spots her and walks over with a smile so wide all her upper teeth show. Behind her, the Protestant chaplain Matt calls Padre Vogel is chatting with other dependents. The cheeriness he radiates looks fake, like a mask hiding intense concern.

Gail brushes off Bonnie's compliment about her dress. "Any news?"

The secretary shakes her permed head without dislodging the toothy smile. "Will's going to fill us in soon as he can get away from the office. Meanwhile, come sit with me and have a drink. They're on the house today."

On the house? That can only mean they're expecting bad news. "Maybe later. The drink, I mean. Right now I want to know what's going on."

Bonnie leads her to a table where two women she doesn't know are drinking, one something that looks like a Bloody Mary, the other a pale green concoction in a stemmed glass. After introductions, Gail realizes they're enlisted wives from Admiralty Village. They've left their kids with a neighbor whose husband is surface Navy but who, one says, "Seems friendlier than most surface wives." That Gail is recognizably pregnant provides a happier meeting ground. And prompts advice about the sort of care she can expect in the base hospital maternity clinic.

But when they find out her husband's a lieutenant commander, they clam up, as if in tacit protest of the rumor that officers' wives are treated much better than enlisted. That they don't expect "the straight skinny" about this accident is obvious in their skeptical expressions.

It's after five when Will comes into the room. A large man, he appears to have slept in his clothes. His gray hair is disheveled, his tie unknotted. When he steps to the lectern, the chatter goes silent. Gail finds herself holding her breath, fingers balled into her palms. Now she wishes she'd had a glass of sherry, or one of her white pills, to disconnect her from the anxiety tightening inside her chest like an invisible vise.

For a few minutes, the shipyard commander uses a variety of euphemisms to assure everyone the Navy has the situation in hand. Even his last sentence is delivered casually: "It's just taking longer to fix the problem than it would if they were at the pier."

"So, where are they?" a shrill voice asks from a front table. "On the bottom?"

Will blinks and swallows but his expression remains rigidly sanguine. "Can't really say. But even if they are, it's not a problem. They've deployed the phone buoy, so we're talking to them. We know what's going on."

Noting the unusual surety of his tone, Gail recognizes propaganda, a sales pitch.

"And what's that?" the same female voice demands. "Or is it a secret?"

A fleeting shadow darkens his expression. "No, ma'am. Just a minor problem they discovered on their last dive this morning. There's no flooding and they haven't lost power. Besides, between ship's company and the crew from the yard, they've got plenty of experts on board. Only a matter of time till they blow tanks and surface. But just to be safe, *Falcon*'s on her way from New London with the McCann chamber. Both yard tugs and one from the city are out there too. Even a PBY from Brunswick. The weather's calm and the ocean's as warm as it ever gets around here. So, don't worry; it's *not* another *Squalus* incident."

He swipes a glance at his wrist watch, broadens his smile. "Gotta get back to the office now. But I'll keep you posted. For now, have some supper, a couple of drinks and make yourself comfortable. Everything's on the house. And if anyone needs a word of prayer, both padres are right here."

He gathers up papers and strides to the exit without glancing in either direction, ignoring hands raised with more questions. Gail watches him leave, excuses herself and jumps up. Outside, he's in his car before she can intercept him. His departure reminds her of a bank robber leaving a crime scene with squealing tires.

She's equally quick to hop into her car and follow through the series of turns that take him to the shop. She pulls up next to his Buick as he bolts toward the entrance. He's so tall and skinny, his hunched-over stride seems cartoonish. Gail can't keep up, but he's still standing at the secretary's desk when she bursts in.

"Will," she calls before he can escape into his office. "Where's Matt?"

His eyes widen and his expression melds from the dark glower into a professional smile. "Oh hello, Gail. Didn't see you behind me. Sorry. What'd you ask?"

She moves closer, stifling desperation in her voice. "Where's Matt?"

He glances toward the open door to the shop. "Why, at his desk, I suppose. Probably on the horn with the boat. I wouldn't interrupt, if I were you."

She walks toward the doorway, and a scene she's come to know well since Matt's been stationed here—a clutter of men at desks and drawing boards, filing cabinets, white-scribbled blackboards, duplicating machines and other mechanical equipment she can't name. Illumination streams from sputtering fluorescents overhead, and high-set windows above rows of framed photos of submarines from as far back as the first war. Only once has she seen them rowed neatly. More often, they're at off-kilter angles, as if there's a breeze in here. Or the walls are vibrating. Between them, a pall of tobacco smoke drifts in oblique slants of sunlight. The smell is the usual—burnt coffee, stale cigarettes, ancient cigars, industrial lubricants, layers of accumulated grease and the rust of old machinery. And overall, the dusty antiquity of the venerable brick building.

Unable to see Matt's desk from the doorway, she enters the space and glances toward the rear corner. Everything appears as it has the other times she's been here. Except that he's not in his swivel chair.

She turns to Will, now staring after her with a deepening scowl. "He isn't at his desk. And from the look of it, he hasn't been for a while."

As she speaks, her eyes take in the evidence—the neatness, the clean coffee mug, the waiting phone, their wedding photo. She walks toward the desk. And on today's page on his desk calendar, the scribbled memo, "Pickup at 1630 for Mrs. B's 50th."

Until this moment, she hasn't let the possibility he might have gone on the test run worm itself into her consciousness. Too far-fetched to be reasonable anyway. His orders to this duty had been explicit—*no underway activity*. He knows that, knows his presence on any sub would be a hazard to the others. His ability to move quickly is compromised by the prosthesis, still unwieldy despite his improvements. Not only would he refuse any invitation to go along, even from the skipper, no one on the team would have tolerated, let alone suggested it.

As this contrary truth forces its way past her reluctance to accept anything other than a reasonable explanation, a sudden weakness suffuses her body. Her heart races even harder than before. Grabbing his chair, she sinks into it. "Oh God," she whispers. "He's out there, isn't he? He's on the damn boat."

Will walks over; one large hand clamps her shoulder in a clumsy attempt at reassurance. "Now, don't jump to conclusions. He's probably just gone over to another shop. One with a better phone connection."

She shakes her head.

"Or maybe he's on the second tug. Yeah, that's probably it. So he can be right there, right on the scene. "

"If that's so, why are you only telling me now?"

"It never occurred to me before. See, it's been so chaotic around here, I've lost track of who's doing what. Honestly, Gail."

This final protestation moves her to say, "Honestly? Then call somebody who knows and let me hear it from them."

Will's massive sigh confirms her suspicions. He rolls a chair over and lowers himself into it, eyes averted, shaggy head wagging. "Sorry. Okay. This morning—not that he asked my permission, but when he went along, he wanted to make sure you didn't find out. See, the first month he was here—before you two married, that is—the skipper invited him to be on the bridge when they sea-tested the diesels. And nothing happened. So we thought today'd be like that. A few dives, then back for chow."

She's amazed at the tidal wave of shock that wallops her. "He went along before? And never told me? But why? I mean, he knows he's not supposed to. Who lets him do this?"

Will shrugs as if it's a mystery, but says, "It's the skipper's call, so everybody looks the other way. Besides, all the men, including the yardbirds, they think Matt hung the moon. Not just for his experience, but his guts. I mean, living through a train wreck, losing a leg, being laid up so long. But fighting to stay in anyway, even when he could've retired and never had to work again."

She nods, accepting this logic…to a point. "But having him aboard, that could've put them all in jeopardy. Oh God, is that what happened?"

Will pats her hand. "No, no, they hit something on the bottom. No idea what, but now they can't blow tanks." His next inhalation's audible. "But don't worry. Nobody tripped over him. Besides, there's this other thing. He ever tell you his nickname's Lucky?"

It's a small relief to be reminded of a time more normal than this one. "That first day on the train. Said it made him nervous, like a jinx."

His smile is weary, verging on sad. "He never told me himself. But word gets around. So between his experience and the nickname, we've come to regard him almost as a…well, a good luck charm. Naturally, nobody objected when he went along today. Especially when he promised not to move from the control room. And keep the peg leg out of the way."

As this scenario takes shape in her mind, its logic seems irrefutable. Except for one piece she can't swallow. "But why? He knows how I'd feel if I found out. He takes special care of me now that I'm…you know, expecting. So, doing this…." Tears flood her eyes, her lips tremble. "That's what I can't understand. Why would he take such a risk?"

Will shakes his head with what looks like genuine puzzlement. "Because he's a submariner. I've worked with guys like him most of my life. I won't say they're all that way. But the good ones are. Officers and enlisted both, they've got diesel oil for blood. Oh, they'll settle down for a while with a wife and kids. But basically, on shore they're fish out of water. Can't understand it myself: even the newest boat's a stinking sardine can. Besides, they know they're a lot less likely to come back than the blackshoes, the men in the surface navy. Sure they make more money. But in my book, it's not enough. I mean, how much is your life worth?"

She stays silent a moment, as if pondering the interesting but irrelevant academic question. "I guess they're obsessed. Matt still is...." She sighs to lessen the intolerable pressure of this evolving knowledge. "Maybe I should've known when he was so determined to stay in the Navy. Even when it made sense for him to retire."

They engage in more verbal ping-pong, volleying between Will's truth and hers. As if the sum of the game will change the outcome, revise the news, tip the scale in favor of the happy ending she's begun to doubt. In that regard, she's back on the train after the wreck, knowing nothing about what's become of a man who means little to her except the dim possibility of future connection.

Now that connection is as secure as any human link can be—formalized, legalized, sealed with a pregnancy. Yet there's still this enormous unknown, this potential for dissolution. A rip in the fabric of her understanding of the universe. And she has no idea how to accommodate it. How to adjust to it. How to live with the possibility Matt may not come back. How to be the wife of an active-duty submariner, even one who, though forbidden from that status, has to risk it. Like a drunk feigning sobriety, a man who stashes bottles in secret places.

Now, she begins to understand what Anna had felt when her husband vanished "somewhere in the Pacific." This disappearance isn't a mystery, nor is the boat's location unknown. It's offshore just some five miles. All over the base, experienced, knowledgeable men are talking to them, and figuring out how to return them, safely and soon. But all she can feel is the enclosed space, the silence, the artificially-regulated air he's breathing. And her own ignorance of the encyclopedic expertise Matt brings to bear on the situation.

That's the worst of it: it feels so impossible, so futile in the light of all she's read about submarine disasters. True, *Squalus* ended happily. But only for half the men aboard.

She turns to Will with an ominous new question: "Are there casualties?"

His benign expression shifts to surprised. "Uh...none they've mentioned."

"None they've mentioned? Do you mean maybe there are some, but none that can still use medical attention?"

His eyes narrow and he shifts in the chair. "Don't know, Gail. Sorry." With what appears great effort, he rises, stretches, cracks his knuckles. "Look, I have to stay near the phone. So why don't you go back to the club with the other wives? I promise you'll know as soon as I hear anything. Okay?"

Faced with pursuing this discussion, she realizes she's pouring good energy into a situation she can't understand. And never be able to change. She sighs as if to admit defeat; her whole body goes limp. She whispers, "Okay."

Will nods, excuses himself and strides from the office, relief obvious in every move.

For a moment—two minutes? Five? Fifteen?—she sits in Matt's chair and tries to connect with his spirit. But the antenna in her head can't locate his wave-length; there's only static where she needs the hum of his presence. Wordless, soundless, just a vibration would be enough. Yet there's nothing.

Finally, feeling massively old and tired, she gets to her feet and retraces her steps without so much as a peek into Will's office, though she can hear his rumbling voice and the phone light's on. She waits a few minutes in case he has news. When he doesn't appear, she gets in her car and drives the few blocks to the club in a mental mist. As if trapped in a dream. Or the stupor of anesthesia.

Inside, the crowd's larger, noisier, the air heavy with cigarette smoke and beer fumes. Aunt June rushes over to pull her in for a tight hug. Behind her is Father Moss with another hug, full of concern. Gail lets them lead her inside, to an empty table. She refuses their offer of a drink, but listens to their explanations of why each is there. As if it matters.

Behind them, one of the chaplains is leading a lengthy, sententious prayer. He's followed by a doctor from the dependents' clinic who volunteers sedatives if anyone needs one. "In case the boat doesn't come back tonight and you can't sleep."

As she takes all this in, the scenario becomes even more drifty and distorted. First there's June's explanation—she's been sent by her paper to report on how the wives of the boat's crew are handling the emergency. Father Moss is there because the Protestant chaplain's asked for his spiritual help. Neither had been aware of Matt's involvement, so now their original purpose has been intensified by the personal connection. Fortunately, neither realizes he's aboard in defiance of rules, so their messages are simple and to the point. Basically: Keep praying, keep believing, keep hoping.

Time becomes distorted as the hours drag on, as no news arrives, as nothing happens. Around her, cheery voices keep repeating clichés like, "No news is good news!" until she wants to scream. At some point, June and the priest order the Friday night special for all three of them—fish and chips, with cole slaw and lemon meringue pie. The noise level rises as others who've had too many free drinks talk more loudly.

From time to time, some officer wearing the sub force dolphins takes the microphone and announces that work to bring the men to the surface is going well, just taking longer than it would normally. He doesn't say, "If they were at the pier" or even "on the surface," but everyone gets the picture. Almost as well as their husbands, they know the cramped spaces, the foul air, the darkness, the myriad of minor connections that need to be checked before they can locate the one that failed. Didn't work, or worked for a while, then blew up.

It's almost eight before Gail runs out of the energy to appear normal. For a while the food revived her. But two hours later, she can barely speak. When June volunteers to drive her home, she doesn't resist, doesn't worry about leaving her car overnight. Instead, she sinks wearily into June's coupe and stares straight ahead as they make the familiar drive to Kittery Point in the fading daylight.

The imminence of night darkens her thoughts further, as if it signals an interruption of the efforts to bring *Spearfish* to safety.

Leaving the car even before June sets the handbrake, Gail stumbles toward the house, key in hand. As she twists it in the lock, the phone rings inside. The door sticks, so she kicks it open, then rushes to the bedroom to grab the set on the nightstand with shaking hands.

Oh God, let it be Matt, roars in her mind as she gasps out, "Hello?" into the receiver.

CHAPTER FORTY
8:20 PM, The Same Day

A t first there's only the faint crackle of long distance, before an operator reports a call from Boston. Not person-to-person, so she has no idea who it is. Until a familiar voice says, "Gail? It's Anna. Is there any news?"

It takes her a moment to weave the threads of possibility into an explanation. Of course: Father Moss has let her know. "Hi, Anna. Thanks for calling. But no, there's no news."

"Any idea what happened?"

Suddenly faint, she eases onto the bed. "Evidently they hit something on the last dive this morning. And now they can't surface. Meanwhile, the rescue ship—the one you mentioned when you were here? It's on the way from New London, with that chamber they used with *Squalus*."

"Oh, I see," is all Anna says. Her reticence resonates with Gail's suspicion that this is an extreme measure. "Meanwhile, how are you doing, under the circumstances?"

She shrugs. "Don't know. Just got home. A doctor gave out sleeping pills, so I'll take one and get into bed. And wait. Not much else I can do."

"Except pray. That's what I'd be doing." She laughs coldly. "That's what I did for almost a year. Till I finally found out Dan's boat had been lost the whole time."

"So your prayers were for nothing."

"No prayer's for nothing." Anna's tone is preachy. "Maybe I didn't get what I wanted, but the Lord strengthened me. See, that's the thing. Prayer's always answered, even when it's not the way you want. The Lord listens, so you don't feel so alone."

Gail sighs. "Easy for you to say. You've probably been praying your whole life. After the train wreck, I let a *total stranger* say the rosary for Matt. A *Catholic* girl. And even after four years at St. Margaret's, I still can't follow the prayer book at your father's church."

"Oh, Gail. You don't need the prayer book. Just talk to God. Tell him what you want. And ask for help." In the background, another female voice murmurs what sounds like, "Are you almost finished?"

Anna doesn't explain, except to say, "Sorry. Margie's waiting. I'll call tomorrow, though, and see how things are. Meanwhile, I'll be praying too, as hard as I can."

By the time Gail hangs up, Aunt June's standing in the doorway, smiling her gentle smile. "Ready for one of those sleeping pills now?"

"I guess. That was Father Moss's daughter. She says I should be praying for Matt."

"Sometimes it's all you can do." Her aunt switches on the bedside lamp, a warm yellow glow in the purple dusk. Her expression turns wistful as she folds down the spread and turns the covers back into a welcoming triangle. Another of the motherly gestures that had warmed Gail during her six weeks with June and Pietro during last winter's scarlet fever quarantine.

"I'm not in the habit of praying."

"Almost no one is at your age. Little by little, though, you learn." She draws a deep breath and hands over a small envelope. "I'll get some water. I told the doctor you're pregnant, but he said they're so safe you can take two if you need to."

"I'll start with one."

After her aunt brings the water, Gail swallows the tablet, then stretches out on the bed without removing anything but her shoes. June lifts her pajamas from a hook on the door, lays them out on Matt's side. "You may want these later. Now, I know you may not *need* me to spend the night, but I'm going to stay anyway. In case you have to go to the base—say, to pick Matt up. Or if you can't sleep and want company." Her smile broadens. "And if you just want to be alone, I promise to stay out of your way."

Tempted by the offer, her only protest is, "But the little bed in the other room isn't made up."

"Don't worry, dear. I know where the linen closet is."

Her concern triggers a new thought. "By the way, does Ma know about this? What's happened to Matt, I mean."

June frowns. "I told her when I left. Thought she should know."

"Did she want to come with you?"

The ensuing pause confirms Gail's hunch that she doesn't really need to ask. "Well, no. But she sent her love. So did Rosalie and your father. The restaurant was short-handed tonight, so they all had to keep working."

All Gail hears is her mother's message, which she doubts. Most likely she'd said nothing, had never considered leaving her birthday party. Past disappointments echo, after a lifetime of being the middle kid of the three born to her parents in their first three years of marriage. From her perspective, a disgusting non-stop orgy.

June reaches over, rubs the hand clutching the sheet. "Sorry, dear. But…well, life's hard for your mom. Your father's a good man. But not easy to live with. Not like Pietro."

Gail nods; tears well. "It's okay, June. You're here. You always take such good care of me. And now…sure, I'd love it if you stayed."

The older woman hands her the Kleenex box. "Then I'll let Pietro know."

While she makes the call, Gail goes into the bathroom and brushes her teeth. Already feeling detached, she wobbles a bit on the return to the bedroom, then collapses on the bed as if she hasn't slept in a week. Still, she isn't sleepy, just grateful she has nothing to do but wait for the phone to ring. And pray, of course.

June finishes her conversation, replaces the receiver and tucks the sheet over Gail. "Pietro sends his love and good thoughts."

"That's nice," Gail says, hearing her voice at a distance.

June switches off the lamp, strokes the hair back from her face and moves away from the bed. "I'll close the door so I don't keep you awake, but I'll be right across the hall if you need anything. Okay?"

"Thanks. Meantime, if you want something to read, there's a new *Ladies' Home Journal* in the living room."

"Don't worry about me, dear. I'll find anything I need. Nightie-night now."

As she drifts toward sleep, Gail tries to imagine what serious praying entails: closed eyes, of course, folded hands, bowed head, bended knees. And the right words. Whatever they are.

All she can think of is, prayer's like a letter to the Lord, in spoken form, but with a proper salutation—*Dear God,* colon, new paragraph, then the message. Maybe first she should introduce herself and explain the situation before she asks for help. As one would in a business letter: here's what I want and here's what I'll do in return. Finally, thanks for your help. Sincerely, Gail Benedetti Ogleby.

After half an hour, true sleep still hovers out of reach. She's on the verge of swallowing the second pill, but decides to try praying before she fogs up her mind with more soporific. Self-conscious, she slides from the bed and kneels, observing the formalities she's just pictured.

"Dear God," she whispers; "You don't know me very well, and I wouldn't bother you if the situation weren't so dire. But I need help. Not for myself, but for my husband. He's such a good man and he loves me more than I deserve. I'm not a very good wife. Especially my attitude toward the baby. I know Matt doesn't want me to give it away. So if you bring him back safe, I'll never mention it again. I promise."

She pauses, wondering what else will convince the deity she's worthy of help; maybe an unselfish gesture. So she adds.

"And please, God, bring the rest of them back too, because they're his friends. And from now on, I promise to love him better than anyone ever did. And love the baby even if he's the spit and image of Frankie. I'll also work hard to be the best wife Matt could ever have, and the best mother any baby could want. I'll have him baptized right away, and take him to church and Sunday School every week. And raise him to be a good Christian."

She pauses to let new ideas blossom. When none do, she concludes with, "Thank you, Lord. Oh, and I promise to come to church every Sunday from now on, no matter how tired I am or how bad the weather is."

For a few moments longer, she remains kneeling in case some message follows her petition, maybe a flash of light, a thunderclap, or a chord like *The Grand Amen*. When nothing happens, she remembers to say "Amen." Then, knees smarting, she gets up, takes the second pill and returns to the bed, satisfied she's done all she can to guarantee her husband's rescue.

For a while, though her prayer may have enlisted some supernal help, it still feels like a gesture...desperate and empty as her hands. Pulling Matt's pillow closer, she burrows her nose into it, absorbing the smell of his hair. A connection, true, but ephemeral and of little comfort. Until the second pill begins to numb her anxiety, blur her sense of tragedy and relax her into sleep.

But this sleep is broken, interrupted by distorted pictures from the gallery of her life. No order, no consistency to them. At times just remembered feelings, like the incessant cold and hunger of her childhood. At other times, images, like the St. Christopher medal on the dashboard of Pop's Pierce-Arrow. Smells, like the burning feathers at Trenton station last year as she waited for the relief train to resume the journey to New York. Tastes, of the bourbon in Jerry Graham's kisses after their wedding; and for the next three days of his incessant hunger—for bourbon, and for her.

Finally, the disappointment she'd felt at age eight, when Rosalie was born, such a beautiful baby Gail knew instinctively she'd usurp whatever bits of love Ma still had left for her three older kids.

Again and again, fragments of recall shake her out of the soft cloak of sleep, awaking with a gasp as remembrance of Matt's peril falls like an avalanche. She senses she should pray more, but all she can manage are whispers of "Dear God, Dear God…." Again and again she drifts into sleep, only to find herself mired once more in the sludge of some metaphorical pond she's been tasked with dredging. And through it all, the silent telephone confirms his continuing absence. Even with impaired consciousness, she realizes each minute of *No News* extends the boat's time on the bottom, further depletes oxygen. And hope. She has no idea what the point of no return is, just that it must be growing closer with every silent passing minute.

Sometime after four, the phone bell shatters the fog and jolts her awake. She grabs the receiver with shaking hands. "Matt? Matt, is that you?"

On the other end, Will Gladwell clears his throat. "Uh…sorry, Gail. Just Will. But I have good news." A pause tightens the suspense before he says, "Matt's safe. He was in the first group we brought up. Just after midnight."

Not quite trusting the words, she says, "Did you say he's *safe?*"

"You bet."

"Oh thank God, thank God." The major prayer answered, she still needs more: "Can I talk to him?"

"Uh, not yet. They took him to the base hospital for observation. But he said to tell you he's fine. And you can come see him tomorrow."

"He can't be fine if they're keeping him."

"They just want to be sure he's all right after…well, what he went through. How are you, by the way?"

She has no idea, but shrugs. "Numb. I took two of those pills the doctor handed out last night. Didn't sleep much, though."

"Well, suppose I come by and drive you to the hospital later? Not before noon, though. They want him to rest. Shall we say thirteen-hundred? One PM?"

She starts to agree, but remembers June. "Thanks. But my aunt's here. She can bring me."

After she hangs up, she tiptoes across the hall to the spare room and taps on the door. "Aunt June," she says, eager to share the good news.

Her aunt answers immediately, is sitting up in the narrow bed when Gail enters. Her tone is anxious. "I heard the phone just now. Was it about Matt?"

She nods, perches on the edge of the bed. "He's safe. Thank God, he's safe. His boss said he's fine, but they're keeping him for observation. I don't know what that means."

June clasps her hands, pulls her in for an embrace. "Probably routine under the circumstances. But it's such good news, you must be anxious to see him."

"Have to wait till after noon. Now I'm so relieved, I'm going to try to sleep for a few more hours. If I'm not up by ten, wake me, all right?"

"Sure. Meanwhile, if you and Matt haven't decided on a name for the baby, you might consider Grace, if it's a girl. Because you two have certainly had your share of it, right from the day you met."

Surprise surfaces through the lingering fog of the pills. "Grace? The day we met was a disaster. And yesterday could have been even worse. How can you say that?"

"You're both still alive, aren't you? And still have everything you had before, don't you? That's not just good luck, dear. That's the Lord blessing you with grace."

She's not sure what June means, nor does she have the energy to ask. She kisses her aunt's cheek. "Whatever you call it, I'm as grateful as I can be. You can tell me more when you drive me in later."

Returning to her own bed, she nestles Matt's pillow as the first pink stripes tinge the eastern sky with the promise of dawn. And a new day. This blessed new day. She sighs, whispers, "Oh God, thank you, thank you." Then, pulling the sheet higher, she closes her eyes and lets herself unwind, senses expanding to encompass the truth that Matt's safe. Safe, out of harm's way.

So she's safe as well—to acknowledge her need, her love for him. And to love the small being fluttering in her belly. And finally, to shed tears of relief, unclasping her fingers and whispering, "*Thank you, thank you, Jesus,*" over and over again as she contemplates the prospect of a new start with Matt.

And a new chance to get this marriage right. Grace indeed.

CHAPTER FORTY-ONE
2:45 PM, Saturday, 18 August

For the past half hour since Matt's examination, the Chief of Orthopedics at the base hospital has been explaining why they're keeping him for another night. Dr. Perry Simon is a seasoned full commander, graying and thick-jowled, with a heavy New York accent. And a message Matt no longer needs to hear. Not only does it echo the one he's heard since he began fighting retirement, yesterday's events have seared it into his brain as effectively as a branding iron marks a bull: since his damaged body will never perform as it did when he was whole, he has to swear off ever going to sea again. Except maybe as a passenger on *Queen Mary.*

"As you found out yesterday," the doctor continues; "at sea—especially on a submerged sub—that's where shit happens. And your body's already had all the shit it can handle."

Confined to the high, narrow bed with neither prosthesis, crutch or cane close enough to grab, Matt's too numb mentally, and in too much pain to defend himself. He can only nod.

The doctor draws a breath. "Look, I admire your guts. But you lost more than your leg in that train wreck: you had multiple fractures of both right-side appendages, broken ribs, a ruptured spleen, and a concussion. Less than a year later, these damaged areas are still trying to heal. Which doesn't happen in the conditions you experienced yesterday."

"Oh, it wasn't that bad," Matt says. "We didn't lose power or go dead in the water. The base knew where we were. The chamber was on the way. And sea state was favorable."

The doctor dismisses this upbeat summary with a toss of his hand, then lights a cigarette from a mashed pack of Luckies. The smoke drifts toward the open window, briefly veiling prosaic waterfront Kittery. "Anyway, they tell me you didn't want to be in the first load out. Until the CO insisted. I give him credit for that. But he should never have let you go to begin with. Even if he knew the shipmates who helped you down to the control room that morning would boost you into the escape hatch later."

Matt shrugs, wishes he smoked too so he'd appear unconcerned. The way John Wayne would play this part. As it is, he can barely speak without quavering.

Puffing rapidly, the doctor scowls. "Now what I'm wondering is, will you do it again?"

Matt shakes his head decisively. "Not only no, but hell no. I don't need to learn that lesson twice."

Before he answers, Simon smokes the cigarette down to a nub, then stubs it into the coffee mug on the lunch tray. "Easy to say now. While doomsday's fresh in your mind. Besides, you got away with it before, didn't you?"

Feeling reprimanded, Matt says, "That was different. I never left the bridge. And we were surfaced the whole time."

The older man's face reflects disbelief. "Look, Ogleby, I'm not going to argue, or forbid you to try it again. Hell, you're not the only submariner who thinks he's immortal. All I can do is warn you what to expect if you keep putting yourself in harm's way like that."

Bracing himself for more preaching, Matt's relieved when someone knocks on the door. After he calls, "Yeah," Gail steps hesitantly in. Her face is pale and drawn, eyes deeply shadowed. A flood of remorse chokes him, prevents him from smiling or tossing off some casual greeting. All he can do is hold out his arms.

To his surprise, she ignores them. Her mouth is grim and she makes no move toward the bed, but stares at him with a look he's never seen on her before. It strikes him as rage too profound to verbalize. With a great effort of will, he pretends not to notice.

"Sweetie, this is Doctor Simon," he says, adding, "Doc, my wife, Gail."

She gives a stiff nod but doesn't extend her hand.

The doctor gets to his feet. "Pleased to meet you, Mrs. Ogleby." Closing the metal cover on Matt's chart, he adds, "I was just leaving. But first I wanted to tell your husband what could happen if he keeps going to sea."

"No need of that, doctor. If he ever tries it again, I'll kill him myself." Folding her arms across her chest, she steps closer. "Hear that, dear? Next time you do anything that stupid, I'll kill you dead. I swear I will."

Stunned, he can only gape. And hope she's joking. Of course she is. Gail's not the sort to hurl idle threats, even in jest.

The doctor's smile is awkward. "I was going to say he runs the risk of becoming permanently disabled. An invalid in a wheelchair. With mandatory retirement after those fractures become arthritic. But your argument's more compelling." Opening the door, he turns his gaze to Matt. "Okay, Commander. I'll look in on you later, after I've seen your x-rays. Meanwhile, strict bed rest, okay?"

Matt snaps a quasi-salute. "Aye-aye, sir."

As if pursued by hounds, the doctor exits so swiftly his coat catches in the closing door. Still poker-faced, he yanks it free and bustles away.

Alone with his irate wife—that normally calm and sunny woman now confronting him with fury radiating from every feature—Matt says feebly, "Sweetheart, I can't tell you how sorry I am."

She steps closer. "Sure you are, now you've been found out. I guess when you got away with it before, you thought you would this time too."

"That was different. There was no risk. Besides, we weren't married yet."

"Not the point. You still weren't supposed to do it."

"But the skipper didn't object. It's not as if I was going against regs."

Sighing, she marches over to the wheelchair he uses for trips to the head. She plops into it without touching him, without brushing a kiss on his cheek or even shaking his hand. "But you know what? When I found out you were on the boat yesterday, I wasn't surprised. Because that's what you do. I mean, always more than you have to. Even that first day on the train, you couldn't wait for me: you had to go ahead to the dining car. And ever since, you've moved heaven and earth to stay in the Navy." Her smile is tight, humorless. "The irony is, I used to admire you for being so determined. Now, though…." She shakes her head as if at a loss for words.

Listening, Matt feels as helpless as he had on the boat the day before, after it had become obvious they were doomed to stay on the bottom, while the batteries ran out and the CO_2 scrubbers stopped working, along with lights and other systems that permitted their survival in a hostile environment…*unless* fate was smiling on them. Unless every step of the rescue process worked perfectly. Meaning that the tug on the scene promptly realized their failure to surface meant they were in trouble. Then immediately radioed the base to send search vessels, and notify New London to dispatch *Falcon* with divers and the McCann Chamber.

But before any of this could happen, they had to spot the smoke flares that marked their position, or the phone buoy that let them communicate with the world. Because if they couldn't be located, none of the other efforts mattered a pinch of shit.

Now, discomfited by Gail's frowning scrutiny, he braces for more wrath. It's understandable, a fine way to mask the fear that must have racked her since she'd learned the boat was down. He decides on a pre-emptive strike: "So now I guess you want to know why I did it."

Her eyes flash. "Not really, Matt. See, I already know why. For the thrill. Being underway again. Being part of the team. Maybe even being a hero. Saving the day. And proving you're still lucky."

The insight is so stunningly accurate, once again he's left with no response except an involuntary nod.

"The worst of it is, for the life of me, I don't understand why you're still that way. I mean, what is it you still want? After all, you're back in the Navy. Working with subs. With a nice home, and a car, and a baby on the way. What more do you need?" She pauses, as if to let him explain. "Unless you have a hero complex. So; is that what happened? Did you save the day?"

Sobered, he shakes his head. "No, not at all. *Not at all.* See, I couldn't move from the control room. On the other hand, I didn't cause the problem. Not like somebody tripped over the leg and wiped out a relay, if that's what you're worried about."

"I'm not. From what Will said, no one caused it. Why? What *did* happen?"

Abruptly emotional at the prospect of recounting yesterday's torture, he slugs down water from the glass on the night stand and coughs to ease his throat. But his voice is still a whisper. "We hit something." Speaking the words transports him to the heart-stopping moments in which that unlikely but altogether believable truth had seized everyone aboard. "It was at the end of the final dive, when we trimmed out for silent running near the bottom. Just a little jolt, then a scraping sound along the starboard side. Not loud enough to worry about. And we left it astern."

His next breath is so deep the splenectomy scar twinges. "But when we blew tanks to surface, the port side started to rise, but the starboard didn't. Which would've turned us over if we let it go on. Then, when we heard air rushing out instead of water in the starboard tanks, we realized we had a breach in the outer hull. As if we'd hit something on the bottom."

She frowns, as if imagining the situation. "Hit something? Like what? A rock?"

He shrugs. "No, that area's pretty well charted. This was something uncharted. If we hadn't been so deep, we could've sent out a diver. But we were on the bottom, a hundred twenty-seven feet. Besides, even if we knew what we hit, we couldn't patch the damage."

Her expression softens. "So what did you do?"

"Well, first we sent up the phone buoy and smoke rockets so the tug could pinpoint our location.   Then we went to emergency status to conserve power.   Which meant staying quiet—I mean, no unnecessary activity that'd raise the carbon dioxide level." His grin's feeble. "No calisthenics."

She dismisses the joke with a flick of her hand.   "But you've told me so much about the McCann chamber, surely you knew it was only a matter of time till they got you out."

"Well, sure. We all knew it worked. But it was 200 miles away. And if the weather deteriorated, we'd be in deep shit. Thank God it stayed good. And everything worked the way it was supposed to." He sighs, sips more water.   "But see, we didn't count on it. Because everybody knows how many things can go wrong in a rescue operation. Any operation for that matter. It doesn't take much to sink a ship. In that regard we were like *Titanic*—doomed by a little gash in the hull."

Gail reaches for his hand, shakes her head as if connecting with the anxiety as he and his shipmates waited for the efforts of men on the surface to save them from that minor but strategic wound. "So…did they get everyone off?"

"Don't know what happened after I came up. Haven't had any news since they brought me here this morning."

The next rap on the door is brisk, authoritative. Even as Matt says, "Enter," Chuck Kellogg comes in, garrison cap under one arm. His khakis are wrinkled and stained, and from the smell of them, soaked with fuel.

Advancing to the bed, he grins and extends his right hand. "Commander Ogleby. How're you doing today?"

Matt forces what he intends as a reassuring grin. "A hell of a lot better than yesterday, thanks. Don't know why they're keeping me."

"Probably just to be on the safe side." The sub's CO nods toward Gail; they'd met before at a cocktail party earlier in the month, when the men were splendid in dress whites, their women dolled up and perfumed. "Sorry to drop in before I had a chance to shower," he adds, "but I thought you'd want to know everybody's safe now. "

"Thank God," Matt breathes. "What about Chief McGill, though? How's he?"

At forty-two, the oldest man aboard had had chest pains while they'd waited for rescue, so had been with Matt in the first recovery run of the chamber. Another was a yard bird whose wife had been about to give birth when he'd left the previous morning. The other six had gone along under protest after drawing straws to make sure there was no favoritism in the order of escape.

Kellogg nods. "Just looked in on him. They're not sure it was a heart attack, but they're keeping him anyway."

"What about the boat? Any chance of bringing her back?"

"Don't know yet. Divers are looking for whatever we hit. Yard birds seem to think it was a wreck that never got on the charts. Easy to imagine with all the U-boat activity off the coast the last two years."

Clearing his throat, Kellogg backs away, glances at his watch, moves closer to the door. "Anyway, thought you'd want to know everybody's safe." He coughs nervously. "Also, I want to apologize for looking the other way when you came aboard yesterday. Shouldn't have let you this time."

He fidgets with his hat. "Sorry, Mrs. Ogleby. I know you went through hell too. But I have to tell you, Matt's presence boosted everyone's morale. He's been in combat. And has so many sea stories. He shouldn't have been there, but the crew thinks he made a difference. They're more convinced than ever, he really is lucky." His voice falters on the last words. "Sure glad you're okay, though." With a quick grin, he strides from the room.

Gail watches the door close, then addresses Matt: "Well, there you go, dear. You were a hero after all."

"That's ridiculous. I was scared shitless the whole time. I only kept talking so I wouldn't try to calculate how long the batteries'd last drawing on them the way we were." He shudders, adds, "And what'd happen to you if we didn't make it."

She blinks rapidly. "Nice of you to think of me...eventually. But you know something, Matt? You aren't really lucky after all. Or you wouldn't have been in the train wreck to begin with. Or on the boat yesterday. Sure, things could've been worse in both cases. And you were lucky they weren't. But your good luck's only relative to the chance things might've been worse. So what you really are is jinxed. Just not fatally."

Listening as she unspools her string of logic, he's unable to refute it. All he can say is, "You're right, dear. Never thought of it that way. Who knows? I sure as hell don't." He squeezes his eyes closed so he doesn't have to observe her reaction to his next words: "See, the only thing I want now's for you to forgive me. And trust me never to do anything like that again. Not ever."

As Gail absorbs his admission, he senses a shift in her emotions. The upturn is gentle, but as palpable as the first rise of the McCann chamber on the long ride up the night before. Has she forgiven him? Or just run out of steam for more accusations? He's aching to know.

Until she adds, "Before we talk about that, I want to tell you what the worst of it was for me."

He doesn't need another argument to realize he's lost this debate. "What was that, dear?"

Her eyes glaze with tears. *"You didn't need to be there.* On the boat. It wasn't your job. Nobody ordered you to go along. It was just another of those irrational impulses to do more than you had to. Right?"

He nods. "Funny. I thought of that too. The other guys— well, it was part of their jobs. If they'd lost their lives, it'd been in the line of duty. But not me. I'd have died for no good reason." He shrugs. "So I can see why that was bad for you."

He's tempted to add, *It would've reminded you of your first husband's death. He got drunk and wrecked a Jeep before his unit left Samoa for Guadalcanal, didn't he?*

But by the time Jerry Graham had died, exposure to his dark side had softened her grief. Whereas in this marriage, with the future aglow with promise, his death would have been an unspeakable irony. Once again, she'd have taken no pride in the gold star in the window.

"All I can say is," he adds, "I hope to God you can forgive me."

As he waits for her verdict, her face softens. It takes a while before her hands unclench. She kicks off her loafers and gets to her feet. Then, inhaling deeply, smiles down at him. Tentatively, just widely enough to deepen the dimples. The effect is that of a rainbow at the end of a storm.

"Now then," she says quietly, "Why don't I get in there with you? Like we did last year in Philadelphia."

Assuming this is a positive response, he scooches over. Though it's late afternoon and his window faces east, sunlight seems to fill the room. While down the hall, someone's radio is playing *All the Things You Are.* Even more remarkable, the various aches in his body—right arm and leg, left hip, his ribs—fade so suddenly it's as if he's just had a morphine shot.

Tossing back the sheet, he pats the space beside him in the narrow bed. "Come on, sweetie. Just don't expect any action. I'm still recovering from my latest brush with death. Besides, whatever we do now is legal. And that takes all the fun out of it."

"Oh Matt. Don't pull that daredevil stuff with me." With an enigmatic smile, she smooths her skirt, stretches out next to him and carefully replaces the sheet over their bodies.

At first, all her can feel is her presence beside him. Until he's inundated by relief so widespread, so profound, he can barely breathe. Tears scorch his eyes as he wraps his arms around her. As time expands to encompass past, present and future in one shining interval filled with the promise that all things are indeed still possible. With unspeakable joy. And most of all, with hope. Not for anything specific, like her forgiveness or trust. More for resumption of the life he might have lost when he'd chosen to go along on sea trials.

Still, he has to ask, "Does this mean all is forgiven?"

She snuggles closer, lips on his cheek. "Conditionally. But you're not out of the woods yet. Because I'm still going to kill you if you ever do anything like that again. Remember that, Matt."

"Oh, I will. I will, sweetie! I'll never forget." He chuckles without intending to. "Have to wonder though—how're you going to do it?"

"Don't worry; Pop probably knows somebody in the Mafia who can...uh...take care of it. A hit man. Somebody who can do it without getting caught. Probably a Chicago gangster."

"Well, okay, I'll be careful. See, I don't want you to go to prison. Which you would no matter who does the job. Because the doctor heard you threaten me. Remember?"

She gasps, as if this hadn't occurred to her. Almost instantly, however, she says, "But I wouldn't. See, no jury'd ever convict me. Because you'd have driven me crazy. So I'd be not guilty by reason of insanity. I might end up in the state asylum for a while. But as looney bins go, they say Concord's one of the best."

He stifles a smile at the absurd claim. "But who'd raise our baby if you were locked up?"

"Well, probably June and Pietro. They never had kids, so they'd love it. By the way, this morning she suggested a name." Her gaze goes distant, shifts to the window. "Grace. For all the troubles the Lord's helped us get through since we met. Of course, it'd have to be a girl. Wouldn't want to name a boy Grace."

"Certainly no son of mine," he says with exaggerated bravura.

"Then we'd better think of a boy's name too. See, even if I have to have you...uh, *rubbed out*, I want you to name our son first."

For a split-second, the urge to quip almost overrides sentiment. But even as he tries to come up with a lighthearted riposte, he's aware the mood is already rising from the dregs of yesterday. And the murk of this absurd discussion.

So all he says is, "Let me think about it, okay? I mean the right name." But as he speaks he realizes her expression has morphed from aggrieved solemnity to amused toleration. As if she's finally figured him out, glimpsed the man beyond his strengths and weaknesses, assessed his humanness. And discovered everything she'd ever wanted to know about him.

Everything he can no longer hide from. Or if not all of it, enough that she can allow herself to love him fully. Finally. Maybe even enough to reconsider the death threat. Time will tell about that, though.

Sighing with relief, he pulls her close enough to sniff the familiar scent of Camay, The Soap of Beautiful Women, on her neck. With the curves of her body pressed to his, he considers telling her she won't have to kill him: he has everything a man could ever want. Besides being lucky, he has access to all the grace the universe has to give. And he's not going to do anything to jeopardize it, not ever again.

But as he kisses her, it comes to him that there's really no need to put these thoughts into words. If she doesn't already know the complete content of his heart, she's got most of it.

In his book, this is close. Certainly close enough for government work.

EPILOGUE
Labor Day, Monday, 2 September, 1963

Having learned his lesson, Matt keeps his promise and doesn't become the target of a hired assassin. But the baby, born in January, 1945, is a boy, so bald he resembles Matt's Uncle Jim, for whom they name him. Eleven months later, a baby girl comes along; with her dark eyes and dark curls, she reminds Gail of her sister Rosalie, but not enough to name her anything but Grace.

So close in age they're almost twins, these children grow up as normal as any kids ever do. As for Matt, even without going to sea again, he's involved in the reconstruction of *Spearfish* after she's retrieved from the sea floor, put back together, renamed and sent off to the Pacific, from which she returns safely after VJ Day with Chuck Kellogg still skipper.

Now, all these years later, Matt and Gail have planned a family excursion to Washington. The kids, however, are reluctant to leave their Kittery Point friends just to spend the last weekend of summer with their *parents*, for God's sake. Even to see the grandeur of our nation's capital.

They're not above being bribed, however, by round trips on the Eastern Airlines shuttle to and from Boston, their own rooms in a shiny new hotel, and anything they want from Room Service. They draw the line though, at returning with Matt and Gail, even to honor the twentieth anniversary of their meeting. So, claiming they have important things to do before school starts tomorrow, they fly out of Washington National

on the morning's first flight. Which gives Matt and Gail eight
hours alone before the New York train leaves. It's just the
Congressional now, apparently renamed as part of the
Pennsylvania's efforts to entice riders back to the rails.

So, in the interests of memory lane, they wander the city
in a cab. There are a few new additions to the tourist
attractions, like the Lincoln Memorial and the Iwo Jima
Memorial. Unfortunately, with the beautiful family who
occupies the White House away for the weekend, there's no
possibility of glimpsing them behind the fence. Even in their
absence, however, America still basks in the Happily-Ever-
After that's followed the war.

While on the far side of the world, the skinny little country
once known as French Indo-China is resisting a communist
takeover with the help of American advisors. As for Korea,
hardly anyone mentions that war now, except folks who lost
sons there. In Matt's case, it was the brother who'd survived
Anzio, and made the Army a career.

Meanwhile, all across America, sleek superhighways are
filled with bulbous new cars responding to the invitation to
"See the USA in your Chevrolet." Overhead, skies are criss-
crossed by passenger planes so swift and safe hardly anyone
goes anywhere by train anymore. Except in suburbs where they
connect city workers to sprawling new towns with cookie-
cutter houses full of labor-saving appliances, the happy
housewives who use them, and a steady stream of new babies.
Times are good and getting better. At least for rock-solid white
Americans.

Including Matt and Gail. Having outgrown the rental on
Admiral Dewey Lane, ten years ago they bought a four-
bedroom, two-and-a-half bath salt box in a spiffy new section
of Kittery Point. His parents too, are part of the prosperity
picture: two years ago they turned over the farm to their
youngest son and invested in an oceanfront condo in Fort
Lauderdale. Gail has problems picturing them enduring such
sun-drenched and luxurious indolence for very long.

Once, after he and Pietro had sold the restaurant in 1957, Gail's father had had the same Florida aspirations. But within a year he'd died of lung cancer. So Ma sold the Portsmouth house and moved in with Pete and his family in Hartford, where he builds jet engines for Pratt and Whitney. Pietro and June invested their share of the restaurant proceeds in a small farm; after failing to produce anything saleable in the thin and rocky soil of southern Maine, now they raise exotic Italian vegetables in hot houses.

The rest of the family is also living the American Dream—Charlotte and her significant other, Elaine, in San Francisco, where they operate a used book store. And Rosalie's married to Ben Finklestein in a Main Line Philadelphia mansion not far from his family's scrapyard. If Pop had known how much money there was in scrap metal, he'd never have noticed his new in-laws were Jewish. Their four children are so beautiful that Gail's abandoned all interest in genetic resemblances. Actually, she stopped worrying about it when she'd realized she adored her own kids so much she didn't give a damn who they looked like.

The only one whose life is less than idyllic is Frankie. Now a gangly twenty-six, he's trying to make it as a dancer in Broadway musicals. From a distance, his life sounds colorful and exotic. Up close, however, it's hand-to-mouth. Unaware he survives by appearing as a female impersonator in sleazy nightclubs, Ma sends money to bail him out of recurring crises. Gail had always thought he'd come to a bad end, but not *this* bad. She's shocked to realize, however, that these days she merely feels sad for him, with no overtones of I-told-you-so.

This holiday afternoon when she and Matt arrive for their train, Union Station's busy but not bustling, more civilians than military waiting. Matt's one of the former, having retired from the Navy eight years before. At fifty, increasing pain and decreasing energy have prepared him for retirement. Gail suspects that mentally, though, he's kicking and screaming Of course, shipyard management's promised him plenty of work as a civilian contractor, on special projects related to the

284 *Joan La Blanc*

nuclear Navy, like the disappearance of *Thresher* the year before. He's also helped evaluate the status of Russian diesel boats during the Cuban Missile Crisis. And worked on tracking the Soviet missile subs playing hide-and-go-seek around the globe. He's not totally out to pasture yet.

As four o'clock approaches, Matt waves over a red cap to carry their luggage to Car 6, then help him board. From the gate, the train looks just as it had both times they'd ridden it before. Inside, however, the smell is no longer fresh and new, but of dust, age, and stale cigarette smoke. The windows are grimy, the upholstery worn, the floor dirt-specked. Rumors are that railroads have become so unprofitable they're going to be nationalized. New government agencies with the futuristic titles of AmTrak and ConRail will manage passenger and freight separately. Matt predicts the Navy could do a hell of a lot better job.

The coach is only half full when they pull out, ten minutes late. Aside from the deterioration, Gail senses the wonder is missing. Gone is the shining contrast between the train's luxury and the dismal right-of- way. And the ride is rougher, despite the fact that they're moving more slowly than she remembers.

As the train rumbles northward, old memories fill her with nostalgia. She'd share them with Matt, but he's absorbed in a new *Reader's Digest.* Until the conductor wanders down the aisle. His uniform is shiny with age, his dark face weary but pleasant.

After he punches their tickets, he hesitates, gaze dropping to Matt's pinned-up trouser leg. "Excuse me, sir. Mind if I ask if you lost that in the war?"

Matt grins. "Actually I lost it right here on this train. I mean, the one that cracked up twenty years ago. Wasn't all bad, though, because I met this lady just before it happened."

"Well, I'll be damned! If that's not a coincidence! See, I was on that run too, in a Pullman at the tail end. Eight cars, only two didn't derail. Fact is, at first we didn't know there'd even been a wreck." His head wags emphatically. "Worst thing

I ever saw. Don't have to tell you, I guess. Where were you when it happened?"

"Seventh car. On the way to the dining car. Still don't remember anything after it started shaking. Never will, I guess."

"Better that way, I'd say." He pauses, gaze swinging to Gail. "You hurt too, ma'am?"

"No. I was in the lavatory in the sixth car. So I was spared."

He shakes his head again, looks back at Matt. "Tell me, sir. Ever think about suing the line?"

"No. Why? Did others?"

"Oh, some. Heard talk, but the line squelched it, I guess so nobody else'd get the idea. Not much in the papers about the hearings either, when they tried to blame somebody." He glances around, lowers his voice. "In the end, though, they did what big companies always do—pinned it on the lowest guy on the totem pole. Refugee from Albania, or some other country nobody cares about." More head shaking.

"You ask me, though, they should've blamed whoever it was decided to make that run non-stop. See, today we make all the stops—Baltimore, Bel Air, Havre de Grace, Wilmington, both Philly stations, plus all the ones in Jersey. Now, if we'd done it that day, the journal boxes would've had a chance to cool off. Speed we were making, they needed it more than usual. So the one caught fire might not have, even without enough lube. But no, some hotshot in the main office figured if we cut half an hour off the run, we could charge more and still fill every car." He snorts with disgust. "Make a buck. Always the name of the game. Make a damned buck."

As Matt listens, Gail notices the shift in his expression from polite to focused, as if recording this latest *If Only* in some mental Journal of Ironic Details. She can only imagine its impact, especially today. He's still smiling, though, as the conductor concludes. "Way things are going nowadays, I'm going to retire while they can still pay me. Before the Pennsy folds up completely."

After a round of good-luck wishes, the employee moves on. Gail waits till he's out of earshot before she says, "That was interesting. Ever hear that before—if we'd stopped along the way, we might have been okay?"

He nods "Don't need a degree from MIT to know running at high speeds makes bearing problems worse."

"And you never thought about suing the railroad?"

He scratches his head. "Another patient at Philly suggested it. So I thought about it, yes. Only problem was, it made me bitter. And didn't bring back the leg. Besides, when you get right down to it, what happened to me wasn't anyone's fault. Here we were, perfectly safe in Car 6. Except I had to impress the cute gal I was sitting with. Had to go ahead to get a table in the dining car." Shakes his head, regret in his eyes. "That's the thing. See, I was on that train by chance. But leaving you, even for a good reason, that was choice." Another long sigh. "Hell of a difference between random chance and conscious choice."

The admission takes her breath away. And fits into place the last piece of the puzzle about the nature of that tragedy: Matt feels responsible for his involvement in the wreck, for his disability, for the way his life has turned out.

She inhales to compose herself. "I had no idea you felt that way."

He only nods and turns his gaze to the window and the dismal outskirts of Baltimore beyond.

As the train slows, Gail's aware of a full-circle sense warming her. Still she wonders if, when they'd ridden this train on the last leg of the Iowa trip, if the pregnancy issue hadn't dominated her mind, would they have eventually come to this intersection of chance and choice? Or hadn't it been up the Lord's sleeve that day? Not in Fate's program? Tabled and comfortably buffered for nineteen more years?

She's about to suggest it to Matt, when he asks, "Say, sweetie; could I borrow that little notebook you keep in your purse?"

Surprised, she reaches into her pocketbook to produce the spiral tablet in which she jots notes for the newsletters she produces—for the base Officers' Wives' Club, St. Margaret's Academy Alumni, Kittery-York Consolidated High School PTA, and parishioners of St. Stephen's Episcopal Church. "Here. Shall I ask why you need it?"

He chuckles. "Actually, I've been thinking about…uh, writing something. A novel, maybe. I mean, I'm going to have lots of time now I'm finally retired. I'd start with this Navy officer—a submariner they call Lucky—who's on his way to Portsmouth to be exec of a new boat. He has a ticket on the Congressional Limited, but decides to take an earlier train. Next day, when he hears about the wreck, he realizes he really is lucky."

She laughs. "Oh that guy. I've met him somewhere. But not on the earlier train. That day, I only made this one by the skin of my teeth."

He grins, clasps her hand between them on the seat, leans closer, gestures toward the notebook. "See, I've been thinking about it a long while—that *what if* we talk about? Now I want to make some notes while they're fresh in my mind. So I can start writing soon as we get home."

Questions crowd, starting with, "Are you talking about the life you might have had if the train hadn't wrecked?"

He nods. "Or if I'd taken an earlier one."

The words thud into her mind, as if he's been waiting twenty years to speak them. She swallows the sense that this admission marks another pivotal moment, a blinking red light at the crossroads of his history and all that lost potential. Of *faits accompli* and the unknown territory he's drawn to explore. But never has, perhaps for fear of finding riches—a brilliant career, a war hero's reputation, a strong dependable body, perfect love—which might have been his. *If only.*

She forces a smile. "I see. A memoir of *what if.*"

"Guess you could call it that." He glances out at a dingy station and a straggle of seen-better-days folks waiting to board. "Problem is, all I've ever written are official reports.

Cut and dried stuff. So I'd need a lot of editorial help with this. Because it'd be fiction. Or maybe fantasy. Anyway, sound like something you'd be interested in?"

She hesitates, aware that most fiction is rarely pure story, rarely unalloyed by unconscious autobiography or repressed secrets. Could she and Matt work together on a project with the potential to turn into an emotional minefield?

Finally, she nods. "Well, okay. If you promise Lucky'll end up with a red-headed English teacher, once he gets the adventures out of his system."

Matt's smile is the gentle one she's loved for two decades. A blend of enthusiasm and apprehension about revising his personal story, about transforming the man he is to a man he's never met, but might have become. And though he never will, now and then still longs to be. Like a twin he knew only in the womb, but still misses.

As the train edges out of the station and accelerates through the shabby city, Gail squeezes her husband's hand, then settles back to ponder this new development. Even aware of its pitfalls, she senses its promise. Like being pregnant, at the threshold of a new adventure, another great unknown.

She's deep in reverie when Matt's voice interrupts: "Sorry to bother you, sweetie, but now I need a pen."

As she fishes in her purse for a new ballpoint, it dawns on her that she's into happily-ever-after without realizing she's crossed the border. How amazing, that this is the day and this train the place where so many ephemeral lines have converged to complete the story she and Matt had begun twenty years before.

No, not complete it, she reminds herself. Train trips are finite, but the journey she and Matt share is "'til death do us part."

About as infinite as you can get this side of the promised land.

–The End–

ACKNOWLEDGMENTS

On a May evening in 2015, a northbound AmTrak train suddenly accelerated to 106 MPH on a tight curve near Philadelphia. The ensuing derailment resulted in numerous injuries and eight deaths, one a Naval Academy midshipman. News of this disaster stirred memories of another wreck at that same spot when I was a teen-ager in that city. With my brother's help, I learned it involved the crack Congressional Limited in 1943, a freak accident in which all casualties—79 dead, 117 injured—occurred in cars 7 and 8, the other fourteen being untouched.

As I delved into history, I concocted a plot based on the chance meeting of two strangers in Car 6, and a budding attraction that's shattered in the wreck. Now, three years and 93,000 words later, their story's as complete as I can make it, thanks to help from a village of knowledgeable friends and relatives. Chief among them is my brother, Bob Hartzel, a semi-retired genius who supplied technical background not only for the railroading segments but throughout the process, starting with his recall that the wreck happened the night before his tenth birthday. My gratitude to him is boundless.

Thanks also to fellow Philly ex-pat Carol O'Toole for supplying photos and information about the Naval Hospital there. And to Nurse-Practitioner Tammy Hedspeth for her insights into long-term problems of amputees. To Tom Bertrand, Esq., for inspiring the setting of the New England segment of the novel. And to my amazing daughter, Barbara Iobst-Gonda, for trouble-shooting the text from ten thousand miles away in Australia. My son David Iobst, too, has encouraged me to keep writing even when I'd rather have a nap.

Thanks to early readers, like my BFF Joan Brown, as well as to her daughter, Beth, for online research into the love life of amputees. Another source was former submarine officer Collins "Schatzie" Snyder, who even at 92 was quick to answer questions like, "How does a sub communicate when submerged?" And to his wife Pat Moody and other friends—Nancy Thibodeaux, Betty Mariner, Amy Betit, Dolores Tyler and Lynn Steel—for their comments. I'm beyond grateful to Lenore Hart for her superb editing, and to other writers in her workshop—David McCaleb, Ken Sutton and Mark Nuckols—for their patience with my nonogenarian ways.

Finally, profound thanks to novelist, editor, and publisher David Poyer for the various touches large and small that have enhanced my efforts. To everyone, my sincere appreciation. Writing this novel hasn't been easy, but without y'all's help, I'd still be stuck on Page One, never knowing what became of that cute young couple in Car 6.

ABOUT THE AUTHOR

Born in 1929, Joan Hartzel La Blanc discovered the joy of writing during her childhood in Philadelphia. While she set this addiction aside to raise four children, it later enabled her to survive marriages to two career Navy men and one with Alzheimer's. Now, in her golden years, it continues to offer romance, travel, and the adventures of an international spy without the dangers. After a "real" career as a PR and non-fiction writer, she crafts circumspect prose for church publications between visits to the parallel universes that still provide inspiration and creative fulfillment.

THE ANNA DONOVAN NOVELS

If you enjoyed this book, you'll like Joan's series of World War II-era novels about young Anna Donovan. The first, INNOCENCE OF ANGELS, recounts her romance and short-lived marriage to submarine officer Dan Donovan. The second, MINISTRY OF ANGELS, follows a newly-widowed Anna to a Maine coastal island, where she expects to be able to forget her losses. ODYSSEY OF ANGELS takes her into the hell of the Pacific War as a nurse aboard USS *Compassion*, a hospital ship in the final year of the conflict. ORDINARY ANGELS follows her return to civilian life, a new marriage, and eventually, a measure of peace. All are available from Northampton House Press in both ebook and paper formats.

Northampton House Press

Northampton House publishes selected fiction, lifestyle nonfiction, memoir, and poetry. Our logo represents the muse Polyhymnia. Our mission is to discover great new writers and make their books available in inexpensive forms. See our list at www.northampton-house.com, or Like us on Facebook – "Northampton House Press" – for more innovative works from brilliant new writers.